BOUNDARIES *of* EDEN

BY

GLENN ARBERY

Wiseblood Books

Wiseblood Books
506 Belmont Mt. Holly Rd.
Belmont, North Carolina 28021

ISBN-13: 978-1-951319-13-7

Cover Design by L. Maltese
Book Interior Design by L. Maltese

Wiseblood Books
Belmont, North Carolina
www.wisebloodbooks.com

Printed in the United States of America

Set in BaskervilleURW

For Ginny

It was all
Shining, it was Adam and maiden
The sky gathered again
And the sun grew round that very day.
So it must have been after the birth of the simple light
In the first, spinning place, the spellbound horses walking warm
Out of the whinnying green stable
On to the fields of praise.

Dylan Thomas, "Fern Hill"

PROLOGUE

Bill Sharpe

Monday, June 23, 2014

7:04 a.m.

A boy was standing dead in the middle of the kudzu off Hopewell Road. The look on his face made Sharpe hit the brakes. The boy's mouth hung open, and there was a peculiar desperate vacancy in the way his head turned at the sound of the pickup. Sharpe's little brother would get that open-mouthed look, but this boy did not have Down syndrome.

Sharpe put the truck in park and switched off the radio and pushed the button to lower the passenger-side window.

"You okay?" he called.

The boy was looking back at the shrouded house. He turned and saw Sharpe and then started wading out, holding his elbows above the leaves and picking up his legs like a swimmer coming out of the ocean. Missy's Garden. Old black people claimed Missy had been a conjure woman, but Miss Emma Fields said she had been a fine lady with statues on the grounds. Whatever was down under there, the abandoned place between Vernon Jenkins and Jimmy Proctor hadn't been anybody's garden except Lord Kudzu's for as long as Sharpe could remember.

He turned off the truck and got out. The boy came up through the ditch onto Hopewell Road, tearing through the vines of morning glories just unrolling their blossoms. His white t-shirt, stained with green, rode up his abdomen, and the skin of his knees showed through the laddered threads of his wet jeans.

"You okay?" Sharpe asked. "What were you doing out there? I wouldn't go in that snaky mess to save my life."

The boy had hit his head on something; an ugly contusion bulged from his forehead. "Have you seen Mama?" he said. "I was just coming up from the creek for breakfast, and I don't know where she went."

"Nobody was making breakfast in that house. You must have gotten lost."

"No sir, that's my house," he said.

"Okay, come on, hop in the truck. I'll run you up to the store. I'm Bill Sharpe from just down the road here. What's your name, son?"

The boy's mouth opened to answer, and no sound came out. His eyes wavered.

"I don't know," he finally said.

1

"You don't know?"

"No sir."

Bad news flickered in the fine tissue around the boy's eyes.

"Tell you what," Sharpe said. "Hop on up in the truck. We'll figure out who you are and get you home. Get you to the doctor if we need to."

He was supposed to be at the dealership early to meet Nolan Adams. His cell wouldn't have a signal until he got closer to town, but he could call Chick Lee on Ed Watkins' landline and tell him he would be a little late. Nolan wanted to trade in his old pickup and get a new F-150, and he didn't need Sharpe for that—but the commission would have helped. Spartan Dog was faltering. His partners were getting distracted, it wasn't their baby, they were drifting off to other things. A tech startup needed imagination and endless energy. His had run out when Deirdre died.

He got in the truck and settled behind the steering wheel. The boy opened the door, climbed in, and sat there like a zombie. A smell came off his clothes.

"Did you find something dead?"

"Sir?"

"Roll down your window. And fasten your seat belt."

The boy nodded and did it obediently, but after a moment he seemed to forget Sharpe. He turned to stare out the open window at the kudzu.

"What's the last thing you remember?" Sharpe asked.

After a long moment the boy said, "Mama was making breakfast. But when I came in—she was—she was—"

"Gone?"

"There was a man in a truck."

"A man in a truck."

"Yes sir."

"Somebody left you here?" Sharpe hoped to God whoever it was hadn't done something evil and that's why the boy's memory had shut down. Children were raped, starved, abused—you wanted it not to be true, but God let it happen all the time. The familiar darkness came over him. The black wing, his mama called it.

"No sir," the boy said. "I was down at the creek and I came up and she was—I was looking for Mama—and somebody called me, and it was a man in a truck," the boy said. After a moment, he added, "It was you. You called me."

A shiver went up Sharpe's neck. He leaned up and started the engine. "That's right. I called you," he said.

"All I did was turn around."

"I saw you."

"What happened to my house?" the boy asked plaintively.

"What do you mean?"

"What happened to it? It's all covered up with that stuff. And where's Mama?"

NORA

Part I

Come slowly – Eden!
Lips unused to Thee –
Bashful – sip thy Jessamines –
As the fainting Bee –

Reaching late his flower,
Round her chamber hums –
Counts his nectars –
Enters – and is lost in Balms.

Emily Dickinson

Walter Peach

September 13, 2013

Peach was struggling left-handed to get the key in the lock of the *Tribune* office when Mary Rose Ryburn came out next door with the menu chalkboard for the Left Bank. She paused and stared at him, cocking her head.

"You went to McDonald's," she said in flat accusation.

"You weren't open yet," he said.

She shook her head and turned her back on him and started chalking the morning's specials on the board in her elegant cursive.

"You know I'm in there by six in the morning, Walter," she said without turning her head. "Just knock on the window—I'll bring you some decent coffee and a croissant."

Her coffee was good, but not as good as Teresa's Ethiopian Yirgacheffe, which he had just had in their morning ritual an hour ago. The McDonald's coffee was more to accompany the sausage biscuit he shouldn't have eaten. He was about to fend her off with a joke when he heard the phone ringing inside his office.

"Somebody's already calling." He turned the key and pushed the door open and set down the McDonald's cup too hard: black coffee shot out the tiny sipping hole and burned his knuckles.

He cursed at the empty room, licking his fingers and blowing on them, waving his hand in the air. Friday the Thirteenth kicking in already. It wasn't even seven. Who the hell could be calling? He dropped the keys on the desk and left-handed the phone on the fourth ring, letting his laptop bag slide off his shoulder onto the chair, as he looked around the room at the empty desks.

"*Tribune*," he said.

"Walter Peach?" Heavy emphasis on the first syllable of *Walter*. Soft male voice, strong Hispanic accent.

"Speaking. Who's this?"

"Is Paco."

"Okay, Paco."

Peach waited a beat. The man did not speak. Was he supposed to recognize the name? He turned the coffee toward him and took a scalding sip, wrenching his head back away from it and almost spilling it again. Good God. Somebody had sued McDonald's about that. How did they get it so hot?

"So good morning, Paco. What can I do for you, buddy?"

When Paco still said nothing, Peach sighed through his nose and started to hang up. Maybe he should have called him amigo.

But then Paco said, "You dunno me?" Not *dunno*, exactly. More a nasally *donno*.

"I meet lots of people."

"Is *bueno*," said Paco pleasantly. "*Te conozco*." And Paco hung up.

What the hell? *Te conozco*. What did that mean?

A faint disquiet shadowed him. Several copies of yesterday's paper lay stacked on his desk, and he swung the top one around. **CARTELS IN GALLATIN?** A photo of a handcuffed cartel boss recently extradited from Mexico to face charges up in Gwinnett County, Walter Peach on the byline. The headline ought to sell a few extra papers—stir up the Jaycees and the Lion's Club. Maybe it's what Paco was calling about. Maybe a disgruntled immigrant was calling instead of the disgruntled farmers or football parents who usually berated him after one of his stories had somehow insulted them.

Or maybe his latest "Ask Socrates Johnson" column had ticked Paco off.

Listen, Socrates, let's say 70% of world terrorism is caused by Sunni Muslims with connections to the Middle East. So if you see some guy who looks like a Muslim from the Middle East, is it bad if you think he's more likely to be a terrorist than some black dude with a beer belly and his Braves baseball cap on backwards?

Hell, no, says Socrates. Makes sense to me.

And the more Mexicans you see in Middle Georgia, the more likely it is that cartels are coming with them. So it makes sense to, you know, be a little worried, right?

Damn right, buddy. Be stupid not to.

So **CARTELS IN GALLATIN?**

He had tested the logic of the question on Braxton Forrest during their weekly call on Monday morning. The locally notorious Forrest, as Peach would explain to anybody who made a crack about him, was a different man these days. He had pulled Peach from a dead-end job teaching English in a tech school, put him in charge of reviving the historic newspaper started by Josiah Graves, and made him resident caretaker of Stonewall Hill, the antebellum Farquhar McIntosh plantation rebuilt as the showpiece of T.J. Forrest's textile fortune. Since his troubles four years earlier, Forrest had come into that money, just enough of which had been cannily reinvested in Texas Instruments by his prescient father after World War II.

Forrest was still teaching a few classes at Walcott College in New

Hampshire, but he took the same kind of interest in Gallatin that Zeus took in the Trojan War when he was seated on Mount Ida. His motives were complicated; sometimes he could reach in and stir a character to do something, maybe just to see what would happen. His motives were complicated, but Peach chose to interpret them as more or less benign.

They sometimes spent an hour on the phone planning the next issue of the paper. Peach's argument on Monday had been that Gallatin was a quiet town with an Interstate running through it, Miami to Detroit. It had lots of woods and fields around it. It was an hour from Atlanta, a major international hub. And with people like Dexter Watkins around, drugs had already been in the county for decades. Why wouldn't the cartels want to use the resources of Middle Georgia?

Look, just don't forget football, Forrest had said. *It's September, Walter.* But he said to go with the cartel story and see what happened.

So far, Paco had happened.

Peach yawned, suddenly grinning. *Dexter Watkins.* He ought to do a "Friends and Neighbors" profile on him. This week it had been the tiny and fearsome Adele Lawson, for decades the head librarian at the Gallatin County Public Library. Next week—Dexter Watkins. *So Dexter, what's the best kind of weed on the street these days?*

The front door of the *Tribune* office opened, and Peach looked up. A tall, thin man, a casual elegance about him. He wore a Panama hat and a white summer suit with brown snakeskin loafers. Something was wrong with his face, a disfiguration or scar—hard to tell in the shadow of the hat. He stood just inside the door, holding it open, looking over his sunglasses. Very dark eyes, as though his irises were the same color as the pupils.

"Come on in, sir," Peach said, "before all the air conditioning sneaks out past you."

The man closed the door and stood just inside it, pushing the sunglasses back up over his eyes. He did not remove his hat. The room felt distinctly colder with him inside it. He looked around and picked up a copy of yesterday's paper.

"'Cartels?'" he said. "What an interesting suggestion." He had an accent, probably British, and a voice that sounded wet around the s's. He covered his mouth when he spoke as though he were ashamed of his teeth. "Might you be Walter Peach?"

"I might indeed," said Peach. "I don't think we've met."

"No, but we have a mutual acquaintance from Chicago."

Chicago? Possible. And he had done readings there back in the day. He remembered his hostess at a library in Highland Park. Or maybe somebody he had known in the writing program at Iowa or later at

Georgia.

"So are you going to tell me?" he said.

"Alison?" the man said slowly, teasing out the syllables wetly, insinuating something. Strange, the hand over his mouth and the way he lowered his sunglasses to look Peach in the eye.

"You must have me mixed up with someone else."

"Oh, absolutely not, sir. Not at all. I know you very well."

The man gazed at him steadily, as if accusing him of something. Peach smiled, raised his eyebrows, shrugged.

"Sorry, my friend. I don't know you, and I don't know anybody named Alison."

"Really? How interesting."

"Not a soul."

"Well, oh my." Flirtatious, almost. Certainly mocking. "How rude of me. Please, pardon my intrusion." He lifted the paper about cartels. "May I?"

"By all means," said Peach.

When he left, a gust of warm air came in. Peach sat for a moment, unsettled. A faint scent of fruit lingered—or maybe he had just noticed it. Probably a banana peel the graphics girl had left in the trash can. He set up his laptop and checked his email. A few letters to the editor. He would read those later. Nothing from Forrest. Something from Rowing-in-Eden with *your poetry* on the subject line. He started to erase it, thinking it was a local poetess aspiring to be the next Emmeline Grangerford, but something made him pause. *Rowing in Eden.* He opened it.

```
Dear "Uncle," as they would have it,
    I wanted to meet that author whose mind met
mine some years ago, but the gridiron, they say,
has greater title in Gallatin than the dinner
table. Will it ever be so, or might I hope for
solace? Poetry is the honeybee trapped in my little
room: I watch it buzz against my windowpane. Will
it live? The mind is so near itself it cannot see
distinctly, and I have none to ask.
Your niece—
not by blood, but by all else that's fated
Nora
```

Your niece. Who was this? His *niece*? He didn't have a niece, so it had to be Nora O'Hearn, Teresa's niece from Athens. Buford's pretty fifth-grade teacher. He felt his breath tighten. *Might I hope for solace?* Calling him "that author." *your poetry* in the subject line, all lowercase. Had she actually read his poetry? A dark qualm went through him.

He could still write easily, and his prose had a flow and unexpectedness that made it notable enough to win him a few prizes, but the poetry was long gone. Those moments when he would feel the image come upon him. He would be reading or walking and it would suddenly be there. He would scramble for a notebook, an envelope, whatever lay at hand. Lines would start to form themselves, sounds, as though something wholly new would come to exist only when he found the words. And when it was said, he would stare at the lines he had written, not sure where they had come from: his early sequence on the hidden Southern past, his poems on table manners and sex, the satires on cultural extinctions in modernity.

That gift had vanished on the day his son died, almost in the very moment. Bereft from that day, without a voice to lament his having betrayed his wife and his gift and his son—only when he had lost them had he begun seeking what he once had, what he once was, what would never come again. Then came the bad, forced poems, the bad, faltering classes, the crippling loss of confidence, a growing, half-contemptuous disregard from others. And then came the long downward spiral, like Dante's Geryon descending into the deepest infernal circles of fraud. Teresa had never left him except for that summer when her mother died in Alabama. He remembered first seeing her across the room during his reading at Duquesne, the dusting of freckles across her cheeks and the bridge of her nose, the dark auburn hair, cut almost dismissively short— Rose called it a "nun's cut" when she saw the old pictures—the serious green eyes, that focus of fierce attention that had left an ampersand in the skin of her forehead above the nose. He had recognized her, a face no one would describe as beautiful, but compelling and intelligent and full of attraction. He could not possibly have seen her before. There was something fiery in the very look of her face across the room and something modestly abundant about her when he sought her out at the reception.

Opulent, if he was fair, so much more than one would expect — but being fair to Teresa did not suit him at the moment. He looked back at the email and that sentence he recognized: *The mind is so near itself...* It came back to him: Emily Dickinson in her first letter to that guy—who was it? Higgins? Higginson? The man she had first sent her poems. The abolitionist who was part of the John Brown plot. He googled "abolitionist Dickinson editor" and there he was: *Thomas Wentworth Higginson.*

So was Nora another reclusive little Emily Dickinson? He had missed meeting her a couple of weeks back when Teresa invited her to dinner to get reacquainted with the family. There had been a Booster's Club meeting he had had to cover down at the high school—Coach Lincoln's pre-season assessment of the 2013 schedule for the Sybil Forrest High School Blue Devils. He remembered Nora from ten or so years ago when he had driven everybody up from Waycross to Athens for Thanksgiving. A skinny, waifish girl, a few years older than Rose, her mouth full of braces, but even then, she had seemed an unlikely offspring of the blustering and opinionated Terry O'Hearn or the fidgety Bridget, Teresa's younger sister. The children had found little to talk about; there was a brother who had since passed out of family favor, if he remembered rightly from that alcoholic weekend. Duane. Endless football games on TV, O'Hearn's humorless domination of the remote, his bloviating about stupid coaches and lazy wide receivers and missed tackles. Teresa had driven them home the next day while Peach slumped against the passenger door, hungover and morose.

But skinny little Nora must have turned into something. Several men in town, Bill Fletcher among them, had raised an appreciative eyebrow mentioning her.

Your niece, not by blood, but by all else that's fated. What was he supposed to say to that?

He would have to email her back.

Not yet, though.

The coffee had cooled a little.

He skimmed through his usual news websites—BBC, *Le Monde*, the English edition of *Der Spiegel*, the *New York Times*, the *Wall Street Journal*, CNN, Fox News, the Drudge Report. Most of the attention was on Syria, Assad's use of chemical weapons, Vladimir Putin warning the U.S. not to get involved. He wondered if anyone in Gallatin had Syrian connections. Or any connection to the Arab Spring, which increasingly appeared to be just another liberal fantasy. Or any experience of chemical weapons— maybe some recent veterans nobody would think to ask. He should check it out. *Hey, ask Dexter.*

Peach jotted down a few notes. He liked embedding world stories in local ones, explaining international tensions with names and faces right here in town. He had a theme, too. Everything in their age was part of the unfolding devastations of the modern project—the conquest of nature, the destruction of longstanding organic traditions, the turn from belief to crippling skepticism about any common good and incredible importance afforded to sexual predilections. The mayor's son had just decided he was really a girl, for crying out loud—couldn't write about that. So the cartels instead—the next step from the empty creature comforts of the modern world, a kind of savagely uber-capitalistic enterprise supplying a feel-good antidote to meaninglessness. He could sketch in next week's editorial right now. What's happened to real communities? If people have to make up reality for themselves, it's no surprise they turn to booze or drugs.

Right, Walter? He imagined saying that to Teresa. But for the editorial page, at least, wasn't it true? If you had enough serious people who believed in loyalty and courage and loved their parents and their children, the drug market would dry up.

Wasn't likely to happen. More likely was the legalization of everything that the police had a hard time stopping. Opposition to marijuana was going to crumble. Colorado had already legalized it. Methamphetamines, opioids—the plague wasn't Mexicans or Colombians, but a homegrown nihilism. Hell, working class jobs had been displaced by automation and outsourcing to China, and the old virtues had been destroyed by liberal ideas that never hurt the elites but undercut traditional working families. Obama and his people seemed to be ashamed of America itself—Good Lord, as though the slow suicide of Europe were the answer! Gay marriage: Peach could easily imagine that being legalized. What he couldn't imagine was the return of a self-restraining, self-governing populace. Everybody looked to Washington, D.C. for answers instead of coming up with them for themselves. The very idea of a "virtuous people" was mocked, even though the alternative led to all the problems. The contempt of the Ivy League crowd for the rest of the country was begging for a populist backlash.

So working for a local paper, Peach thought, pushing his notepad away, was a statement in itself, right? Why, he wrote about Gallatin people. He praised the kinds of things Wendell Berry or the old Southern Agrarians would praise—but so what? Gallatin readers didn't understand him. A lot of them thought he was pretentious. Hiram Walker, retired from his hardware store, had come to give him some advice after his second or third month on the job. *Why don't you just write about the goddamned county commissioners? Just write about the goddamned school board and the football team.* Peach had just seen Hiram Walker down at McDonald's with four or five other old men, all of them taking advantage of the senior discount. He could imagine him slapping the headline of yesterday's paper with the back of his hand and holding it up for derision. *Ain't that some bullshit? Cartels?*

But listen, Peach wanted to say, *it's all connected, and it keeps me interested.* He imagined leaning casually on the lectern in front of the Lion's Club. *Gentlemen*—the tones of Tom Brokaw—*just by writing what he writes or choosing what he chooses, a good journalist can form* (he eloquently shapes a great pumpkin in the air) *what might be called the larger consciousness of the community.*

Now *that's* some bullshit.

Still, he cared about the paper being good. He liked tweaking it a little every week, introducing subtle changes in the way it looked—the headlines, the art, the fonts, the cutouts. He got some of the best design students in Macon and Atlanta to work for almost nothing, just to build up their portfolios. Most of his readership had no idea what they were getting. They would have been just as happy to have it mimeographed. Or to have syndicated film reviews instead of the ones he took the time and effort to write. On the other hand, the town was proud when the *Tribune* won state and then national awards, as it had begun to do within six months of the time Braxton Forrest bought the paper and hired Peach as editor.

And old ladies liked him, by God. They stopped him on the street to tell him it was a pleasure, just a *pleasure*, to see the English language used so well in this day and age.

But what did Nora O'Hearn think of the *Gallatin Tribune?*

Peach reread her email.

Will it live?

A little honeybee butted around inside his ventricle. Auricle? Oracle?

He sighed. He had better get to work. He should home in on Georgia with the *Atlanta Journal-Constitution* and then get more local with the *Macon Telegraph.* On the *Journal-Constitution* website, he saw several stories with no local interest—a judge retiring, a woman arrested for fraud of some kind—but then there it was, dated just an hour ago. A truck full of pumpkins a few miles north of Gallatin had overturned and closed the Interstate. Next week's front page—a total switch from cartels. He closed his laptop, dropped it in his bag, and grabbed the digital camera from the drawer of his desk. The traffic was probably backed up halfway to Florida. He could go out the back roads, cut through on Hopewell, and give the old homestead a glance on the way.

*

It was after seven o'clock that night when Peach finally got home. He pulled into the driveway at Stonewall Hill and saw somebody else's car beside the Focus—a blue Corolla, probably some friend of Rose's—and sighed with irritation. Teresa said he sighed a lot. He just wanted to go inside and complain to her about his day, get a stiff drink, balance a few pieces of Friday pizza on a paper plate, wave everybody off, and go up to his armchair, where he could watch a movie on his laptop alone. The idea of having to make conversation annoyed him.

He sat there in the Outback, hoping they had all already eaten, looking up at the house for clues about who it was. He saw Teresa walk past and then come to the door and look out at his car, but then her head turned sharply—somebody calling her—and she disappeared into the kitchen.

This Friday the Thirteenth had lived up to its movie-star billing. He had been out on the Interstate lining up his camera on one of the pumpkins when a passing state patrolman had idly nudged aside another one with his foot. It had wobbled away like an insulted drunkard, loose and lopsided, until another patrolman stopped it with the sole of his boot, and it split open in a soft burst. A packet of white powder appeared from inside it, pale and fugitive, like Jonah from the whale.

Heroin, it turned out.

Suddenly, it was total war on pumpkins. A mound of plastic packets was growing, radios were squawking, and the loudly protesting driver—*Man, all I knew was they was just pumpkins*—was under arrest. Ten minutes later the scene swarmed with GBI; half an hour later, FBI and DEA. *Where had the truck been loaded? Where had it been going?* Meanwhile, the Blue Devils were playing in West Point two hours away, and he had to scramble to get Howard Noles to cover the game for him.

What, you're not even going? Noles had been incredulous. *Don't you want to see their running back? People are already saying he's NFL material. This'll be the first big test of the defense, and you won't even be there? I don't mind doing it, but damn, Walter.*

Unthinkable for the editor of the *Gallatin Tribune* to be absent from a Blue Devils game. What else was the newspaper really for? Homer was to Achilles, Pindar was to the Olympic victors, what the *Gallatin Tribune* was to the heroes of the local blood: the boys in their shining hour, not only the chosen ones who had been watched and discussed in the drugstore and the pool hall and the doctor's office since fifth or sixth grade, but also the common athletes who supported them, blocked for them, cheered them on—all of them drilled like Roman legions for these autumn Friday nights.

It was the first game he had missed, and he knew he would pay for it in community goodwill. He could imagine what Forrest would say. *Walter, come on. People care more about the team than they do about dope that happens to be passing through from one big city to another. What does that have to do with Gallatin?*

He got out of the car into the hot night. When he was halfway up the brick walk, Teresa came to the back door and opened the screen.

"So who's covering the game? Buford really wanted to go."

He had called her hours ago to see if Buford could find another ride.

"Howard Noles. I told him he'd get to sit in the press box. So Buford's still here?"

"His friends had already left. Why Howard Noles?"

"He's seen every Blue Devils game since God created football."

"Can he write?"

Peach shrugged. "What's an editor for?"

She kissed him lightly. "We already ate, but there's some pizza left. Listen," she said, dropping her voice. "Nora's here. To see *you*. Walter, she's read your books. She's been dying to talk to you."

He felt the same qualm he had felt that morning. "She just showed up?"

"After you said you weren't going to the game, I called her and told her you'd be home tonight. Be nice to her."

"I'll be nice."

"What's the matter?"

"Nothing."

Will it live?

"She's in the sitting room with Buford."

He went into the kitchen and put two slices of pizza on a plate and strolled toward the sitting room, as Teresa called it—not the living room or the formal parlor, both of which Forrest had restored, but the small room near the front of the house where, in the old days, callers could sit and wait for the servants to fetch the family. He came in behind the Queen Anne's couch and saw Nora's blonde head bent over a book, the hair caught back in a ponytail. Buford sat beside her, rapt.

She wore a sleeveless dark blue top and white shorts, and her slender legs were crossed at the knee, one thigh molding smoothly onto the other, a leather sandal dangling from her suspended, unconsciously rocking right foot. Neither of them felt his presence as Peach stood watching, taking a bite of cold pizza. The girl's hand, deeply in communion with his son's attention, would hold the page and then turn it unhurriedly, solicitously, as though her whole desire were to let him see each page exactly at his own pace and only then—as if it were a sheet of music and she knew exactly where his eye would be when the last bar ended and the next began—to turn the page.

It was a book of Pieter Breughel's paintings. Dutch, 1500s maybe. The page was turned to *Harvesters*, his own favorite. He saw her finger go unhurriedly to a hay wagon in the middle distance, then to the ships in the faraway harbor, back to the foreground and the sprawled sleeping man, the women in a circle eating beneath the tree, a man reaching back to cut some bread, and then to the gathered sheaves. Her finger traced the line of the cut wheat and paused over the mowers and ended by resting upon a man with a great jug wearily trudging uphill through the lane cut in the still-standing grain. There was a pause, then a delicate, lightly feathered addition to the pause, and then she turned the page to another painting. *The Hunters in the Snow.*

Bliss overwhelmed him.

It reminded him of a time in his childhood soon after Judge Lawton had adopted him. Seeing the sorry state of his clothes, the judge took him to Burbank's Department Store in Macon, and kind old Mr. Burbank stood with them at a rack of shirts, pulling them along the bar, shirt after shirt, unhurriedly, one by one, looking up at Walter, who watched the shirts sliding along, each one catching a little air like a sail, each hanger clicking lightly against the next. He had been mesmerized by the pace of it and still more by Mr. Burbank's patient and solicitous kindness. This same singing bliss had come over his heart. He had not wanted to move, even to breathe; he had wanted it never to end, this selfless, attentive, deeply considerate display; he had loved Mr. Burbank for it; he had felt a foretaste of beatitude: the lovely unhurried solicitude, all time suspended, eternity quietly brimming into a single moment that lasted and lasted, shirt after shirt, page after page; the slightest inhalation or sigh seemed too violent.

A touch on his back startled him. Teresa stood beside him, watching Nora and Buford. "Nora, honey," Teresa said. "Walter's home."

Nora turned suddenly, her face alight—her perfectly lovely face. The book slid from her lap as she stood. Buford grabbed it and put it on the coffee table and stood up.

"Uncle Walter!" she said.

He had not been greeted so warmly even by his own children since they were very small. How had this lovely creature emerged from the weedy undertow of genetic O'Hearn-ness? But here she was, like Botticelli's Venus. It was almost embarrassing now to see her bestow upon him, in his old jeans and his late-Friday weariness, such a welcome.

"Uncle not by blood," he said, "but by all else that's fated."

"You didn't answer me! So do I really have to call you 'uncle'?"

"Call me Walter if you want to."

"Really? Do you mind, Aunt Teresa?"

Teresa looked at her, a crinkle of sharp attention between her eyes. She was letting the gray take over her hair, he noticed.

"That's up to Walter."

"It's because of his poetry! I feel like I know the little boy you were," she said to Peach. "*The Small Gnats Mourn*? Some of those poems I know by heart.

> How can she be a standing full of care
> inside the open door,
> a smiling turn
> (ladle in hand) from the fevered stove
> and then—nobody there—
> no greeting there to consecrate my love,
> no corpse to burn.
> Just absence disquieting the air.

He nodded. The lines struck him painfully—a little misquoted—and sickened him a little with the strangeness of remembering his mother.

"'Her Departure,'" Teresa said. "But it's—"

"Yes!" Nora cried, as though she were surprised that Teresa had read his poetry. "Oh, I'm so happy to meet you as Walter instead of my uncle. Now that I know who you are."

"Who I am," Peach said, glancing up at her. "That's an accomplishment I've never managed myself." He put his arm around Teresa and winked at Buford. Just then Rose, digging a long spoon into a carton of sorbet, wandered in, her red hair disheveled, like some enchanted princess just wakened from a spell.

"Who is it who can tell me who I am?" Peach asked his daughter.

"I think I can," Nora O'Hearn interjected before Rose could speak.

Rose put a spoonful of sorbet in her mouth and then gestured with the spoon as if it were a wand.

"Well aren't you the Little Engine that Could?" she said with her mouth full.

Nora

September 14, 2013

On Saturday morning, the other teachers who boarded with Miss Emma Fields told Nora about the Blue Devils' victory the night before. Gallatin had shut down West Point's famous running back Alfred Harkins and held West Point scoreless. The defense had scored three of Gallatin's four touchdowns, two by interceptions and one on Alfred Harkins' fumble.

"Nora, why didn't you *go*?" Missy Talbot asked her, touching her arm as though she must have some shameful secret.

"I told my aunt I'd come by," Nora said. She sipped her coffee, hoping she looked a little contrite.

"Your uncle wasn't at the game, either," Dixie Jenkins said. "The editor of the newspaper. I'm just saying."

"Oh, come on, Dixie," Nora murmured.

"People notice."

After breakfast, when the other girls dispersed to grade papers or get their assignments ready, Nora sat in the rocking chair on the side porch to browse through the Edward Snow translation of Rilke's *New Poems* she had borrowed from Walter. Many biblical poems—old David impotent with young Abishag, young David singing before Saul, Rilke's "Pieta" in Mary Magdalene's voice: "Your heart stands open and anyone may enter;/it should have been a way in kept for me." She wondered if nuns felt that way.

She had milked Lettie earlier and brought in the warm milk to Miss Emma, who had to leave early for a physical therapy appointment in town. She was supposed to meet Miss Emma and some of the other teachers at the Left Bank for brunch at 11:00. It was a wonderful clear morning, almost cool enough for a sweater, and sunlight slanted down through the oaks and elms onto the lawn that Bobby Thurman was crossing with a push mower that whirred pleasantly and flung little bits of cut grass up into the sunbeams. A blue jay kept raiding the bird feeder that hung from the tree nearest the house and scaring off the sparrows. *Bully!* She wondered whether Rilke would notice a common blue jay. Keats would. Walter would.

A rich sense of harmony came over her as she was taking in the whole scene at once, a feeling of deep peace, like what she had felt with Buford turning the pages of the book of Breughel, just before Walter came in. She gazed out, smiling, innocently watching Bobby, the sixth-grade math teacher, in his t-shirt, his puny neck always turtling forward at an angle that made him seem intrusive. Not a torso to make you change your life, she thought, smiling to herself. He noticed her and raised his hand and pushed his glasses up on his nose. In his self-consciousness, he made the poor inert machine look like an alien invader about to overpower him.

At 10:00 or so, Nora went up to her room, put on her good jeans and a light V-neck sweater and drove into Gallatin. As she got off the interstate and went up Lee Street toward the center of town, cars filled every available parking space for blocks. Was it some kind of parade? Traffic backed up. Almost at the courthouse square, she saw a banner stretched from building to building above Lee Street.

Third Annual Gallatin Fall Festival

Edging forward beneath it, she despaired of finding anywhere to park. As she glanced down an alley, two girls on the sidewalk spotted her and whirled and waved—Katie Vaughn and Sabrina Hayes from her class. She waved back, smiling, and followed the traffic past the courthouse. Main Street was open, but the rest of the courthouse square was blocked off. She tried three bank parking lots, all overflowing, and finally drove down a side street that took her behind the library and into a neighborhood she had never seen.

She found a weedy spot in front of an unpainted house with a collapsed front porch and a CONDEMNED notice on the door. Down the street a skinny boy threw a football toward her just as she got out of the car. She winced. A few feet in front of her another boy she hadn't seen flashed from behind a hedge to her right. He caught the pass and bounded up over the ditch on the other side of the road.

"Wow!" she said, and he stood still and gazed at her for a moment before ducking his head shyly and trotting back down the asphalt toward his friend.

She walked the several blocks back toward the square. As she passed the library, she began to hear the distant glad squeals and cries of children that filled every lull of the music. A country band performing Tammy Wynette's "Your Good Girl's Gonna Go Bad" crowded the steps at the top of the north courthouse entrance. The lead singer pranced down toward her audience and back up the steps as she sang. She tossed her hair back, stamped a foot, and segued into the Allman Brothers' "Ramblin' Man." The whole crowd started shouting *Highway 41!* when they got to that line, because Main Street *was* US 41.

At the corner of Main, Nora turned up toward the square. Ahead of her three toddlers, bowlegged as old cowboys, their bottoms padded with diapers, commandeered the sidewalk, their dimpled arms sawing out for balance. She wanted to draw it somehow, the three planes of motion—the plane of their brave new world, the plane of their sleep-deprived, chatting mothers, and up another half-foot or so, the plane of their twenty-something fathers in their UGA sweatshirts or old letter jackets talking about the Blue Devils game.

You know what Harkins ended up with? Two yards total all night.

I tell you what, this is the best I've seen us play since Coach Fitz retired.

The one in front turned around, walking backwards, his beer belly swelling a long-sleeved khaki work shirt with the tail pulling out, little boy perched on his shoulders.

You see that tackle Bud Holmes made on Harkins?

Oh hell yeah. Reminded me of Dutrelle Jones back in the day. Harkins didn't know what hit him! You see him coming off the field?

Down in the middle plane, one of the mothers suddenly stopped, pointed, and said *OH my LORD!* as the others bumped into her. On the corner across the street, a clown was juggling five or six balls, stepping forward and back, seeming to pay close attention, as though he were balancing on a high wire, but in the middle of it he darted out his hand and snatched a baseball cap from an open-mouthed little boy. He caught one of the balls with the cap and sent it up, not breaking his rhythm, and in the next split second the cap was back on the boy's head.

"Did y'all see that? Come on!" the young mother said.

She grabbed her toddler by one hand and glanced to see if any cars were coming on 41 before she stepped into the street. The other mothers and husbands flowed after her. The sidewalk ahead of Nora was suddenly vacant. Just then three older boys tore past her, almost bumping her. One of them whirled in mid-run—mid-leap—startled to see who it was.

"Good m-m-morning, Miss N-n-n—" he said, his eyes comically wide, and as he came down, his feet tangled, and he windmilled and sprawled headfirst into the boxwoods along the front of the old post office. "Oh!" she cried and started forward to help him—it was the Parmenter boy in her class—but he picked himself up and ran shame-faced after his friends. Thank God he hadn't hit his head on the concrete!

Nora crossed Main Street at the light, passing the clown and his admiring crowd. She paused at the barricade on the other side to watch the slow milling of the townspeople. Football players strolled around in their dirty jerseys from the night before, accepting smiles and handshakes. Booths covered the usual parking spots around the courthouse—displays of watercolors, wood carvings, handmade belts and purses. Inside one booth was a great pyramid of jams in Mason jars; other booths sold corn dogs or turkey legs or shapeless fried things powdered with sugar.

Or cotton candy: she saw a little girl sitting up on the courthouse lawn bawling, a pink cloud of spun sugar melting into her blonde hair, the white cone handle projecting from it at a melancholy angle. Two little boys were laughing at the girl—but then they saw a very large and irate woman approaching and bolted.

Out in the street, carefully warding off little children, men were tending grills with hot dogs and hamburgers smoking on them. Standing near one of them was a big, broad-shouldered man who looked like a Viking warlord. He must have been six-four or six-five with tattoos on both deltoids and a head of blond dreadlocks. The man at the grill said something to him and pointed with his long, wooden-handled spatula— toward her? no, behind her—and the warlord's head turned sharply, dreadlocks swinging. For a moment as he looked for what the cook was pointing at, their eyes met, and she smiled despite herself. His head went back a little.

What was she thinking? She left the barricade and made her way down the block in front of the old stores that Miss Emma said Walmart had put out of business. Excusing herself repeatedly, she cut through the press of people toward the north side of the square where the Left Bank was— and next to it the office of the *Gallatin Tribune*. She glanced through the restaurant window and saw Sybil Truitt, who did not see her. The others had not arrived, and Nora was glad. It gave her a moment to peek inside the newspaper office. She cupped her hands on the glass of the door to look in, and Walter glanced up from his desk. She opened the door.

"Why aren't you out*side*?" Nora said, imitating Missy Talbot's accent. "First you miss the football game, and now you don't even have you a corn dog."

Walter's lower lip came out, and her heart warmed strangely. She finally knew Walter Peach. Nora glanced over her shoulder and stepped inside, letting the door close behind her, glad for a moment to be alone with him. The office felt bare—just three desks, the one in the back with two big flat screen displays angled toward each other above the keyboard.

"Have a seat," he said.

She pulled a chair over from the other front desk. As she sat next to him so she could see the laptop screen she caught her breath. It looked like poetry.

"What are you writing?"

She pulled close enough to smell the soap he had used to shave, close enough to see the Greek meander pattern on the leather band that held his ponytail in place. He let her be there, but he glanced at the door and shifted his chair back a little, closed the laptop and looked at her.

"So Nora O'Hearn."

"Yes I am."

"How's the little honey bee?"

"It might live." She met his eyes. A deep hazel.

Walter shook his head and glanced again at the door. She took the hint and backed her chair away a foot or so.

"George Kilgore remembers reading the first poem you turned in for *The Fire and the Rose*," she said. "He told me he stood up from his desk and went in the hall and yelled 'Who the hell is Walter Peach?'"

"George Kilgore," said Walter, smiling. "He got me to edit it my senior year."

"I know. He got me to do the same thing," Nora said. She reached in her purse and brought out a recent copy of the magazine and handed it to him.

"Nice," he said. His mouth pursed and he met her eyes for a long moment, and something happened inside her, a soft shift or rearrangement, like a seed underground.

"What are you doing in town this morning?" he asked, again glancing out through the front door.

"Meeting some friends I've made at the school. Other teachers."

"Teresa said you could have had a full ride at Yale. Why are you teaching fifth grade in Gallatin?"

Yes, that would be his question.

"Maybe I want to get to know *you*."

"Me?"

"The best poet of your generation. Where else would I get such an opportunity?"

He shook his head, avoiding her eyes. "I haven't written poetry in a long time."

She sat silent a moment, watching him.

"What are you working on this morning?" she asked.

"A story about the game. Its author is entirely innocent of grammar and syntax. And I'm thinking about a message I got."

"What message?"

"A picture of Rose."

"What do you mean?"

"Come here."

As he opened his laptop, he moved closer than before, shoulder to shoulder, and he clicked on an email with *Leukostoma* in the subject line. There was no text, just a picture of Rose coming out the back door of the high school. She stood erect in mid-stride, but her head was slightly bowed, and she had her hand on the top of her head as if she were trying to control her mass of whipping red hair. Her blouse and skirt were molded tightly against her; the Greeks would have said that the enamored wind embraced her. She looked unconsciously beautiful, unconsciously provocative.

"Rose has a boyfriend," she said,

"I don't know who took it," he said. "It's from somebody named Josiah on Hotmail. Sent from his iPhone."

She saw the worry in his face. The fact that there was no message with the picture felt ominous. Just then there was a tap on the door. Ginger Robertson raised her eyebrows and tilted her head at the Left Bank, tapping her wrist. Nora waved back and nodded.

"Brunch with Ginger," Walter said. "Just you two? You'd better have some more coffee."

A divorced woman in her late thirties, Ginger was always brimming with energy. Seeing her small frame running or cycling along the roads outside Gallatin was like seeing one of those fires above a refinery that burns up escaping fumes. Ginger also loved whitewater kayaking, and she had been trying for a month to get Nora to go with her to drive up to North Georgia and go down the Chattooga River before the weather changed, but Nora kept putting her off. Someday Nora would have to take her up on it, if only to experience Ginger's energy.

"Ginger's a legend in the classroom," Nora said. "This inspector from Atlanta came down to observe her—"

"I heard something about this."

"Right, because her kids' scores on standardized tests always set the bar for the state. This observer more or less staggered out into the hallway after an hour of watching her teach the sixth graders. *Not that scores are the point,* Ginger would say. And no, it's not just us. Sybil Truitt and Miss Emma Fields are on their way."

"I haven't seen Miss Emma since we got back to Gallatin. You stay out in the country with her?"

"I just love her," Nora said. "I would have driven her in with me, but she had a physical therapy appointment early this morning for her knee, so she's meeting us. I'd better go on. Maybe I'll see you later?"

"Could be," he said. The trouble had not left his face when she left.

*

Ginger had already organized the table, and since Nora was the guest—or the one being initiated—they seated her facing the window to let her take in the festival as they talked. Sybil Truitt, a plump and genial fourth-grade teacher, sat to Nora's left, guiltlessly spreading raspberry jam on her English muffin. Miss Emma sat to Nora's right.

"That boy almost killed me, but it does feel better," Miss Emma sighed, rubbing her left knee.

"You go to Ty?" Ginger asked.

"He's a sweet boy."

"He goes rock-climbing out in Wyoming every summer, did you know that? He got into physical therapy after he fell and broke his leg and dislocated both shoulders."

Miss Emma smiled and nodded. Nora suspected that the allure of rock-climbing eluded her.

"So," Ginger said, turning her focus to Nora, her forefinger drumming unconsciously. "How's it been this first month? Are you finding your way around?"

Nora smiled and tilted her head and was about to speak when a movement outside lifted her eyes past Ginger. The big man with blond dreadlocks had stopped on the sidewalk. He was staring in at them, focused on Sybil Truitt. When Nora did not speak, Sybil and Miss Emma followed her gaze. Both of them started.

"Oh my Lord," Sybil said, putting her fingers to her mouth. The man disappeared.

"It's Dexter Watkins," Miss Emma said with infinite deprecation.

A moment later, he came striding into the Left Bank, powerful and easy, casually defiant of the murmurs around him. He looked splendid. He was so big and handsome, with those blond dreadlocks and ice-blue eyes. As he approached their table, Dexter gave his dreadlocks a toss, nodded at a startled couple as he grabbed an unused ladderback from their table and swung the chair around to sit backward in it right beside Sybil. His eyebrows were pierced, full of rings. The tattoos on his shoulders looked Mayan or Aztec. The deltoid six inches from Nora displayed a fierce warrior whose helmet made a beak. Big arm muscles tensed and surged and then relaxed as he leaned his elbows on their table.

Then the effluvium of him enveloped her: deodorant, barbecue smoke, marijuana.

"So *Miss Truitt*," he said, as if calling her that were a private joke they shared. He leaned close to her ear. "How come you don't answer my calls? I just want to know how my little girl's doing. I heard somebody in her class made her cry talking about me."

Ginger Robertson's finger had stopped.

"Emily's doing just fine," Sybil said, not looking at him.

"If you'll excuse us, Mr. Watkins," Ginger said, "we're trying to order some breakfast."

"You could have gone to the parent-teacher conference, Dexter," Miss Emma said.

"Is that right?" Watkins said loudly, glancing around the room. "Well, I had the sheriff outside the goddamn school door telling me not to."

Mary Rose Ryburn came around the corner and stood looking a question at them.

Miss Emma put up a hand to hold her in place and tilted her head at Watkins as though he were a misbehaving fifth-grader.

"See," Watkins said, lowering his voice, "what happened was Ellen didn't want me there at the same time as that teeny little husband she got herself. What's his name? Something Wolf, but he don't look big and he don't look bad." He wiggled his little finger and sat back so the other women could savor his humor. And then his eyes fell on Nora.

"You a teacher? I would of stayed after school for you." He held out his hand. "Dexter Watkins."

"Hi," she said, letting him take hers. "Nora O'Hearn."

"Nora O'Hearn," he said, not letting go. "Mmm. I like the taste of that." The other women sat back, appalled. He let go and winked at Nora and then touched Sybil Truitt on the shoulder. "Just call me back," he whispered. He swung his chair into place at the other table and left.

"Who was *that*?" Nora asked.

"Oh, sugar," said Miss Emma. "Oh, baby."

They told her how many times he had been arrested and for what. They told her he had been locked up for war crimes. Sybil told how his daughter Emily had begged to have her name changed from Watkins to Wolf. She thought it would protect her from Dexter, who kept scaring her by showing up when she would be trying to do something with her friends.

Miss Emma insisted on paying for brunch, but Nora could hardly taste the seafood quiche she had ordered. The conversation about her first month would start—and then somebody would remember another detail about Dexter Watkins. They all apologized for it; they said they would have another get-together sometime soon. They told her that if she needed help with anything to be sure to ask them, because they would be just tickled to help her.

Ginger invited her to go for a long run that afternoon; Nora demurred.

Outside the door of the Left Bank, they had a little breaking huddle of departures. As she got free, she thought of checking on Walter again, but then the idea of the afternoon opened before her—a walk at Miss Emma's place, a good hour or two on the porch with a novel or a book of poems. She started back to her car, and suddenly Dexter Watkins stood in front of her on the sidewalk.

"Nora O'Hearn," he said. "I do like the taste of that name. Like a chocolate with cream inside."

Somehow, without touching her, he pinned her to the brick wall of the old movie theater so that her back was against the cool brick and she was looking up into his face.

"You and me, we're gon have a good time," he said, as though she had already conceded something to him. "Introduce you to my friends." He retracted the arm extended above her shoulder and tensed his huge deltoid for her. "My amigo Huitzilopochtli, god of war." Feathered headdress, shield, mask, flaming weapons. He turned the other shoulder, bunching the massive biceps of his left arm as he did. "And this here is Quetzalcoatl. These boys take care of me."

Beneath his cocksure bravado was something so injured and melancholy that it stopped her. Then the odor of him encompassed her.

Ginger Robertson—she must have been on the way to her car—hurried up to them.

"Oh Nora," she said, and then stopped and waved her hand in front of her face. "My God! What is that *smell?*"

Dexter drew back sharply, ran his tongue over his teeth, and shook his dreadlocks away from his face. He tried strenuously—the effort was visible on his face—to come up with something to say, but instead he turned and strode down into the milling crowd.

"Good Lord," Nora said.

"Are you okay?" Ginger said. She put her hand gently on Nora's arm. "You're shaking, sweetheart."

But Nora looked up at her, open-mouthed. "He showed me his Aztec tattoos!" she said, trying to laugh it off. "I'll be okay. I just—"

"Where did you park?" Ginger said. "I'll give you a ride to your car."

As they left, she saw Dexter Watkins across the street on the courthouse lawn, staring at her. He met her eyes and sighted along his finger at her like a pistol.

Gallatin

Friday night. Griffin's Memorial Stadium is filled to capacity, and everyone in it is shouting. Fourth quarter, quarter-finals of the AAAA state playoffs. The Sybil Forrest Blue Devils have driven all the way down the field to the Tate County eight-yard line. It's the last possible play, fourth down, Blue Devils down by three. The linemen take their stances. Benton Ashley, the Blue Devils quarterback, barks out numbers, takes the snap, and scrambles to his right, looking for an open receiver. Time expires on the clock as he spots Darrell Sanderson in the end-zone—hands like flypaper, first-team All-State since his freshman year. The pass is high, but Sanderson has a three-foot vertical leap. But before he can jump, the Tate County safety, like a man drowning, claws Sanderson down without once looking back, and the ball sails past overhead—the most blatant interference anyone has ever seen.

Everyone waits for the flag.

The closest referee waves it an incomplete pass.

There is a collective gasp, a long, appalled inhalation, like what happens when a baby in church hits his head on the hard edge of the next pew: a hush, a gathering of the resources of sound, a withdrawing tide before the tsunami, and then the earsplitting outrage.

Coach Lincoln bolts onto the field bellowing, which draws a flag—as if there were anything left to penalize with no time left and the game itself over. Coach whirls toward the stands and jabs his finger at the scoreboard, where the score reads HOME 17 VISITORS 14, and then lifts his hands palm upward in disbelieving protest. It brings the crowd, already on its feet, to a decibel level that would have brought down Jericho. Blue Devil supporters on the Gallatin side of the stadium boo with such climbing intensity that an infuriated mob of them—most of them former players—bursts down from the stands toward the referee who blew the call, now suddenly surrounded by a phalanx of policemen, as though they had been expecting trouble. They escort him toward the Tate County sidelines as Gallatin fans shout profanities after him. Boys of ten or twelve start flinging things at him, hitting policemen and innocent bystanders, but at least one clod of dirt bursts across the back of the fleeing referee's head.

The opposing coach had started toward the center of field to shake hands with Coach Lincoln, but seeing the melee, he waves his team back to the sidelines, where they nervously walk toward the gymnasium without celebration. The Blue Devils, beside themselves with outrage, will not leave the field. They kept punching the air furiously to rile up themselves and the crowd. Not a man, woman, or child from Gallatin leaves the stadium. A minute or so into the orgy of protest, someone starts a chant that instantly catches on—Bull-*SHIT!* Bull-*SHIT!*—all their arms chopping in unison. Bull-*SHIT!* Bull-*SHIT!* Bull-*SHIT!*

A preacher from Griffin gets on the loudspeaker to try to calm down the crowd.

Brothers and sisters, please. Think about the example you're setting for the children.

It doesn't help. The children know bullshit when they see it. Then there come two or three hard thumps on the microphone.

Quiet, a sharp, distinctive voice says. Everyone instantly recognizes it. He taps the microphone again. A hush falls.

I never saw such a sorry spectacle.

Coach Dan Fitzgerald, retired after four decades as the Blue Devils head coach. The man with the most victories in Georgia football history.

The words hang there.

You folks are making the Blue Devils look bad. You're making the town look bad.

Out on the field, all through the stands, people look at the ground. No one meets anyone else's eye.

You folks go home. Go on home.

After a few seconds, Coach Lincoln and his players, embarrassed now to be on the field, start trudging back toward the stadium's locker rooms. It is so quiet everybody can hear it from the press box when their cleats scrabble across the concrete into the gym. The crowd disperses; the parking lot empties.

Walter Peach

November 23, 2013

Peach drove home from Griffin with Prof. Braxton Forrest, heir of the Forrest fortune, former Blue Devils football hero, and owner of the *Gallatin Tribune*. Forrest had flown down from Boston just for the game, and he was so furious afterward he wanted an early special edition of the *Tribune* published by Monday morning, instead of the usual Thursday. He and Peach had argued until midnight.

Now, barely at eight o'clock on Saturday morning, Forrest repeatedly bumped his fist on Peach's desk in the *Tribune* office, unconsciously devouring his second croissant—Mary Rose Ryburn had brought them over with coffee—in great, fierce bites.

Forrest was always bigger than Peach remembered him. His blond mane was grayer, his face more lined. There were sometimes blank spots in his conversation, occasional lapses of balance when he walked, but his intelligence and force had largely regathered after a head injury five years before during what Forrest's wife had called the Calamities, which had left him almost disabled for a year or two. At six-five, he still moved with the leonine grace that Peach remembered from the hallways of the English department at the University of Georgia, where pretty girls always seemed to have an urgent need to talk to Forrest. He was the next thing to famous; he had his own page on Wikipedia recounting the controversial career that came after Harvard University Press published his book on cultural "meiotics," *The Gameme.* He had a chaired professorship at Walcott College in New Hampshire. He had unexpectedly inherited millions of dollars five years earlier in the middle of a town scandal. Then came his conversion to Catholicism and his new book, *The Ark in Ashdod.* When famous academics converted, the media usually went silent. Peach remembered Teresa's excitement about Elizabeth Fox-Genovese, the feminist bellwether at Emory, whom Teresa had met after her conversion, and her husband Eugene Genovese, the lifelong Marxist: stars of the left who became Roman Catholic communicants. Other academics had been embarrassed, probably assuming that some emotional crisis had crippled their intellects—or, more cynically, that it was a late excitement, a canny betrayal, a bid for attention. Those who knew them, of course, knew otherwise.

Five years into being a Catholic, Forrest seemed much the same as before—huge, overwhelming, infuriating. At the moment, his only cause was the injustice of the stolen football season. Forty-five years earlier, he had led the Blue Devils to the first state championship in their history, and this morning he was still as furious as he had been the night before.

"There's a good shot of it? Let me see it." His fingers beckoned impatiently.

Peach scrolled through the images his photographer had sent him after the game. He found the ones he needed and clicked through them. There: the Tate County safety, his back toward the ball, all over Darrell Sanderson, the ball close and reachable overhead. As it came up on his laptop screen, Peach turned it toward Forrest.

"Sweet Jesus," Forrest said, and then checked himself. "Sorry, old habit. That's fantastic. Who took this?"

"Boy named Rob Waldrop. He's in Southern Studies at Mercer. He's read your books."

"Southern Studies?" Forrest looked across the desk at Peach and then shook his head. "Fill the whole page with it. *Robbed.* One word at the bottom. All caps, exclamation point. Can you print it in red?"

"It will cost us."

"I don't care. Do it."

Peach nodded. Forrest got up and walked over to the iMac on the desk with two screens and put his hand on the keyboard. "So who uses this?"

"Whoever's doing layout and graphics for me."

"Can you get somebody in today?"

"Maybe the Haygood girl if she's not busy. Rose could do it in a pinch. She's pretty good."

"Do it yourself if you have to. I'll write an editorial. You write the main piece. Interview Coach Lincoln and the Sanderson boy. Get something from Coach Fitz if you can. See if we've already appealed the game."

"Where would they appeal it?"

"Hell, Walter, I don't know. Find out."

"Can you even appeal a bad call?" Peach asked.

Forrest was pacing back and forth. He stopped to stare unseeing at the wall of framed award-winning stories, the certificates, the trophies, and then started off again like a caged panther.

"Find out how an appeal works. Hell, there was something fishy about the whole damn game. Remember that holding call on that third-down play when the Blue Devils were driving? We made the first down, but it got called back, and we ended up having to punt. Somebody paid off the referees, I can smell it—and you saw those cops. They were expecting it. Somebody's behind this."

"It wasn't Tate County, it was the referee. There's no guarantee Darrell would have even caught it. I don't see how they can just give us the game. And weren't those Griffin police? They weren't from Tate County. You sound like me on the cartels."

Forrest stopped by the front door and gazed out through the glass at the courthouse square with his hands in the back pockets of his jeans.

"Somebody stopped me last night to ask me why the paper was paying so much attention to cartels."

"Was it Hiram Walker?" Peach said.

"No, a woman from out in the county. A teacher. I can't remember her name. She said your niece Nora lives with her."

"Emma Fields." Peach's heart lightened at the mere mention of Nora. "What did she say?"

"She told me the school board was talking about cutting back funding for art and music. She wanted to know why Mexican cartels were getting more attention than educating our children. I've let you run with it. But it's time to let it go. You don't have any proof."

"They must think so. I've gotten threats from them."

"What threats?" said Forrest, turning around to face him.

"Mexicans calling me. Telling me they know me. That's happened twice now."

"Like they know where you live?"

"And a picture of Rose coming out of school. Things like that. Cartels are already in the suburbs north of Atlanta," he said. "And they're moving south. There was a Sinaloa deputy arrested last week in Butts County."

"Listen, Walter. Not this week. I mean, if Tate County's quarterback is named Gonzalez and you can prove that his daddy runs a cartel that threatened to murder the referees' families unless they made the right calls—"

"I hear you."

"The game is the story."

"Okay, okay."

"Did this Waldrop boy get a picture of those cops?"

"No, just the game."

"Well, somebody must have been taking pictures. Somebody probably got a video on their phone that we could put up on our website. Get a picture of that goddamn referee. See if he's got a Facebook page. Let's get this to the printer today. I want the Atlanta papers to pick this up. I want it on the Atlanta TV news by Monday night."

"Seriously, Braxton? You want me to do all this in one day?"

"I'm serious as hell. Let's get it done. Get on the phone."

Braxton Forrest

On Tuesday afternoon, a day later than Forrest had hoped, one of the Atlanta TV stations picked up the story about the Griffin game. One of Peach's former interns, now working in television, had called Peach to watch the News at Five. The anchor on NBC, Gloria Nabors—radiating actual intelligence, in Forrest's opinion, and pretty without looking like a Fox News mannequin—held up the *Tribune's* front page. *ROBBED!* The sports announcer, Dewey Stroud, took the handoff. Dewey had played linebacker for the Atlanta Falcons. He had a bulging face and a seen-it-all attitude, but he did not made a joke of it. He hadn't used the referee's name and picture, as the *Tribune* had—a man named Tim Dibbler, a county tax assessor in Newnan—but he had shamelessly editorialized. He said he knew how much work and how much hope went into a high school football season. He said that the Georgia Officials Athletic Association claimed to be taking the incident seriously, but then he showed a few seconds of video (where had he gotten that?) proving the interference on Darrell Sanderson and the non-call.

"You see that, folks?" he said to the camera. "And there's nothing to do about it. No appeal on that call. No instant replay. Tate County goes to the next round, and the Sybil Forrest Blue Devils? Well, as the *Gallatin Tribune* says…" He held up Rob Waldrop's full-page photo and the huge word at the bottom: ROBBED! "If you ask me," Dewey said as the camera pulled in for a close-up, "it's time for some rule changes in Georgia high school football." He glared into the camera. "Gloria."

Forrest stared at the television for a moment from the big leather armchair—Gloria Nabors talking about a street tirade by Alex Baldwin caught on somebody's phone—and then turned off the power with the remote.

"I guess that's all," Teresa said from the couch, sighing.

"Listen," Peach said, leaning forward, "did you see a man in a suit standing on the sidelines in that video? Skinny, wearing some kind of black fedora?"

"Didn't notice him," Forrest said.

"It's frustrating we can't run in back and stop the video. I could swear I've seen him. Several months ago."

"You think it's important?"

Peach lifted his hands noncommittally.

"Another lost cause," Forrest said. "But ma'am," he said to Teresa, "the *Gallatin Tribune,* edited by your award-winning husband, just got statewide attention, and we need to celebrate."

"I bet you do." Teresa gave him a sardonic look.

Forrest nodded, frowning judiciously, and led Peach to the back stairs. They went up half a flight to the landing and Forrest opened the door to the study. Inside, Peach took an armchair. Forrest found the heavy old glasses and opened the bottle of bourbon he had bought on the way over. He poured himself a glass, drank it off, feeling the sweet burn of it down his throat. He poured Peach a glass and refilled his own.

Outside, the pecans and elms were stripped of all but the last few leaves. A squirrel clambered up the swaying branches to a high nest. From this height halfway between the second and third floors, Forrest could see the curve in Johnson's Mill Road and the cut cornstalks in the fields beyond the last houses. He lifted the bottle and held it against the late November light slanting through the picture window above the desk.

"Isn't that just goddamn beautiful?" he said.

"Shading into sublime," Peach said. He was sitting back in the shadows. Sunlight touched his right hand, his glass, which was already empty, and his blue-jeaned legs crossed at the ankle above his scuffed brown loafers. Forrest reached forward to pour him more whiskey. Peach leaned into the sun and nodded as Forrest half-filled his glass.

Forrest regarded the fine aristocratic head, the graying hair swept back into a ponytail. Twenty years ago, he would have sworn that Peach would be the most famous poet in America, but then Walter's son had died in an accident. Forrest remembered the lucid, ironic man, still not yet thirty, whose office had been a few doors down from his in Park Hall. No occasion was lost on him, no display of personality. His unofficial accounts of faculty meetings—he called them "Seconds"—circulated hilariously through the younger members of the English department. The best students loved him. When he drank at parties, which he did without coarseness or loss of self-control, he could call up whole poems by Yeats or Keats or Marvell, passages from *Ulysses* or *Lolita*, sections of the *Iliad* in Greek and the *Aeneid* in Latin, Biblical parables in Anglo-Saxon.

"You remember that passage about bourbon you used to recite?" Forrest asked. "The one from Faulkner?"

"Give me a second," Peach said. He set down his glass and straightened up, thinking. "*He would forever remember*—No, that's not it. *It would seem to him*—yes. *It would seem to him that those fine fierce instants of heart and brain and courage and wiliness and speed were concentrated and distilled into that brown liquor which not women, not boys and children, but only hunters drank, drinking not of the blood they spilled but some condensation of the wild immortal spirit, drinking it moderately, humbly even, not with the pagan's base and baseless hope of acquiring thereby the virtues of cunning and speed but in salute to them.*"

"To the wild immortal spirit," Forrest said, raising his glass. He leaned forward and Peach reached over to tap his glass.

Forrest's grandfather, Thomas Jefferson Forrest, founder of Forrest Mills, had conceived of Stonewall Hill with this study in mind, for just this kind of occasion. The room had its own plumbing, its own liquor cabinet, its own set of deep leather armchairs and standing lamps to match the desk chair, and its own fireplace and chimney, which Forrest had restored. A cherry-wood humidor sat on one side of the desk, and cigar smells permeated the room. Old T.J. must have brought guests here to escape the notorious Sybil, Forrest thought. Her name adorned the high school in Gallatin—less in honor than in recompense for old T.J.'s amorous transgressions with Ella, one of the household maids. The room was full of old books, complete sets of Shakespeare, Dickens, and Browning, the writers of the Southern renascence of the last century—novels by William Faulkner and Caroline Gordon and Robert Penn Warren, books of poetry by Allen Tate, John Crowe Ransom, and Donald Davidson, the short stories of Eudora Welty, a first edition of Flannery O'Connor's *Wise Blood*. Forrest's father Robert had collected them in the years after World War II.

Until Forrest had taken possession of the house after the death of Cousin Emily Barron Hayes, he had never suspected the existence of this secret masculine haven. Apparently Cousin Emily—Forrest remembered lifting that ancient crone to eye level as she shrank back in her chair—had never bothered to explore it. She was too obsessed with Robert Forrest and his marriage to Inger Glatt, not to mention his abandonment of his family and inheritance for Pearl Parker, Aunt Ella's daughter, mother of Marilyn Harkins. The whole tangle of family lore. Forrest had spent a week in the study four years ago before the Peach family moved in. He had gone through old T.J. Forrest's private letters and papers, uncovering matters that even Mary Louise Gibson, with all her experience growing up in the house and seeing its secrets, had never suspected.

Under the house, carefully built over, was a deeper history. A century and a half ago, during the last autumn of the war when Gen. William Tecumseh Sherman was pillaging and raiding his way south to Savannah with a huge Union army—making his March to the Sea—Major-General Peter J. Osterhaus and his Fifteenth Corps had passed to the east of Gallatin and spared the town, but a few stray raiders had come through in search of chickens or unguarded silver. One of them had famously been shot in the heart by ten-year-old Bessie May Willingham as he emerged from the smokehouse with a ham in each hand. And then there was the other faction, so to speak. The slaves of the plantation, a thousand acres owned by Col. Farquhar McIntosh, had heard the great wind of the

Union passing and vanished overnight after the liberating army. Forrest's daughter Hermia had looked up the name of every slave in the McIntosh family records. She had interviewed all the descendants she could find for her book, *Tell Old Pharaoh*, which had caused a minor stir and had earned her a chair at Northwestern.

Hermia Watson. Good Lord.

"And this also," Forrest said aloud, "has been one of the dark places of the earth."

Peach leaned over to get Forrest to pour him some more bourbon.

"You know, it's a consolation," Forrest said, "to have a history of actual wrong. A heritage of real injustice instead of all the bullshit whining about gender identity and microaggression. All those lives lived in actual mastery or slavery, real aristocracy, real servitude, in the heart of the modern democratic industrial world."

Peach was silent. After a long moment, he asked, "How exactly is that a consolation?"

"It was forthright injustice. Nobody vilifies all those Yankee mill owners who depended on the slave labor of plantation cotton. The whole smug economy supporting Boston. Were they better men than the slaveowners? Not a chance, but now everybody just wants to—what? Rewrite it all? Moralize it to some prim drivel."

"Okay," Peach said.

"Think about what you have to *be* to actually hold another man in bondage. Think of the ancients. Slaves were an everyday part of the household, even for philosophers and statesmen like Cicero. Slaves were a *measure*. If you owned slaves and you had any moral integrity, you had to be worthy to own them. And that meant that being a free man was in effect defined by what your slaves were—and not just by their bondage. You had to rise above whatever you had in common with them in order to be worthy to own them."

"Seriously, Braxton?"

"Hell, yes. Now everybody thinks like a slave, as though the only reason they can't be happy and do whatever they want is because of something holding them in bondage—including nature itself. Look, Mama, mean old Nature gave me a winkie when I didn't want one! Human greatness comes from genius working within strong limits, not getting *rid* of limits. It's impossible to imagine a statesman like Cicero in our age. But it wasn't impossible to imagine men of real complexity and stature in the Old South."

"Like Cicero?" said Peach, lifting his glass with a slight twist.

"You never could stand Cicero."

"Did you ever see anybody so eager to groom his own reputation? I'm not convinced he ever did anything good except to be praised for it."

"Okay, Walter, but look. I'm talking about men who owned other human beings as their property, but they were expected to be courteous, brave, prudent in their dealings. And then in public, they were expected to defend and perpetuate slavery in the face of righteous abolitionist condemnation. It was insane. But at least they had to take care of the victims of their own injustice personally and for life. They had to be strong enough to bear the contradiction."

"That has a certain Nietzschean nose to it, doesn't it?" Peach said, raising his glass toward the bust of Nathan Bedford Forrest, who glared down on them from the bookshelf.

"Genovese says the slaves themselves admired the aristocratic ethos, especially their masters' dignity and courtesy and coolness under fire."

"They admired virtues. All men admire real virtues. And yes, slaveowners with any conscience exercised a certain noblesse oblige, I suspect," Peach said. "But remember Jefferson writing about the effects of slavery on the owner? The boy working himself into a frenzy to whip the slave? Besides, it's easy to define yourself over against your slave if you can deny his humanity. It reminds me of Gulliver with the Yahoos."

"Is that what you think I'm saying? "

"Not exactly. And you may be right about the ancient world. There's an undeniable height, an undeniable nobility, but it was different then. Slaves could be freed and then just melt into the general population— Cicero's Tiro, for example. I'm thinking about being defined at birth by blackness. If you're born into chattel slavery in the Old South, you don't have any way to disappear. You bear the visible sign of the peculiar institution even when you're no longer legally a slave. To me that's the intractable problem of race in America."

"I admit all the injustice!" Forrest said. "God knows I've thought about that. I'm talking about the displacement of your own servility onto another man. I'm talking about what constitutes honor and dignity for a man who owns slaves—the forms, the manners, clothing, modes of speech, the deliberate elevation of bearing, the upward transformation of the body and the passions. Race just confuses the essential issue."

Peach took a sip of his bourbon and regarded Forrest with his gray eyes. "I would have said it distills the issue."

Forrest stood up and gazed through the picture window. What if the land itself held the curse? What if that old injustice underlay his own story of dark erotic recompense? His head turned at a sound. Again, it came, a light knock at the door onto the landing.

"I thought your family was out," Forrest said.

Peach shrugged and Forrest took two steps down the passage and opened the door. A girl in a yellow dress stood there. She was looking away down the stairway toward the second floor, but when she heard the door open, she turned back with such perfect grace that his heart hurt. When she saw that it was not Peach, her mouth opened and she drew back, watchful.

"I thought—is Walter here?" she said. Before he could answer, she cried, "Oh! You must be Professor Forrest." By now, Peach stood in the entryway beside him, and the girl brightened to see him. All the habitual irony was gone from Peach's face.

"This is Nora O'Hearn. Buford's teacher," he explained to Forrest. "Teresa's niece."

"I need to ask you something," Nora said. "I'm sorry to just bust in like this. I didn't see anybody downstairs, so I just came up."

She did not stay long. She wanted to talk about the next poem she was having her fifth graders memorize. She turned her gaze on Peach for guidance. Forrest admired the sideways inclining of her head. She had a face full of quicksilver concerns and pleasures. There was a speed, a fleetness, in her person. When she stood to go, he thought of a pronghorn antelope he had seen once on his way through Wyoming, poised at the edge of a field of sagebrush, alert and gathered, on the verge of graceful alarm.

"Wait just a minute," Walter said. "Did I tell you how Braxton got me up here?"

"I don't think so." She sat back down.

"So four years ago, I was teaching English at South Georgia Technical College down in Waycross. I had this one pot-bellied guy in class, thirty or so, with an ugly bristle of a mustache. A stalker type. He always wore NASCAR pit crew shirts and he never let up on his chewing gum. He'd sit in the far corner of the room tipped back in his chair, chewing and eyeing the women—not a choice selection, in all fairness. I remember the exact second when I got him to stop. Jaws on pause, mouth open. We were about five weeks into the course, and I had just read out loud the last lines of the poem we were doing: 'Let the lamp affix its beam./The only emperor is the emperor of ice cream.'"

"Wallace Stevens," Nora murmured.

"So WHAM, the front legs of the chair come crashing down onto the floor and the whole class jumps. *Jesus Christ Almighty*, he says. *I'm paying for this shit.*"

Forrest laughed, but Nora looked at him with concern.

"What did you say?"

"I called him the Rajah of Juicy Fruit."

"You did not!"

"No, I think I told him he should go get his money back. Anyway, at the end of that class, I go out in the hallway, and there's Braxton."

Nora turned her gaze on Forrest. "And you invited him here?"

"I did. I hated to see him wasted on Waycross."

They talked for a few more minutes. When she left, the study seemed desolate. The two men sat without speaking for a long moment.

"Walter," Forrest said at last. He turned on the desk lamp. "You know what Mary Louise Gibson used to tell me when I was little and she was ironing clothes in the laundry room and I'd come in upset?"

"What?"

"She'd say, *Man is born to trouble as surely as the sparks fly upward*."

Peach finished his whiskey and said, "I'm writing again. Two poems in the past week. Eleven in the last two months."

Forrest sighed and shook his head. "God help you," he said. "I'd better get to bed."

Buford

Halfway down the hallway toward his room, Buford heard Mr. Forrest coming upstairs from the office. No escape. In the dim hallway light on the second floor, Mr. Forrest loomed up, a little startled to see Buford, and put out his huge hand.

"Hey, buddy. Good to see you. I just met your pretty teacher."

Buford shifted the books to squeeze them under his left arm and offered his right hand sacrificially. Mr. Forrest seemed to have no idea how strong his grip was. Buford squeezed back as hard as he could, shifting his feet and smiling awkwardly. He always felt timid with Mr. Forrest because his family owed him so much.

"What are you reading?" Mr. Forrest asked.

Buford held out the books he had checked out from the library that afternoon: one on astronomy with good illustrations, an atlas, a book *about* atlases, a Civil War novel called *The Killer Angels*, and a French edition of Descartes, *Les Meditations Metaphysiques*, which had made Mrs. Lawson tilt her head at him.

Mr. Forrest looked through them, his lips pursed.

"Descartes in French?" Mr. Forrest said, lifting his eyes. Buford could smell the whiskey. Whenever Mr. Forrest visited, he would go up and drink and talk to Buford's father, usually until very late.

"Yes sir."

"You know what it's about?"

"I think, therefore I am?"

"Here's what you want to ask yourself: why would Descartes think that he had to doubt everything but himself? Do you doubt that the sun will come up in the morning?"

Buford knew there must be a trick in the question, maybe something about the difference between probability and certainty, but he decided to give the answer he thought he was supposed to give.

"No sir."

"So, tomorrow morning, the sun will come up at the eastern horizon and climb through the trees and rise into the sky."

"Yes sir."

"But it won't really come up."

"No sir. Because it's the earth—"

"Right, the rotation of the earth, not the motion of the sun."

"Yes sir."

"And even though you know it's happening, you can't sense the earth whipping along at a thousand miles an hour with you and everything else."

"No sir."

"And so what else should you doubt? Your senses fool you. Your mind itself fools you. What you think you're looking at is really just information being reconstituted in your brain. Everything seems real to you when you're in a dream. How do you know that what's happening right now— you think you're awake, right?— isn't really a dream?"

"Because I can smell whiskey?"

Mr. Forrest laughed out loud and clapped him on the shoulder. "I have to get up early. See you next time, buddy."

"Yes sir. Good night."

"Listen, if you're going to read Descartes, you should read some Aristotle."

"He makes fun of Aristotle."

"Read Aristotle anyway. Actually, read him for that very reason."

"Yes sir."

Buford went to his room, buzzing a little from the conversation, and opened his laptop.

Buddy, Mr. Forrest had called him. Could a man so much older be his buddy? He checked his email. Nothing there except a link to an old map of Wyoming somebody on his online forum had sent him. He needed some friends his own age. But most of the boys his own age didn't know anything and didn't care that they didn't. It was all video games and sports, which he liked, but not the way they did. Mr. Forrest didn't talk down to him, at least. *Why would you doubt everything?* That was the key to Descartes—that's what he meant. Coming to realize that everything was a trick. Everything you thought was real wasn't. The sun coming up was a trick. So Descartes saw this huge difference between what he knew from science and what he knew through his senses. It would be even worse now, because Descartes didn't even know about molecules and stuff like that. How you smell, how you taste. Nerve endings, receptors, little floating molecules of whiskey smell.

Or Miss Nora.

Or how you see—how reverse images curve on your retina and go up the optic nerve and get straightened out in your brain so you think you "see" something, but it's all a kind of show in your head that you think is real. That's what he was saying. So how do you know what's really real?

That was the whole thing. I *think*; therefore, I *am*. Even if nothing else is real, *I* have to be here to think. To be thinking, I have to exist.

But that puts everything back on me. The only real world I can be sure of is me thinking. Me and the Happy Neuron Show.

Suddenly the idea made him feel like he was suffocating, like he was stuck in a dark closet. Or blind and deaf and dumb and paralyzed. Or buried alive, lying there trapped in a coffin like Madeleine Usher in the Edgar Allan Poe story.

Buried alive. He stood up panicked and walked around clenching his hands, trying to get rid of the thought.

The world wasn't a trick. That couldn't be true. What about Rose? What could be realer than Rose, sitting across from him in her t-shirt at the breakfast table with the fork dangling backward from her hand? What could be realer than Rose calling herself Raïssa because she saw the name on a book her mother liked and thought it sounded better than plain old *Rose*? Or his mom, or Martin Sams, who sat on the bench at the corner of the courthouse square dressed in a police uniform? Or Evelyn Watson, who sat in the next row in Miss Nora's classroom with hair so long and smooth it looked like the grain in polished wood?

It wasn't a trick! Your senses gave you the live world, the way you were supposed to have it. That's what his mom always said—that it was *given* to you. It struck him that for Descartes, the world was always *taken* except for that last thing that couldn't be taken, which was your own thinking, even if you were being tricked.

But you weren't being tricked. He thought of the big raucous crows in the bare branches of the pecan tree that morning. They were just as real as he was. Sunlight on the grass. The dog who came and visited from next door, wagging his tail and ducking his head, stopping right in the middle of greeting him to scratch behind his ear with his back foot and then getting up with his tongue lolling out, friendly as could be.

His mother and the way she smelled after she had been baking bread. Miss Nora.

A sense of the goodness of God overwhelmed him and his heart felt so warm with it he walked around the room again the other way. You're always being given something that's yours, more than you could possibly take in. This very minute, being given everything.

He saw himself in the mirror and stopped. Was that him? What he saw was not what he felt like. His face looking at his face. His body. He was of two minds about his body. On the one hand, he was just a chance combination of genes that his mother and his father had passed on, without meaning for him to be anything in particular. On the other hand, this body was what God had given him. It was what his own individual soul looked like to everybody else. His father had explained to him that the Latin word for soul, *anima*, was the word that described anything animate. Animals were things with souls.

Wait, so animals have souls?

You can't be an animal without one, his father said.

Souls like ours?

Souls as different as their bodies. Horse, cow, mouse, blue jay.

But your body isn't your soul.

So what holds your body together? What makes your heart beat? What makes you dream? How do you keep breathing? Animals have all that going on. So I look at your body, and I see what your soul looks like.

What about Janice Knowlton? Is her soul as ugly as she is?

Describe your soul to me.

Isn't it what I am inside? Like my personality? like what I think? something immortal that's—you know—?

The Greeks in the age of Homer never used the word for body for a living man, only for his corpse, and they never used the word soul for a living person, either. Only at death did they become body and soul. Don't you think there's something right about that?

I don't know. What do you mean?

If you kill something, you divide it into a soul and a body. This thing in front of you, this thing you killed, is now just a body. But that doesn't mean that the body was what made it alive. Its life, whose form was the soul, was the condition for the body. You shoot an animal, and then its brain won't work or its heart can't pump, and then what happens to it? It dies, which means that it becomes two things. Its soul leaves the body, and the body becomes a thing, like ice cream that holds the shape of the scoop for a little while and then starts to melt. Maybe it's best to say that life is the condition for life. Do you realize that there's nothing now living that has not always been alive, since the very first living thing? If you're alive now, the life in you has been alive ever since the first thing that lived.

He had thought about that a lot: everything now alive has the life in it that has always been alive; otherwise, how could it be alive now?

But he got confused. He wasn't sure his father wasn't confused, too. *Buford* hadn't always been alive—that didn't make sense—but what about the stuff going on in him that knew how to circulate his blood and fight bacteria and breathe and hold all his memories? You came into stuff going on that grew "you" which was you thinking, you conscious, and the going matured you and aged you and died as you and left the body behind like a shell washed up on the beach while the huge sea of going never died.

Okay, but what happened to you, to your soul? All the bodies in the cemetery, all the Confederate soldiers?

You woke up already in the going and then got used to the going as if *you* were *it* but then you died and had to leave the going and you became what? Became what?

Braxton Forrest

Forrest's flight from Atlanta left at seven the next morning, and he had to drop off the rental car in time to check in an hour ahead of time. He would need to leave Gallatin by 4:30 or so. He used the bathroom, put out his clothes for the morning, set his phone for 4:00, and got undressed for bed. He had replaced the mattresses on all the beds in the house, but the ornately carved headboard and footboard of the bed were original, already a hundred years old, as were the heavy dresser, the armoire, the deep leather armchair, and the full-length mirror. He had told Walter and Teresa that he wanted this room reserved just for his visits, because it was the master bedroom his grandfather had fashioned just for himself. His grandmother Sybil had her own room on the opposite end of the house. Like the office, the room gave Forrest a feel for the original life of the house, even its civil wars; it brought him a little way toward his father and the family he had never known. All he really wanted from Stonewall Hill was the occasional sense of lineage, he supposed. He was happy to have the Peach family inhabit it.

Closing his eyes, he thought about what else he might have said to Peach. He had spent so many years of his own life with a disregard for ordinary standards of virtue that it was hard to explain what exactly he dreaded, seeing the look on Walter's face or that bright adoration in the girl's eyes. Maybe part of his penance was seeing it all happen to someone else and being helpless to intervene.

The man had fallen in love with his niece. Well, his wife's niece—at least no blood relation. Of course, Forrest had never thought there was a blood relation with Marilyn, had he? Or with Hermia, their daughter. Maybe it had taken the death of Marilyn Harkins to make Forrest see with his whole soul the relentless weave of the old Sisters, the way all things came around. It felt like Fate, or Hardy's Hap. Only after a very long time, —sitting in his house in Portsmouth and musing over everything, trying to recover from the damage to his brain and his psyche—had he been able to call it "providence," as if there were something good in these disasters. He felt numb to what his wife Marisa called "the delicate hand of providence," quoting somebody—Mother Teresa, perhaps.

The hand had hardly been delicate with him, in any case. Why should there be providence with respect to Braxton Forrest, anyway? Hardest of all to imagine was that God Almighty, with the whole universe to look after, cared anything about the peccadilloes of a middle-aged literature professor. The apparent absurdity of it had to be balanced against the overwhelmingly convincing sense of an inner witness, an exacting (if often ignored) conscience, a kind of co-knowing whose ground lay deeper than his own conscious mind. So yes. Acceptance of providence brought him to see himself differently. It even brought him, if only occasionally, to the Gospels, where he did not encounter the sweet, naïve, androgynous, new version of the fierce Old Testament God that he expected, but the Old Testament God incarnate, the fierce, severe, enigmatic otherness of a man whose absolute authority overflowed any apparent warrant for it. This Jesus was the one whose kingly power had startled him when he saw the golden apse of the Monreale Cathedral built by the Normans two hundred years before Dante was born. It was the iconic Christ whose face Flannery O'Connor's character O.E. Parker chose to have tattooed on his back—a Christ without sentimentality, one whose eyes saw man for what he was, whose gaze penetrated to whatever was hidden in Forrest's depths, especially what was hidden from himself.

Forrest didn't know if he stood a chance. He didn't think he would ever know. Unseemly images were always coming into his head, unprompted, from a lifetime of indulgence. Sometimes, waking in the middle of the night, he looked back over the wreckage he had left in his wake, the hurt and damage to people who had loved him. He thought that he must have felt like a curse for anybody who cared about him. How could he make up for what he had done so carelessly, so arrogantly? All he could say, when it came down to it, was that now, in all truth, he loved God, actually loved Him, and found the familiar pull of sin tawdry by contrast. He sinned all the time, but he prayed, too, startled whenever he remembered he could do it, just turn to God and talk.

He prayed for Walter Peach and Nora and Teresa and Rose and the boy Buford. He prayed for Marisa and his daughters. He prayed for Hermia, his daughter with Marilyn Harkins, and for his son with Hermia, John Bell Hudson, the brilliant young quarterback who was also his grandson. He prayed for the soul of Marilyn Harkins. He prayed for his father and his grandfather. He prayed for his grandmother Sybil, who had despised him—prayed even for Cousin Emily Barron Hayes, who had cheated his father out of his inheritance.

Falling asleep, he found himself bound by hooded Muslims, forced to face a camera before they beheaded him. He was saying the psalm he had memorized, what David sang after sinning with Bathsheba and sending Uriah to die. *Have mercy on me, O God, according to thy steadfast love; according to thy abundant mercy, blot out my transgressions.*

A swing of the machete. His head rolled free.

But he kept speaking.

Wash me thoroughly from my iniquities and cleanse me from my sin.

Ask Socrates

> Ain't nothing wrong with chasing the truth if
> it ain't attached to your own behind.
> --Socrates Johnson

Hey Socrates, what do you do if somebody steals a game by buying the referee?

Mrs. Tilda Poptart

Well, Mrs. Poptart, it's kind of hard to prove, ain't it? I mean unless you can track the money right from the CARTEL into the referee's back pocket with the camera on your iPhone, you know what I'm saying? Hard to make it stick even if the quarterback is named Mictlantecuhtli Gomez and his daddy has a nickname like El Serpiente—that's The Snake in real English—and built him a McMansion just far enough inside the Tate County Line, say, to get his boy on the team, and a bunch of bodyguards with AK-47s stand around at the gate and meanwhile the high school just announced a big donation to put up a statue of Pablo Escobar. I mean, don't get me started, honey. All I'm saying, it might not just be *the referee.*

Hey Socrates, I'm confused. I had Miss McGill for Spanish in 10th grade and got a C, and if you was to say The Snake in Mexican, wouldn't it be La Serpiente which it's kind of girly, like calling him Miss Snake?

Bucky G. Whillikers

You know what, Bucky? Them people in the CARTELS couldn't read the warning on a pack of firecrackers, you ask me, so it won't make no difference. Let's just call this TexMex rattlesnake El Serpiente like we didn't know no better. But hey, um—listen up, who is this Miss Snake? I think I saw her in the beauty pageant— kinda slinky black dress, right? Whoo, I guess I need me a date.

Hey Socrates, I heard on the radio ignorance is bliss, which it sounds better than this weed I got, so how do I get me some?

Upton Hodgewaller

Don't you worry, Upton, it ain't a thing to it and you're halfway home already. Step one: Get you a beer and sit down in your lawn chair and calm way the hell down and say to yourself *Congratulations. You don't know nothing, buddy.* Just go on and be up front and admit it: *Upton, you don't know pee-pie diddly.* You oughta start feeling better right away. Step two is the tricky one: Say *back* to yourself, *Yeah well listen, I know* one *thing, which it's I don't know nothing.* Then just let not knowing diddly—listen, I hate to get all mystical on you. But seriously, now—have you a sip of beer, close your eyes, and just let *not-knowing-diddly* sink in like a suntan. We're talking 101-proof glory-to-God ignorance-is-bliss. Upton, my man, this one's on Socrates and you're welcome. My problem is I close my eyes, I see a Mexican with a doobie and a machete.

Teresa Peach

Christmas Eve, 2013

Her children knew not to interrupt her morning ritual. If anyone happened to be up at 5:30 or 6:00—no one was stirring today—she would enforce a strict silence until she finished. Much of the year, she could sit outside, but on rainy days or winter mornings like this one, she used her favorite chair in the front sitting room, where she kept her icon on the table in the corner. Her friend from college, little round Brother Juniper, smitten with the Eastern tradition, had gotten permission from the monastery at Conyers to spend months in Ukraine learning iconography, and he had written the icon for her after her first son died. The sorrowful Virgin held the luminous form of the Christ-child, whose lips rose to meet hers, but it was almost as if she were not touching Him, as if he were never hers to hold, her son, yes, but more than hers. *Mother of God of Tenderness.* A harsh comfort.

She lit a votive candle in front of the icon and sat down to read the morning office from the breviary she treasured. She had been with Walter the day she found it in a vintage bookstore in Pittsburgh during her second year of graduate school at Duquesne—beautiful, leather-bound, printed in England. She loved its colored cloth ribbons in her fingers, and she had learned to navigate the seasons and feasts. The book spilled over with collected prayer cards, and she sifted through them, remembering the dead. No card for her mother, but she said a daily prayer, remembering her last days filled with bitter, unfiltered, and often-repeated castigations of Teresa for marrying Walter. And then her hand's clutching desperation as she died, the feel of it still on Teresa's wrist after fifteen years.

When she finished the readings, Teresa put the breviary aside and pulled herself into a stricter posture to meditate, trying to empty her mind of everything but God, not thinking of her mother or of forgiving Walter his darkness or Rose her irksome narcissism and pretension or Buford his oddness, trying to forget the emotional tethers, bringing her attention back—and back again—to focus on the Jesus prayer, *Lord Jesus Christ, son of the living God, have mercy on me, a sinner.* When she could manage it, she would be like Mount Zion and her thoughts would be the weather on Mount Zion. She loved that image: she could watch thoughts rise and set without entering them. She was not the thoughts. On some blessed days she felt herself wholly present to God, wholly here.

Not today, it seemed. Christmas Eve. She was anxious about the next morning, the gifts, decorating the tree that Walter would get later in the morning if there was still one left in town. She would usually pray for twenty or thirty minutes, but something felt amiss today, and she was already too impatient for her coffee. Rose said she could have been a nun except for the coffee. But her coffee ceremony was a kind of prayer, her way to honor her dear, holy, Ethiopian friend, Belen Senai, to feel Belen's blessings on her marriage and her children. Walter had met Belen one memorable evening in Pittsburgh when Belen's parents were visiting, and for a long time he would join Teresa in the ceremony every morning. They would share the coffee, plan for the day, and end with the St. Michael prayer that Belen had loved. A month after Nora started showing up every Friday and their meetings solidified into "poetry sessions," Walter had missed a Saturday morning, then a Monday, and soon there was always some excuse.

At the quick burn of jealousy, she stood and crossed herself and walked over to blow out the candle in front of the icon. Smoke trailed away above the stack of Christmas cards into one of the old house's drafts. Thank God the girl had gone back to Athens for Christmas. She heard Walter moving upstairs, rousing himself to go out and get that tree.

She should try again. In the kitchen, she started the kettle on the stovetop and got down the bag of Ethiopian Yirgacheffe coffee beans—she needed to order another one this week after the Christmas rush—and shook them into the hollow of her left palm. It was a *felt measure*, as Belen always said—the look in the hand, the weight. She loved the feel and smell of the beans—four palmfuls, one by one, into the coffee grinder. When she pressed the button, the grinder roared for a few seconds. She tapped it to settle the beans, ground again, not too much, and then emptied the grounds into the French press and waited for the water in the kettle.

Out the window over the sink, crows swapped perches and cawed at each other from the bare branches of the pecan trees.

No one could say she had not tried to be kind to the girl. She had sent up pies for their poetry nights, Nora, Rose, and Walter up in the study reading together. Early on, she had even joined them a few times. She warmed seeing Walter's genius revive, though it stung that she was not the occasion.

When the water came to a boil, she was halfway through a third biscotti, hardly conscious of having taken out the container. She poured the boiling water, stirring the mixture with a wooden spoon, twice, before closing the top.

Belen, her guide into mysteries.

Small-boned, colorful as a tanager in her native dress, she had an elegant formal command of situations, and her eyes were always full of merry courtesy. She addressed people as though she were inwardly awed by the very fact of their presence. She had been full of half-pagan stories— the great serpent that lived in a cleft of the rock and guarded their farm. She had made *doro wat* once at Teresa's apartment, and one morning she had come over to show her their coffee ritual. Belen's grandfather had owned a small plot where he tended coffee plants. Her grandmother had roasted the just-picked beans in a stove pan, had then ground them by hand and stirred the coffee into the boiling water of a clay *jebena*.

Oh Teresa, Belen would say in her lilting way, her face shining, *the house smelled so good. My grandfather and his friends had cups only this big,* her hands shaping the size of a child's teacup, *and my beautiful āyatē would hold the jebena high up, this high, and pour it without spilling or splashing, and everyone would talk and laugh all morning.*

Her family had fled Ethiopia to escape the Marxist regime that would have forced Belen into the army. On the phone in her last months, on medication, she had told Teresa in whispers how many people on her block in New Jersey were possessed by demons. When Belen died of cancer in her mid-thirties, luminous and full of spirit to the ravaged end, it took Teresa a year or so of grieving to develop this honorary ceremony, and now it was her way of remembering Belen every day. Praying for her, yes, but also praying for her intercession and help.

Walter came down the back stairs on his way somewhere. He waved as he looked into the kitchen.

"Don't you want some coffee?" Teresa asked. "I just poured it."

He already had his hand on the door, but he stopped—jeans, running shoes, an old hoodie, the neat gray ponytail, the habitually sardonic expression that suddenly softened.

"It's been a while, I guess," he said.

"I was just remembering Belen. Wasn't she lovely? I remember your expression when she tore off that piece of injera and fed you the *doro wat* her mother made."

She watched him remember and nod.

"I loved her very much," Teresa said.

He stood across the island from her and met her eyes. She loved Walter, too, and when he lifted the cup she poured and took a sip of it, her heart filled. He lifted his eyebrows.

"I'd forgotten how strong it is."

"Will you say the prayer with me?"

"You go ahead."

He stood back with a respectful tentativeness that brought out all her impatience.

Walter Peach

There was a poignancy to the way Teresa looked, still in her robe, fit and self-contained and somehow opulent, rich with hidden treasures, her face alight with some of that hopeful innocence that he remembered from before the accident with little Walter. It always moved him to see the ampersand of concentration dissolve between her eyes, a flush rising into those freckles he had fallen in love with long ago. Such *life* in her eyes. He thought about her all the way out the drive and into town.

What had happened there at the end? Wanting him to pray. She knew he didn't pray. And then the mild sarcasm about the cartels. *Right. The cartels*—as though she knew it was something else altogether that distracted him.

Which was Nora. Yes, yes, she was jealous of Nora. He thought back over the past few months. The niece so pretty and so adoring who brought with her the return of his poetry, which had once lived for Teresa but had died with their first son. Did Teresa want it to stay dead? Maybe she did.

He should let it go. It was Christmas. Nora was away for the holidays. They could just be a family.

He passed the disconsolate Confederate soldier on the square and headed downhill toward Walmart. Walmart had killed the downtown businesses years ago, but at least they still had Christmas trees on Christmas Eve. The ones at the grocery stores were gone by early December. The Baptists, Methodists, and Presbyterians in town all got their trees early, sometimes the day after Thanksgiving, went into a flurry of last-minute shopping, pretended to be Santa Claus on Christmas Eve, and indulged in a ritual binge of gifts the next morning. The day after Christmas, they stripped the tree of ornaments like a dishonored soldier and heaved it out to the curb, shamed, naked, shedding needles and dripping foil icicles. They might have sung "The Twelve Days of Christmas" once upon a time in school, but they had no notion of why there were twelve days. Lucinda Devereaux Lawton had taught him that much, at least. He ought to do a story about why the early Puritans rejected Christmas altogether. Startle some Baptists.

Peach wandered the vast aisles, scanning overhead for signs, until he found the gardening and lawn department, which they had moved since his last visit the year before. When he asked if they had any trees, a woman in a Walmart uniform said *Yes sir* and pointed him toward the nursery section and turned back to her stock inventory.

"I mean a Christmas tree," Peach said.

"A Christmas tree?" she said, looking a little scandalized. "Well, we might still have one or two if you look outside."

He bargained them down to $30—who else were they going to sell it to?—for a noble eight-foot Colorado blue spruce originally marked for $200. He even persuaded a couple of guys working a forklift to stop and help him tie it to the top of the Subaru.

Walter drove up Lee Street to the courthouse square, attracting stares. Going through the light at Jackson Street, he waved genially at Hiram Walker, who was coming out of the Good Scents gift shop. It used to be Rockwell's Pharmacy, but now it was a chichi place smelling of expensive scented candles. Hiram looked a little stricken to be spotted there. He held up a bag—Christmas present for the wife—and recovered by opening his other palm toward the tree on top of the van and looking a question at Peach.

Peach slowed and rolled down the window and called through the cold air, "It's a whole lot cheaper the day before Christmas," and Hiram shook his head dismissively.

After the ROBBED! issue, Hiram had warmed to him. When Peach pursued the story at Forrest's urging, he discovered that the Tate County quarterback was not Hispanic, but one of the wide receivers was. Javier Alejandro. In his editorial a week before, Peach had not used the boy's name and he had not accused the Tate County coaches, but he had asked whether there might be Mexican cartel money behind the referee's call.

Why would there be, though, seriously? If there was a clear pattern of bad referees that led to a Tate County championship, there might be a case to make, but Tate County had lost badly and uncontroversially in the next round of the playoffs. Peach wondered if he was getting a little unhinged because of the calls that kept coming. *Se donde vives.* A voice that sounded somehow familiar, a little juicy—where had he heard it? Maybe that was why he indulged his fury in the guise of Socrates Johnson. Was it responsible journalism? Not at all, but he could not kill his strong conviction that the referee had been bought off. The last Socrates Johnson feature had been a bit much, he had to admit, but he had been surprised when Mrs. Elton Buckwalter, who taught Sunday School at the Baptist Church, called him up and told him he was a racist. He had never thought about it as *racial*, but maybe, he would admit, as xenophobic, a feeling that the old American way, the old Southern story with all its tragedies and injustices, was being displaced by a culture that was not a culture at all but an amorphous set of accusations, disrespectful of hard-earned understandings about freedom and responsibility and the common good. Maybe that's what Americans used to feel about the Irish, the Italians, the Poles—all those Catholics. Not exactly racism, but close.

Hiram had come by the *Tribune* office a few days before to tell him the Touchdown Club would be behind him if he had any trouble about last week's issue. So was he just off track, just playing to the prejudices of his clientele? He would have admitted that if it were true, but he did not think so. He *knew* that that referee, Tim Dibbler, had been bought off. Or had been threatened, it suddenly struck him. It had something to do with the cartels. Maybe it had something to do with Dibbler's job as country tax assessor up in Griffin, some kind of pressure or blackmail they were putting on him—but why a football game? Who benefited from the blown call if not ultimately Tate County's football team? And they lost the next week.

Maybe it wasn't about benefit. Maybe it was just a message. But what kind of message? He could not get it to make sense.

And then, with a sudden onset of dread, he felt an absolute conviction: the blown interference call was directed at *him*, at *Walter Peach*, and it had something to do with that man in the suit and the fedora on the sidelines. He knew who he was: the thin man who had come into the *Tribune* office. The one who thought Peach knew somebody named Alison.

Peach tried to shake off his trepidation. It was Christmas Eve. He drove down the hill from the courthouse square, waving at a few more outraged neighbors. When he pulled into the drive behind the house, he honked for Buford. A yellow Prius sat beside Teresa's Focus. He parked and got out to cut the twine the men at Walmart had used to tie down the tree. The merry forklift elves hadn't used slipknots, he discovered, and the strings were pulled so tight they twanged when he plucked them.

Where was Buford? He reached in and honked the horn again, and now his son came running out the back door, pulling on a jacket.

"Bring me a knife," Peach called. "A sharp one. Or a boxcutter. Or some scissors."

Buford ran back in. Out toward the old barn, Peach heard a dog bark. He walked around to the front of the car and looked out through the vegetable garden. A big Irish setter he didn't recognize pushed through the gate and came bounding toward him. It sniffed his offered hand, licked it, and then trotted back out, breaking into a brief sprint after a panicked squirrel. So it must belong to the owner of the Prius.

Buford came out with a small paring knife that Peach used to cut the stressed twine. At an angle, Peach rocked the tree toward his side of the car, taking the thick end and most of the weight as it tilted off the roof. Buford reached up carefully through the prickly branches and caught the slender end of the trunk. They eased the tree to the ground, Peach's end first. Buford walked it upright and then backed away to look at it.

"That's awesome!"

"Let's take it in through the front door so we don't get needles all over the house. Is the stand ready?"

"Yes sir."

"Whose car is that?"

"Mr. Forrest's daughter," Buford said.

"Cate?"

Forrest's older daughter had spent Thanksgiving with them during her sophomore year at Emory. But did she have a dog? And wouldn't she have gone home to Portsmouth for Christmas?

"No sir. Hermia something. She's about your age."

"*Hermia Watson?*"

Peach glanced up toward the house, suddenly apprehensive. He had not seen Hermia since his childhood. Since they were in the bathtub together.

"She says she used to work here."

"Did she say what's she doing here now?"

"No sir."

Peach tipped the tree toward his son, who caught the top gingerly. The boy circled as Peach backed the stump around the side of house. They took it up the steps and across the porch. Peach reached awkwardly behind him and tried the huge old knob while he supported the weight of the tree against his belt.

"Run around and unlock the door," he said to Buford. The boy dropped his end and ran back around to the kitchen. He heard voices inside. Half a minute later, after some work with the unused lock and the big sliding bolt, the big door behind him swung open and Peach backed the tree into the foyer. Buford picked up his end and they took the tree past the sitting room and across the hardwood floor into the living room, where the stand waited in the corner.

"That's huge!" Rose exclaimed as he backed it into the room.

The first Christmas at Stonewall Hill with its high ceilings, he had bought a stand that could accommodate a trunk with a large diameter. Last night, he had made sure the gripping screws were all the way out to the rim. At Walmart he had cut half an inch off the hardened base of the tree so it would absorb water, and he had checked the lower branches before the men put it on top of the van. Now he guided the tree into the opening of the stand, Buford tilted it upright, and they let it fall with a deep, satisfying *thunk* onto the spikes. Buford knelt and tightened the screws while Rose brought a gallon jug of water and poured it in.

"Beautiful," said an unfamiliar voice behind him.

Hermia was almost as tall as he was, both ample and slender, dressed in tight jeans and a black top and a long knobby-textured off-white cardigan sweater that came down past her hips. With an easy languor, she stepped toward him and offered her hand.

"Walter, it's been a very long time. You look good."

"Hermia. My God."

"I bet you saw Eumaios outside."

"That's your dog's name?"

She smiled. Her black hair, cut short against her head, had streaks of grey in it. Her olive eyes took him in, quick with intelligence. She gave his hand a squeeze that lingered off into softness as she let go. Peach thought about Hermia's mother, his beloved Adara Watson, which—though he had certainly not known it at the time—was the new married name for Marilyn Harkins, the legendary streetwalker of Gallatin. He thought about the baths she used to give them and felt a blush rise in his neck. Teresa stood behind Hermia, her face not wary or suspicious, but alert. Hermia met his eyes hotly and then glanced away.

"I was just apologizing to Teresa for dropping in unannounced on Christmas Eve," she said. "I'm on my way down to Macon to visit my aunt. I thought I'd stop in Gallatin to see my friend LaCourvette Todd and her grandmother, old Mrs. Gibson, who's not doing very well. And I had to see the old place after Braxton's renovations."

"Now which aunt is this?" asked Teresa.

"Daddy Watson's sister."

"Forgive me," Teresa said, "but who is Daddy Watson?"

"My father," Hermia said.

"Oh, of course," Teresa said, meeting her calm gaze with that wrinkle of attention in her forehead and then looking down.

"So you worked here?" asked Rose in the uncomfortable silence.

"Yes, I did. While I was working on my book," said Hermia. "Stonewall Hill looks *so* much better now." Her gesture encompassed the whole house. "Old Mrs. Hayes—God rest her mean old soul—never left the back room upstairs if she could help it. She'd sit up there every day and stare out toward the garden and the barn and think it was still the 1940s."

"That's my room now," said Rose.

"Really?" Hermia smiled. "Do you see any ghosts up there?"

"Not too often," said Rose. "So what was your job? What did you do?"

"Kept Mrs. Hayes alive. And I was doing research for my book. I'd imagine I was a slave woman named Tillie."

"Were you writing a novel?"

"Not exactly. A meditation on memory and race."

"*A Mumbalin Word*," Teresa said.

"Yes!" exclaimed Hermia.

"Braxton gave us a copy. Didn't you win an award for it?"

"No, that was for *Tell Old Pharaoh*, sweetheart," Hermia said, touching Teresa's hand. "About the slaves in this house. Or the house inside this house, the old McIntosh place. Oh! I have to show you something I got a year or two ago. I've kept it for the next time I came by."

It was a worn email, printed out and folded in four, dated April 10, 2011.

os.bombacio@gmail.com
to me
Dear Prof. Watson,

Allow me to express my admiration (however belatedly) for *Tell Old Pharaoh*, which I have just finished. It gives a local habitation and a name to the matriarch my mother spoke of in my childhood. *Stonewall Hill*, she would whisper to me at night, and a magical image would rise before my inner eye. "A long, long time ago," she would say, "a great woman my grandmama lived with was just a girl in that house and still a slave."

What a pleasure it has been to read Zilpha's story in your book. I must visit the old place. My business might be taking me near Gallatin in the next several years, and if my presence should ever coincide with yours, I think we would find much in common. Of late I have become interested in family history. Do you recognize, by any chance, the name Walter Peach? You may reach me at this email address.
Most sincerely,
Os Bombacio
Durango, Mexico

"Did you write him back?" Peach asked.

"Well, I did. In fact, I told him that, as a matter of fact, you were living at Stonewall Hill. Nothing since then. I love fan mail, and I've hung onto it because I want to figure out who his grandmother was. I'm sure she must have visited Stonewall Hill, but I suspect she lived at Zilpha's place out in the county." She smiled at Peach. "Do you mind if I just take a quick tour? Don't let me interrupt your decorating. I'll just look through the house and be on my way."

"I'll come with you," Rose said.

"Wonderful!"

On their way out of the room, Hermia hugged Rose against her. "You are just gorgeous," she said. "I want you to meet my son."

In the silence, Teresa's eyes rose to meet Walter's.

Teresa

Since the Peach family first moved into Stonewall Hill in 2010, Teresa had grown closer every year to Marisa Forrest, Braxton's wife. Three or four times, Marisa had come down with Braxton to visit, and at least three times, most recently in October, she had come by herself or with one of her girls. She and Teresa had as much in common as Braxton and Walter did. They shared their faith—an idiom of favorite saints and devotions—and their sense of beauty. Marisa gravitated toward the Post-Impressionists, as did Teresa. Marisa sometimes brought gifts of her own work; at least once she had spent the morning painting while Teresa sat nearby and read, more contented than she had been since the accident.

They could talk for hours about the still-life paintings of Cezanne. Without having read a word of Husserl, Marisa instantly understood her when Teresa said that "the earth does not move" in our primordial experience and that Cezanne knew it. Marisa understood what Teresa meant about things being "given," and she said that the *givenness* in things was what she most wanted to paint.

Teresa could never talk to Walter these days with the same kind of depth. *You go ahead*, he had said that morning when she asked him to pray. *You go ahead*. Nothing to do with him, was it?

But Marisa shared her faith. She remembered sitting on the porch of Stonewall Hill with Marisa on a warm October day, the leaves falling, a bottle of wine beside them and even, on occasion, the smoke of a cigarette or two rising languidly from their hands, and she was reminded of days in college, picnics in Tuscany, meals with Belen, intervals of pure communion. Sometimes when she and Marisa talked, worries dropped away and the original world, naked and unfallen, came from behind its veil and pressed upon them.

One deep worry that never quite left Marisa (as Teresa came to understand through her friend's indirect comments and offhand allusions) was Hermia Watson. In the summer of 2009, Hermia had caused the Calamities, as Marisa called them—the endangerment of Cate and Bernadette, who had arrived in Gallatin in the expectation of welcome to meet instead the contempt of old Mrs. Hayes, not to mention the wholesale surprise of the community; Braxton's brain injury; the death of Gallatin's only NFL star, Dutrelle Jones; the death of the woman no one had recognized as Marilyn Harkins. There was something about Hermia that seemed to bring destruction in its wake. Marisa was a woman of deep charity, but Hermia troubled her. When Teresa had finally asked Braxton's wife about it on her last visit, her friend had been a long time answering her.

She remembered exactly where they were. It was late at night, in the living room. Marisa sat at one end of the couch, musing and quiet, swirling the cognac in her snifter. Teresa sat across from her in the armchair, her face bent almost comically into the warm fumes of her glass. Marisa looked up at her.

You know she's Braxton's daughter.

Yes, I knew that.

And she has a son.

Yes. The football player.

There had been a longer pause.

He's her son with Braxton.

Teresa's eyes met Marisa's.

Hermia's son with her own father.

Yes.

Teresa stared into her friend's impassive face, and a chill of horror held her so still she could not move or speak.

Have you seen her son? Marisa asked. *He's the quarterback at Alabama, an NFL prospect. He looks just like Braxton at that age. And she's so proud of him. Do you know what I feel like when she looks at Braxton?*

You've seen her with him?

She came to our house in Portsmouth last summer. Not a sign of guilt.

Oh, my Lord. Marisa. What does he say about it?

He told me after the Calamities. He actually wrote it down, and I've kept it for so long that I've memorized one sentence: "Fate searches its way unfelt into the smallest capillaries of the will, and then at the opportune time, it burns from within like a million filaments." He quoted King Lear *to me. "I am bound upon a wheel of fire/That mine own tears do scald like molten lead." He told me he had been singled out for damnation.*

Walter says that same thing to me sometimes.

Braxton has changed. He got past that darkness, thank God.

Do you hate Hermia?

Marisa paused for a long time before she spoke.

You know, she gave the boy up for adoption when he was born. She discovered him again through a friend in Dallas back before the Calamities, and that's why she got back in touch with Braxton that summer. It all seems intended, but not by her. I don't think she knew until he came to Gallatin that he was her father.

Oh God, Marisa.

And now Hermia Watson was in Stonewall Hill. She was upstairs, talking to Rose. *I want you to meet my son*—her son with her own father, with

64

Braxton Forrest, who owned this house, who had been their benefactor and friend. After Marisa's revelation, Teresa had looked up pictures of the son. With macabre fascination, she had examined him for evidence of genetic defects, but everything about him seemed almost uncannily enhanced—intelligence, looks, athletic ability—as though he were a more sophisticated version of Braxton in his youth. Where was the aura of evil? The visible genetic flaw? But Teresa could see nothing amiss in him. And Hermia Watson spoke of him openly, as though the spirit of this confessional age had absolved him of any shame attached to his origin.

Or Hermia's own. She puzzled over what Hermia meant by saying that "Daddy Watson" was her father. She had not said it defiantly. She simply seemed to have decided against naming Braxton as her father. Standing in the foyer, Teresa heard the woman's laughter upstairs as Rose took her from room to room.

With a sudden urgency, she went to the landline telephone in the butler's pantry and closed the doors into the kitchen and the dining room.

"Teresa!" Marisa answered. "Merry Christmas, sweetheart! I've been meaning to call you."

"Merry Christmas to you! Is everybody safely at home? How are Cate and Bernadette?"

"They're fine. Bernadette's trying not to think about colleges, and Cate's up in her room reading, as usual. She's gotten obsessed with the Old South."

"The poor thing!"

"I know. How are Rose and Buford doing?"

"They're okay," she said vaguely. "But do you know who just showed up? Hermia Watson." After a moment, Teresa thought the line had gone dead. "Marisa?"

"What does she want." Marisa said, as though she didn't want an answer to her question.

"To see the renovations, she says. She told us she was on the way to spend Christmas with her aunt."

"What aunt?"

"Daddy Watson's sister in Macon. I asked her who Daddy Watson was and she told me he was her father." When Marisa did not answer, she added, "I don't know what to make of it. I guess she doesn't know we know."

"I think she's just accustomed to keeping up appearances."

Teresa considered that possibility and began to soften.

"Well, of course," she said.

"Oh, I've poisoned you against her. If I could think of her outside the fact of what she did to my family four years ago, I might even like her. She's a thoughtful person."

Teresa sighed. "Well now I feel bad for calling about her."

"No, don't. There's no telling what's really going on with her, Teresa. It could be that she's simply owning the fiction she was given by her mother. Until that summer, she couldn't have known that Braxton was her father—well, unless her mother had told her, which she obviously didn't. As far as she knew, her father was the old man who had been there when she was a child, the one she called Daddy Watson. This aunt must be someone she remembers from her childhood."

"Well that makes sense," Teresa said.

"I've spent a lot of time trying to figure her out," Marisa said. "Have you ever talked to LaCourvette Todd?"

"The police chief? Not except in passing. Why? Hermia said she was going to try to see her today."

"Ask LaCourvette sometime about Hermia. I bet Hermia is still trying to work things out. It might be why she's visiting Daddy Watson's sister."

"I guess you're right. I just panicked a little when she wanted Rose to meet her son."

"She wanted Cate to meet him!" Marisa cried. "At least Rose isn't his half-sister!"

"Oh, my Lord," Teresa said, laughing despite herself.

"No, seriously, Teresa," Marisa said. "Listen, I'd better finish wrapping my presents." She sounded subdued, a little distant.

"Marisa, I'm so sorry to trouble you. I feel terrible now."

"No, it's okay. I just wish we could sit and talk and have a glass of wine. I miss you."

"And I miss you. Please think when you can come back down."

"We'll see."

When she did not speak again, Teresa said, "Well, Walter just brought in the tree, so we'd better put on the lights and ornaments. They tell me it will soon be Christmas."

"I bet you're a scandal to the whole town, getting your tree so late."

"I think it's Walter's favorite thing to do."

"How is Walter? Are you getting along with Nora O'Hearn?"

"Nora?" Hearing the name from Marisa sobered her mood. "She's gone home to Athens for Christmas. Why?"

"Oh nothing," Marisa said, suddenly contrite and apologetic in her turn. "Nothing, sweetheart. Merry Christmas! Give my love to everybody! I can't wait to see you."

"Bye, Marisa. Love to everybody there, too."

After she hung up, she stood for a moment with her hand on the phone. Why had Marisa brought up Nora O'Hearn? Braxton must have said something about her niece and the way she hung on Walter's every word. She closed her eyes and lowered her head, sighing through her nose. She hadn't thought about Nora for a whole hour. She shook her head.

Lord Jesus Christ, son of God, have mercy on me, a sinner.

She pushed open the door into the dining room.

"Buford!" she called.

"Yes ma'am!"

"Come help me string up the lights!"

Buford

Pressed into the tree as he tried to reach the higher branches, Buford concentrated on getting the little hooks and loops of the ornaments onto the twigs of the blue spruce without stripping off the needles.

"Spread them out a little," Rose said irritably. "It looks like the tree has a tumor."

Miss Watson was telling his parents about her current project on windows and gardens. Buford could not imagine why someone would write a book on windows and gardens, but he did not say so.

"Windows and gardens," repeated his mother, looking at Miss Watson with the expression she usually reserved for the homeless people who sometimes accosted her in downtown Macon: blank, forgiving, dramatically serene.

"It's all because of Mrs. Hayes," Miss Watson said. "Watching her spend her days sitting up in that window. I started thinking about the idea of a downward perspective—a *fashioned* outside, you know? An outside meant not so much to be experienced from within its own space but framed from inside and made into an object." She held up her hands like a photographer planning a shot. "It struck me as a mode of possession. In fact, that seems like the whole idea of gardens and grounds—everything ordered for the eye to possess."

"You don't think gardening can be a way of coming to know the natures of things?" his mother said.

"That's just it, Teresa. Knowing their natures is already a mode of possession. You're saying you know in advance what something will be, and you put this plant here and that one there, granting them their existences in order to watch them and possess them."

"There's no window overlooking Eden."

"God's, maybe?" said Miss Watson. "A kind of absolute and privileged oversight?" She was about to say something else when her dog began barking ferociously at something outside. Her expression clouded.

"That's not—I'd better go see what's bothering Eumaios."

"Buford, you go," his mother said, and he gratefully broke away from the tree, handing Rose a big, red, gleaming ornament with a tiny wire loop. He ran through the foyer and out the front door. The dog was on the driveway just in front of the steps, bristling and growling at a slight brown man who was frozen in place. When he saw Buford, the man lifted a card in one hand above his head.

"Señor Peach. ¿Está el aquí?"

The dog turned and looked at Buford, still growling, but uncertain

69

now.

"Eumaios!" Miss Watson called sharply from behind him.

The dog's head dropped. He looked at the man, barked once, and then wagged his tail and ran up the steps to Miss Watson. Buford descended and took the card from the man, who nodded at him and trotted down the drive, which set the dog into another frenzy of barking. Buford stood for a second wondering how the man had squeezed through the chained gate. People who knew them always came to the back door. He watched him disappear into the shrubbery.

"Who was that?" Miss Watson asked.

"I don't know," he said, holding up the square envelope. The card had no name on it.

"Eumaios," Miss Watson said to the dog, kneeling and holding his head in her hands. The dog licked her face and sat back panting. "Now you be good, okay? Okay?" Eumaios wagged his tail and writhed with pleasure as she stroked his back.

The dog went carefully down the steps, his nails clicking on the wood, and then raced across the lawn after a squirrel. Miss Watson turned her attention toward Buford.

"Now let me look at you," she said, beckoning him to her. She took him by the shoulders, tilting her head as she gazed into his eyes with her green ones, which seemed alight with mischievous interest. "Strong," she said, squeezing the muscles of his arms. "And aren't you a handsome thing? Smart as a whip, too, I hear."

"Thank you, ma'am," he said.

"I didn't get to have my son when he was your age," she said, and suddenly she pulled him into her, pressing his head against her bosom. The smell of her—cottony, lemony, with something under it that reminded him of night flowers—made him a little dizzy. He stood stiffly at first, holding the envelope in his right hand against his leg, aware of her breasts, but after a moment, he realized that she wanted him to feel what he felt, and the softness of her overwhelmed him. He relaxed into her as she stroked the back of his head and held him tighter. He thought after a moment that he should break free, but when he moved to do so, she whispered, "Oh don't," and held him a moment longer. "Aren't you something?" she whispered into his ear. She released him and touched his cheek and went slowly back in through the door.

He stood for a moment, his heart pounding, and then followed her. He was embarrassed to see his parents. His mother in particular looked at him strangely as he brought the card in and handed it to her. He did not meet her eyes.

"What's this?" she asked.

"A man brought it to the front door and said something in Spanish."

"He asked if Walter was here," said Miss Watson.

His mother handed it to his father, who took out a card from the envelope. It had a comic Santa Claus in a sombrero on the front. Inside were several photographs. His father stared down at them, sorting through them slowly, his face suddenly somber.

"What are they?" asked his mother.

"Pictures of us," he said.

"Who sent them?"

"No signature. Just *¡Feliz Navidad!*"

Buford stood next to his mother as she took them from his father. On top was a picture of Rose taken at an angle from below her room. She was standing just inside the window holding a book in her left hand. It was dark outside; she was in her nightgown; her hair was wild about her head; the light inside the room silhouetted her body through the cloth.

"Who could have taken this?" his mother cried.

When Rose looked at it, a fear he had never seen before crossed her face.

"Somebody was out there watching me?" she said. She seemed to shrink into herself as she looked at it. "They had to be out in the garden. Or closer."

"You know, I hadn't thought about a window quite that way," said Miss Watson, and he saw his mother's quick wince of irritation.

The other pictures showed them all doing various things around the house—his mother at the kitchen sink, this one also taken from outside and below; his father getting out of the car, a level shot from behind; someone, it had to be Miss Nora, coming out of the back door, looking back inside; and Buford lying on his back, asleep in his bed.

He must have left the light on in his room. It was taken from just above him, close up.

"Walter," his mother said, "somebody was inside his bedroom."

Buford's flesh crawled.

"You don't remember hearing anything?" his father asked.

"No! But there was a funny smell one morning when I woke up."

"Funny how?"

"Like rotten bananas. I even looked in the trashcan."

His father tilted his head, as though he were trying to remember something.

"How long ago?"

"I don't know. Last week?"

"You should call the police," said Miss Watson.

His father soberly examined the photograph, front and back, then gathered the pictures, looked through them again, and put the stack back inside the card.

"It's the cartel," he said quietly.

"Call the police," his mother said.

"I will," he said.

"Oh Walter," his mother said. "Even Braxton has been saying—"

"It's just what I've been telling everybody. This is what those people do. This is how they corrupt everything. They know people care more about their families than anything else."

He put the card on the coffee table and went to the butler's pantry to call the police.

"I think I'd better be on my way," said Miss Watson.

His mother raised her eyebrows and shrugged.

"Thank you for coming by."

After she gathered up her dog and said her goodbyes, after she gave Buford a wink and a soft we-have-a-secret squeeze of the hand, Miss Watson drove off in her Prius.

"So that was Hermia Watson," his mother said. "My goodness."

When the police came, they went up to Buford's room and looked around, but they didn't know what to look for. Nobody knew when the picture had been taken. They went around the big house checking all the locks on the doors and windows, speculating about how someone got in. One of them found some footprints and a cigarette butt in the garden. They would look down at the picture of Rose and then up at the window.

"I do a little photography, and that's a really good picture," one of them said. "I mean just as a picture."

His mother took it away from him. "You wouldn't think so if it were your daughter," she said.

"Who's this one? You can't see her face."

"My niece."

"Any idea when it was taken?"

"She went home to Athens two days ago."

"Let me see that one," his father said. He gazed at the picture. "Is that what she had on when she came by last?"

Rose and his mother looked at the picture. She was halfway out the door, and her head was turned to look back inside. She had on jeans, a light sweater, a jacket over it, some kind of scarf; she was in motion but pausing in it. Her face was not in the picture, but you could feel the smile going through her whole body, whatever she was hearing or saying, the joy of her.

"Sunday," Rose said. "Remember? She came by after Mass in Macon and brought the presents."

"He must have been right over there," her mother said, pointing to the shrubbery on the other side of the driveway.

The holiday mood was spoiled. They had a quiet dinner, said prayers, and sang "Joy to the World" while they put a Baby Jesus in three different creches. Afterwards, they had eggnog and watched *It's a Wonderful Life*, which they did every Christmas. After the movie his mother and father stayed downstairs talking while he and Rose started up to their rooms.

"Are you scared?" she asked Buford on the back stairs.

He hated to admit it to her, but he nodded. He kept thinking about somebody coming into his room and standing over his bed and taking his picture. Suppose he woke up and some stranger was standing in his room?

"The idea of somebody out there watching me just makes me feel—I mean, I don't even want to go in my room," Rose said. "What if they're out there now? What if they waited until the police left and now they're back out there?"

"I'll go in and turn off the lights," Buford said. "They won't be able to see anything then."

"Would you?"

He turned off the hall light first and went into her room and turned off the bedside lamp. She came in then and they went and stood a little back from the window looking down into the garden. Somebody could be down there in the dark. He watched for a match or the glint of a lens, but he couldn't see anything.

"Can I stay in your room tonight?" Rose asked.

"I don't want to sleep in my room," he said.

"I don't blame you," she said. After a moment she added, "Let's go in Mr. Forrest's room."

"Both of us? In the same bed?"

"It's a big bed. I won't kick you."

She lay on the far side with a line of pillows between them. It was a cold night, and it felt good to be under the heavy covers. Christmas Eve. A few years earlier, he would have been waiting for Santa Claus. His parents had never made too much of the Big Lie to Kids, as Rose called it, but he missed the fun of running downstairs early in the morning and finding the Christmas cookies half-eaten, everybody conspiring to pretend Santa had left in a hurry.

Now all the emphasis was where it should be, his mother said, on the birth of Jesus, the gift of the Incarnation, as she called it. He thought about the card with the Santa in the sombrero. Those people had *chosen* Christmas Eve just to scare them and ruin the holiday.

Anger flared up inside him. His father said the cartel wanted to show how easy it would be to kill them or kidnap them. Or other things. Vague images of girls struggling to escape came to him. And then in a rush he remembered the way Miss Watson had taken his shoulders in her hands and exclaimed about his muscles. She talked about not having her son when he was growing up. He felt again the softness of her when she squeezed him against her, took him *into* her almost, a moment too long and then longer than that.

But then he remembered the card he had held against his leg and the pictures inside it, including the one of Rose and the one of himself sleeping.

Somebody standing right over him.

Rose was snoring lightly. It was strange that people had to sleep. You had to give up being awake every single night, but when you did it, you were lying there helpless, and somebody could come in and stand over you and take your picture.

Or kill you.

Buford prayed *O Lord, please protect us.*

He thought about the newborn Jesus being God and lying there kicking out his little baby arms and legs. Being in a body.

His thoughts were beginning to drift on their own and speed along. Mary had been overshadowed by the Holy Spirit. Overshadowed and made big-bellied like pretty Mrs. Godwin in church. *Pregnant,* her other children beside her in the pew, the husband sitting at the other end. The one who made her pregnant. Mary pregnant too, but a virgin still, with God sleeping inside her body. Origin of everything tucked into that tiny curled godbody like a little sea horse.

He curled deeper into the blessed inner sea and the galaxies brimmed around him and drifted and *O God* he started to pray and

March 2014

Nora

March 7, 2014

When Aunt Teresa called after school and invited her for dinner at Stonewall Hill—*Please, Nora, you're done for the week. We'd love to have you*—the very fact of the invitation made Walter seem familial and a little common, a daddy, a pass-the-sweet-potatoes man, not the poet of eyebeams and ecstasies. Nora imagined Buford and Rose at the table, quipping and sardonic. She pictured Aunt Teresa, with her small ambiguous smile, regarding Nora's enthusiasms with clipped forbearance, and it took the keen edge off the pleasure of having Walter almost to herself for the reading that would come later.

She declined with the excuse that Miss Emma was expecting her. Natasha Simmons, another girl rooming in the big house, also stayed home and ate a leisurely dinner with their landlord—fresh broccoli, a roasted chicken, Miss Emma's light, buttery rolls from her grandmother's recipe, and collard greens done the way her own anxiety-ridden mother considered threateningly unhealthy, with fatback and onions and pepper. Natasha left before dessert to meet some friends in town. Nora helped clear the table and put the dishes in the dishwasher while Miss Emma limped around humming, pleased to have Nora to herself. She had been working in her vegetable garden since they got home from school, and she still had on the big shirt and the jeans she always wore outside. A wonderful baking smell permeated the whole downstairs.

"What *is* that, Miss Emma?"

"A surprise. I'll call you in a few minutes."

She took a cup of decaf into the sitting room and sat flipping through the book that Walter had sent her that day through Buford. He usually made copies of poems and brought them when they gathered in his study on Friday nights, but this time he had sent a book. Buford had come up to her after school, just before Walter called, and handed it to her. A new copy of the poet Louise Gluck's *The Wild Iris*. When he called, she had asked Walter if she should read anything in particular in it, but he had just said to browse around in it.

She had opened it there in the schoolroom, by herself, after Buford and the other children left. *For Nora* said the inscription on the first page, and three lines followed:

whatever
returns from oblivion
returns to find a voice

And then his signature, but not just his name. Not just Walter. It said *Love, Walter.*

Love, it said. Not *Uncle Walter* but *Walter*. She had wondered nervously if Buford had seen it. Or Aunt Teresa. No, he wouldn't have let her see it.

Now, waiting for Miss Emma, she read the first lines of the first poem.

At the end of my suffering
there was a door.
Hear me out: that which you call death I remember.

She stirred in her chair, gazing out the window at a wide expanse of lawn under huge old pecan trees just coming into leaf behind the house. What would Walter—what would Walter be like? She let herself ask it.

He would adore her.

She would be the beauty he was only just able to bear.

He would read her body in exaltation.

A terrible joy surged through her.

Because she knew what he meant by *Love, Walter*. She had known for a long time what he meant, hadn't she? She had felt it now for weeks, Friday after Friday, even as she dated Bill Sharpe. She had felt it always in the background, Walter Peach like a Bach cello suite next to Bill Sharpe's Dickie Betts. No, that wasn't fair. But what she felt for Walter was truer and deeper. *Love, Walter.* He meant exactly what he said. He loved her, not as his niece but as herself, as who she really was, as no one else had ever known her or loved her. He loved her as a woman is loved. This sad and brilliant man loved her.

Of course, he loved Aunt Teresa and his children, too. Her heart pinched with jealousy. Did they truly understand who he was—Rose, Aunt Teresa? Could wise, reserved, suffering Aunt Teresa ever give Walter the supreme and delicate attention he deserved, a man with such a gift, a soul so brilliant that his first critics had heralded the young poet as the major voice of his generation?

At the end of my suffering/there was a door.

Nora herself. Nora was the door.

She lifted her head, her eyes wet with joy, and just then Miss Emma limped through the door carrying a Pyrex dish with a hot pad in one hand and a small saucepan in the other.

"What are you smiling about?" she asked.

"Oh, nothing. This book Walter sent me."

"*Walter* is it? What does Teresa have to say about that?"

"Oh Miss Emma. We're all grownups."

Miss Emma regarded her skeptically.

"Well here's the surprise—and pardon the informality."

She set the dish down on a trivet and pulled off the kitchen towel that covered it. "I hope you like gingerbread."

"I love gingerbread!" she exclaimed.

"I made some sauce to go with it. But I forgot to bring plates."

Nora leapt up and ran into the kitchen and brought back two small plates, quickly rummaging in the silverware drawer for smaller forks. When she got back, Miss Emma had already cut her a large piece and was holding it up.

"I can't eat that much!"

Miss Emma tucked in her chin in mock disgust, shaking her head at such an obvious lie. She put it on the plate and picked up the saucepan: a hot lemon sauce, which she poured copiously over the gingerbread as Nora danced in protest at the abundance of it. She loved the way Miss Emma took pleasure in serving her.

"I've got some news for you," Miss Emma said as they sat down and cut into their dessert.

"News? This is *so good*," Nora said, savoring the spongy gingerbread, still hot from the oven, and the tart sweetness of the sauce. "I feel guilty being the only one eating it."

"*I'm* eating it, you goose. I would have made it just for you anyway," said the older woman, not looking up from her plate. After a moment, she added, "Besides, is that all you have to feel guilty about?"

She shrank a little from the question as Miss Emma lifted her eyes and met her gaze.

"What do you mean?"

"Dexter Watkins came by last night."

"Dexter Watkins! What did he want?"

"What do you think? To see you."

Nora gazed at Miss Emma, her fork in midair. "To see me?" she said.

"I ran him off. If I'd had a shotgun I might have shot him."

"Oh he's not that bad, is he, Miss Emma?"

"Child, you are just too sweet to people. It's going to get you in trouble." She pointed a dripping piece of gingerbread at Nora before putting it in her mouth. "You don't know what he did to get kicked out of the army?" she said around it. "Didn't we tell you months ago?"

"But he seems like he's just the kind of man people around here can't—"

Miss Emma raised a hand to stop her from saying anything else.

"He killed a whole family in Afghanistan, children and all." She stared at Miss Emma, her heart going cold.

"Killed them?"

"His unit was looking for snipers."

"He killed children?"

"Three of them. Literally shot them to pieces. A little girl and two little boys, not to mention the father and mother. Like they weren't people at all."

"But why?"

"They did have weapons in their house, and that's why they didn't keep him in jail. They also said he had PTSD or some such thing, because he'd been over there a year and he'd seen several friends of his die, but I think it was drugs. Drugs and meanness. And they just let him go after doing that. Do you need some more coffee?"

Nora nodded distractedly, and Miss Emma got up and limped into the kitchen.

She remembered him standing above her at the table, the way he looked at her that first time, and now his expression made more sense, almost as though he had seen her as a hope of some kind, a way out. She wondered if he looked at all women that way at first, then used them, fed them to his need, discarded them.

Killed a whole family. Something already monstrous had to open the door for such a deed. She could picture him, almost as though she stood inside the room, watching. His eyes were glazed with terror and rage that gave him a hair-trigger ferocity. A door swinging open, a cry and sudden movement, and after holding himself ready for too long, the burst of bullets. And then some terrible recognition that it was all wrong, all askew—a woman, a child. Sprawled and bleeding, looking up at him. And then a rage against whatever had allowed it to happen, that absence where God used to be, rage against that absence for bringing him here, into this living hell. And then his finger cramping on the trigger in the reflex of protest and self-loathing, as though the one or two he had already killed were to blame for the horror of what he had already become, the transgression already committed, the meaning already ruptured forever, forever ruptured.

And so he killed them all. He shot them and shot them in an eternity of satanic permission, an ecstasy of the abyss, a god beyond the human frame of feeling.

And how must he have felt once he came back to himself and saw what he had done?

When he looked down at those bodies?

Oh God.

She pitied that poor family.

She pitied Dexter for what he must have suffered in the aftermath.

"Nora?"

She looked up at Miss Emma, who was pouring her a fresh cup of coffee. She wiped the tears from her eyes.

The older woman covered her mouth in astonishment. "Oh you sweet child. You feel sorry for him, don't you?"

"Yes ma'am," she said.

Miss Emma set down the coffee carafe and came around to her and Nora turned to hug the older woman, pressing her face into the softness of her, smelling the outdoors on her shirt. For a good moment, Nora was convulsed with weeping.

"Well, now listen," said Miss Emma, stroking her hair. "Just don't let your judgment be turned by your pity. Dexter used to be a decent boy— not perfect, but decent. Not a good student but a fine athlete. Something happened to him over there, and you can't do anything about it." When Nora did not answer, she shook her gently and said, "You hear me, Nora? Sometimes you just have to leave these things to God."

Nora nodded into Miss Emma's comforting body.

But an hour later she drove to the Peach house thinking about the dark need in Dexter's eyes. She knew that Miss Emma was right: any slightest kindness on her part would mislead him and feed his imagination in exactly the wrong way. She would be something he had to possess and immolate. For a moment a dark sexual thrill passed through her, but she saw it for what it was and repudiated it. That must be what Dexter's women felt. Overmastered, annihilated, sacrificed to whatever demon he served to keep his own horror at bay.

She said a prayer for him.

Walter

He waited, sitting at the desk of his study—this room that still felt like a gift, this place of conversation and wit and poetry. He could write here, if that strong and unexpected urging ever took him over again. Forrest had given him a sleek new MacBook Pro, and Walter had tried to write, no question, but without experiencing again that sudden opening in the imagination that had come to him starting in his late teens and continuing all through his twenties and into his thirties. After his son died, it had never come back. He could labor at verse, he could write skillful lines full of wit and metrical interest, but the poetry, where the gods could feel their holy space again, where the angel could stand in the threshold—not until lately, not until Nora.

Outside, the March twilight lingered in the azaleas. He had seen her car turn off Johnson's Mill Road into the back driveway; he had watched with a dangerous exhilaration as she stepped from her car, light, like the most graceful of animals, with that lovely alertness you saw in her whole body, an avian lightness. But also moving through her was a slow, almost tidal, sexual power. He felt her in his abdomen, beneath his navel, in the webwork of his subtle body, as he had felt it long ago with Lydia Downs when she touched the chakra there with her fingernails, so lightly, just there below the navel, in his office. He had written a poem to her, hadn't he? Yes, on the bottom of one of her essays that he had graded late at night, alone in his office. He didn't remember a line of that poem, but he remembered the one she had written in reply. She had slid it under the door of his office, unsigned, just with a telephone number at the bottom.

> *Your sentences*
> *I heft against my palate*
> *my lips shape them*
> *syllable O syllable syllable*
>
> *your words in my mouth*
> *run live upon my tongue*
> *their sudden honey and salt*
> *beget me O beget me beget me*

He had stood there reading it and reading it. Trembling, he had called her. She had been so knowing. So young and so knowing—

He heard the light knock on the landing door.

"Walter?" Nora said. And then she was in the inner threshold.

"Nora," he said.

"I got the book," she said. "Thank you so much." She gave him her hand and he held it in his for a moment too long, he knew, and she squeezed his lightly as she released it. Rose was with her. She had a curious expression on her face, and she turned her head a little sideways, as though she were averting her gaze.

"I brought it," Nora said, faltering a little, "just in case you want to read some of them. Have you read Louise Glück?" she asked Rose.

"Who? No."

"You really should," she said distractedly, but she did not offer the book for Rose's perusal. Nora's eyes met his for an instant, and he knew. It was the inscription that she did not want Rose to see. *Love, Walter.*

"Maybe we'll read some," he said as if they were stepping together, trying not to be heard, on the surface of a forest floor where small new ferns, still not fully unfurled, thrust upward among the dry leaves and fallen twigs.

They read poems and talked them out for half an hour or so, and his mood of entrancement did not change. Rose said something about a poem by Henry Vaughan.

"Very good, Rose," Walter said after a moment.

She looked up at him crossly, he thought, which puzzled him.

They went over another poem, and Rose's mood darkened more. She suddenly got up and put her poems on the desk.

"What's the matter?" Nora asked her, unable to mute her alarm.

Rose shook her head and left them.

"Rose," Walter called after her, but she did not return.

They were reading a poem by John Donne.

"I guess we should stop for tonight?" Nora said.

"What, with our souls out in the air?" he said. "Rose is just moody. I guess we weren't paying enough attention to her. You read the next part."

She spoke the lines very softly. He could hardly hear her. She met his gaze for a moment. He poured his eyes upon her.

"I should go," she said.

But she did not go.

Raïssa

"So you got your feelings hurt?" her mother said. They stood in the middle of the kitchen.

"All he cares about is what Nora says."

"He brags about you, honey. Go back up there. It's important to your father for you to be there."

Raïssa crossed her arms. "He calls me *Rose* in front of her. It's like my feelings don't matter at all. *I'm* not the point when we're reading."

"Everybody calls you Rose—and do you know why, Rose? Because that's the name we gave you. Your name isn't Raïssa."

"But I feel like myself as Raïssa, like being in my own poem, and I don't know why Dad can't see that—but I say something and he says *Good, Rose*, like I'm a puppy. You ought to see the way he looks at Nora when *she* says something."

Her mother turned uneasily, and Raïssa knew at once that she should not have said it.

"Your father needs these readings. I can see what a difference they've made for him these last few months. Rose," her mother said, "Raïssa." She touched Raïssa's cheek. "Go back up there. Please."

She caught her mother's hand and squeezed it, suddenly moved by her need. She left the butler's pantry and made her way to the foot of the back stairs, where she hesitated before climbing to the landing. She knocked, imagining them tearing their eyes from each other and looking up at her, but when she went in, her father was standing and looking out the window.

"So you haven't been back there?" she heard Nora ask.

"Never. Except to lock it up," he said, turning and waving Raïssa to her chair, as though she had never left.

"And when did you write 'Her Departure'?" Nora asked him.

"A long time ago. When I was a teenager."

"Walter, I think about all this time of letting it get overgrown—"

"Why? What about it?" he said, turning to look at her.

"I think you should go back out there and open it up."

"Just open it up," he said with a trace of sarcasm that silenced her. He leaned across the desk and lifted the window more and the March night air came in, too cold. After a moment, he closed it and sat down without looking at Nora.

"We're talking about your grandmother," he said to Raïssa. "My mother, Rosemary."

Raïssa nodded, puzzled by this turn in the conversation. She had heard her father and mother speculate about Rosemary's disappearance ever since she could remember.

"I don't understand what you mean at the end about *following Shedir*," Nora said.

So they must have read her Dad's poem, "Andromeda."

"Because she taught him the constellations," Raïssa said. "They would go out at night and lie down and look up at the stars. Shedir is the brightest star in Cassiopeia, and it points to the Andromeda galaxy, which is the most distant thing you can see with the naked eye."

Nora raised her eyebrows, and her father smiled at her.

"So," Nora said, "your mother used to show it to you?"

For a moment he did not speak.

"She used to say"—his voice was heavy with irony—"that if she ever went away, that's where she'd be."

Raïssa's heart sank, it was so cheesy. But Nora seemed electrified.

"Let's go look for it!" she cried, starting up. "Come on!"

"Stop it," he said, wincing.

"No, seriously, come on," Nora said, looking to Raïssa for encouragement. "It's a clear night, and you can always see Cassiopeia. Let's find Shedir. I bet we can see Andromeda."

Nora was as excited as a child. Over his protests, she pulled him from the study and down the back stairs. Raïssa followed them to the back door and even out a little into the yard. Nora was holding her father's arm as she remembered doing when she was little. She remembered when they went to the zoo in Atlanta and she first saw the heads of the giraffes looming in the treetops, nibbling the leaves.

After a moment, watching them, she stopped. They did not notice her. They went on happily, and she turned back. Avoiding her mother, Raissa went up to her room.

Nora

March 14, 2014

When the bell rang at 3:00, the fifth graders broke into their clamor of leave-taking. Gathering their books, heaving up their backpacks, making faces, teasing each other—the boys were still children, but some of the girls had matured into women at eleven—they quickly reverted to the dense atmosphere of status (Bill Sharpe called it primate behavior) that prevailed on the playground or in the lunchroom. It was all about popularity and power, as though out of primordial instinct, and there was virtually nothing an adult could do about it. She remembered being in it, and she felt lucky to be above it now, in a thinner, more reasonable level of the atmosphere.

The children seemed to genuinely love her. And she loved them, every single one of them, even red-headed, freckled Hershey Parmenter, whose face went into a frenzy of blinks and tics and the oddest involuntary puckering whenever she looked at him. The other boys called him Kiss—and not just because of his first name. He was reputed to adore her.

"Goodbye, Miss Nora!"

"See you Monday, Miss Nora! Have a good weekend!"

She stood at her desk, nodding and smiling and saying goodbye. In half a minute, they had all taken their leave except her cousin, Buford Peach, who came to a stop halfway up the aisle, either thinking about something or pretending to. One strap of his loaded backpack strained his body uncomfortably to the side.

"How many light years is it to your solar system?" she asked him, and he looked up, startled, quickly shrugging the pack up onto both his shoulders.

"Dad told me the compensation for my cosmic insignificance was my capacity to conceive of the whole universe."

"Oh, I see."

She could not help smiling. Anything his father said amused her.

"I like your earrings—well, not *rings*, but—" He flipped two fingers beneath his ear.

She had on her favorite ones, three delicate leaves of hammered gold dangling on each side. Her high school English teacher, Mrs. Allen, had given them to her when she graduated. *My best Portia ever.*

"Thank you, Buford," she said, touching them lightly with both hands. "I'm surprised you notice things like that."

He stared at her for a moment with an odd look on his face and then looked down as he swung his backpack onto the top of a desk.

"So anyway, I've reconciled myself to being a momentary speck of random organic matter," he said with the flat irony she could easily imagine in his father at that age.

"Oh, have you?"

"Almost. I'm a speck with perspective. But just now I was thinking about time—how you kind of think of times as equal even though they're not even close."

"So—"

"So, like the weekend is equal to a whole week of school, you know? And summer is equal to the whole school year. Maybe it's because you take the time you don't like now and push it over into the time you're going to like, the time you actually want to be in, so it equals out."

"Okay." She humored him to see what he would say so she could report it to Walter.

"But then there's the other side of it. When you're doing something you *like*, you don't notice the time. It just goes away. So, summer's already over, the weekend's already over, and you're already back in the classroom like the time away never happened. So, if that's true, I was wondering, you know, whether it was even worth it for me to go home—I mean, if the weekend's already over and I'm already back here."

"Buford, I can't tell you how good you're making me feel." Her eyes went out to a momentary flash outside, a red Jeep slowing at the crosswalk across the schoolyard, a quick glare from its mirror.

"Oh, I didn't mean you, Miss Nora. I just meant school in general."

"Go home, Buford. I'll see you tonight."

"Yes ma'am."

"And don't call me ma'am. I'm your first cousin."

As soon as he was out the door, the weekend opened up before her—poetry at Stonewall Hill tonight, her very favorite thing, the greatest pleasure of mind and heart she had experienced in her life, better than any class she had ever taken or any conversation she had had, even with her best and most intelligent friends.

Then tomorrow a leisurely day reading and weeding with Miss Emma in the garden, maybe a movie in Macon tomorrow night. Maybe Bill would take her. On Sunday, if the weather held out, he was taking her on a picnic to a beautiful spot he had found on the Ikahalpi River. He promised he would bring the fishing gear she had seen him use last weekend at the lake above the falls. She had gone there to walk on the trails, and she had stood unseen in the shade and watched him, entranced by the elegance of it—the way the tip of the rod whipped over, and the lure flew out to just the desired spot. As she watched those big hands, powerful and exact and patient, as he handled the bending rod and reeled in the fish, she had fallen into a pure reverie of looking. He had caught two big bass in quick succession before she decided she was spying and called out to him. Even thinking about the look on his face, the warm, delighted surprise, filled her heart. He was a deep man. Deep and good and strong. Just not Walter.

A whole weekend with no tests to grade, no papers to read, no big new preparation. On Monday she would start *The Secret Garden* with the children, a book she knew almost by heart. Walter said it would be okay to do *The Secret Garden*, because they had just done *Treasure Island*, which the boys had liked, even though some of the older teachers had thought it would be too hard for them. Some of the boys would rebel at *The Secret Garden*, which they would consider a girl's book, but all it really took to get any book across was reading it aloud—if you knew how to read. And Walter said she was spellbinding. Walter said it, Walter, who could plant the words of a poem so far inside you, you felt them growing in your cells, pushing up through the humus of your old self, feeling for light. That little poem of Theodore Roethke's: *One nub of growth/Nudges a sand-crumb loose.*

It was a mild, fair, spring day. She could hear the children outside, the loud cries, the calls. She got her things together, and she was just closing the door behind her and starting down the hall toward the exit when Buford reappeared from outside.

"Buford!" she cried in exasperation. "Go home!"

"Dad's in the car," he said sullenly. "He wants to talk to you."

"What about? Did he say?"

Buford shrugged. His demeanor puzzled her, his mood seemed so much darker than it had just a few minutes before.

"Are you going to talk to him? I can tell him you're busy or something."

"Of course, I'll talk to him."

He looked at her, as though he were weighing what he ought to say. "He's been drinking."

Her spirits sank. She had seen him drink once or twice earlier in the year, even once or twice in the poetry sessions. He either got morose or flirtatious in a way that disquieted her.

"I'm sorry to hear that."

"Don't pay too much attention to what he says, because he sometimes says things he doesn't mean."

"Don't talk that way about your father."

"Rose says he's…"

He faltered and could not look at her.

"What? Rose says he's what?"

"Nothing. He's out in the parking lot. I'm going to walk home."

"Buford!" she called, but he had already turned and pushed the bar that opened the door. Outside, she saw him break into a run.

What had Rose said? She thought of Rose's nervousness with the two of them when they read poetry. She had not come with them to look for Andromeda, when she and Walter stood close beside each other in the dark behind the old barn. The night of stars a week ago.

Rose says he's... what?

A veil of dread fell over her heart. She stood inside the row of doors at the end of the hallway, looking out through the glass until she spotted the Subaru, tucked in the back corner of the parking lot, in the shade of the big pecan trees. He had parked out of the way of the other teachers and the parents picking up their children. He must have thought they would not notice him, but he immediately aroused suspicion. She supposed she had seen too many crime shows on television. It was entirely her father's fault: he loved that kind of thing—serial killers, child molesters, forensic investigations—especially if Gillian Anderson was in it.

She wondered whether to walk all the way across the lot to his car, which would call even more attention to Walter, or to get her car first. Get her car first. That was the way to do it. She could start to drive off and then pretend to see the Outback and change direction and go over and park next to Walter, as though it were all spontaneous. She pushed through the door, not looking in his direction, and started walking to her car.

"Nora!" she heard after a few steps, and she faltered and looked in his direction. He had gotten out and was waving at her. "Nora!"

She saw several of the teachers in the parking lot glance at Walter and then back at her. They knew he was married to her aunt.

She was not going to seem embarrassed. She lifted her arm and smiled and waved.

"Hi Uncle Walter!"

"I need to talk to you!" he called.

"Let me get my car!" she called back.

But he beckoned her over insistently.

"I have to put my things down!" she called.

Nora walked quickly to her car and put her satchel and purse in the back seat and locked it.

"Have a great weekend," Ginger Robertson called. She was already in running clothes, doing some stretches beside her car.

Nora waved at her. Then she cut across the grass past the flagpole and hurried toward Walter as he stood impatiently. Something must be very wrong for him to drink in the middle of Friday afternoon with the next week's paper to get ready. When she reached the asphalt of the lot, she was almost running.

Dexter Watson

Sweet Jesus, look at that. She ran and then slowed down and then hurried again. He held the smoke in his lungs and watched her from his Jeep. Almost worth being in fifth grade again. Sit there and look at her all day long. She was heading toward a dark blue SUV, where a man, looked familiar, was standing by the front. Had to be in his forties. Gray hair in a ponytail like an old hippie. Gesturing to her. *Come here.*

Goddamn if it wasn't Walter Peach. Newspaper. Lived up in the big house. Rich old Forrest had wanted a caretaker, something like that.

Drunk, way he was acting.

He let the smoke go from his mouth in a long plume. Quetzal feather for his boy Quetzalcoatl. Decent weed, not great. He held the joint below the level of the window and glanced in his mirrors to see if anybody was coming up from behind. Nobody.

So what was Peach doing with her?

He watched as she reached him. Peach took her hand and pulled her toward him, and she had to backpedal to keep him from grabbing her on the spot. Drunk as hell. She glanced back over her shoulder. Worried about somebody seeing them.

Somebody *was* seeing them. He winked and raised the joint to his lips and took another hit.

Look at her. Sweet she'd be, like a honey tree. Poem. What a bear must feel breaking into a tree, bees all around him. Headfirst in that honeycomb.

He rolled his shoulders and tensed his shoulder muscles and relaxed them. Sweet just to see her. Everything about her.

Peach was saying something to her, leaning toward her. She didn't want to hear it.

Something nagging at his memory. She had a relative, aunt in town. He blew the smoke out all at once when he remembered. By God, Peach was married to her aunt.

Why she got a job in Gallatin.

And look at him. In love with her at his age. Telling her how he felt. That's what he was doing. Drunk so he'd be brave enough to tell her.

Couldn't blame him.

But she didn't want to hear it. Wasn't buying it. *No.* Shaking her head. *No sir.*

But then she looked up at him, tilted her head, smiled, came close and put her hand on his arm, said something to him.

Peach looking down at the ground then up at her. Taking her hand, trying to touch her face. But she's backing off, sweet to him, saying something. He nods. She turns to walk away. Peach standing there watching her go. Good god at that caboose.

Sweet to watch her.

He's slow to get back in the car. But he does it, starts it, puts it in gear, pulls out of the parking lot like a zombie in driver's ed, turns. He passes Watkins five feet away, doesn't glance over. Sober now. Face like stone. And what was she doing? At her car now, unlocking it. That little blue Corolla.

Everybody else gone by now. Should he pull over now? Better hurry. He starts the engine. She's looking for something in the back seat. She stands up straight, looks back at the building. Forgot something. She's hurrying toward the entrance, waving at somebody inside. Runs up the walk, up the steps. Door opens from the inside. Janitor. She goes in.

So now he can catch her coming back out. Just right.

He takes one more hit, squeezes the fire from the joint out the window, and tucks the roach under the dashboard. Checks his mirrors. Still nobody. He pulls over into the parking lot, close to the entrance, between the door and her car. Lets his breath out, a plume, long and smooth, another feather for Quetzalcoatl's headdress. Gets out, stretching, buzzed.

He walks over and sits on the bench beside the sidewalk, waiting for the schoolteacher. He can smell her honey on the breeze.

Buford

Your dad tells you not to get in the car. What is that?

So here he is, Friday afternoon, a backpack as heavy as something you would take into the mountains for a month, having to walk home. Either that or hang around— watching what? Rose had been whispering that his dad was in love with Miss Nora, but he had never paid any attention. So what? Who wasn't in love with Miss Nora?

So, what was "Walter" going to do now? Leave his mother?

Bill Tompkins had asked Buford to come out to his house in the country tomorrow and go squirrel-hunting, but instead of feeling good, he was feeling the same dread he had known when they lived in Waycross and he used to find his father drinking by himself in the backyard. Once, a Monday morning, Buford had eaten breakfast and started for school and there was his father facedown in the oxalis with a robin pecking at his ponytail. Not dead, anyway. Another night he fell into the fire-ant bed under the redbud tree and screamed for an hour. For months he looked like he had survived smallpox.

Everything had been better since their move to Gallatin. His father seemed to like running the paper. Buford had begun to trust him, even talk to him. Just now, he had gotten into the car wanting to ask him about the past and how long the past felt when you were older. Did it ever feel as long when you remembered it as it was when you lived it?

And instead, *Hey, buddy, don't get in yet. Send Nora out here and then make yourself scarce for a few minutes.*

Seriously? *Make yourself scarce.* Who made that up?

Past the playground of the old school was the cemetery with its two brick entrance posts. He walked past the Confederate graves, three hundred of them the plaque said, men who had died in the tent hospitals in town when the facilities in Atlanta overflowed and trains brought them south to Gallatin and Macon, before Sherman burned his way toward Savannah. Most of the graves didn't even have names. He thought about dying like that. All you want to do is go home and see your mama or your girlfriend or your brothers and sisters and not die at Rose's age like you're about to do, and some surgeon who doesn't have enough whiskey left to give you saws off your arm or your leg and throws it in a pile. And it doesn't do any good. The fever burns you up like a piece of bacon, and people who don't know you carry your body out of the tent to make room for somebody still thinking about his mama's smile and the way his dog would be glad to see him.

Make yourself scarce.

He walked along through the cemetery, praying vaguely. He stepped on a beer can in the grass with his foot, and the two round ends bent up to grip the sides of his shoe and he had to kick it off with the other foot. Now it was litter, now that he knew it was there. Like Purgatory. His mother said that they used to tell you in church to pray for the souls in Purgatory, because the souls needed prayers. He thought of those dead men sitting around in Purgatory, still in their ragged uniforms, waiting a hundred and fifty years, second by second, minute by minute, for something to help them move, like sailors in a calm at sea. When it was over, would it feel like it had all been the blink of eye, like summer? Somebody would have an answer. Mr. Forrest once told him to read Thomas Aquinas. He wondered what it would feel like to be in Purgatory when the prayers began to stir them.

He stopped and turned around and prayed for them. It couldn't hurt. Looking back up the road toward the school, his heart lightened. That's exactly what Miss Nora was like. She wanted to give people joy. She couldn't imagine not giving joy if she could. Of course, his father loved her. Buford loved her, too. Everybody loved her. It was just that if his father loved her the wrong way—

The Subaru came around the corner beyond the old elementary school and started toward him. Buford raised his hand to wave and started taking off his backpack. But as the Outback got closer, it did not slow down. His father didn't seem to see him. His face was as rigid and blind as the face on the statue of the Confederate soldier on the courthouse square.

"Dad!" Buford shouted as he went by.

The Outback swerved over into the shallow opposite ditch then back up onto the road, where it jolted to a stop. Buford ran to the passenger's door and opened it and slung his backpack onto the floor and got in.

"Didn't you see me?"

"What did you say?" he asked after a moment.

They rolled down the lane through the cemetery and up to the stop sign on Lee Street.

"You didn't see me standing there?"

His dad passed his hand over his face and rubbed his chin.

"I'm sorry, what?"

Buford's heart swerved into alarm.

"I said it didn't look like you saw me."

"When?"

"Just now."

"No, I didn't see you."

Buford looked at him as they made the turn onto Lee Street and started toward Stonewall Hill.

"Dad?" His father did not seem to hear him at all. Buford reached and touched his arm; he looked as if he were just waking up. His father focused on him. He looked pale and sick, older, grayer, spotted with age.

"Did you talk to Miss Nora?"

"Yeah, I talked to her."

"What's the matter?"

"Nothing."

They pulled into the driveway and rode up to the gravel where they parked the cars near the back door. His father did not turn off the Outback but sat waiting for Buford to get out.

"Where are you going?"

His father shook his head, shrugged lightly.

"Out," he said.

"Dad," Buford said.

But his father would not look at him.

Nora

Mr. Watts would be wondering why it took her so long to pick up the book she had left behind. Pushing that big broom down the long hallway, limping a little on his bad leg, keeping his eye on her door. She couldn't let him see her crying, because he would ask her questions, and how would she answer him?

It mortified her to think that she had let Walter believe that he could be interested in her romantically. But of course she had let him believe it. *Love, Walter.* Holding hands and looking up at the stars for his lost mother.

Her aunt's husband, a married man with children, one of whom she taught.

Her *uncle. Uncle Walter.*

She had been the one to erase the word uncle. *Your niece, not by blood, but by all that's fated.* What had that been but a provocation? Had she thought that their intimacy was safe because he was supposedly off limits? Of course not. She wanted to be free to feel what she felt, free to touch his arm, to smile at him, so often thrilled by the poetry they read together. She had imagined being with him, what he would be like.

That night last week they had gone out in the dark, half-heartedly trying to get Rose to come with them, and she had leaned on his arm and held his hand—to steady her, to guide her—as they went down the path through the vegetable garden and out toward the old barn to a place where they could look up at the stars without lights all around them. They found Cassiopeia, then used it to find Pegasus and the constellation of Andromeda. Close together, their arms up to point, they traced with their fingers in the night sky the crossing lines that let them find the cloud of the Andromeda galaxy two and a half million light years away. A trillion stars. He had squeezed her against him, turned her face toward him and kissed her so lightly on the lips that *it was just a game. Just a game,* she had told herself, as she turned away laughing in the dark to run back toward the house.

But of course, she had known what he felt, because she had felt it. What had she thought? Did she think nothing could happen? He knew she was dating Bill Sharpe. She had talked about Bill partly to keep her aunt from being jealous—she had sensed the coolness growing there. But had she simply been using Bill to shield from Aunt Teresa, and from herself, what she in fact felt for Walter? She had told herself that the effect she had on Walter was just intimacy over the poems they read, and she had let herself believe that he understood it that way, too—impossible, unthinkable. But she could see, now, exactly what she was doing to him.

And she loved it. This superb mind. Rose was there to read with them, to be part of the conversation, but Nora had soon begun to feel her as her chaperone—the check on the emotion she was feeling. A middle-aged man, forty-seven years old, but with a fire she had never experienced before. Not with Ezekiel, her first lover in high school, fumbling madly through her clothes in the backseat of his parents' Chevrolet, or Mark, her boyfriend through junior year, with his one earring and an air of Elizabethan pretension, as though he knew Marlowe and Chapman personally, and his coffee pour-over every morning and his way of proffering himself.

Aunt Teresa's husband. Buford's father. She said the phrases to herself, but they would not carry their plain prose correctives into her heart of hearts. She should never have stopped calling him Uncle Walter. She would never dream of calling Aunt Teresa simply Teresa. She would always be Aunt Teresa, as she had been from Nora's childhood, when she and Duane and her parents had visited them in Athens, where Walter taught before the accident with little Walter, when Rose was still little, before the Peach family had moved, under its cloud of tragedy and doom, to Waycross and Walter had completely lost his way.

But Uncle Walter had become Walter so easily, so sweetly.

And now she had made him lose his way again. She had done it. She felt it so deeply her knees weakened and she sagged against her desk. She wiped the tears from her cheeks and took from her desk the book she had come to retrieve. Louise Glück. *The Wild Iris. Love, Walter.*

Useless now. *They couldn't still read it together.* She couldn't possibly go over to Stonewall Hill tonight. No, he wouldn't be there now. He could never act as though nothing had happened between them. They couldn't read together now, not ever again, could not look up from the poems and find each other there, as they had so often, for so long.

Never again could it happen. Never again.

She bent over sobbing.

"Miss Nora?" said a gentle voice from the door. Mr. Watts stood there with his broom, full of solicitude. "You alright, Miss Nora?"

She could not speak. She nodded and smiled at Mr. Watts, wiping her tears away. He tilted his head as if to let her explain but she shook her head and gently waved him away.

"Yes ma'am, I just—"

He backed from the room. On Monday, after a weekend without seeing Walter, knowing she had driven him into despair, she would have to go in and teach *The Secret Garden*, and Buford would be sitting there—Buford, who had been his father's unwilling messenger, who had tried to warn her.

Then the thought struck her. All those trusting faces. How could she teach? The very idea of it terrified her. They would smell out her guilt, like dogs sniffing baggage for drugs. Blindly, she gathered up her treasured books, the ones she had left because she thought she would not need them this weekend. She put *The Wild Iris* on the stack and glanced around the classroom. The maps and star charts and lists and posters all suddenly looked alien. With her arms filled, she left the room, nodding to Mr. Watts, who bowed his head to acknowledge her departure and express his sympathy for whatever had happened. She went carefully down the steps at the end of the hall, turned slightly to bump the bar with her hip and slid through the opening, leaning against the door as she got outside to make sure it clicked shut and spared Mr. Watts that trouble.

When she turned to start for her car, a man on the bench between the walkway and the brick wall rose and stood astride the sidewalk, smiling, his hands thrust into his back pockets.

Dexter Watkins.

She stared at the huge man blocking her way, tossing his blond dreadlocks like a Viking raider who would cheerfully murder and rape his way through a village of innocents, the eyebrows glinting with rings. This murderer she had pitied.

"Miss Emma tell you I came calling on you the other day?"

He had a piece of gum in his mouth, and he chewed it with an insolence that maddened her. The stupidity of his self-assurance. Fury ignited within her, but she knew she must not reveal anything.

"You upset Miss Emma," she said.

"I thought we could go to ride. Go up to the falls. Get to know each other." He stepped closer to her. "Look at all them books," he said, as though the stack she held were keeping him from her. "You look like you been crying. Something wrong?"

He asked it knowingly. She met his eyes quickly and then tried to step around him, but he got in her way. A bully on the playground. She sighed through her nostrils and looked at the ground.

"Mr. Watkins, please."

"You don't know me is all. I just want you to get to know me."

"I know you as well as I want to. Let me pass or Mr. Watts will call the police."

"Mr. Watts," he said mockingly. "Listen," he said, stepping closer, forcing her to step back. When she tried to get around him again, she found herself pinned back against the brick wall as she had that day in September when she had first seen him. He put both arms over her shoulders to box her in. "I saw you out there with Peach," he said.

She met his eyes.

"I saw you," he said. "Old Peach trying to talk you up."

She stared at him. He saw the effect of his words, and his jaw began to work the gum again.

"So how about this," he said, leaning close. She recognized the smell of Dubble Bubble from the gum she was always telling Rufus Grimes to spit out. Dexter was forming a bubble with the tip of his tongue. She viewed the pores of his nose, the errant hair protruding from his nostril. One of the rings in his eyebrows oozed a little pus. "You and me go for a ride," he said, popping the bubble between his teeth, "and I don't tell your aunt about you and Peach." His tongue rode out a little over his bottom lip.

"You don't know the first thing about Walter," she said.

"*Walter?*" he said, mocking her. "You turned Walter down, but you're sweet on him. A man with a wife and children."

"Mr. Watkins, let me go."

"Listen, sugar, I just want to go to ride," he said, pulling her against him, enveloping her in his aura of marijuana and deodorant. The books pressed against his chest seemed to irritate him, and he relaxed his hold, running his hand over the curve of her bottom. "I got some decent weed. We can talk. I won't do a thing you don't want me to. But you're gon want me to."

She broke free and burst past him and ran for her car. Some of the books spilled loose, and she grabbed at them, but let them fall. She had left the car unlocked, and when she got to it, she yanked open the driver's door, dropping more books, spilling the rest onto the seat, and climbed in over them, locking the doors.

But he had not chased her. Through the windshield, she saw Watkins standing where he had accosted her, his hands back in his hip pockets, smiling at her, still chewing. He shook his head and shrugged his regret.

She drove a block, then pulled over to the curb and turned off the car. She dug in her purse for her cell phone. She had to warn Walter. But when she glanced in the rearview mirror, she saw Dexter Watkins' red Jeep pulling from the school lot and coming her way. She fought down her panic and held up the phone to her ear, meeting his eye and moving her lips, as though she were calling the police. He stopped and grinned and pointed his index finger at her. *POW*—the recoil jerked his hand upward. And instantly, a stream of smoke blew from his mouth across the fingertip. Marijuana, she thought.

He paused, looking at her, still grinning. Again, his tongue came out over his lip.

But then he drove on.

Thank God. She sat trembling. Thank God. She watched the Jeep disappear around the curve toward town, and when it did not reappear, she sank back into the seat, weeping again for a moment. Then, collecting herself, she turned the key and took the wheel.

But where would she go now? Back to Miss Emma's? Without being able to see Walter? She would be without Walter from now on. She had never been happier anywhere. And how could she ever face Rose? Because red-headed Rose—*Raïssa*, as she called herself—had seen through their double entendres, their denials and evasions, Nora's naïveté about the power of love. A terrible hot shame spread beneath her ribs. But then she stiffened with a fierce resentment. This teenager presuming to judge her. Or had her cousin only seen the obvious? Nora and Walter right in front of her. Anybody could have seen it.

Nora sighed and let it go.

Oh God, how would she get through the weekend? Every joy seemed blocked. And with a sudden access of panic, she thought of Bill Sharpe. The date on Sunday. No consolation to think of him now. She felt what it meant, felt it suddenly and deeply. He planned to propose to her, that's what, and today, before this very hour, she would have let him. Before Walter said he loved her, she might even have accepted, because Walter would still be available to her, and he would understand that she could have Bill as he had Aunt Teresa. And their souls could still meet in poetry, when deep in that preserve of language they entered each other, as Donne said, and flowed into each other and became that "abler soul," that one from two. She had never known with Bill Sharpe anything near what Walter had opened in her—that deeper thing, withheld from Bill or entirely inaccessible to his practical mind. Reserved for Walter alone.

She found much to admire in Bill, but now even speaking to him seemed like a betrayal. A betrayal of Walter, who loved her. And what she felt for him! That high, intense pleasure of the mind and heart. Panic of losing him seized her, a wild longing.

For adultery.

The word burned into her heart with its scarlet-lettered horror. It had not been adultery until now, never sinful—had it? O never, never, never. How could such glory of soul be sinful at all—much less *adultery*, that vicious word smelling of cigarette butts and spilled liquor?

Walter

Slumped behind the wheel of the Subaru, already halfway down the day's second pint, sipping it, taking it slow, Peach was watching customers cross the Ingles parking lot. It was splendidly depressing. Women fierce of mien and vastly overweight proceeded into the store in gym clothes, and their buttocks shook enough at each step to intimidate a sumo wrestler. What would Walt Whitman do with them? *Apostrophize me, O Walt! Make me a song triumphant! O celebrate each tremor and aftershock of my ungirdled amplitude! Of my largesse of flesh make for America its live and undulant reserves!*

Over to you, Wallace Stevens: *Fat! Fat! Fat! Fat!*

Near him a minivan pulled up hesitantly and stopped, straddling a yellow line. A young woman, plump but not yet elephantine, got out of her car and carefully extracted her baby from the infant seat in the back. She glanced around, momentarily met Walter's eyes, and went into the store clutching the child with both arms.

He took another swallow of bourbon and leaned his head back, closing his eyes.

What is it, Walter? What's wrong?

Nothing's wrong, except that I love you. My God, don't you know I love you?

Walter...

O maiden, muse, and maiden, o my love!

And the look in her eyes. The look in her eyes when what he was saying became unmistakable to her. When he took her hand and tried to pull her to him.

He sighed through his nostrils. What the hell had possessed him? He rubbed his eyelids and opened them blearily.

Quick trip: the young mother was already coming back out of the store, still clutching her baby. A fat bag dangled from one hand. Diapers. The husband must have a night job, or maybe he was boozing it up with his buddies and that's why she had to go out by herself with the baby. Glancing around anxiously, she hurried toward her car as though she might be attacked at any moment. At the last second, fumbling for her keys, she spotted Walter behind his windshield and froze. What was he still doing there, just sitting there watching her?

She averted her eyes and hurriedly opened the door.

Right. What was a middle-aged man doing sitting alone in an Ingles parking lot on a Friday night?

Seeing himself as she saw him, he felt like the bad news about what babies might grow up to become. A lurking presence, a man whose natural desires had soured and curdled into dark imaginings and unnerving fantasies, a creature of sick appetites, one of those men who has wrenched himself from the vine and withered into his own evil nature. Child porn, the whole deal.

He shuddered with self-loathing as she buckled in her baby and drove off quickly.

So was that how Nora saw him, too?

No. That was what moved him about her. She never saw him that way, not even today. She would make the best of what he had said, as she had made the best of him all year, encouraging him, reviving in him the passion for finding the right word and rhythm that had been the bright motive power of his youth. In her presence, he felt a clearing, an airing-out, an opening.

After being with Nora on those Friday nights, he realized how much he had been a prisoner of Teresa's forgiveness, not that she ever intended it. With Nora he felt the horizons opening in every direction. He ran and he flew. He was free, climbing into unknown skies above a vast patchwork of forests and fields and cities—

And then *Quack! Quack! Quack! Don't you know I love you?*

And now Sir Walter Mallard was plummeting shot-ridden from her brilliant eyes. Old Chaucer. "Your eyen two wol slee me sodenly,/I may the beautè of hem not sustene,/So woundeth hit through-out my herte kene." He held up his bottle and swirled the contents. Back to what he was destined to be after all his early promise. He took another drink, and just as he did, his phone buzzed— Teresa wondering where he was—and a red Jeep pulled slowly into the parking lot. He picked up the phone and glanced at it.

Not Teresa. Nora. His heart rose, and yet he answered with dread.

"Nora?"

"I have to leave Gallatin."

"Because of me?"

She was silent for a moment before she answered him. "I just can't do this to Aunt Teresa. Somebody saw us."

He sat up straighter.

"There was nobody there."

"Dexter Watkins saw us."

"Dexter Watkins? I'm looking at him right now."

The red Jeep came steadily toward him across the Ingles parking lot, slowing as it got closer.

"Walter?" Nora was saying. "Call me back, please."

Dexter Watkins rolled up beside him facing the opposite way and motioned for Walter to lower the window. His right hand drooped over the steering wheel, and in his left, he held a cigarette that he put to his lips, sucking in the smoke, holding it, eyeing Walter as he did. Not a cigarette, a joint. Walter could smell it now. With an air of casual menace, Watkins blew the smoke in a thin stream up into the space between the Subaru and the Jeep and then held the joint toward Walter, who shook his head and held up his bottle.

Watkins' head went back in amusement.

"I figured," he said. "Girl like that turns you down."

"A girl like what?"

Not meeting Walter's eyes, ignoring his question, Watkins took another hit and neatly pinched the fire from the end of the joint with the long yellow nails on his thumb and forefinger. He tamped the end of the joint and squeezed the paper around it and tucked it somewhere under his dashboard.

"I have to say, it was pretty funny to watch."

A burn started in Walter's abdomen.

"I don't know what you're talking about."

"What I'm thinking is you help me out and I'll help you out."

"How exactly can you help me out, Watkins?"

"Call me Dexter," said Watkins, making a fist. "The mighty right hand."

Walter snorted and took another swallow of bourbon.

"How can I help you out?" Watkins said. "That's your question? Starters, I can keep quiet about what I saw. Your wife don't need to know you're hitting on her niece. And to make sure I don't slip up, all I need is one little favor."

"What's that?"

"Give me the girl."

After a moment, despite himself, Walter started to laugh.

"Give you the girl?"

"You know damn well you can't have her. Alls I want is a chance to talk to her," Watkins said, holding his hand out, palm up. "Just take her to ride. She thinks I'm some kind of criminal. People say all kinds of shit about me. But she'll listen to you. Tell her all I want is to take her to ride. Let her get to know me."

He could have been running for mayor. The man actually believed himself.

"She's not mine to give you," Walter said.

Watkins stared at him and shook his head, as if in resignation. "Come here," he said. "Let me make you a proposition."

Walter narrowed his eyes.

"What kind of proposition?"

"Come here."

"No, you come here."

Watkins sighed but then pulled his Jeep around to the other side of the Subaru, got out, shut his door, and leaned in the Subaru's passenger door.

"Come on. Get in," Walter said.

"Okay, you ready to hear it?" he said as he sat down and closed the door. Watkins' ripe cloud of weed and cologne drifted over Peach.

"Go ahead."

"You own five acres out on Hopewell Road," Watkins said.

Walter felt a sharp cold in his heart.

"How do you know that?"

"I got this foreign dude looked me up. Might be"—Watkins fluttered his hand. "You know what I'm saying? Gives me the creeps—but sharp, my sweet Jesus. He tells me you got this land between Vernon Jenkins and Jimmy Proctor. Caleb Creek cuts through it. It's flat down there on both sides for about a hundred yards. Nobody's been back there for thirty years. Most of it's overgrown with kudzu. But not down by the creek."

Walter stared at him and shrugged and shook his head. "So?"

Watkins stared back without speaking, and suddenly Walter's comprehension ignited, and he sat up.

"My God, you mean a trade?"

Watkins tilted his head noncommittally.

"You leave her alone?" Walter said.

When Watkins thrust out his lower lip and nodded, raising his eyebrows, Walter blew out his breath and sat back in the seat. His fingertips went to his ponytail and worried it.

"I mean," Watkins said, "when I set my mind on a really, really sweet piece of—"

"Shut up," Walter said.

"If that ain't true love," said Watkins, his tongue coming out over his bottom lip. "There's good sun down there," Watkins said. "We're talking about—I mean, a shit load of weed, which it's the only reason. What do you think? Deal?"

He offered his hand and after a moment Walter shook it. "Deal."

Watkins smiled at him.

"But you know damn well you can't have her," Watkins said again.

Nora

By the time Walter called her back, Nora had been sitting on her bed at Miss Emma's for twenty minutes, holding the phone on her hot, open palms, unable to pack, unable to move.

"Walter?" she said, instantly putting it to her ear when it buzzed. "What happened?"

"I made a deal with him."

"What do you mean? Did he threaten you? What kind of deal?" He was silent for a moment.

"He won't bother you again."

"What did you do?"

"It's okay, Nora. And listen, listen, darling. Please don't leave Gallatin. You should keep your job. I won't bother you again."

A sob broke raggedly from her chest.

"Walter, you don't—you don't ever—it's not because you bother me. You understand that. It's because you *don't* bother me."

Her heart would not stop hammering. She wondered at herself. Desire mastered her body, demanding, demanding. Must! Must! Wicked. And she was so willing. So willing. Hungering stigma and pistil and ovule and scent. It had not happened, but she had wanted it to happen. She still wanted it. She was guilty of it now. Before she could stop it, a cry broke from her, a sob. She did not know who she was.

This time he was silent for so long that she knew she had hurt him again.

"Nora…"

"Oh, Walter, don't make me say anything else, please. I just have to go home."

"Will you call me?"

"You know I can't. I need to go home and start over. Just start over."

"What should I tell Teresa?"

"I don't know," she said. She was shaking with sobs now, and Miss Emma, limping down the hall, must have heard her. She stopped, tapping at the door.

"Just a minute," Nora whispered into the phone. "What is it Miss Emma?" she called.

"Are you all right?"

"I am, Miss Emma. Thank you."

Miss Emma waited for a moment before she went away.

"Walter?" Nora whispered.

"Yes, I'm here."

"I don't know what to tell Aunt Teresa," she whispered. "I don't know what to tell Miss Emma. Or Bill Sharpe. Or my mother when I get home."

"I'm so sorry I said anything."

"No. Don't be." Her heart was high, wild, urgent. "But it can't ever happen," she said, weeping.

"So a great prince in prison lies."

She would think about it later. She waited until she could answer. "Goodbye, Walter."

"Goodbye, Nora," he said.

She sat there for a long time, bent above the phone as if it were the body of a dead child. Finally, she stirred and began to gather her things.

Walter Peach

March 17, 2014

It was at least ten in the morning, and Peach was still sitting at his desk with his head in his hands, unable to concentrate on work. He had a paper to get out, and he did not care. The breaking news, the headline story in his life—**Fifth-Grade Teacher Nora O'Hearn Abandons Classroom**—he would not write. He felt like getting another bottle of bourbon and renting a motel room and watching cable TV for two or three days.

When the door of the *Tribune* swung open, he sighed and looked up.

It was the tall thin man from the summer. The one who claimed that Peach knew somebody named Alison. The dandy. Peach could almost hear a hushed golf-commentator voice describing his outfit: *Beneath a simple brown fedora our mystery guest wears an elegant brown leather jacket, tan slacks with a belt of Everglades python, and a soft lime V-neck sweater over an ivory T-shirt of pure silk.*

"Mr. Peach," he said, casually covering his mouth as he spoke. Something about him triggered an association with Forrest, but he could not remember why.

"Back again," said Peach. "You have the advantage of me. You know my name."

"Oh, I have incalculable advantages," the man said in his British accent. "But to business. Might one still purchase a classified advertisement?"

The ripe voice, the manicured hand, the face somehow turned aside or blocked from view. There was just one accented syllable, ad*ver*tisement, Peach noticed, not the local *ad*vertisement. *Might one still purchase*—as though he were asking, with his mannered subjunctive, if classified ads were even printed any more.

"Tight for this week," Peach said. "We can get it up online. What do you need an ad for?"

"Workers in the vineyard, so to say."

"Some kind of revival?" Peach said, lifting an eyebrow.

"Gimme that old-time religion," the man said merrily. "Perhaps I might write the advertisement out?" the man said.

Peach opened his desk drawer and found a legal pad and pushed it across the desk.

"Need a pen?"

Shading his face with his hat, the man pulled his own pen from the inside pocket of his jacket and jotted down several sentences and turned the pad back toward Peach.

"Spanish?" Peach said, trying to read it. Something about *marimba*. "I don't know if we have a Spanish-speaking clientele."

"Is that a problem for you?"

"For me? No sir. But if you want anybody to answer it, you should put your contact information."

Once again, the man lowered his sunglasses and Peach felt the strange, dead, black-iris effect of his eyes. The man got out his wallet and counted ten hundred-dollar bills onto the desk and then covered his mouth with his hand.

"I'll pay for a year in advance. If this exceeds the necessary amount, please continue to run the advertisement longer."

"Yes sir."

"Do we have an agreement?"

"You bet."

"Or should we call it a *deal?*"

The man seemed to be making a point—maybe the difference between British English and American English. It reminded him of his deal with Watkins, and remembering Watkins brought the idea of Nora. Thinking of Nora brought nothing but darkness.

"Suit yourself." He took the money and put it in the desk. He would have to deposit it, and the idea of a trip to the bank wearied him. "Anything else?" he said.

But the man was gone.

KUDZU

Part II

Throughout the 1930s and 1940s, the Soil Erosion Service and its successor, the Soil Conservation Service, touted Kudzu as the remedy to the South's soil problems. In a little more than a decade, these agencies provided about 84 million Kudzu seedlings . . . to southern landowners for erosion control and land revitalization. . . . Religious metaphors comparing the Kudzu invasion to biblical scourges are apt and appropriately evocative of the degradation the plant has visited upon the ecosystems of the South.

From *The Great Reshuffling: Human Dimensions of Invasive Species.* IUCN, Gland, Switzerland and Cambridge, UK. The World Conservation Union: 55-62.

Teresa

June 14, 2014

When Nora O'Hearn left Gallatin in March, Teresa had watched Walter fume. He would get over it in a few days, she thought, and then resume his real life. One morning, she imagined, he would come in a little shame-faced and join her for coffee, and they would talk about Belen, plan the day, smile at each other. Say a prayer together. But week after week went by, and nothing changed. For three months now, he had been sinking into worse and worse listlessness and depression. He avoided her in the morning when he left for work. At meals, he would answer direct questions but otherwise initiate no conversation, exhibit no interest in the children. At night, he would come back and have two or three stiff drinks and sit in front of the television streaming one dark Netflix series after another, usually about cartels. Having a family and responsibilities appeared to irritate him. If she reminded him of simple things—to take out the trash or pay the electric bill online or get the oil changed in the Outback—he would flare up. Once he stormed out of the house over a spilled drop of coffee on his shirt, once because Rose made a sardonic comment about how they never read poetry anymore, once over nothing at all, as though merely being there were intolerable to him. At night, he lay beside her like a prisoner whose punishment was to sleep in her bed.

The *Gallatin Tribune* sank with him. Pick up an issue now, and there would be a tepid account of the school board or the city council, a front-page photo of a cute child, syndicated political columns and movie reviews, a high school sports story, a few photos of the basketball team. He stopped writing editorials. After several weeks of obvious decline in the quality of the newspaper, Braxton Forrest had called him at home. Teresa overheard Walter's replies—*Jesus, these yahoos don't know the difference. They like it better now.* He sounded so bitterly sarcastic that she marveled at Forrest's patience. *Right, right. Man is born to trouble, you told me. .... A vacation? Hell, I don't need a vacation, just—you know, just—just*—How long would Braxton put up with him? Teresa lost her temper with him several times a day.

This Saturday morning in June, a week after Rose and Buford had completed the school year, she finished her coffee ritual alone and, after making breakfast, called everyone down. They sat at the breakfast table, the morning still cool enough to keep the windows open. Teresa asked Rose to serve the bowls while she set out the yogurt and walnuts and raspberries.

"No books at the table," she said to Buford.

It was a book of chess problems Nora's substitute had given him. Buford dropped the book under his chair.

"Mr. Parker was good after all, wasn't he?" Teresa said.

"He was okay, but not like—". He left the sentence unfinished and glanced at Walter, who felt the pause and lifted his eyes from a page of the *New Yorker*.

"What's the matter? Just go on and say it."

Just then, Rose came in and set down a bowl in front of him. Walter stared at the steaming steel-cut oats, and then abruptly pushed the bowl away with the back of his hand.

"*Every* goddamn morning? Seriously? Why can't I get a decent breakfast?"

Rose and Buford looked at Teresa, and before she could think, Teresa savagely swept his bowl and cup crashing into the wall, oatmeal and coffee spattering everywhere.

"Just get the *fuck* out of here, Walter!" she shouted, leaning toward him.

She never used that word. Never. And now, and now, right in front of the children.

Walter worked his tongue under his upper lip, not looking up.

"Just walk out?" he said. "That's what you'd like?"

"You're making everybody miserable. If you're so unhappy, Walter, just go on."

"What if the only good thing I've ever done is not to disappear like everybody else in my life?"

"What do you mean, *everybody else*?" she cried, waving her hand at Rose and Buford. "Here we are, Walter. And let me tell you something. Look at me!"

He would not look up. She reached over and lifted his chin.

"Look at me!"

He looked up at her and met her eyes.

"Did I ever disappear? Did I?"

Walter dropped his eyes. He got up and went over to pick up the fallen bowl and the pieces of the shattered mug. From the kitchen, he got paper towels and a broom and a dustpan to clean up the mess. The children sat tensely, expecting another explosion, but when he finished, he came back and stood at the head of the table.

"Look, I'm sorry," he said, looking at each of them. "I'm sorry I'm not a better father and a better husband. Teresa, I'm sorry."

His calm terrified them. After the screen door closed behind him and

116

they heard the Outback start, Buford asked, "What's the matter with him, Mom? I mean, it's been—I mean, he kind of . . . when Miss Nora left . . . "

He faltered to a stop. She sat at the table for a moment turning her mug in her hands and then broke down sobbing. Rose rushed to her and hugged her.

"Mom," she said. "Oh Mom. I'm so sorry. You need to talk to somebody. Dad's just not—why don't you call Mrs. Forrest? I bet she could help."

She almost did it. Later that morning, she sat in her bedroom with the phone in her lap. It would be good to talk to Marisa.

But about this? Was Teresa ready to tell her the whole saga of betrayal that began long before Nora? Marisa had been through things as bad, no, things far worse, and Teresa could imagine her friend's genuine sympathy, the way she had of opening her heart to take in someone else's suffering. Yes, and her friend would pray for her and do whatever she could to make the situation right. But imagining that intervention was exactly where Teresa faltered. Walter was the problem. He sensed every nuance in other people's attempts to help him or interpret him. The problem went deeper than Nora O'Hearn. His whole being was a dark psychological tangle, but God help you if you tried to root out or even start to discover what allowed that thicket to grow. He had a way of saying the phrase "abandonment issues" with such deliberate delicacy that you realized he was making fun of you before you even tried to help.

No, she would simply have to wait him out. She set the phone back on the bedside table. She felt her life coming to a crisis. She had no idea what Walter might do. But it might end with divorce, she realized. After all they had been through, it might actually end that way. The family torn apart.

She bowed her head, breathing slowly, taking a long breath in through her nostrils—*Lord Jesus Christ, son of God*—and then letting it out again *have mercy on me a sinner.*

Lord Jesus Christ, son of God,
have mercy on me a sinner.

Forrest

On the big screen of Forrest's desktop the facsimile of the print edition lit up, large. The *Gallatin Tribune* had come out that morning—always on Thursday to anticipate the weekend. **Fathers Honored** said the headline for June 19. Two big pictures from Father's Day, the previous Sunday, sat side by side: on the left, Hosea Hubbard, a beaming old black man (103, according to the caption) surrounded by five generations of his male descendants; on the right, a very young and very serious white insurance agent named Steve Colter, who stood outdoors in his Sunday clothes, stiffly holding his little girl's hand and warning off the yahoos who would show up as her suitors a decade or so from now. And inside on the editorial page, where Peach now ran syndicated columns (Ann Coulter, David Brooks, Clarence Page), he had printed a treacly commemoration of her dead daddy by a local teenager named Angie Pearson. Peach knew well that Angie would warm the *Tribune* readers' hearts: many a grandmother would *just love it.* Circulation had already increased—not much, but some—since Peach had stopped writing his own columns and reviews.

All of which would have been fine in Cuthbert, Georgia, or Londonderry, New Hampshire, but not in Gallatin—at least, not in the *Gallatin Tribune,* the paper Forrest had given CPR by putting Walter in charge. It wasn't even this issue itself; it was the fact that, coming from Walter Peach, it emanated a kind of ironic contempt for its audience. Ever since Walter took over the paper four years ago, he had downplayed made-up holidays that tapped complex emotions and reduced them to generic Hallmark syrup—Valentine's Day, Mother's Day, Father's Day. He ran holiday ads, but he would not write a frontpage story about mothers or fathers or hundred-year-old sweethearts to save his life. Printing Angie Pearson's tribute felt almost cruel, a provocation—but for whom? Teresa? Or Rose, who would curl her lips at such sentiments? Or was it aimed at Forrest himself? *What are you complaining about? This is just like football. This is what makes money.*

The man was in despair, worse even than his exile in Waycross. The new position as editor had saved him four years ago, but now it was just another job. If Nora O'Hearn had not come along, he would have kept himself entertained by tying local stories to national and international developments. Cartels, for example—that had kept him going for months. But ever since Nora O'Hearn left town, Walter had been in a death spiral. Forrest had tried to warn Walter, but what could you say when that kind of love took over a man, that kind of incurable disease? With gloomy recognition, Forrest remembered his own obsession with Marilyn Harkins. Peach could not get over Nora O'Hearn. The poor fool thought his poetry had returned with her arrival, and now her departure had drained his motivation for everything. Teresa had suffered it in silence, but just last night she had called Marisa to confess her worries. Every Monday, she said, after Walter put that week's issue to bed, he would run everybody off and sit in front of the TV, streaming violent shows and drinking bourbon by himself until he passed out. When she tried to talk to him, he would say things about wanting to be dead, about feeling damned. Even in Waycross, she had never sensed such dark fatalism, such furies in him.

What could he do? Despite all Walter's faults, Forrest loved the man.

He pushed back from his desk. Soon, maybe even next week, he would be going down to Gallatin. Something was coming. He felt it. Remembering that he could pray, he said a Memorare. Through the north-facing window, he watched the middle section of Memorial Bridge slowly crank upward over the Piscataqua River. A moment later, heading seaward, came one of the cruise boats that went out to the Isles of Shoals, where old Thomas Morton had been exiled by the Plymouth Pilgrims after his escapades with the Maypole at Merry Mount—a little much for their Calvinist tastes.

Forrest thought of first seeing Nora O'Hearn outside the office at Stonewall Hill, looking up, thinking he was Walter. God help him. The sweet breeze out of Eden could ruin a man.

Walter

Mary Jane Ryburn was writing her daily specials—Eggs Benedict for breakfast, Reubens for lunch—on her sidewalk chalkboard when Walter crossed the sidewalk to the *Tribune* office.

"Morning," she said brightly.

He nodded at her and tried to put the key in the lock, but it would not go in.

"Walter," she said. "Hold on a minute."

Wearily, he waited for whatever she would say. Sensing his rudeness, he turned to face her. Fit in her fifties, she stood next to the sign in her jeans and her light blue Left Bank t-shirt, her left hand on her hip and the pink chalk poised in her right.

"Listen, what's happened to the cartels?" she asked. "You haven't written a word about them for months. In fact, you haven't written much of anything. 'Fathers Honored'? Seriously? You've got me worried."

"You and Teresa," he said, turning back to the problem of the lock.

"Come on, I know depression when I see it. Come inside. You can try the eggs benedict on the house."

He looked at her.

"And free coffee," she said. "Come on. Talk to me."

"I'm scared of you."

"Faint heart never won fair lady," she said. "Can't you spare me five minutes?"

"Well," he said, "I can't seem to get into my office."

Inside the Left Bank, two early customers—middle-aged women Walter did not know—sat at a table by the front window, leaning toward each other and speaking in whispers with considerable headshaking and eyerolling. Mary Jane situated Walter at the table nearest the kitchen. She disappeared for a moment and came back with two cups of coffee and a small pitcher of cream.

"Tell me if you need anything," she called to the two women, who looked up a little startled and lifted their hands toward her. Mary Jane sat down opposite Walter, her crossed legs aimed outward into the restaurant and her torso turned toward him. As she lifted her cup to take a sip, she regarded him with a slight, disapproving smile.

"What's going on with you?" she asked.

For the next few minutes, she grilled him. Had he seen anybody for help? What kinds of medications was he on? Had something happened to trigger this depression?

"You have to know there are rumors," she said, leaning toward him, but just then the waiter, a high school boy Walter recognized from the band, came out and reached across the table to set down Walter's eggs benedict.

"Herschel!" Mary Jane said. "Serve from the left, clear from the right. I told you that before."

"Yes ma'am," Herschel said. "I just, you know—"

"You thought I was teasing?"

"No ma'am."

He looked at her, a little scared—Walter sympathized—and went back into the kitchen. Mary Jane shook her head as Walter started in on the eggs benedict.

"There are rumors," she resumed, "that you got your niece pregnant and that's why she left suddenly back in March."

"That's ridiculous," he said.

"Okay," she said. "What's the real story? Because you started phoning it in right after she left town."

"Really good eggs," he said.

"Did it have something to do with Nora?"

He took another bite, fighting down the impulse to flip over the table and crash cursing out of the restaurant.

"Mary Jane," he said, "it's really none of your business."

"Just help me squelch the rumors, Walter. Being here all day, I overhear things."

He speared one of the home fries.

"Are you in love with her?" she asked quietly.

He slammed his fork down on his plate and stood up. The two women at the window stopped talking and looked at him.

Mary Jane did not lift her eyes.

"*Sit. Down.*"

He sat back down.

"Okay," she said. "That part's true. But not the other part."

"So, that's what you're going to tell everybody," Walter said bitterly.

"No," she said, "I'm going to tell them that what they're saying is ridiculous, just like you told me. It's ridiculous, right?" She smiled at him, shaking her head with a knowing sympathy. "Look at me." When he met her gaze, she put her hand on his for the briefest moment. "Just *ridiculous.*"

His heart burned with hurt, and he felt his eyes water. When he stood to go a few minutes later, he thanked Mary Jane perfunctorily for the meal and the coffee.

"Walter," she said, "I'm sorry. I know this is hard on you. It's men in their forties. Did you know Frank left me once, around your age?"

He raised his eyebrows and shook his head, but he did not care about Frank.

"May I see those keys," she said. He glanced at her open palm and shrugged, not realizing until that moment that he already had them out. He handed them to her. She held up the key to the Outback. "Did you really think this was going to open your office door?"

For a full hour, Walter sat at his desk, not even turning on his computer. The stupid, prying town with its commentaries, Mary Jane's seen-it-all air. Of everything Mary Jane had said, one sentence kept coming back to mind.

Faint heart never won fair lady.

Rosemary had once said that to him.

Faint heart never won fair lady. Something to do with Vernon Jenkins— no, with his father. He had asked her why Cletus McBride had a father and he did not. Rosemary told him that his father had abandoned her because he was afraid.

Why was he afraid? he asked her.

Because he didn't love me enough. If he had, he would have given up everything for me. Other things meant more to him than I did. If you really love somebody, you will give up the whole world for that person. Faint heart never won fair lady.

I love you, Rosemary he told her. *I would give up everything for you.*

Oh, Walter. I love you, too. She had squeezed him against her. *But I mean grownup love.*

That was when Vernon Jenkins started coming over.

Faint heart never won fair lady. Months ago, Nora wanted to know why he never went into the old house on Hopewell Road. He had just shrugged off the suggestion, as if she could not possibly understand how much it terrified him to think about it. How could he even think of going back into that house, hideously overgrown, where he had searched in such desperation for Rosemary? But Nora did understand, she understood too well, because she was like Rosemary. It was easy enough to pretend that she was just a pretty girl who had infatuated him and to strip away her aura, drawing her back down into the bourgeois world, as Mary Jane had just done. But a woman like Nora needed risk and danger and sacrifice as homage to her beauty, because, in being given such a high treasure, she had been called to serve it by making great demands and asking for great love. She had asked him for an act of courage. She wanted him to go back into the past and find Rosemary, and he had failed her and failed Rosemary. He had to weigh his passion for Nora against everything else in his life and without hesitation throw the rest of it away, no matter how much pain and condemnation it would bring. She wanted him to be a hero, not a guilty, forty-something, down-in-the-mouth husband. She wanted him to love her in the full and rare meaning of a great love. She should be a Helen or a Cleopatra or a Guinevere, desired and envied, beyond the reach of ordinary morality, remembered with disapproval but never contempt long beyond her time.

But what did he have of momentous counterpoise to her great beauty? Not Troy, not Rome or Camelot, but a job as editor of a small-town paper. He had his family, but what kind of grand gesture would it be to leave them?

Just get the fuck out of here Teresa had told him, sick of his bad humor and defensive moroseness. For Mary Jane, he was just a typically foolish middle-aged man like Frank facing the long decades of growing old. No, he wanted to come just once, with full knowledge, early and alone, upon his young Eve in a cloud of fragrance, still naked and guiltless. He wanted beauty's archetype to look openly upon him and swear the unconditional *yes* whose radiance would transfigure his sour and melancholy heart.

As he gazed out the window at the courthouse across Johnston Street, a new resolve began to take shape in him. This time, Eurydice would lead Orpheus out of hell. He could do only one thing: what most terrified him. He would do it, and when he did it, Nora would somehow know.

Buford

June 20, 2014

"*What?*" the boy shouted, opening his eyes in a panic and swinging his elbow up sharply to ward off whatever terrible thing was coming. He hit something hard.

"God d—Ow! *Shit!*"

Whoever he hit backed off. Buford sat up, ready to swing again. It was not somebody taking his picture. It was his father in a baseball cap, an old t-shirt, and a pair of jeans. He was standing in the lamplight a few feet from the bed, holding his jaw.

"You always wake up like that?" his father said. "You could have broken a couple of my teeth."

Buford tensed, not knowing what to expect. "I was having a bad dream."

It was still half-dark outside. Of all the times somebody had shaken him awake, he could not remember once when his father had done it. The long, graying hair was neatly pulled back in a ponytail. The intelligent eyes, the habitual expression—bemused, sardonic, angry.

"Get some old clothes on. I want to take you out to our property."

"What day is it?"

"Friday."

By now he could see the clock.

"At 5:30 in the morning? There's nothing out there but kudzu."

"Come on. Get your jeans and your boots."

Reluctantly, he got out of bed. As his father waited, he shucked off the gym shorts he wore to sleep in, pulled on old jeans and a Braves t-shirt, and then sat on the edge of his bed lacing up the boots, pulling them taut over two pairs of hooks and then threading the ends through the eyes at the top, wrapping the long leather laces around his ankles, pulling them tight, and doing double-knots.

"You'd better bring a sweatshirt until it warms up."

"I'm okay," Buford said.

"Suit yourself. So what were you dreaming? Something about those pictures?"

Buford glanced up to see if his father, still working his jaw, was really interested in hearing it. His mother would have been, but his dad just went through the motions of paying attention.

"Not exactly," he said, deciding to trust him. "We were driving up this black road in the mountains. I was in the front seat with you and the

125

car ahead of us kept slowing down because the road was melting and the car was sinking down like a dinosaur in a tar pit. And then all of a sudden, all four tires started spinning and caught on fire, and the car started rising and turning around toward us like some kind of spaceship. I could see faces inside the car. And these animals. All these eyes staring out at us."

His father's forehead wrinkled. "Hmm," he said.

He seemed to lose interest.

"Everything was shaking," Buford said. "These big trees were jerking back and forth, like somebody was trying to tear them out. And I heard this voice. That's when I woke up."

"What did the voice say?"

"My name."

"So it was me, right?"

"I guess."

But it had not been his father, and the name He said wasn't Buford. It was his Real Name, and it swallowed him up and made him huge at the same time. The thought made him shiver.

"Put on the sweatshirt," his father said.

"I'm okay."

When he came out of the bathroom, his father held a finger up to his lips as he led the way down the front stairs. "Grab a banana," he whispered as they passed the kitchen.

"How long are we going to be gone?"

"Couple of hours."

He got a banana from the basket on the counter where his mother left them to ripen. He closed the screen door quietly behind them and went down the back steps and across the yard to the Outback.

Buford expected some explanation, but on the way up Lee Street toward the square, his father turned on NPR. Some group that wasn't the Taliban and wasn't al Qaida was conquering big sections of Iraq. Ancient Mesopotamia. The Tigris and Euphrates flowed south out of Eastern Turkey past Nineveh and Babylon and Ur of the Chaldees, where Abram heard the voice of God.

Walter

Walter's hands trembled on the steering wheel. Nothing had ever terrified him as much as the idea of going into the house on Hopewell Road alone. With Buford, it was possible, somehow. He would have to be brave in front of his son. The boy reminded him of himself at that age. He had a good look to him—clean-limbed, clear-eyed, intelligent—and he had a better disposition than Walter had ever had. He had absorbed French from Rosa Loomis, who had tutored him last summer and who said she had never seen anything like him. He soaked up the grammar effortlessly, and he shot past her, reading *Les Miserables* and *The Count of Monte Cristo* in the original within a few months. He had pulled down Euclid from the set of Great Books that his father had bought in college, and after puzzling over the proofs a bit, Buford had started going through it on his own, absorbing the definitions and postulates and common notions. His idea of a game was to work out a proposition—something like "To draw a straight line at right angles to the radius of a circle from a given point on the circumference"—and come up with the proof himself and only then check to see if Euclid did it the same way.

Lately, maps absorbed him. Walter had seen him musing over Forrest's big globe in the sitting room, finding the ancient empires. He liked to think about the relation between the curvature of the earth on the globe and the scale of things on a flat map; he would put a Mercator projection map next to the globe and look at what gets distorted when you flatten it. He seemed obsessed with knowing where he was, historically and geographically. He brought histories and atlases home from the library and pored over them. He spent hours a day online, switching between Google Maps and Google Earth, fascinated with Gallatin and Gallatin County, but also with the possibility of exploring every address in America from his computer. He would Google their own address and zoom out—county, state, nation—then zoom back in until he could see the car in the driveway.

Nora had always marveled at Buford. One day he had stayed after school when they were studying the solar system. He had asked her how far away from the sun they were. She was sure he already knew, and she thought it was a trick question, so she told him it varied but it was usually about 93 million miles.

How long does it take the light to get from the sun to the earth? he had asked.

Well, light travels at 186,000 miles per second, so you divide 93 million by 186,000, she reminded him, but too late. He held up his calculator to show her the answer already on it.

500 seconds exactly. Then he divided 500 by 60: *8.33 minutes. It takes me twice as long to walk to school as it takes the light outside on that car to cross 93 million miles.*

She had smiled at him, she said, not knowing what to say.

A light year is the number of seconds in a whole year times 186,000, right?

She had nodded.

So in one day, you have 24 hours. Every hour is sixty minutes, so 24 times 60 is 1,440 minutes in a day. All of those minutes have sixty seconds, so one day is 1,440 minutes times sixty seconds, which is 86,400 seconds. So, to get how far light travels in one whole day, you multiply 86,400 seconds by 186,000 miles, right?

She nodded again.

He did the calculation and held it up to her.

That's over 16 billion miles in one day. So a light year would be 16 billion miles times 365 days.

That's right.

Which is—he held up the calculator—*almost six trillion miles. That's just one light year. And the closest star is 4.3 light years away? I'm talking about the closest neighbor in our own galaxy.*

Yes, that's right.

And the Andromeda galaxy, which you can see with the naked eye, is 2.5 million light years away? So, when we're looking at Andromeda, it's six trillion miles times 2.5 million years?

Walter imagined her tilting her lovely head at Buford and saying *Yes.*

But she had not expected his next question.

So what does that mean I am? he asked her. *What am I supposed to believe about who I am, Miss Nora? What am I supposed to think?*

What do you mean?

But she knew what Buford meant, and so did Walter, who had told her it used to make him dizzy thinking about how minuscule he was in the universe. He and Nora had gone out behind the old barn to look up at the stars and find Andromeda. It had been cold that night, a Saturday night in early March—a short night because Daylight Savings Time started the next day. That was the week before she left.

Here was Orion, the downslant of stars in his belt pointing to Sirius, the brightest star; over there was Cassiopeia, and you followed the line of the stars in the right of the W to find a star in the big square of Pegasus, and from there to the constellation Andromeda, then you aligned a star in Cassiopeia with a star in Andromeda—he forgot the name. But they saw the oval cloud of the Andromeda galaxy. There was the Big Dipper, as always; there was the North Star. He had shown her how to find the Twins, holding her arm to point it, her cheek that close, the smell of her hair, her breast against his chest.

Yes, he told her, to be under a sun that seemed to be moving around the earth, when actually it was moving in some other way altogether, and meanwhile the earth you stood on was spinning along at a thousand miles an hour and yet you never sensed it. As though you were not supposed to have found out, and you were fine until you did, after which the apple couldn't be unbitten.

It was like being inside a spaceship, living your whole life there, and knowing but never seeing that what seemed real to you was part of something so much bigger you could never even begin to get your mind around it. Here you were on this planet spinning on its axis around a minor sun in a run-of-the-mill galaxy among millions of other galaxies. And yet you were made of elements that were just as infinitely small as the universe was big. You were this phenomenon between two infinities.

Except you were conscious, and what were you most conscious of? What was it that made you most conscious that you were conscious? The knowledge that you were going to die. That someday, as W.S. Merwin put it,

the last fires will wave to me
And the silence will set out
Tireless traveler
Like the beam of a lightless star.

This temporary coalescence of matter and energy, scars and fingerprints and bad habits and wretched memories of sweaty high school dances, this person that loved and felt and knew things, *you* were going to come to an end someday, once and for all, never to be repeated in all the ages upon ages.

And here they were next to each other on this starry night.

His beloved, his own golden Nora.

And for three months now, not a word.

He was doing this for her. He turned up the radio.

Buford

The news was still on, but his father, as usual, was thinking about something else. Miss Nora, probably.

Gallatin County sat in the middle of Georgia, and the town of Gallatin sat in the middle of the county, the nucleus of a cell of gathered roads—state roads, US 41, Interstate 75. Right in the middle of Gallatin was the courthouse and the square of stores around it. North of the square were rundown old neighborhoods. Some houses were being renovated by young doctors and lawyers, his mother said, but other old ones had been torn down, and nothing had replaced them. Southwest of downtown was a mostly black neighborhood where his friend Carlton Hobbs lived. New subdivisions had sprung up where the interstate turned northwest toward Atlanta, and more of them were being built southeast toward Macon.

Right now, they were heading northwest of town to the part of the county where the Ikahalpi River was, between Jackson Road and I-75. He had studied the county map so thoroughly he could pinpoint the old place his father had inherited, either from Judge Lawton or from his vanished mother's family. Buford did not understand it.

Suddenly, he wondered if somebody had offered his father money for the land.

They pulled up to the window at McDonald's.

"You want something?" his dad said.

"No sir." He was still holding the banana. He couldn't imagine eating this early. His father got a large coffee, and Buford noticed his hand trembling when he settled it in the cupholder.

"We'll pick up something out there a little later," his father said. "A honey bun, maybe."

A honey bun? Bleak dread came over him. Buford was being spiritually kidnapped and lured into some agreement he didn't want to make. He was being disinherited, and his father wanted to break it to him with a honey bun. Before now, he had never felt anything but a mild curiosity about the old property, but now he wanted it more than anything.

As they pulled out of the parking lot, NPR had a report about where the group called ISIS got its money. They listened for a minute or two as they went under the interstate and then turned west onto the road into the country.

"A hundred years ago," his father said, turning off the radio, "after Darwin and Nietzsche and Marx and Freud, it seemed like religion was over."

Buford flinched. He was used to these little lectures at the dinner table, but he'd never had one directed at him. Just at him.

"Yes sir," he said.

"Getting rid of God was supposed to liberate us into huge transformations, but all that's happened after a century of wars is that the Europeans are Nietzsche's last men."

"What do you mean?"

"The ones at the end of history. The ones who just want their little comforts. While the last men putter around finding the best latte, Europe's being taken over by Islam. Religion is huge in the rest of the world. Do you remember what you were doing on 9/11?"

"I wasn't born then."

It took a moment for his father to nod. They were passing the retirement center on the right, then came the telephone tower and the entrance to a new subdivision. Past it was a new 7-Eleven with three separate islands of gas pumps. Across the road from it, the land had been cleared by a bulldozer: red clay crisscrossed with tracks, mad mounds of roots and stumps at the edge of the property. On the left past the bare field was a stand of pine trees in strict rows perpendicular to the road. The rising sun strobed through them row by row, and then on both sides the land opened up—a pasture on the right side with a creek cutting through it, bordered by young hardwoods that the sunlight hit high up in the branches. On the left were short bushy crops—probably soybeans or peanuts.

The car slowed at an intersection with a blinking yellow light and turned left onto Hopewell Road. Father and son rode in silence. Buford had been in this part of the county only once, on a family trip one Sunday afternoon just after they moved to Gallatin, but he remembered it well. After a few miles of pine woods, there was a farm on the right and then the property covered with kudzu.

On cue, the farm appeared. His father slowed and pulled off the road just past the fenced end of the cornfield. And there it was, a kingdom of green. Kudzu draped the house and the trees, climbed the guy wires, smothering everything.

For a moment, they stared at it, saying nothing. Swarms of insects rose and fell, sunshot against the deep shadow of the shrouded trees behind them. His father reached to the backseat behind them and handed Buford a long, rolled piece of paper. Buford worked the roll free from the rubber band and unscrolled it carefully. It was blue-tinted, a little stiff and slick to the touch, some sort of map of the property with Hopewell Road lettered onto it.

"We're at the southwest corner, about here. Here's the line between us and Vernon Jenkins on the south. The other two sides on the north and east are Jimmy Proctor's land. This is ours, this five acres." He pointed north on Hopewell Road. "Caleb Creek comes into the property on the north side, a little less than halfway in. See it right here on the plat?"

"You call this a plat?"

"Right. Surveyors draw them up. So you see the creek?"

"Yes sir."

"It flows northwest to southeast through our property, and then it bends back due east on Vernon's land and on toward the Ikahalpi River."

"Yes sir."

His father got out his side of the Outback, closed the door, and walked around in front to stand at the very edge of the property, hands in his back pockets. Buford watched him take a few steps along the ditch. The broad kudzu leaves gleamed with dew in the early sunlight. Papery morning glories were opening along the fence line, and bees intermittently flared into the sunlight, alighted, crept headlong into flowers. Fifty yards or so back from the road, the blurred shape of the old house rose from the dense blanket of vegetation in a grove of shrouded trees.

He looked back down at the plat in his lap that showed the boundaries of the property. It was dated October 4, 1951, and signed by the surveyor, Bradley Hendricks. It had compass bearings and distances neatly lettered above every line. Exactly marked were the location of the house, the well, and the outbuildings. All of them must still be there under the kudzu. He had to convince his father to keep the land, no matter how much they needed the money. Buford felt a burn of resentment in his abdomen, like the time he found out he had an older brother who had died.

"What are you waiting for?" his father called. "Come on."

He got out and closed the door.

"Dad, you can't sell it!" he cried.

"*Sell it?* I'm not going to sell it. Who told you that?"

"Nobody. I just thought that's what you were going to tell me."

"God, no. I'm not going to sell it."

A flock of birds rose from the next field, taking shape in the air, a single, fluid form forming and changing and reforming in the early light. High cirrus clouds gleamed in a brilliant row like a blare of trumpets.

Nobody else was up this early. Everywhere it was quiet, except for the insects and the river-rapids sound of the interstate a few miles away. Down Hopewell Road, a young buck stepped out of the corn and paused at the edge of the right-of-way. Ears lifting, it turned to watch Buford before leaping across the road in two bounds, white tail flashing, disappearing into the thick pine woods.

"Let's get our stuff," his father said.

"What stuff?"

In the trunk were hedge-clippers, a machete, and a two-sided ax-like weapon that an ancient Assyrian might have carried into battle or an executioner might have used for beheadings. It had a flat blade more than a foot long and as broad as a big man's hand, wickedly curved at the end, gleaming and sharp both on the inside of the arc and all down the long outer side. Bolts and metal plates secured it to a handle longer than a baseball bat. His father handed the machete and the hedge-clippers to Buford. "Hold your breath," he said, then sprayed him all over with insect repellent. After getting Buford to spray his back, he tossed the can inside and locked the car. He hooked up a gallon of water with a finger and lifted the big curved weapon.

Buford followed him over the roadside ditch, steadying himself by grabbing the wooden fence post at the corner of Vernon Jenkins' property. There was enough space for a tractor around the edge of Mr. Jenkins' field, and, just on the other side of it, tall rows of corn stretched away, broad leaves and ripening ears and tassels at the top. Shadowy tunnels ran between the rows down to their right. They walked up until they stood under a tree so big it shaded part of the cornfield. The smothered house was directly to their left.

"Dad, what are we going to do?"

His father glanced at him and then turned to look at the house.

"Cut our way in."

A dark qualm went through Buford.

"In where?"

"To the house. We'll cut our way through and then we'll find a way inside," his father said.

"*Inside?*" Buford asked. He stared across the kudzu at the shrouded form, the obscured corners, the live, lifting feelers of the plant that lay across the house like a monstrous organism, eerie and sublime. "Why do we have to go *inside?*"

For a moment, his father did not answer. When he did, Buford felt even more afraid.

"I left something there."

"What do you mean?"

When his father looked at him, Buford saw such fear in his eyes that he felt a pang of pity that confused him. He knew his father would have hidden this fear if he could have. So why was he going inside the old house where he had lived when his mother abandoned him? *I left something there.*

"What did you leave?"

"I don't know yet. I have to find out."

"And you want me to help you?"

Walter

The boy was terrified, but no more than Walter. It was not too late to change his mind. Back down the fence line he could see Hopewell Road and the side of the Subaru. A pickup truck slowed, and the curious driver leaned over and glanced up toward where he was, but Walter and Buford were hidden under the low-hanging limbs. The man drove on. Over on the Jenkins property, a rutted and weedy field road went all the way down to the yard, where a tractor crossed behind the barn and disappeared to the left, the sound of it barely audible. A woman was hanging sheets on the clothesline, and, far in the distance, the cupola of the county courthouse rose above the miles of intervening woods and ponds and expanding subdivisions.

This had to be the new Mrs. Jenkins. The old one had died a long time ago. Once or twice, people dropping by the *Tribune* office had mentioned rumors of her suicide, but he had been in Macon in those days, and Judge Lawton had hidden any news about Vernon Jenkins from him. *Vernon Jenkins.* An old burn of hatred rose in him, a quick image of the big young farmer forty years ago, his easy, sardonic contempt as he came down the hall with Rosemary, his big hand smoothing her bottom before he reached in with a wink and closed Walter's door.

"Look at this, Dad."

Buford pointed out an empty pint bottle of Jim Beam and a scatter of cigarette butts around the trunk of the oak. Somebody had been sitting there. And those weren't cigarette butts. They were the crimped remainders of joints. Roaches, if that was still the name.

A sudden uneasiness ran over him. Dexter Watkins was here.

Nora

Still in her robe, Nora sat reading *The Wild Iris* for the first time since she left Gallatin in March. She loved the early morning coolness, sitting and sipping her first cup of coffee on the back patio of her parents' house in Athens. She once told Miss Emma that she had a vocation to "matutinal languor." *Gracious sakes,* Miss Emma had said with a downturned mouth. *That sounds like something a girl would have to earn the night before.*

Naughty old thing.

She stretched her arms over her head and twisted each way. Sweet Miss Emma. Nora had been happy there, teaching the fifth-graders during the day, coming back in the afternoon to Miss Emma's welcome, the wide lawns and the magnolias, the great banks of azaleas just breaking into bloom around the house when she left. The vegetable garden had already been full of early lettuces for the salads at dinner. And the strawberries! Miss Emma had sat there at the breakfast table with her cheek on her hand, smiling to see Nora eat them. She wondered again whether she had done the right thing when she left. She had upset so many people, and her heart hurt thinking of what she had done to Bill Sharpe, that sad and lovely man.

She was thinking of the powerful way his hands commanded the small of her back when her phone rang beside her. After a moment of hesitation—she did not recognize the number on the display—she answered it.

"Well, Nora O Hearn," said a slow male voice. "It's been way too long."

It was not Bill, but the voice sounded familiar

"Has it been too long?" she said. "Who's this?"

"You know who this is."

The knowing, iniquitous assurance of his voice.

She stood up.

"Listen, sweetheart," he said, "your man Walter has planted quite a crop of weed out on that property of his."

Your man Walter. Anger spilled through her, but she had to keep him from hearing any emotion in her voice. More than anything she had ever done, she regretted the attention she had shown Dexter Watkins that Saturday back in the early fall, the smile and flush Miss Emma warned her against displaying so easily.

She had no idea what he was talking about now.

"Don't call me sweetheart, Mr. Watkins. Are you talking about the kudzu, because he obviously did not plant that?"

He snorted. "I'm talking ganja. Marijuana."

"Walter Peach wouldn't plant marijuana on his property," she said contemptuously.

"Is that right? Well there's about half an acre of it down there by Caleb Creek. I wouldn't of thought he had that kind of hard work in him."

"Why are you telling me this?"

"Ever since I saw you, it's just one thing I've wanted. As soon as I first got your name in my mouth and rolled it around a little, it tasted so good, I knew I'd get you. If you wasn't part of the deal I'd have got you already. But listen, that deal's almost over. Pretty soon I'm going to make you a happy girl."

Dry-mouthed, she said, "What deal?" She remembered Walter mentioning a deal. "How did you get my number?"

He ignored the question.

"You think about me before you go to sleep tonight."

"Leave me alone, Mr. Watkins."

"Baby, you *know* what I'm talking about."

She pressed the button to end the call and stood there trembling at the brutal stupidity of him. If there was any marijuana planted on Walter's property, Watkins had planted it. But what kind of deal? What did he mean she was "part of the deal" or he would have would gotten what he wanted already?

She set her phone on the table and walked out on the grass toward the pear tree in the back corner of the yard. She remembered how solemnly Dexter had displayed his shoulder tattoos to her on the sidewalk outside the Left Bank, pulling his shirt-sleeve up over grim Huitzilopochtli on the left and feathered Quetzalcoatl on the right, tensing his big muscles for her. *These boys get me what I want.* Ginger Robertson waving her hand at his smell.

She bent over with sudden laughter. Nestor, their old hound, came over worried and nudged her thigh with his head as she convulsed helplessly.

"What in the world?" her mother called, wanting to know what was so funny, leaning out from the kitchen door with a spatula in her hand.

Nora waved a hand helplessly. She backed into a low branch, half-ripe pears bumping her neck, twigs tangling her hair. In the moment it took to get free, she began to collect herself.

She had asked Walter one night after they had been reading poetry why he hadn't cleaned up the place on Hopewell Road. He had been evasive, but he had told her—was it on the night of stars?—about his mother's disappearance and his childhood with Judge Lawton. He did not know why his mother left. Judge Lawton had made sure the house was in Walter's name when he came of age, but he would have had to spend thousands of dollars to do anything with it, he told her, and he barely had enough to pay the taxes on it. The only time he had been there since his mother left it in 1974 was to make sure it was locked. That was in 1988, the year he graduated from Georgia, and he did not go inside it then. The place terrified him. Year after year, for more than two decades, the kudzu had fingered every surface, climbed every wall or branch or wire, until it had taken complete possession.

Whatever scares you like that, you have to face it, she had said to him, *or it will ruin your life.*

Says your A in psychology? The whole discipline is just a bribe to the consciousness you can't seem to get rid of after you reduce man to material and efficient causes.

I'm just talking about courage, she told him.

"Nora!" Her mother was in the kitchen door again. "Your father needs to get to work."

"I'm coming."

Walter would face criminal charges if they found marijuana growing on his property. She would have to call him. She had told herself she never would, for Aunt Teresa's sake. But Dexter Watkins had forced her hand.

Buford

He looked back down the fence line toward the road, then over at the house, and then at the creek. According to the plat, the property lines on the north and south sides ran due east off Hopewell Road, which bore slightly west of north. The front right corner of the house, looking at it from the road, was more than a hundred and forty feet from the right of way, situated about midway between the two fences. The big tree on the ridge where they stood was about fifty yards from the road; a line perpendicular to Vernon Jenkins' fence would go directly to the southern side of the house. If he kept following the fence due east, he would get to the creek that glimmered up to him, gleamed and then ran away, alive and going.

"Can we go down to the creek?"

"After we get inside the house."

Buford shuddered.

"What do you want me to do?"

"Let me cut the big vines, and you clean out the smaller stuff after me. Trim all the way to the dirt if you can—I mean really clear a path. Let me get ahead of you ten feet or so."

His father swung the hooked side of the thing he called a "bush hook" down through a tangle of kudzu. The drapery of leaves drooped apart like cut cloth, and he stepped into the gap, already swinging again, hacking through vines. When he was at a safe distance, Buford started in after him. The machete was harder to wield than he had imagined. He was trying to clear a path about three feet wide through bushes and dead branches that the kudzu had overwhelmed.

"This stuff grows a foot a day during the summer," his father said back over his shoulder.

"Yes sir."

A foot a day. He thought about how fast that was: twelve inches in twenty-four hours. Half an inch an hour. If you sat there watching it, it would grow one-sixtieth of a half-inch in a minute. Too slow to actually see—unless you had a microscope, maybe. Distractedly, he swung the machete at some small hardwood branches, but it glanced off something and came loose from his hand. The back of it bounced sharply off his kneecap as it spun down. It nicked the toe of his boot.

"Damn it!" he howled as he jumped backward.

"Be careful with that thing!"

"I hurt my knee," he said, still jumping around.

"Let's see."

Buford pulled up the leg of his jeans. There was a red spot on his kneecap but no cut. He stood up and flexed his knee and walked in a circle several times. His father, sweating as the sun rose, turned back to the vines with ferocious intensity. In fifteen or twenty minutes, quicker than Buford had thought possible, they cut a rough path from the fence to the old house. Their t-shirts clung to their backs, and Buford had to keep wiping his palms on his jeans to get a good grip on the machete as he chopped through vines as live as fingers, as thick as children's wrists. Clusters of broad, hairy leaves caught at his hands. To his right, the ground fell away toward the creek, invisible now, and on the left it sloped more gently down toward Hopewell Road. It had been a beautiful setting once, but the closer they got to the veiled structure itself, the more an obscure terror rose in his spine.

Between him and the road, kudzu as high as his chest broke toward him in the early light like an incoming tide. Wasps floated up from it, bees and dragonflies and gnats. Green wove onto green, surging upward and sideways, reaching everywhere with tender, innocuous tendrils, grasping at anything that could hold it, enwrapping—if nothing else—its own leaves and vines, growing onto itself. By tomorrow *a foot more of it* would have grown, everywhere, in every direction. More than anything he wanted to be back on the seat of the Outback with the belt fastened across him, heading home to see his mother and eat breakfast with his sister.

A mockingbird sang from a telephone pole and a crow flew past, chased by two or three smaller birds. His stomach was growling now, and he wished he had eaten something when he had a chance.

"Look at this," his father said, startling him. As he turned to look, his father reached through the vines with his bush hook, and the whole blade and part of the handle disappeared before it tapped the solid wall of the house. Kudzu had consumed the house so completely it made the interior horrible and alien to imagine. Buford could already feel it, as though he had dreamed it before. The green undersea light. Underfoot, a scatter of bones, loose hanks of the hair of dead things, skulls of small animals. Vines fingering in under the doorsill and through the windows, dark snakes flowing beneath them. With every footstep, the sound of rats scurrying. Around a corner, behind a half-closed door, waiting for him, something, someone, that had always known him.

"More than a foot of the stuff," his father said. "Let's go around to the back. There's a door we should be able to get in. I just found the key last night."

"*The key?*"

The idea of a key somehow horrified him. The skin crawled on his neck.

"You aren't going to chicken out on me, are you buddy? We've got to stick together."

"What's in there?"

"What's always been in there."

"Dad…" said Buford.

"Just come on." His father led him around to the back and pointed up to an overhang. Kudzu cascaded from it on all sides. His father prodded into the vines with the bush hook, reaching in and in. Buford saw him shudder. The whole length of the handle disappeared before the blade touched something solid.

"That's it," his father said. "Hand me the machete."

They swapped weapons, and Buford stepped backward, steadying himself by pushing the bush hook's blade into the ground behind him, as though he were holding himself still against a current that wanted to sweep him away. His father severed a tangle of vines with one swing, revealing a post and the edge of a concrete stoop. Leaves sagged down to touch his neck, and he whirled around as though a snake had dropped on him. He swore at himself and kept hacking, clearing a space beneath the overhang. Leaning forward, Buford could see a screen door whose rusted mesh was coming loose from one side in a jagged triangle. His father pulled left-handed at the handle, but it did not open; it must have been latched from the inside. The last person out of the house had gone out another way.

But his father was the last person out of the house.

Wasn't he? What if there's somebody in there? Buford thought with horror.

His father yanked hard, the inner latch broke, and he staggered backward and almost fell, flailing dangerously with the machete. Buford leapt backward, stumbling into the vines. His father dropped the machete and turned back to the screen door. With two heaves, he yanked it loose from its hinges and threw it out onto the surface of vines.

And there stood the door itself. Its plain wooden intactness seemed strange and out of place, denuded and abject, like an uncomprehending hostage dragged out into the daylight of some larger drama. His father tried the doorknob, but the door would not open. Buford saw a shudder go through him. He wiped his face with his left hand, stepping back from the door. Smeared dirt and bits of leaf clung to his skin, and his clothes were wet and stained with green.

He saw Buford and started, as though he had forgotten him.

"Come here," his father said roughly, and Buford, trailing the bush hook, stepped beneath the overhang, mutilated vines dangling around him. He shivered as if he had stepped into a freezer.

"Dad, I don't want t—"

"Look!"

His father had dug the old key from his left pocket. He held it up to Buford. Fumbling it a little, leaning down to blow the flecks of leaf and dust from the keyhole, he almost got it into the lock of the dead bolt, but his hands were wet with sweat and he dropped it into the tangle of cut vines and dead leaves at his feet. He cursed and knelt down to look for it. After a moment he found it, handed it to Buford, wiped his hands on his shirt, and took it back, inserting it in the lock, which would not yield. Buford felt a brief, cowardly relief. But his father jiggled the key and tried again, and then the tumblers gave, and the bolt shot back. With his shoulder against the door, his father pushed it open. Already backing away, Buford saw it swing inward with a shriek of hinges. He saw his father outlined, crouching in the threshold against the darkness. He saw him sway as if he were drunk, looking to his right. His face turned back toward Buford, naked with terror.

"Come on," he said.

Walter

It was smaller, blinded with vegetation, the windows as useless as the portholes of a sunken ship. At least the glass was still intact. Thank God for that. And the table was still there, the round kitchen table where they had always eaten. Dust over everything. Not dust exactly but more like actual dirt, mealy, the encompassing kudzu sifting it down from its own half-alive winter decay, preparing its own soil against the day the roof collapsed. They were inside the kudzu's vast, blindly purposing body, as if the house were being digested. A humid, rank, oppressive smell pervaded everything. As he stood paralyzed, staring at the gas stove, images rose unbidden. Once he had stood there watching three eggs bob and jostle in shallow boiling water over the blue flame. Another time, something cooking. Curry? He was stepping inside, someone just behind him, his mother at the hot stove, gleaming with sweat, turning to smile at him, ladle dripping.

He stepped backward and bumped into Buford. Off balance, he set his hand down on the table and snatched it up when he touched the dust.

"What?" Buford yelled, jumping away.

"Nothing," he said. "Sorry."

"Dad," Buford said. The boy's eyes kept flicking toward the open door and the daylight outside.

He had remembered his mother turning to greet them, glistening like a primitive goddess, naked from the waist up. Cletus McBride was with him, a black boy his age he sometimes met down at the creek. It would be cold now in the early morning, and small fish would be flitting through it, crossing the current, finding the deeper pools as the day got hotter. Minnows, tadpoles in the eddies, water striders, gnats. He and Cletus would build dams or catch tadpoles in Mason jars or lie on their stomachs in the water when the heat rose. They pretended to be Indians tracking animals along the creek.

That day, Walter had stepped on a water moccasin coiled in the grass on the bank. It dropped into the water and turned and came right back at him, its head a foot in the air, its fanged, cottony mouth wide open. He bolted halfway up the hill to the house before he could look back, and when he did he saw Cletus striking the snake with a big stick until it was dead. He went back down to where Cletus was, pressing the end of his stick down into the head of the cottonmouth. Cletus picked up the snake with the stick and held it up, dead and undead, looped over the end of the stick. *Won't die sure enough till sundown.* Walter had been embarrassed at his own cowardice but hot with admiration for his friend's courage. He wanted his mother to meet Cletus. He asked Cletus up to the house to get some breakfast, but Cletus was reluctant, almost scared.

Your mama don't want to see none of me.

But Walter insisted. *Come on. She'll want to meet you. You just killed a water moccasin! I'll introduce you.*

Cletus came along with him, embarrassed. *She won't be dressed for no company,* he said.

Later Walter thought about what he meant, what must have been said about her in other houses, but it did not occur to him then. They came up to the house and in through the back screen door, and there she was in her jean shorts—long-legged, barefooted, beautiful, her slender tan naked back glistening with sweat—and as she turned, her globular bare breasts, gleaming with the heat, swung into view. Cletus cried *Sweet Godamighty!* and fled. Walter saw him disappearing down the steps to the creek, flying in his panic, and when he turned, he saw his mother for the first time as others saw her, and it shamed him. *Why don't you put some clothes on, Mama?* he cried. The word hurt her. She always told him to call her Rosemary, not Mama. She stood there all aglow, looking down at him, the ladle dripping onto the floor, sweat dripping from her nipples.

We don't have to act like other people, she said.

Years later, after he was living in town with Judge Lawton, he saw Cletus on the sidewalk in Macon, but Cletus pretended not to know him.

"Dad?" Buford said again, his voice high and tight. He was edging toward the door.

Walter had to say something to him. Something rational to calm him. And he needed the boy with him.

"The taxes have been going up on this place," he said.

"We have to pay taxes on it? Why?" the boy asked, waving his hand at the dark hallway, at the very idea of being taxed for this this tomblike gloom, grown over and abandoned, this dead past. "Why would the taxes go *up?*"

"Because of all the subdivisions being built between here and I-75," Walter said.

Something scurried across the hallway, and Buford drew up against him. He tried to sound normal.

"The tax assessors see acreage on the county map and they see the land values around it and they raise the taxes on it. They more or less bully you into selling it, because if you break it up and put a subdivision on it, they get a lot more revenue coming into the county. It gets taxed lot by lot, every single property owner."

"So you *are* selling it?"

"I told you I would never sell it. I just want to see whether it might be worth fixing up."

"Fixing up?" Buford asked incredulously.

"Like it was. Like I remember it." He stepped toward the dark to hide the tremor that went up his spine. As soon as he moved, they heard more scurrying.

"Dad, let's go!"

"I haven't been in here since I was younger than you are," Walter said as lightly as he could, touching the hallway wall. "I was coming up from the creek early in the morning. Mama was making breakfast. I could smell the bacon. I came inside and it was still in the frying pan, right over there, and I went through the house to find her."

"And she was gone?"

"I never saw her again. I remember the exact date. June 23, 1974."

"What about your father?"

"I didn't know my father."

"You mean he was already gone?"

Walter shook his head and took a step into the hallway. The window at the northern end, blinded with vegetation, allowed a faint light.

"Dad," Buford said.

Walter turned to look at him.

"I'll wait outside, okay?" Buford said.

"No, come on with me. I need you, son."

His bedroom was halfway down on the left. All the way down the hall to the right was his mother's bedroom. He had never had the furniture removed, so the beds would still be there in both rooms. Rats would have found the mattresses long ago. The soft, dank mattresses. His own bed from childhood, the mattress he had slept on as a boy, now animate with furtive bodies, live squirming litters, blind, naked, like boneless fingers with mouths—

"Dad!" said Buford, and Walter, startled, turned toward him again. "What are you trying to find?"

Looking back out through the open door, past the posts that supported the overhang, Walter could see sunlight on the kudzu, a cloud of gnats. A mockingbird flitted past. He put his hand on his son's shoulder. He thought he heard voices—probably a trick of sound, Vernon Jenkins or Jimmy Proctor far away.

"Dad!" Buford said again as Walter took another step into the dark. "What are you looking for? What are we doing?"

"Come on with me."

147

Walter forced himself to walk down the dark hall. It seemed strange that the doors were not standing open. In the gloom of the hallway, he turned the knob to his old bedroom door and almost knocked Buford over as a rat rushed out. Steeling himself, he opened the door wide; there was a flurry of scurrying and small shrieks on the other side of the room that subsided into tense silence after a few seconds. A dim, green, underwater light suffused the foot-thick overlay of leaves on the window. Feelers of kudzu that had once prized their way through the window frame curled brown and stiff across the sill. His old dresser was intact, the drawers neatly shut. The mirror above it dusty. On the floor was a black plastic comb he must have dropped forty years before. Bits of torn paper, rat droppings, a thin hardcover book splayed open.

Leaning down, he lifted it. The paper was mottled, partially eaten.

His heart heaved strangely.

"My God," he said. "I wrote this book,"

Buford was still tight against him. He felt a tremor go through the boy's body.

"My God, it's *The Small Gnats Mourn*," Peach said. "My first book. Look at this." He showed it to his son.

"Dad, let's get out of here. Please," Buford said, almost whimpering now, pulling Walter's arm. "Come on, Dad."

"I haven't been in this house since the day my mother left."

A centipede darted from between the pages of the book onto his hand, and Walter brushed at it, shuddering, dropping the book, backing into the hall. He stood stupidly for a moment. His book, published in 1992, inside the house?

"Dad?"

He turned and blindly tried the doorknob of his mother's old room. It was locked. He tried it again. In a sudden fury, he slapped his hand on the wood.

"Who the hell locked it?" he shouted. He backed away and raised his foot to kick it, but Buford grabbed him.

"Don't!" he cried. "There's somebody in there!"

Walter stared down at his son.

"Somebody in there? What are you talking about?"

"The back screen was latched from the inside. These doors don't have keyholes, so they lock from the inside, too."

"So—"

"Somebody's in there! Somebody's dead!"

Buford

They came leaping out of the house like madmen and ran, tripping and crashing, into the kudzu.

"The hell was that?" they heard someone say from the direction of the creek. The voice came plain and clear through the morning air. "You hear that?"

"Of course," another voice replied.

In one motion, his father pulled Buford down deeper into the kudzu. Steps came up toward them, ambitious at first and then waning until the man cursed steadily and then stopped.

"Stuff's like trying to get out of bed with my first wife," the voice said. "I'd say, just let me go, sugar, I got my life to lead, but no, unh-unh."

The silence lengthened. A hairy, heart-shaped kudzu leaf bobbed close to Buford's nose as an inchworm made his way across it. The vines sang with insects in the hot Georgia morning. They heard a car pass behind them on Hopewell Road.

"Nah," said the voice again. "Must of been a animal. Deer starting up, maybe."

"Dexter Watkins," his dad whispered. The name meant nothing to Buford.

They heard Watkins retreating toward the creek. After a few minutes, his father carefully got up, watching behind him. He went back to the house, beckoning Buford. He reached inside, quietly pulled the door shut, and fished the key from his pocket to lock it.

"Where's the machete?" he whispered.

"You must have dropped it."

His father handed him the key and stooped to look around in the weeds for the machete. When he found it, he gave it to Buford, who also took the bush hook leaning against the post. His father waded out quietly and fetched the screen door from where he had thrown it. He pushed it back into the frame, draped some of the cut vines across the door, and nodded toward the path they had cut. There was no way to hide that.

Once they were at the live oak beside the fence, his father whispered, "I need to see who's there with Watkins. I'll be right back."

"Dad!" Buford said, suddenly panicked.

"Come here," his father said. He went over to the barbed wire fence, held open a gap between two strands, and gestured Buford toward it. "Go back this way. If I don't come in a minute or two, run down to Mr. Jenkins' house and call the sheriff."

Buford stared into his father's pale and serious face.

"Why don't you call him now?" Buford said.

His father sighed and let go of the wire. "Just wait here." Holding the bush hook in both hands like a soldier on patrol, he started down the path beside the fence, stepping carefully, making no noise. Before he got to the creek, he stepped off the path. He was out of sight for a minute, maybe two, and then came loud curses and thrashing.

"The hell?" Watkins shouted.

Buford tensed to run, and then someone else said, "Welcome, Walter! My, what an entrance!"

"Goddamn it, Peach!" shouted Dexter Watkins. "Come here!"

A second later, his father broke from the underbrush, running up the path at full speed with the bush hook in his right hand, already waving with his left for Buford to turn and run. Buford bolted. Once they were over the crest of the hill, they raced down to the Outback. Buford fumbled the machete. It whanged off the car and into the ditch.

"Leave it!" his father cried, yanking open the back door and throwing the bush hook onto the seat. They leapt inside and gunned it north on Hopewell Road before they even had the doors closed. After a few seconds, both of them panting, his father reached over and slapped Buford on the thigh.

"Who *was* that?" Buford asked.

"Dexter Watkins and a man I've seen before a couple of times."

"Who's Dexter Watkins?"

"Sort of a local drug lord. Dexter's brother runs the store right up here. You want that honey bun?"

"No sir." The smell of the house was still in his nostrils.

"Country Corner" was painted above the front door of the store. Buford saw a gasoline pump out front, a big, vintage Coca-Cola sign on the side of the building, notices and ads stuck on the window. They turned left on County Road 73, west toward the interstate.

His father's elation faded. The anxious look came back. Buford thought about the inside of the house. That terrible smell, that dead hallway, the locked door. He imagined it breaking open, and a violent shudder ran over him.

"You're thinking about what's in that room."

"Yes sir."

"I'll get the sheriff out here."

"Yes sir."

"Right now, I'm worried about Dexter Watkins."

"What were they doing?"

"Something illegal."

Just then his father's cell phone rang.

"Uh-oh," his father said.

But when he looked at the phone, his face changed. He took a deep breath, glanced at Buford, and pressed the button.

"*Nora?* … When? Because I just saw him on my property…. Well, Buford and I went out to the old homestead. I wanted to go inside the house. … That's right. It was time…. Yes, he is, right here…." His father glanced at him. "I'll tell you about it later. … But why did he call you? What did he say?"

There was a long silence.

"I can't tell you on the phone. I'm coming up there," his father said. "Yes, I can. I'll be there tonight."

Walter

He pulled off onto the shoulder of the road near the entrance to a new subdivision called Phoenix Estates. His heart was beating with a curious empty flutter that made his head light. A kind of ringing veil dropped momentarily over his hearing; his blood sang.

"Is she okay?" Buford asked.

"I hope so."

"What do you mean?"

"I can't get into it right now."

"Are you okay?"

"A little shaky. I'm not used to running that fast."

But that wasn't it. He held up both hands—both of them trembling slightly—to forestall more questions. He tried to breathe calmly through his nostrils.

"What's the matter, Dad?"

"Give me a minute, okay?"

Buford shrugged and turned his head to stare out the window, and Walter followed his gaze. Fifty yards away, the blade of a big yellow bulldozer gouged into the red clay, pushing everything before it—saplings that went down flinging their arms like ravished maidens, wildflowers, weeds, a scalp of matted grasses that curled up onto the steel. A half-buried barbed-wire fence coiled up in wild, emancipated loops. Peach could hear the tank-like clanking of the treads. A crew of laborers stood and watched, mostly Latinos, he noticed. A couple of young black guys. When a fat white foreman came out of a portable toilet, hitching up his pants, the men lifted their shovels listlessly and started toward some concrete forms up the rise.

Watkins must have called Nora on his way out to the property, Walter thought. So Watkins had been showing the stranger a marijuana crop on his land. He felt a sudden fierce sense of vindication and terror. The man had to be a buyer, one of the cartel's deputies in a drug trafficking network. All his work on cartels, all the veiled threats, the photographs—and now he had them on his own property. They knew who he was. *Te conozco.* Of course they knew him. They had known him all along. They had been in his house. Watkins could use the threat of the cartel on Nora. *You ever seen what they do to families in Mexico?* Dexter was just starting on her, putting ideas in her mind to scare her—

"Listen, I need to be out of town for a while," he said to Buford. "I'll take you home."

"Because of something Miss Nora said?"

153

"Yes, but I can't explain it right now."

He put the car in gear, drove the half-mile to the interstate, and did not speak again on the way home. On NPR, a woman named Susan Page, sitting in for Diane Rehm, introduced a story about a surge in the number of immigrant children detained at the border with Mexico. Fleeing the cartels, Peach thought.

When they pulled into the driveway, it was still barely mid-morning, a few minutes before 9:00. Walter parked the Outback in its spot beneath the oak tree. He could see Teresa moving around in the kitchen.

"Are you leaving Mom?" Buford said.

Walter shook his head. The boy sat back against the passenger door, as far away as he could get.

"Look," he sighed. "Dexter Watkins is growing a big crop of marijuana on our land. But for God's sake, Buford, don't say a word about this to anybody! Not to your mother, not to Rose. Nobody. Do you understand me?"

"Why don't you call the sheriff?"

"There was a man down there with Watkins, and I've seen him before, which makes me think Dexter's gotten into some kind of business arrangement with a cartel. Those people will do anything. They don't care about the sheriff. They're like this ISIS group, or even worse. They'll kill your whole family even after they kill you, just to set an example for other people."

Buford stared at him solemnly.

"These are the people who took the pictures, aren't they?"

"I think so."

"What's this got to do with Miss Nora?"

"Dexter Watkins called her about the marijuana on the property."

"Why would he tell *her*?" Buford asked.

"To scare her into something she doesn't want to do."

He saw the boy's face change.

"What are you going to do?" the boy asked.

"I don't know yet. Just let me deal with it."

"Okay." Tears sprang to his son's eyes.

"I love your mother very much. I love you all very much."

"Okay, Dad," Buford said, reaching behind him for the handle. He got out and stood on the gravel, speaking back through the open door. "But can't we call the sheriff about what's in that room? And then while he was out there, he'd find the other stuff."

"Buford," he said, holding his open palm toward the boy to stop him.

"Give me a few days."

Buford slammed the door.

"Where have y'all been this early?" Teresa called from the door, wiping her hands on her apron. Walter sat behind the wheel. His heart fluttered strangely in his chest.

"Out on Hopewell Road," he heard Buford say.

"Are you coming in for breakfast?" Teresa called.

"Yes ma'am."

But Walter was already backing up the car.

THE BOY

Part III

"No one among all the peoples, neither base man nor noble, is altogether nameless, once he has been born, but always his parents as soon as they bring him forth put upon him a name."

Odyssey VIII

Ed Watkins

Monday, June 23, 2014

Ed Watkins edged his head around the doorframe of the back room where he kept the extra stock and held the occasional poker game. The boy was sitting at the card table by the front window holding the old *National Geographic* that Ed had given him, the one with the story about the supervolcano under Yellowstone National Park. Ed kept it for people who didn't have the good sense to realize the end times were coming. But the boy was staring at it like Ed used to stare at the picture of Noah's Flood in the book of Bible stories his mama gave him, all the frantic naked sinners crawling up the mountaintop to escape the water, but knowing they were about to drown with all the snakes and wolves and rats that the Ark would not take.

"You think he's simple?" Ed whispered to Sharpe, who had brought the boy in. "Maybe got loose from somewhere?"

"I don't know," Sharpe said.

"Just standing out in the kudzu?"

"That's what I'm saying."

Watkins wet his lips. "And don't know his own name."

"That's right. When I called him, he looked at me and then back at the house. In the time it took to turn his head, he says everything changed into what it looks like now. He doesn't know how he conked his head. He says he was coming back from the creek for breakfast—"

"The creek?" Watkins stepped back and turned to look at Sharpe. "What was he doing at the creek?"

"Hell, Ed, I don't know. His mama was in the kitchen and he could smell the bacon frying. He went in and couldn't find her and so he went outside looking for her."

"Wasn't nobody frying bacon in that house."

"That's what I told him."

"You didn't ask him why he was at the creek?"

Sharpe straightened up. Ed always forgot how tall he was, because he didn't act tall.

"Look, I need to get to the dealership. I told Chick I'd be there by now."

"You just gon leave him? What am I supposed to do with him?"

"Call the sheriff. See if anybody's been reported missing."

"How come I—"

"For Christ's sake!" Sharpe exclaimed and yanked out his wallet. He took out a ten and pushed it at Watkins' chest. "Give him something to eat. I'll come back and get him in a couple of hours if you can't lift a goddamn finger. What if it was Martin who wandered off?"

"Who's Martin?"

"You probably call him 'Not-Too' like everybody else."

Watkins flushed. Sharpe's retarded little brother. He pushed the money away. "Go on. I'll take care of him."

"Call Sheriff Bennett," Sharpe said. As he left the store, he said something to the boy and dropped the ten on the counter by the register.

Ed closed the door to the back room and dusted his hands as though he had been cleaning up. He wandered through the store, touching cans, pretending to flick things from the shelves, glancing over at the boy, who had finally opened the magazine.

Watkins could see the cutaway picture of the earth beneath the U.S. with that big load of glowing hot magma forcing up under Yellowstone.

"Scary, ain't it?" he said. "That thing blows up, we're all dead."

The boy looked up at him emptily. Both his hands lay limp in his lap.

"We're all dead," he repeated flatly, and the way he said it froze Ed in place.

What would you be if you didn't remember your name and you thought you were going home to breakfast in a house nobody had lived in for forty years?

The walking dead is what.

And you would smell like whatever you crawled out of. He had never seen his dog Burton drop his ears and slink off like that after sniffing somebody. Ed brushed the back of his neck because it felt like something was creeping up it.

A car pulled up at the pump in front and Ed recollected himself. Closed his mouth. He must be losing his mind. *Walking dead.* On a hot Monday morning? The boy had just gotten loose from somewhere.

"Hey, you ever been to Milledgeville?"

"Milledgeville?" The boy's face was blank. "If I knew who I was, I might could tell you."

Ed went behind the counter and picked up Sharpe's ten-dollar bill and put it in the cash register.

"You want something to eat?" he said. He was still a little wobbly from the scare. "I ain't got nothing hot, but." He grabbed things from the jars and open boxes on the counter. "Here's you some Slim Jims and peanut-butter crackers and a moon pie." He took them over and arrayed them in front of the boy, whose hands did not stir. "You like Vienna sausages?" He took a can from the shelf and set it down, but the boy still did not react.

Ed stepped over to the glass door where the refrigerated soft drinks and milk were and got a can of Coke and a quart jar full of hard-boiled eggs.

"You like pickled eggs?"

"I don't know," the boy said.

"Wife makes 'em with dill weed and vinegar," Ed explained, tapping the jar. Unscrewing the lid, he fished one out, shook off the liquid, and bit into it, jerking his head back with astonishment.

"Mighty good. Try one," he said, pushing the jar toward the boy. "It don't need no salt."

The boy reached toward the jar and Ed almost said something about washing his hands. Out in all that kudzu. Smelling like that. The boy bit into the egg and finished it hungrily and was already reaching again when his hand stopped.

"Do you mind if I have another one?" he asked.

Had some manners anyway.

"You go on," Ed said.

"Mama was making me eggs," the boy said.

"What's her name?" Ed said, hoping to ambush the boy's memory. "I bet you I know her."

"Mama." The boy swallowed and wiped his lips.

He couldn't be that simple. "You go to church?"

"I don't know."

"You know the name Jesus?"

"Yes sir."

"If one of your friends was to see you after church—let's say they wanted you to come over in the afternoon and play baseball and they had to ask your mama—what would they call her? Mrs. What?"

The boy gazed up at him. Nothing. Ed sighed and went over to the screen door. It had looked like a decent day until Bill Sharpe showed up with this boy telling him to call the sheriff. The last thing he wanted was the sheriff sniffing around. He thought about the stand of marijuana his brother had planted in the clearing down by the creek on that property his mama and daddy had always called Missy's Garden. Missy. Some lady who lived there a long time ago and had azaleas and boxwoods and irises and fountains and sculptures of naked women and such like. People would drive in to see it. Put Betty to shame. And this boy was about to get everybody stomping all over it looking for his mama.

He turned toward the boy.

"Mrs. Butterworth?" he said.

"Sir?"

"Say one of her friends seen her and come over and said, 'Hey, Aunt

Sally, I hear you been sick.'"

The boy stared at him.

"Well, hell, son, I must have her mixed up with somebody else. I can almost call her name," he said, trying to soften his exasperation. "It's right on the tip of my tongue."

"Mama," said the boy.

Ed stared down at him for a few seconds and then shook his head. "I don't reckon you know what people call your daddy."

"No sir. What?"

Ed screwed the top back on the pickled eggs and set the jar in the refrigerator and walked back behind the counter.

"You got enough to eat there?"

"Yes sir," the boy said, peeling a Slim Jim wrapper off and opening the Coke.

He was going to have to call the sheriff. Look bad if Sharpe beat him to it. Ed hated to use the phone with the boy sitting there, but he didn't see any other way. He found the number in the directory and punched it in, hoping Ellen Wolf answered. She had been married to Dexter for two or three years right out of high school before he got caught dealing dope the first time. She knew a little too much about Dexter, but she was sweet as pie.

"Hey, is this Ellen?"

"It sure is," she said brightly. "And who's this?"

"It's Ed Watkins."

"Oh Lord. Dexter's not in our jail, if you're wondering."

"Heh heh," Ed said nervously.

"Betty all right?" Ellen asked.

"She's getting enough to eat."

"You ought to be ashamed. What can I do for you, sugar?"

Watkins glanced at the boy, who seemed absorbed by the magazine again. He took the receiver over to the corner by the cigarettes and chewing tobacco and gazed out the window. Two flies kept bumping the glass, trying to get out.

"Listen," he whispered, "Bill Sharpe found a boy out here in a field of kudzu on that old place on Hopewell Road."

"Okay."

"Just standing out in the middle of it. Boy don't remember his name."

"Is he there? That's why you're whispering?"

"That's right."

"Is he hurt?"

"Big knot on his head but he looks okay except for not knowing who he is. Y'all got anybody reported missing?"

"Not that I know of. Hold on a second."

She must have palmed the mouthpiece. He could picture her swinging around in her swivel chair.

"Ed?" she said a few seconds later. "Nobody's been reported. Tell you what, Hudson's out that way, so I'll tell him to swing by the store. We'll get it straightened out. So you're saying you don't recognize him?"

"He looks sort of familiar, but."

"You take care of yourself, Ed. Say hey to Betty."

Hudson Bennett

Bennett was just pulling down the southbound ramp onto the interstate to head back into town when Ellen Wolf said *Hudson?* on his radio and then there was a storm of static. He couldn't understand the first thing she was telling him.

"Getting a lot of interference, Ellen. Say again."

"I said he can't remember his name."

"Who?"

"I said there's a boy out at Ed Watkins' store who can't remember his name. Nobody recognizes him."

"Something happen to him?"

"A knock on the head, sounds like. Aren't you out that way? Bill Sharpe found him in the kudzu in Missy's Garden."

"What's Missy's Garden?"

"The overgrown place between Jimmy Proctor and Vernon Jenkins."

"I'll have to turn around," he said.

"Well, Ed's expecting you. He sounded funny. I bet you he knows something."

"Okay, I'll head over there."

Bennett sighed through his nose. It had already been a bad day—a dispute up near High Falls between old Marion Feulner and some nephews of Helen White's who had a band called Flint Hatchet. Helen was in Florida with her sister, and these scraggly nephews from Macon were using her backyard to practice. The afternoon before, Marion had driven his pickup to the fence that divided his property from Helen's and fired a shot in the air. The lead singer said they stopped playing for a second and looked at him. When Marion held his hand to his ear, the lead guitarist gave him the finger and then started back up.

Flint Hatchet had waited until this morning to call Bennett, who had to drive out and see the damages and then go tell Marion they were filing charges. When they resumed playing, Marion had shot one of their outdoor speakers. When they backed off peaceably, he shot the rest of the amps. He shot the guitars. He shot the drums.

Marion was not surprised they had waited overnight to call. *Hiding their dope,* Marion said. *Look here, Hudson. It ain't like I didn't warn them. I drove over there yesterday and told them sorry pieces of shit, I said that goddamned caterwauling comes over the fence on my property, it's trespassing and I'll shoot. So I did shoot. They all ducked and hollered. Dropped everything and ran like chickens.*

Bennett saw his point, but still. A bullet did its own trespassing.

He turned around at a cut-through usually occupied by State Patrol cars and headed back north. Bennett would not have thought Ed Watkins could make a living out here. The store sat at the crossroads of Hopewell Road and County 73 a couple of miles east of Interstate 75, six or seven miles northeast of Gallatin as the crow flies. People went into town for real groceries, but if they ran out of gas or needed something they forgot, they came to Ed. The place wasn't like a 7-Eleven, though. Ed managed to keep up some of the old country store traditions—big candy jars, bins of local vegetables, even some hardware and farm supplies.

When Bennett pulled up to the front, Rev. Holiness McGee was filling his old black Ford sedan at the gas pump. Rev. McGee, wearing a formal black suit and hat, touched his brim as the sheriff got out in the shade of Ed's massive pecan trees.

"How you doing, Sheriff?"

"I could complain, but I better not."

"Give it to the Lord Jesus."

Ed's spotted hound roused himself after a bout of furious scratching and came shambling over, ducking his head and bumping Bennett's knee until the sheriff reached down and patted him.

Ed stood waiting with the screen door open. Unlike his brother, who was tall and broad-shouldered, with tattoos and blond dreadlocks, Ed was a short, soft, balding, freckled, round-faced man who took after his mother, hips and all.

"Church account, Mr. Ed," called Rev. McGee, removing the nozzle from his gas tank.

"Church, hell. You know you're just out tomcatting, Reverend," said Ed. He stepped out the door toward the pump and gave the sheriff a wink.

"No sir," the old man said sternly. "I'm doing the Lord's business."

"Must be one of those young girls needs dipping in the river, Rev. Holiness," Ed said. "Needs a little more instruction." He caught the sheriff's eye and made a wry face.

"God won't be mocked," said the preacher, incensed by Ed's insinuation. "No sir. Sister Mary Louise Gibson, she sick, God help her." He carefully got in the car and shook his head as he started it. "The Lord won't be mocked," he said out the window as he drove off.

"You better listen to him," said Bennett.

Ed put his hands in his back pockets and stood sideways in the door, holding the screen open for the sheriff to enter the store. He tipped his head toward a boy at a table near the front.

"That's him," he whispered.

Bennett remembered the face, but he couldn't place him.

"Hello, son," he said carefully, taking off his hat.

The boy looked up vacantly and then focused. His eyes went from the sheriff's face, to his badge, to his gun, to the hat he was turning in his hands, and back to his face.

"Did you find her?" he asked.

"Find who?"

"Mama."

Ed was at Bennett's elbow. "He says he was about to have breakfast at that old place they call Missy's Garden and his mama just disappeared."

"About to have breakfast," Bennett repeated. "At that place covered with kudzu?"

He was about to ask the boy how he got there when tires crunched to a stop on the parking lot gravel and a door slammed and a second later the screen swung open. Bennett had thought many times that Bill Sharpe ought to start over somewhere up North or out West where nobody knew him and there wouldn't be the twinge of pity people felt at seeing that stoop that came into him, body and soul, the summer Deirdre Harper died. He had been something before that, a star—best forward the Blue Devils ever had, best athlete and scholar at Tech, owner of a successful startup.

"Missed my customer," Sharpe said. "So what happened?"

There was an unusual keenness in him, Bennett thought. Sharpe stared down with proprietary concern at the boy, who glanced up and nodded, bit a peanut-butter cracker and absently brushed the crumbs from his mouth with his knuckles.

"He's okay?" Sharpe said.

"Four pickled eggs before he started in on them things," Ed said.

"You're the one found him?" Bennett said to Sharpe. When Sharpe repeated the story, Bennett nodded.

"Coming back from the creek, that's what he said?"

Sharpe nodded, and Bennett watched Ed back himself carefully behind the counter, pick up a carton of Doral Lights, and tear off the end to begin restocking the dispenser slot. Ellen was right: Ed knew something.

Bennett turned to the boy.

"Mr. Watkins tells me you're having some trouble remembering your name."

The boy nodded. Bennett went around to the other side of the table so he could see Ed without having to turn.

"What were you doing down at the creek?" Bennett asked. Ed's hand paused in midair with a pack of cigarettes. For a long moment the boy did not answer.

"I don't know."

"You just like going down there?"

"It's going away all the time, but there it is."

No one said anything. Bennett met Sharpe's eyes.

"What you call the creek is just the shape of the way it's going away," the boy said.

"What the hell?" murmured Ed.

"If you stopped going you'd be dead," the boy said. His lip began to quiver. "You'd be lying there dead."

Bennett leaned forward. Now the boy's demeanor made sense.

"Did you see somebody dead?" Bennett asked. "Was there somebody dead down there at the creek?"

The boy looked up at him forlornly and tremors went through him.

"No sir," he said.

"Nobody did anything to you?"

Ed was fiddling with the jars of candy and ball point pens next to the cash register.

"No sir."

Well, something had sure as hell terrified him. And Bennett would bet that Ed knew something about it.

"I tell you what," Bennett said to the boy, keeping his voice calm. "You come with me. Come on out to my car, and we'll run over there and look around and get all this straightened out."

Ed fumbled a carton of Marlboros behind the counter.

"Bill? Want to ride with us?" Bennett asked.

"Might as well."

Bennett moved the seat up and put the boy in the front seat of the Bronco so Bill Sharpe could fold himself in the back behind him. Half a mile down Hopewell Road on the left was the kingdom of kudzu. Bennett eased along.

"That's where he was standing," Sharpe said. "You can see where he waded out."

Bennett nodded and glanced at the boy, who stared at the house blankly.

"Where's my mama?" he said.

"We'll find her," Bennett told him.

Just before Vernon Jenkins' cornfield, a cleared path went up along the fence. Bennett did a three-point turnaround and pulled up beside it.

"You want to show us the creek?" he said, and the boy nodded.

Sharpe found a machete in the ditch and handed it to Bennett, who wiped a light film of rust and recent flecks of vegetation from the blade. He set it down it in the trunk of the car and followed Sharpe and the boy up the path. At the top, someone had cut his way through the kudzu over to the house—he'd check that later—but right now he needed to know what was down at the creek.

"Just keep going?" he asked the boy.

"I think so," he said.

As they started down the other side, Bennett could see the gleam of the water through the foliage. A clump of shrubbery blocked the path. They fought their way through the branches—and by God.

"This is what you saw?" he asked the boy. "Did anybody see you? Is that what happened to your head?"

"No sir," he said, clearly baffled.

"You didn't see this?"

Almost an acre of marijuana was growing in the clearing along both sides of Caleb Creek. Dexter Watkins' work.

"No sir."

The creek was neatly dammed, and PVC pipes came out from the bottom of the dam and connected to several two-inch polyurethane irrigation tubes with turn-off valves. These fed a network of sprinkler hoses running down the furrows between the plants. Bennett could see a path through the hardwoods on the other side of the creek, which meant Dexter had been coming in through Jimmy Proctor's land. Jimmy would be pretty upset to find that out. First thing was to get his deputies out here and then talk to Jimmy.

He got out his cell phone. No signal.

"Mine either," Sharpe said.

"We'd better head back to the car," Bennett said. "I need to get in touch with a few folks."

"Can you drop me off at my truck?" Sharpe asked. "I'd better get back into town."

Bennett radioed Ellen Wolf and told her to get his deputies out to the property immediately and to get in touch with Jimmy Proctor. When he dropped Sharpe off at the Country Corner, he saw Ed inside, carefully avoiding his eye. He honked the horn. Ed looked up and Bennett gestured him outside. At first, he did not advance past the doorway, as though he were safe as long as he stayed in his store.

"You want everybody to hear what I'm going to say?" Bennett called, nodding to a car just pulling in.

Ed sighed and came out to the window of the Bronco. The old dog heaved himself up and came up beside him, wagging his tail.

"What's the deal, Sheriff?" Ed said.

"Tell Dexter we found something of his down by that creek," Bennett said. "Tell him there's two ways this can go."

Ed shook his head. "I don't know what you're talking about. What Dexter does, it ain't none of my business."

"You better hope not," Bennett said. "Anybody called about this boy?"

"Ain't nobody called me."

"I'm taking him with me into town, anybody comes looking for him."

Ed cocked his head and raised his hands.

"My god, Hudson," Ellen Wolf said when she called him back on his radio, "you think Dexter got that little boy doped up?"

He looked over at the boy, who looked back at him, puzzled but clear-eyed.

"No. I wouldn't think that of him," Bennett said. "Nobody's called in missing him yet?"

"Not a word," she sighed. "Poor little thing. Well, listen, Jimmy Proctor's expecting you."

The Proctor house was about half a mile east on 73, set back in an old pecan grove, and the Proctors met him on their porch. Jimmy was a placid, broad-faced man with a stomach that conveyed the resolved character of his opinions. Jimmy's wife—well, Bennett was satisfied not being married to her. She always had the air of having just caught somebody trying to get away with something.

"I told Jimmy," she said. "Listen, I says, I was coming by that weedy old place Friday—this was out on Hopewell Road—and I saw a car stopped at the front down there by Vernon's corner. I says, *Jimmy something's going on in there*. And then Jimmy, he says—well, you tell him, Jimmy."

"Well," Jimmy said, slowly raising his coffee cup toward the soybean field, "matter of fact a while back I saw some them ATV tracks—"

"That's right!" said Mrs. Proctor, as Jimmy lowered his head and nodded judiciously. "Saw some tracks that went edging along our field at the back line of that old place. Jimmy says to me, you know how Jimmy talks, he says, *Somebody been coming in there at night, using my road. Cut the barb wire on that fence. I'moan go see.* I say, unh-unh, sugar, don't you go down there. You gon surprise somebody making that meth stuff and end up dead."

She put her hand fondly on the back of Jimmy's head.

"How long ago was this when you saw the tracks?" Bennett asked.

"Month, maybe," Jimmy said.

"You could have called me," Bennett said.

Jimmy frowned. "Hate to get the law in it."

"Let's drive over there," Bennett said. "Ma'am," he said when she started up, "thank you, but you don't need to come."

Inside the Bronco, Jimmy was confused to see the boy. He shook hands and said his name and the boy did not say a name back.

"You don't happen to know him, do you?" Bennett asked.

"Sure don't." This confused Jimmy but Bennett did not want to introduce another complex idea too soon. They drove down the field road to the closest corner behind the old property.

"Yonder's the cut wire," Jimmy said.

In the right angle enclosing the old property and bordered by soybeans, the top two strands of rusty barbed wire were cut, and a faint path went down into the creek bottom. Bennett walked Proctor down through a stand of hardwoods and showed him the marijuana growing in the clearing along the creek. Bennett's deputies had tramped in from the Hopewell side of the property. Matt Casper stood in the middle of the crop on the other side of the creek with his hands on his hips, looking around in astonishment. Red Scott was up beside the dam.

"What's this?" Jimmy asked.

"Marijuana. A couple of million dollars' worth," Bennett said.

"*A couple of million dollars?*" Proctor said, no longer placid.

Red heard them talking and waved.

"You thinking Dexter?" he called.

"Couldn't be just Dexter," Bennett said. "Too professional. I think we need the state boys, maybe the FBI. Get all that PVC dusted for prints, the whole show. You boys handle this? I got to take care of something else, and then I'll be back out here."

"We got it." They waved him away.

"I'll drop you back off," he told Proctor.

All the way home, Jimmy gazed out at his soybeans with growing dismay.

"I don't get no two million dollars for my beans," Proctor said.

Emma Fields

Emma would have been a sight if there had been anybody to see her—baggy old jeans and broad boat shoes slit open to relieve her bunions, no bra under her Blue Devils t-shirt. Dew soaked her ankles, her knees were dirty, her hands itched inside the rough gloves as she jabbed her trowel into the weeds and turned aside the leaves to find the last good strawberries, which made her think of Nora. Emma carefully plucked the ripest one of the morning and sat back on her knees and held it to her nose: she remembered the girl at breakfast looking up laughing from the bitten strawberry in her fingers, a trace of fresh cream on the bow of her upper lip, no cliché about her. Lovely, lovely.

Emma's heart burned with a longing that startled her each time it came. It had become an affliction. She asked herself several times a day why Nora had left in March, why she had suddenly turned in her resignation to the elementary school and disappeared from the county and Emma's life. She didn't believe for a second the rumors that Nora was pregnant, but then what was it? The children had loved her, everybody had loved her—a girl open and trusting and smart, with her love of poetry and her nights with her aunt and uncle, her smitten beaus and her moody silences and her books and prayers.

And, O Lord, the way she looked. And here Emma was, seventy-two years old, kneeling in the dirt like a bedazzled worshipper, daydreaming about a girl, as though she were turning sapphic in her old age. Ginger Robertson, whom she always pictured panting from her latest triathlon, told her earnestly it was "okay." *Emma, women sometimes feel that way about other women.* She had touched Emma's arm when she said it. *Just be honest with yourself. It's a new world.* These earnest young women. Ginger had not grown up on the Bible. Emma would not turn her back on the Lord God Almighty just to trick her conscience. Besides, she *had* always been honest with herself. She had never hidden from her feelings, good or bad.

Her real feeling was simpler than idolatry. No less obsessive, but simpler: she wanted Nora to be hers, the way an infant would want her mother to be hers alone, no matter how many other children there were. Emma knelt in a daze with the strawberry lightly held to her lips. If she went to heaven it would be like that, she thought, when Jesus turned His eyes and His smile and His whole brimming and joyous attention just on Emma. Nora would be with Him. Her head would tilt to the side and that dimpled smile would flash out like hallelujah and Emma's turgid old blood would dash through her body in spangles.

She heard a car slowing down out on the county road and then the sound of tires on her driveway. Oh Lord, look at her. She got up stiffly, leaving her tools and brushing off her knees. She would need another cortisone shot before too long. She plucked up a pile of Johnson grass and dandelions and tough little oak seedlings and dropped it on the compost heap at the corner of the garden as she limped toward the front of the house. If it was somebody who wanted to kill her and rob the place, she wouldn't be able to do a thing about it. She would just tell them to go ahead and shoot her.

Every time someone visited, she pictured what Nora had described first seeing—the magnolias on each side that lined the drive, the lawn spreading away to hedges of myrtle that separated the yard from the surrounding fields, the two-story Victorian farmhouse her great-grandfather had built in 1902. It would make him proud if he saw it now, Nora told her. She kept the house and yard as immaculate as any in town—the grass mowed, the azaleas and boxwoods trimmed, the porch swept. The porch columns and the clapboard sides were as smooth and white as fresh milk. In the summer, she had the place all to herself unless one of the teachers had nowhere else to go. During the school year, she always kept several teachers as boarders—male or female, black or white or Hispanic, it didn't matter to her, and she didn't care what any local nitwit said. Once or twice she had put up young couples with children. Free room and board was a way to attract talented young people to teach in Gallatin, so they stayed at no cost, but she expected help with the upkeep of the place—mowing and trimming, sweeping and scraping and painting, not to mention milking the cow. Nora O'Hearn loved milking: her cheek against Lettie's brown flank, her eyes off in dreamland, and her strong hands easing Lettie's need.

As she came around the corner of the house, she saw the sheriff's car pulling to a stop in front of the steps and felt a cold qualm in her heart. Hudson Bennett was getting out.

"What is it?" she called. "What's wrong?"

He took off his hat to speak to her, averting his eyes after the first glance.

"Nothing's wrong, Miss Emma. I'm sorry to scare you."

"Oh Lord," she said, panting and putting one hand on her heart, feeling the cloth wet with perspiration and recalling at the same instant that she had no bra on. "I didn't expect anybody this morning."

"I just have a question for you. I meant to give you a call," he said.

"I wouldn't have heard it," she said, waving at the strawberry patch. "What's the matter?"

He looked so sincere it moved her. He wasn't much over six feet but seemed bigger. He had an unstudied authority she had always admired. She remembered the tenth-grader better than the man before her—a calm, gathered boy, sober and respectful, unperturbed by adolescence, competent but not brilliant in his schoolwork. Always a fine athlete, a natural leader. Cornerback and wide receiver in football, point guard in basketball, third baseman and sometimes pitcher in baseball.

He nodded at the car and called, "Come on out, son."

A boy on the passenger's side hesitated and then opened the door and got out and came around the car to stand in front of her. He had a big ugly knot on his forehead but otherwise looked fine. Thin, but not scrawny, wearing a t-shirt and worn-out jeans. He had a clean proportion to his limbs, clear hazel eyes, a whorl of cowlick on the crown of his blond head, a slight widow's peak. She ought to know him. Good Lord, come on. If she had seen him—and she knew she had—she couldn't remember where.

"Good morning, sugar. What's your name?" she asked the boy kindly, folding her arms over her chest in sudden embarrassment when he glanced up at her.

"He says he can't remember," Hudson said.

"You don't remember your name?"

"No ma'am," said the boy.

"That's a nasty bump on his head." She looked at Hudson for an explanation.

"Bill Sharpe found him out in the middle of the kudzu on that property next to Vernon Jenkins and brought him to Ed Watkins' store."

"Missy's Garden?"

"Yes ma'am."

She gazed down at the boy, who met her eyes without defiance.

"Do you go to school in Gallatin?" she asked him.

"I don't know," he said.

An inspiration struck her, because he looked like he might be in fifth or sixth grade. "All my teachers have left for the summer, but do you know Nora O'Hearn? Miss O'Hearn?"

She saw the name register and then disappear.

"I don't know."

"You go on and get back in the car, son," Hudson said. "I'm going to run you into town."

When the door slammed, the sheriff walked a few steps toward the house with Emma, turning his hat in his hands. By now the tabby kittens had come from under the porch and gamboled around his boot strings.

"Nobody's gone missing," he said, bending over and gently detaching an attacker. "I'm wondering how to find out who he is. It turns out Dexter

Watkins had a big stand of marijuana growing down by the creek. That flat part if you've ever been back there."

"When my daddy was just back from World War II, somebody took us behind that house and down into the garden."

It was one of her earliest memories. Roses, benches, low stone walls defining the slope, dogwoods in bloom back in the recesses of the surrounding woods, azaleas in profusion. Even then, it was all overgrown. The paths were weedy, the shrubs in need of pruning. *It's because of the war* the woman had said. They had come around the curve of a stone wall and there in a sunny corner under the tall trees was a goldfish pool and a statue of a naked child squatting with his hand in the water. She remembered small reddish fish in the depths, the too-sweet smell of flowers. And now that whole place was covered in kudzu.

"Miss Emma?" Hudson said.

"Do you think Dexter did something to that boy?"

"I don't know. Could be. I want to think better of him."

"I believe he had something to do with Nora leaving back in March."

"Nora?"

"Nora O'Hearn. The teacher who was living with me."

"The pretty one?"

"Men in this town had no business being around her." Hudson looked up at the hot asperity in her voice and dropped his eyes again. "Do you know Dexter Watkins had the gall to come to the front door of my house asking for her? When I saw your car, the first thing I thought was something had happened to Nora. I think the boy recognized her name," she whispered. "I bet she knows who he is."

"How would I get in touch with her?"

"Talk to her aunt, Teresa Peach?"

"Lives at Stonewall Hill. Married to the editor?"

"Ask her. But tell you what," she said. "In the meantime, take him to Adele Lawson at the library. She'll know him if he's from Gallatin."

"Yes ma'am."

As Hudson thanked her and drove away with the boy, she started back to her strawberries, and another image came to her. The playground of the old grammar school—a boy pumping his legs on the swing, leaning back on the chains and then at the highest point letting go and flying out, landing catlike and clean-limbed in the dirt and gravel. Not this boy. This was a long time ago, decades ago. It was summer or a weekend because he was the only one there. Something about a judge from Macon. They said he had been with his mother out in the country—living in that house in Missy's Garden. The mother had *left him*, that was it. And they had found the boy out by the road, looking for her. She was a criminal wanted for something.

Emma turned to call the sheriff back, but the drive was already empty.

MACON, GEORGIA

Judge Harold Lawton

June 23, 1974

Coming back from the Presbyterian service at a little before eleven, Judge Lawton parked the Cadillac in the back of the house and stood for a minute looking out over the meticulous lawn and garden. He ought to pay Samson more, as much as the man put up with to keep Lucinda happy. It wasn't easy, even for the Judge. At the screen door, he stopped and called inside.

"Lucinda?"

She usually changed to comfortable clothes as soon as she returned from Mass, but he hoped she hadn't this morning. He felt like taking her out to eat. He heard quick footsteps—high heels, good—and she met him in the kitchen, still in the dress she had worn to church. When he pulled her to him, a becoming flush rose in her neck, and another thought occurred to him.

"Oh Harold," she said, pushing him away.

"What's the matter?" he said, pulling her toward him again to kiss her. She smelled wonderful. Mattie was off on Sunday mornings, and they had the house to themselves.

"I just got the strangest call. A woman asking for you."

"One of my many admirers," he said, kissing her neck beneath her ear.

She pushed him away again.

"No, listen to me. She sounded desperate. The phone was ringing when I came in."

He sighed. "Let's sit down. I could use some more coffee, anyway. I'll make it."

"Not right now," she said. "This sounded urgent."

He sat down at the kitchen table and reached out and smoothed his hands down the sides of her fine slim waist and across the flare of her hips.

"Harold, listen, please."

"Okay, I'm listening."

"The phone was ringing when I came into the house." She held both hands out before her dramatically, palm downward, like a pianist stilling

179

the audience before the first notes—the delicate wrists, the perfectly polished red nails. "So I hurried into the kitchen. When I said *Hello*, there was no answer, which of course alarmed me. *Hello?* I said again, and a woman said, *Is this–is Mr. Lawton there?* She sounded as though she were not even sure of your name. I tried to think who might call you Mr. Lawton. *No* I said. *Judge Lawton should be home soon. May I take a message?* She did not say anything, then I heard her sob. *Oh my god* she said. *Oh my god. Judge Lawton. Okay, please. I'm on a pay phone at the airport, and I just–can you just tell him* graves? *Say* graves *and tell him I had to leave my son in Missy's Garden. He's just seven. Oh my god I don't have any more coins.* And it cut her off. That was all. She sounded desperate. What graves could she mean?"

"It's a proper name," he said. His heartbeat had begun to accelerate as soon as he heard it. He stared down at the pattern in the kitchen tile. *Graves.* He thought of the ancient, inherited files in his office, his father's solemn confidences. He had never thought he would actually be called on to do anything.

"She said she had to leave her son in Missy's Garden?"

"Yes, what is that?"

"It's an old place outside Gallatin. I should go. Right now."

"Yes, go, go," she said, urging him up. "Do you know who she is?"

"I think so," he said, and a great wave of dread went through him. "God help me."

Forty-five minutes later, when he drove up to the place on Hopewell Road, he found it abandoned. There was no boy at Missy's Garden. He had seen the place once with his father when he was just out of college, when it had only recently been in use. Now boxwoods and nandinas grew wild across the front of the old house, and what had once been a lawn was a weedy mess of fallen limbs, unraked leaves, beer cans, sodden newspapers, random debris blown from the road. No one had used the front door in decades, and the windows were shuttered up. The driveway around the left side showed faint occasional use, as if teenagers had discovered it for parking.

He would check it out just in case. He stopped on the right of way, not risking his Cadillac on the driveway, and stepped carefully through the weeds in his cordovan wingtips. Nothing stirred except the grasshoppers that leapt away before him. It was noon; the heat of the day bore down on him. When he paused, the Sunday silence gave way to the background throb of insects. He walked down the faint trail someone's tires had pressed in the long grasses and saplings and stopped cold as soon as he turned the corner.

"Good God," he muttered. The front yard was pure disguise.

"*Hello?*" he called. "Is anybody here?"

Along the back of the house and past the door at the far end, the broad flagstones of a patio shaded by the great old live oaks and elms had been cleared of debris. Flowers and herbs grew in large pots in the corners, stone benches sat beneath crepe myrtles in full bloom, and on the back side, stone steps went down in a lane roughly cut through brush whose ragged ends showed along the sides. More crepe myrtles, interspersed with dogwoods and redbuds now past their season, continued along the downward path. The descent to the creek was broken by terraces. A sunlit flat rock in the water, broad enough for a picnic, anchored the view. Someone had recently been scraping and sanding the back of the house in preparation for repainting it. The windows were open to the faint breeze, new screens in all of them.

He looked down toward the creek and started when he saw a woman stepping toward him from the nearest of the terraces, her hand raised in greeting.

"Sweet Lord!" he said, "I didn't—"

He broke off when he saw the utter stillness, the green tarnish of her limbs. A statue. Her back leg was embedded in the tree close behind her, but she was so lifelike, she kept fooling his eye. A shiver shot through him, as though he had encountered Missy herself. He turned and walked across the patio to the back door.

"Hello?" he called. Finding the back screen unlatched, he went into the kitchen. A stovetop still-life: burned bacon in the congealing grease of a cast iron frying pan; an unopened carton of eggs beside a mixing bowl; a hand-cranked eggbeater; a loaf of homemade bread on a cutting board.

"Anybody here?"

He walked past the kitchen table and down the hallway. On the left was a boy's room and a bathroom. In the back right corner was a woman's room. Unmade bed, books of poetry and philosophy, pencil drawings all over the desk with its view of the garden—a boy sitting naked on the rock above the creek, a doe poised at the edge of the woods, the boy again. Various watercolors.

So where was the boy?

When he heard a sound outside, he hurried back up the hall and through the kitchen and out across the patio to the side of the house where he had come in. A pickup truck was parked behind the Cadillac, and a woman was standing at the edge of the road, a woman as bleak and flat-chested and bitter-looking as if she had stepped from the front porch of a

Depression photograph. When she saw him, she waited, a little accusatory in her posture, her arms crossed over her chest.

"She left out of here," she said. "Run like a rabbit."

She held toward him a newspaper clipping from the inside pages of the *Atlanta Journal-Constitution*.

"I seen him here before," she said, poking the photograph of a man coming out of an Illinois courthouse surrounded by police, "and I told her I did. All's I did was show that whore that picture," she said triumphantly, "and she just tore out of here. Left that boy like she didn't even know him. I showed her this one, too." A picture of a badly burned child wrapped in bandages.

He skimmed it—the sentencing of a radical in Chicago named Akers who had blown up an elementary school with a female accomplice named Alison Graves.

The Judge stared into her palpable and repellent meanness.

"Where is he? Where's the boy?"

"None of your goddamn business. Who are you?"

"Judge Harold Lawton," he said. "United States District Court, District of Middle Georgia."

"The law!" she said. "Well, so I guessed right. You come to get her."

"Where is the boy?"

"Well, I took him."

"*You* took him? On whose authority?" he asked harshly. She took a step backward, startled. "What is your name?" he demanded.

A kind of cringing obsequiousness came over her.

"Minnie," she said faintly, almost coyly, trying to sweeten her voice. "Minnie Jenkins." She offered her hand but then withdrew it in embarrassment, as though it had acted on its own. She took another step back and began to turn toward the pickup.

"The boy, he's—well, you know—he seemed like he was hungry, so—"

"Is he at your home?"

"Well I thought a church might could—"

"What church?"

Ten minutes later he pulled into the unpaved parking lot of a little ramshackle church in a clearing above the Ikahalpi River. A hand-lettered sign was nailed above the door:

182

✝

Holy Saints of Siloam
Rev. Holiness McGee

Under the shade of the trees were three picnic tables spread with tablecloths and weighted with platters and pitchers of iced tea. As the judge got out of his Cadillac and walked toward them, twenty or so black men and women seated at the tables in their Sunday finest turned to watch, some of the men standing and smiling in welcome.

"How you doing this afternoon?"

"Welcome to Holy Saints. Yes sir. Come on and get you something to eat. We got plenty."

But several of the smaller children playing around the tables ran over and hid behind their mothers, as if they had been warned from the cradle about tall white men in suits. Knowing why he was there, several men and women nodded him toward a little white boy, six or seven years old, shirtless and deeply tanned, seated on the other side of the middle table all alone. His blond hair was as long as a girl's. Light filtered through the branches and over his thin shoulders and bare skin. He was bent over his paper plate, eating country ham and potato salad and baked beans. Sensing a change in the crowd, the boy looked up, his face dirty and tear-stained. A man in an old-fashioned suit stepped in quietly behind the boy to put a protective left hand on his shoulder as he held out his right to the judge.

"Rev. Holiness McGee. And you, sir?"

"Judge Harold Lawton, District of Middle Georgia."

"Here come da judge!" one of the younger men said, and the whole group around him leaned against each other. Rev. McGee glanced at them sternly, and the laughter died.

"Do you know this child?" he asked the judge. "Or why Mrs. Jenkins left him here?"

"I received a call at my home in Macon informing me that a boy had been left at Missy's Garden."

Murmurs went through the brothers and sisters—raised eyebrows, drawn-back heads, significant looks.

"That's where he was? At Missy's Garden?" the preacher repeated.

"Yes sir, so I understand."

"Lord have mercy."

183

At the advice of Rev. McGee, the judge decided to take the boy to the nearby home of Dr. Calhoun Fields, a general practitioner in Gallatin who was also a county commissioner. His unmarried daughter Emma taught in the elementary school in Gallatin.

The boy had a feral look, especially the way he would shake his hair back out of his eyes, but he spoke with mature clarity. On the way over, disturbed by the account the preacher had taken him aside to give him, the judge asked him who his mother was.

"Rosemary," the boy said. "Do you know where she is?"

"No, I don't. I was going to ask you."

"I was down on the rock catching tadpoles, and when I came up from the creek for breakfast, she was gone."

"What's your name, son?"

"Rosemary said to say Walter Peach."

"What do you mean she said to say it?"

"She said if somebody asks me my name, I'm supposed to say Walter Peach."

He glanced at the boy.

"But what's your real name?"

"My real name? What's a real name?"

"The name you got from your parents. Is your surname—I mean, the name you got from your father—is that Peach?"

"I don't know my father. Rosemary says my father is a coward."

"I see. Did he pass away?"

"Rosemary just said to tell people my name is Walter Peach."

Dr. Fields called the judge on Monday to say that the boy was in excellent health. "Clear eyes, excellent reflexes. He's obviously been eating well—and I don't mean junk food. His teeth are perfect."

"Well, good," the Judge murmured.

"And he's flabbergasted Emma," Dr. Fields said.

"What do you mean?"

"She was an English major at Georgia, and the boy knows more poems than she does. He knows plants, birds, trees. He knows the constellations. She says he's the most brilliant child she's ever met, but—"

"But what?"

"Well, I don't know exactly what went on at Missy's Garden. Let's call it problems with manners. I expect he'll work it out after a slap or two."

On Saturday, the judge had enough paperwork done to take custody of the child. He picked him up and took him into Gallatin to get a haircut before he met Lucinda. Miss Emma had suggested her own hairdresser, because she feared that the men and boys in the barbershop might mock the boy for a head of hair any woman would die to have. She didn't want him going into a hairdresser's salon either, not with the way women talked. She gave the judge an address, and he took Walter to the side door of the woman's home as though they were doing something illegal. He sat in his car thinking about how this obligation had come to rest on him.

Half an hour later, the boy came out clean-cut. The young woman waved away the judge's money.

"No sir," she said quickly, touching the top button of her blouse and turning away with another wave over her shoulder. "No sir. Never mind."

Walter

A beautiful lady came walking with small steps from a room deeper in the house. When she crossed over rugs he could not hear her, but on the wooden floor, the high heels of her shoes struck with a sharp, determined sound, like when Mr. Jenkins hammered. She was smiling and carrying a tray with glasses on it. Her blonde hair was swept back from the front of her head into a knot on top. She had on a tight blue dress with white polka dots, and when she turned to set down the tray, she was as graceful as a doe. She straightened up and faced him and ran her hands down the sides of her dress and then reached out toward him—glad, open hands, palms upward. He gave her his hands and she held them soft as petals in both of hers.

"Now what's his name?" she said, looking at him but speaking to the man he was supposed to call Judge Lawton

"Walter. Walter Peach. He says that's what his mother called him."

"Hello Walter."

The lady gently squeezed his hands and then knelt to his height, turning her knees aside, balancing on her shoes, and pulled him toward her and held him there in a light hug. She smelled like nights when Rosemary would take him out under the jasmine and listen to the mockingbird. Unfurled nights. Then the lady pushed him lightly away and tilted her head while she looked at him. *Oh sugar,* she said. *Aren't you a precious little thing?* He did not answer. Her irises were deep blue with black rays bursting out through them, and they made him feel the way he did when Rosemary sang about stardust. The pupils were so huge and close he could see his face in them. Her eyelashes were thick and black, crusted like crystallized honey. Her cheeks were as finely powdered as if bees had brushed them with pollen.

His heart was full of buzz and murmur. The lady's eyes closed into crusty lashes and her mouth made a kiss so red it looked painted with strawberries. He leaned forward and kissed it and felt the lady's lips come off soft but tasting like soap.

"Oh!" she said. She stood up suddenly and looked at the judge, who smiled and put his hand on Walter's back.

"Walter, this is Mrs. Lawton."

Walter nodded.

"A precious little *wild* thing," Mrs. Lawton said. She smiled over him at the judge and pressed her lips together and then pursed them again and ran the tip of her little fingernail along the edge of her bottom one. She remembered the drinks and gave Walter a cold glass. He tasted it.

Lemonade, sharp and sugary but not too sweet. Cletus's mama made it too sweet.

"Do you want to see your room?"

He said he did.

He had been in big places. There was a city he remembered full of big buildings, but the only place he remembered being *inside* in the city was small and cold. He used to ask Rosemary what city it was. *I can't tell you its name*, Rosemary would say, and she would raise her eyebrows and put her finger straight up over her smiling lips, which meant *be quiet*, like the times Mr. Jenkins came in the back door and went into her room and he would hear them making their noises.

But he had never been on the inside of a place this big.

The house was painted white outside with a square tower going straight up above the front door (*Tuscan*, the man he was supposed to call Judge Lawton said). Judge Lawton had parked his big green car in front (a Cadillac, he told Walter) on the brick drive that came off a shadowy street of other big houses and up between the flowering trees.

He wanted to tell Rosemary. He thought how he would describe Mrs. Lawton to Rosemary—but Rosemary was gone and everyone in Macon, Georgia, was furled and now Mrs. Lawton was going to show him his room in the house in Macon a long way from Missy's Garden.

"You go on up," Judge Lawton said.

Mrs. Lawton softly took his hand. She led him through a room with a long table. Stacks of plates and arrays of glasses showed behind windows in a big cabinet. They went into a hallway and started up the stairs. Twice she looked down at him, first when they passed a painting of Judge Lawton and Mrs. Lawton when they were younger.

"What do you think?"

"You're more beautiful than the picture."

She smiled at him and put her hand in his hair.

"You *are* precious."

A few seconds later she stopped on the flat place between the set of stairs that came up and the set of stairs that went up more. Through the wide window he could see down into the shady yard—huge trees and smooth short grass and stone paths and places to sit. A white bench without legs was hanging on chains from one of the tree limbs. He saw a rectangle of water where white flowers grew up from broad leaves that lay flat on the surface; a slow stir went through it like the breath going through the skin of Rosemary's stomach when she lay sleeping on her back unfurled on a hot afternoon.

Something red-gold—fish!—flitted under the leaves and moved the dark water. He watched until something else caught his eye, a motion, a flash. A black man stood hoeing in a bed of tall white flowers further back, and the hoe caught the sunlight as it rose. Along a hedge far across the yard in sunlight was a bed of deep red flowers. Beds. A *bed* of bright yellow flowers stretched out along a low building toward the back. *Beds where they stay all day* Rosemary would say about the flowers Missy planted and tended. Big *beds* of irises. Like his where he would sit up late, looking through books of paintings Rosemary loved. Or where he would learn the feel of words on his tongue from the books she would give him. He would read and look at books in his bed because Rosemary said he was so smart. Trace the words of a poem with his finger and say them. *One nub of growth / Nudges a sand-crumb loose.*

Nub—like what's left of a burned candle. Or like his little pee-thing. His pee-nis.

Nudge—like what he did to her shoulder when he wanted her to scratch his back.

Crumb—like cake she let him take from her lips. But *sand*-crumb. Not sweet.

These were *lines*, Rosemary said, like rows of flowers. Some lines he liked, but some scared him. *Pokes through a musty sheath / Its pale tendrilous horn* scared him. The word *musty* got in his nose like the things left in Missy's dusty closet. *Sheath* scared him because the sword that came out of it was a *Pale tendrilous horn*. It made him think a ghost was waiting in his mother's closet to get in bed with her. Maybe it would scare away Mr. Jenkins. He read or looked at books of paintings with Rosemary, too, but he read mostly when he was not in Rosemary's bed, when she was in her bed being tended by the man with the long hair who came once and whose name she would never say. The one she cried for when he left but called a coward. The one who said he could not live this way. Or big Mr. Jenkins lately, who made him angry. Walter would ask what they were doing in there and she would smile and tease him and say *I'm being tended. Like Missy's flowers when the bees go up inside them and come out covered with pollen.* He would say he could tend her too and she would smile and squeeze his nose and shake her head.

"Do you like it?" Mrs. Lawton asked. "This is your new home."

He nodded.

"Now listen to me, Walter."

He looked up at her.

"Where did you learn to kiss like that?"

His heart filled.

"Rosemary taught me."

"Rosemary—I'm sorry. Who is Rosemary? A little girl you knew out in the country?"

"My mama. She doesn't like me to call her mama."

After a second Mrs. Lawton made a sound.

"She taught you? How did she teach you?"

"She puts honey on her lips and lets me have it. Or cake or jam. Mr. Jenkins brings raspberry jam."

Mrs. Lawton stood looking out the window without saying anything.

"Oh, you poor thing," she finally said.

He did not understand her. They stood for so long that the black man saw them when he straightened up and stretched. He lifted his straw hat at them, and Mrs. Lawton waved.

"Now, Walter," she said. "Judge Lawton has a few things to explain to you. But first come on upstairs and I'll show you your room."

At the top of the next set of stairs they went across the wooden floor toward the front of the house. Her shoes made the sharp sound all the way. She led him through a door and up a stairway that went up and bent and went up and bent again and up again and into the top of the tower. It was his room. There was his bed, she told him. It had a white cover and many pillows. A big box in the wall cooled the room so much he shivered even though it was a hot day outside. Many books filled a bookcase. At the edge of the bed a new baseball glove lay untouched, its leather better than Cletus's even, and a bat and a baseball still in the box.

The clatter above his head was a train that went around the whole room on its own railroad shelf. A chugging locomotive pulled a long train of boxcars clattering along. He watched it go all around the room once and then again, and he thought about the freight train schedule he and Cletus figured out and how they put pennies on the tracks, falling back into the bushes, hiding and grinning a few feet from the train that clanked by as big as a house and louder than thunder and sparking and clamoring. And afterward there among the gravel and railroad ties was the flattened penny that he made into a necklace for Rosemary.

He gave it to Rosemary and her smile kept brimming up. Her face would finally go still, then another smile would brim through and she would hold him and let him be there against her. And every day the penny hung on its cord and she would tie it different ways, sometimes up at her collarbone, sometimes just between the tops of her breasts, sometimes dark as another nipple, slung below her breasts on the flat of her stomach when she was lying down with the cord loose between them.

And now Rosemary was gone. Judge Lawton said Rosemary was gone.

Would she come back? Judge Lawton did not think so.

"What's the matter, sugar? Oh now, what's the matter? Don't cry."

When Mrs. Lawton knelt and held out her arms, his heart melted, and she pulled him against her and he tried to put his hand under the top of her dress.

All the air went out of the world.

"What are you doing!"

She slapped his face and shoved him back so hard he fell on the floor and hit his head on the bookcase.

"You don't *do* that, do you understand?" He stared up in confusion at her horrified expression. She looked so disgusted, so disfigured, he was sorry for her. "You don't *do* that!"

Her heels made gunshots down the stairs, and he went over and lay on the bed. He had tried to think she was Rosemary, and she had turned into a witch.

It was worse when he came up from the creek into the house and Rosemary was gone. That was worse. When he went out to the road looking for her. This was not as bad as that. *Forlorn* was what he felt then. Rosemary would read him the poem with the word *forlorn* in it and tell him about how she once heard a bell in the fog that made her think of *fairy lands forlorn*. It was summer, she told him, and the fog was everywhere and she was with her friends on the beach of Lake Michigan—this was before he was born—and she was watching a nearby seagull just hanging in the air and then she could not find the others and as she was wandering she heard a bell somewhere out on the lake say

FOR. LORN.

Forlorn! The very word is like a bell/To toll me back from thee to my sole self!

Rosemary would read him that poem. That was by the poet who died young. The poem about hearing the bird singing at night and wanting to get away from being himself and having to die—and almost getting away into the bird—but then having to come back and be himself again.

Sole self. It was like that without Rosemary.

Forlorn. Yes, his sole self. Forlorn.

The little train chugged along above him on its track.

Samson Wills

Miss Lucinda she always wanted a baby but couldn't have none. Say she went to every doctor, all kind of tests. I used to tell Brother James at church it seem to me it ain't much to it. *How many babies you make?* he say and I say *No telling.* Back in my day you know. Whoo. But now listen what I'm saying. Miss Lucinda, she fix up that room a long time ago like she already had a son and when that boy come home with the Judge she kind of go crazy. At first it like the boy something she got to tame before he be what she want. Like the Judge brought her a pup and it turn out a wolf. Some kind of wildness in him she got to get out. I ain't talking mean. Just wild. Quiet. He watch all the time and he see everything but it ain't his house and he ain't studying to make it his. Like he know he in a cage. Like he come from some place he can't get back to.

They say his mama run off and left him by himself at that place in the country outside Gallatin. They plenty of stories about his mama. How she go around half naked. Free love. Anyway, it ain't like the boy won't do what Miss Lucinda say because he do it just exactly, but he do it quiet and watching. He don't smile. He smile at the judge, he smile at Mattie, he smile at me, but ain't smile at her. That's what drive her crazy. He don't trust her.

One time I need to ask Miss Lucinda about where she want me to plant the azaleas. I hear her inside the house with the boy. She talking to him and I stand at the back screen. Miss Lucinda inside the kitchen with the boy at the table. I hear her and I tap at the wood on the screen door but she don't hear, not even when I knock, louder and louder. She whispering and begging. *Walter* she say. *Just call me mama. Look. Look what I'm doing.*

I can't see what she doing. Judge he done gone to work and Mattie— you know Mattie Hawks?—she gone that morning. *Miss Lucinda* I call and I hear a chair go back but it must be the boy. She don't hear me. She say *Please Walter. It's strawberry. You like strawberry don't you?* I figure she trying to feed him something. *Please Walter* she say. *There's somebody at the door* he say. *At the door?* she say. I hear her chair push back and her steps and there she is. *Oh, Samson* she say. *What is it?* I tell her I need to know where to put the azaleas and she say she be out in a little bit. I don't say what I'm thinking but what I'm seeing is she got strawberry jam all over her mouth, like she put on lipstick crooked. I'm thinking great God in heaven. My stomach turn over. *What's the matter?* she say. *Why are you still standing there, you fool? I told you I'd be out soon.* She ain't whispering now. That boy stand behind her looking at me still and quiet and wild.

So she got sick in her head first. I had to call the judge to come home one morning because she come outside. I'm trimming the boxwoods and I look up and there she stand like she Eve in the garden of Eden. You know what I'm saying. Something strange going on in her head. A fine woman my opinion. Judge Lawton a lucky man. The boy he just standing there on the back step, looking like a wild animal look it had just come up to the edge of the woods, watching to see what somebody would do.

So the judge come home and threw something over her. It wasn't long after that the cancer showed. Six months later she was dead as the azaleas I never planted to suit her, and it was just the judge and the boy and Mattie. And it wasn't long it was the undertaker's wife visiting sometime with her daughter in the day and a night every week or so by herself. Mattie say to call her the nanny.

Tell you what. Call her what you want to. Judge Lawton a lucky man.

Judge Lawton

What distressed him most was not Lucinda's passing, though he loved her from the heart, but the manner of it. After over a year of seeing the boy's capacities, she wanted legal claim to Walter, which meant rushing through adoption papers and establishing that she was a fit parent—this despite the fact that for the last three months of her life she rarely left her bed. She wanted the boy's name changed to honor her family, not the judge's. The Lawtons were middle class, in her view, and she accepted as her due the judge's rise from humble origins—nobodies in Gallatin—to achievement and prominence. Walter did not appear to have a birth certificate that the judge could find; he suspected that the boy's mother had used the name *Walter* simply for convenience around others, the same way, apparently, she had used clothing. Favors from his friends in the law—potentially expensive in quid pro quo—helped the judge satisfy Lucinda's stubborn will, and the boy became their legal son, Walter Devereaux Lawton, in time for her last few weeks.

The boy would come in holding the judge's hand while Mattie Hawks hovered at the tall window, half-hidden behind the curtains, more a referee than a maid. The big armoire doors were open to display Lucinda's neatly ordered antique fabrics, her inherited wools and linens and laces. Her dressing table shone with sundry perfumes, enough expensive creams to soothe a Cleopatra; her reading chair waited in its pool of gentle light, and her books waited beside it.

The room was as still and calm as always, and the light would slant through the fissure in the curtains, and the dust motes would swirl upward through the sunbeam like souls soaring aloft in paradisal light, but Lucinda herself would lie tormented there, a knot of pain impossible to loosen. Her lovely body shrank into mere bone, and her skin seemed to web down into the cotton sheets. But her eyes never rested, her demanding eyes, alive and full of silent judgment.

Whenever she saw the boy, she would lift a hand and beckon him.

"Walter!" The boy would stand impassive at the foot of the bed. "Come where I can see you." The boy would go and stand beside her. Her wasted hand would rake at him. "Won't you kiss me?" her voice plaintive and despairing.

He would not.

"He's afraid of the way I look," she would say, almost accusatorily, to the judge. And then she would turn back to the boy.

"What are you reading?" her voice querulous and tyrannical.

"Plutarch. About Camillus."

"Good. You see how the common people treat him? The man who saved Rome?"

"Yes."

"Say '*yes ma'am*.'"

"Yes ma'am."

"And so what's the lesson here?"

Walter thought. "Piety by itself doesn't work. You have to flatter the people."

"*Excellent!* Isn't that excellent, Harold? A Devereaux needs to know what common people are like. Keep them thinking well of themselves, and you can do anything you want. But always disguise what you really think of them. Have you read yet about Caesar?"

"Yes ma'am."

The judge intervened. "We wouldn't want Walter to be a Caesar."

Walter was to be a governor or senator, perhaps even the president. She had demanded, the previous year, that he be kept away from the public school, which she considered a mere instrument of low democratic indoctrination. When Judge Lawton suggested Cumbrian Academy, the best private school in all of Macon, she read their materials and agreed that he could go after a year of her own steady tutoring. He needed to understand what was expected of a Devereaux, and to her mind this meant that he should be reading noble things well beyond the commoners' capacities—Homer, Shakespeare's history plays, Plutarch's *Lives,* Herodotus, Thucydides: books her father had loved as his ancestors had before him. Of all her demands, these were the least burdensome to the boy, because he read easily and with immediate intelligence.

Lucinda meant to instill in the boy a real aristocratic mind and character, to inoculate him against the baseness and the ease of an egalitarian age. She needed above all to undo the work of "Rosemary," whose name she never spoke without contempt. A Devereaux also required an early and intense schooling in his *innate*—she would emphasize the word as though to ward off the unseemly fact that he was not of her own blood—his *innate* superiority to all but a few others of equal standing. He would grasp the reins of his high responsibility; he would be kind to his inferiors; in all situations he would exhibit *noblesse oblige.* For Lucinda, the development of this capacity required something more: a complex and ambivalent relation to black people. He needed a servant whom he *obeyed* out of love and humility and yet *commanded* out of his inborn superiority. Early in his life, he had been spiritually malformed and deprived of his hereditary right to a black woman—his *right* as a Devereaux. But now he must have a black nanny. Mattie was as fine as they came as a maid, but she could by no means be a nanny.

Lucinda forced Mattie to bring in aunts and friends and women from her church as possible nannies. All were inspected with a noble hauteur.

"Boy don't need no damn nanny," Mattie would grumble to the judge when she left the room. "He tall as I am and smart as a whip." The judge would ask her to humor Mrs. Lawton because the drugs for pain affected her mind. "Same mind she always had," Mattie would say, and walk away.

In February of 1976, a few weeks before Lucinda died, Mattie brought in an elegant and beautiful young woman. Wearing a matching yellow skirt and jacket, she stood for a moment in the foyer and smiled at the judge—startlingly green-eyed, feline in grace, quietly knowing in manner—and followed Mattie, who treated her with a curious distance and respect, down the hall to the stairs. The judge wanted to see how Lucinda would react. He caught Mattie at the top of the landing as the woman stepped out into the upstairs hallway and began examining the portraits.

"Who is she?"

"Name Adara," she whispered to the judge. "She married to Mr. Watson, the undertaker, but she too much for that old buzzard, you know what I'm saying. I'm talking watch out. They got a little girl five or six years old, whiter than most white people. Ain't no child of old man Watson."

When they arrived at the door of Lucinda's room, Mattie knocked and opened. Adara Watson hung back and tilted her head at the judge, her face full of irony and bemused speculation. He opened a hand toward the room's prevailing gloom, and she went in and walked to the side of the bed. Without prompting she immediately took Lucinda's hand. Lucinda started and stared up, confused. Adara smiled at her and touched her cheek, already intimate, and Lucinda's hostile reserve shattered.

"*Tildy?*" she said. She sobbed, clinging to Adara's hand and kissing it so pitiably that Judge Lawton had to turn aside. "I don't feel good, Tildy."

"That's all right, baby," Adara told her, stroking her cheek, her hair. "I'll help you."

Mattie quietly intervened.

"This ain't Tildy, Miss Lucinda. This here Adara Watson," she said. "She come to—"

Understanding came back into Lucinda's eyes, but she did not change. "Yes," she said, still kissing her hands. "Yes, Adara. You'll come back and help me, won't you?"

"Of course, I will, baby." She leaned down and kissed Lucinda on the forehead.

197

"Oh, thank God. Thank God."

Afterward in the hallway, the judge thanked the young woman, whose eyes lifted frankly to his own.

"You are most welcome," she said. "Mattie said you were Judge Lawton. Judge of what, if I may ask?"

So that was how it was. She was already *his* judge. He saw himself in her eyes: six-four, graying, serious, athletic but slightly stooped from his habit of listening patiently to intemperate people shorter than he was. A kind man, usually calm, but definitely held attentive by her beauty.

"United States District Court, District of Middle Georgia," he said.

"I am happy to help, Judge Lawton, but I fail to understand entirely what Mrs. Lawton desires of me. Is there a boy? Mattie mentioned a boy."

"Walter. He's up in his room. I am not sure that Mrs. Lawton *knows* entirely what she wants. But she does want you to help Walter—to help draw him out."

"Draw him out?"

"He's very bright but very shy."

"How might I help draw him out? Perhaps by bringing my daughter sometimes? She's a very bright little girl."

"That might be just the thing."

Her eyes met his. She reached and took his hand for a fraction of a second longer than was needed to convey her sympathy, and a shock ran through his whole body.

"How might I help *you?*" she said.

Walter Devereaux Lawton

He had never wanted Rosemary to leave, not for a single second, but he wanted Mrs. Lawton to be gone forever. And she refused to go. She would not go to the hospital, even though the judge begged her. The judge hired nurses to stay in her room and give the dying woman her daily shots, which sometimes worked but more often didn't. One night she demanded Adara spend the night in the room with her. In the middle of the night Adara came up and woke him. *Mrs. Lawton wants you, baby.* She wore nothing but her nightgown, and he could see the shape of her kneeling body against the light of the stairway. *What?* he said. *What?* She pulled him against her. *You need to wake up, baby.* She held his head like Rosemary used to do and her hand scratched his back, lazily, not letting up.

He got up and she led him down the steep tower stairs to the hallway and across to Mrs. Lawton's room. Adara knew he was afraid of Mrs. Lawton; she held his hand all the way in. He stood back from the bed just outside the arc of light made by the bedside lamp, and the judge stood near him, both of them watching with hands folded in front of them.

The crickets throbbed outside the open screen and somewhere a dog barked in the night. A bird was singing. A mockingbird. Mattie had told him they sang all night long in the springtime because they were showing off to their girlfriends. He missed Rosemary. But he missed her less because of Adara.

Adara in her nightgown knelt next to Mrs. Lawton rising slightly to whisper in her ear. Mrs. Lawton whispered back and kept touching her face.

Yes, you will, won't you? The boxwoods? And the azaleas. Boxwoods for definition. And the tiger lilies. And the koi in the pool. You will, won't you? And little Walter's lessons. Yes, I know you will, you sweet thing, you darling.

She kissed Adara's face—her eyelids, her cheeks—and then she lay back, exhausted. Minute after minute passed. And suddenly she sat straight up in the bed with a cry, staring into a corner of the room. She called out in a language Walter did not know. He did not know why, but he remembered the exact sound of it even into his teens and later wrote it down over and over, trying to spell what it sounded like and understand what it meant: *Inwistolon monaskator petragrammatain musistilonus notanorispura!* She pointed, full of elation, her face alight with something she saw. And then she fell back and missed the pillow. Her frail body slumped off the bedside, but Adara caught her scant weight and lifted her up, arranged her head on the big feather pillow, and tucked the sheet up to her chin. Adara waited a moment. Waited while time gathered like honey at the lid of the jar. Then she glanced over at Judge Lawton.

She's passed, Judge Lawton. Shall I leave you?

When he shook his head, she pulled the sheet up over Mrs. Lawton's face. That was *death*, Walter knew, like a frog flattened on Hopewell Road or the deer the buzzards found on the other side of the creek or the cottonmouth Cletus killed with a stick. Whatever was in you that made you alive left behind a thing that looked like you. Adara stood and turned and again and Walter could see the shape of her body under the nightgown against the low lamp. Everything that made her alive was still everywhere in her.

Like Rosemary.

The newspaper had a picture of Mrs. Lawton when she was young and very beautiful. She stood in her wedding gown beneath a magnolia tree, glowing, almost, against the darkness of its shade. She was embraced on her left by a bough of broad blossoms whose soft white petals you should not touch because it would bruise them, as she had told him many times.

> Mrs. Lucinda Devereaux Lawton, graduate of Sarah Lawrence College *summa cum laude*, past president of the Macon chapter of the United Daughters of the Confederacy, author of *The Classic South* and *The Garden of Recollection*, died during the early morning hours of March 18, 1976.

Walter wore a new black suit to the funeral. He would not look at her dead body in the coffin. He sat in the pew beside Judge Lawton and held Mattie Hawks's hand. Adara and her daughter Hermia sat several rows behind them in the crowded Catholic church on Poplar Street. The priest finished and everyone left the church and drove to the cemetery, and the priest said more prayers, and they put the coffin in the ground.

That was the end of her. She would not bother him anymore. She was dead, and he was glad. She was in the ground in the cemetery—but where was Rosemary?

They went back to the big house, and he lived in the square room at the top of the tower. That summer of 1976, Hermia and Adara would come and visit him. He and Hermia would play in the backyard and talk about books they liked and fossils in rocks and the barks of different trees and whether birds had dreams and the shapes of insects. They would help Samson water the plants in the vegetable garden and pluck out the weeds. They would come inside filthy.

You ain't gone put them chirrun in the same tub! Mattie would cry.

Oh stop it, Mattie, Adara would say. *They're just children.*
They chirrun, they ain't babies.

Adara would get them out of all their clothes and fill the bath just enough not to splash out and, smiling with all her beautiful shining teeth, she'd ask *should I come in? Yes* they would cry, but she would say there wasn't room. *Unfurl!* he would say. *That's what you call it?* she would say. She would unfurl for him and it made him happy to see her so beautiful and lightly brown. She would lather her hands and start washing them and she would tease them about how Hermia was different from Walter, see, and her light brown hands would soap them all over and then she would make them stand up and rinse off under the shower. When they got out, she would dry them herself, Hermia first and then Walter, and they would be as excited as puppies.

He loved Adara. Sometimes after she visited Judge Lawton at night she would come up to his room and unfurl, turn him on his stomach and scratch his back. She had long fingernails, as hard and perfect as Mrs. Lawton's but painted with complicated designs. She would trace patterns and circles all over his skin, and he would lie in such bliss in the smell of her body that he was afraid to breathe because it might disturb her. He never wanted it to stop.

But it did stop. When Adara's husband died, she married a Nigerian man, a professor at Morehouse in Atlanta. She and Hermia left with one brief goodbye, and then it was just himself and the Judge, Mattie and Samson. Just meals and Cumbrian Academy. Discussions sometimes in the Judge's study. Books, many books of history, biography, but many more of poetry—especially poetry. A few friends, a few girls, and a fading ache for Missy's Garden where it was Adam and maiden and the birth of the simple light.

Mattie Hawks

Long as she came I ain't said nothing. First time she come in dressed up and say *Good evening, Miss Mattie. The Judge is expecting me* and she walk over—you ever see a woman walk like that?—and tap on his study door. I wouldn't watch him open it after that first time. The way he say *Come in, Adara.* It ain't for me to judge. *He* the Judge and I ain't talking Judge Harold P. Lawton. But you ever see a woman do like that? Her married or supposed to be and him just lost his wife.

When old Mr. Watson finally died, the funeral man, I mean, she wasn't six weeks marrying that man from Africa. Her and her girl move to Atlanta, and I tell you what, it was bad. Both of them, the judge and the boy. It was bad. Miss Lucinda die, the judge just fine. Sober, you know, but just fine. But when Adara leave, ain't nothing fine. The judge start to complain about every little thing. *Why can't you fix my coffee the way I like it?* Ain't nothing change about the way I make his coffee. Holler at Samson for being too slow. Samson been slow his whole life at everything but women. But the boy he took it harder. First his mama and now Adara. He go to school and they send home notes about how come he ain't doing like he did. He go up to his room and don't come down for dinner. I go up to get him and he just lying there, staring at the wall, still got on that tight-neck uniform. He come down and they sit in the dining room and I put the food in front of them. My meat loaf—ain't nobody ever complain about my meat loaf—and sweet potatoes and fresh pole beans cooked with ham hock and my good rolls.

The judge he at least poke at it. He start to say something but don't finish his sentence. Wants to say something mean but won't—because he the judge. I wouldn't want to be in court when the judge like that.

Boy don't even poke at it. Sit there like stone.

Timothy Branch

April 10, 1985
TO: Martin Scholarship Committee, Department of
English, University of Georgia
FROM: Timothy Branch, Dean of Faculty, Cumbrian
Academy, Macon
RE: Walter Devereaux Lawton

I have taught for thirty years, and I have
seen many bright students, but I have never
encountered one like Walter Lawton. I hardly
feel it necessary to praise him. He surpasses—
indeed, makes inconsequential—all the usual
academic measures (a fact which should already
be clear from his records); he has a poetic
sensibility that remains extraordinary despite
the incomprehension of his peers and the
mores of normative mediocrity at a school for
the privileged; he performs at a high level
athletically, especially in baseball, track, and
tennis; and he comports himself well socially.

Yet, in all candor, I would prefer *not* to
recommend Walter Devereaux Lawton—though I do
so—for the Martin Scholarship in Literature.
There is something unsettling about Walter
that I find hard to define and that others also
have mentioned to me, not exactly a coldness or
indifference, but something off-putting, cooling
if not chilling, that inflects the rest of his
qualities. I do not mention this indeterminate
"something" in order to warn you away from his
excellences, which certainly make him worthy of
the scholarship, but simply to explain my own
reservations in recommending him. Let me try
with three examples.

First was when Walter won the school-wide
literary competition at Cumbrian Academy in
the ninth grade. He submitted a poem called
"Rosemary's Departure," which I include here:

How could she be my sanctum—beauty bare
inside the Garden's back screen door—
and show me glad day's unfurled smiling
turn,
ladle in hand, from the fevered stove
and then—
nobody there?
No body there to congregate my love,
no corpse to bury—or to burn.
Just absence disquieting the air.

Not so remarkable, perhaps, but his entry
aroused the interested suspicion of the committee
of judges made up of faculty from local colleges;
plagiarism seemed likely, even though Walter's
stellar reputation had preceded him from our
middle school.

Part of the competition included an interview
with the students about their works. Walter was
a slender fourteen-year-old, just coming into
his growth, a little nervous around so many
strangers. When he was asked about the unusual
use of "unfurled," his face clouded, and he
mumbled that it was just a word he liked—an
answer that convinced most of us the poem was in
fact plagiarized. But then a man from Wesleyan
asked about the play on "nobody" and "no body."
Walter responded that he was breaking open the
word to distinguish it from *no one*. "What's
missing is Rosemary's *body*," he said. I asked
about the word "congregate," and he said he was
thinking of the Roman Catholic Mass and comparing
Rosemary's body to the Eucharist, which draws a
congregation into church, except in this case it
was a congregation of one. Her body *congregates*
the speaker's disparate desires, unifies him
in worship. "*Worship?*" I asked with a shade of
sarcasm. It struck me as almost blasphemous.
"That's a strong word." He looked at me with those
blue eyes and pointed back to *sanctum* in the first
line as the preparation for the metaphor.

We moved on. A woman from Mercer asked why he put the dash after "bury." He answered that all the dashes in the poem were an homage to Emily Dickinson's use of them. He also wanted to suggest Rosemary's reclusive nature and the speaker's doubts. "To bury" suggested Christianity and resurrection, whereas "to burn" was pagan, like the funerals in the *Iliad* or the pyres in *Beowulf*. It hinted at a darker finality in death.

Any suspicions had of course evaporated by this point. One of the judges said that the last line sounded a little off to her ear. Wouldn't it be better to make *absence* plural: "Just *absences* disquieting the air"? She felt the need for another syllable. "That's exactly right," he said, the only time he smiled. "You *feel* the absence, and you feel it at the unaccented syllable *dis-*, which already means the negation of something." The whole committee was by this point exchanging glances whenever he happened not to be looking. *Ninth grade?* It was unnerving to me to think what it would be like to have him in class.

At the end, we thanked him, and we all got up to see him out. Just as he was passing through the doorway into the hall, I called after him—I thought in a jocular tone—"So who's Rosemary?" He stopped and stood completely rigid for a moment and then left without turning or answering me. Everyone was taken aback. We speculated for a minute or two. Did he realize he was being rude? Didn't he know he was still in the interview? Was the question too personal? But then we let it pass. Who else could have won the competition? "A Daniel come to judgment," the professor from Mercer said.

The second example is more disturbing, at least to me. Cumbrian Academy was hosting an event for important donors in late October a year ago. It was the afternoon before our homecoming game, perfect football weather, one of those

Saturdays when the old maples are golden, and the air is like chilled white wine. The campus looked beautiful. Guests were dropped off at the top of the circular drive, and they came into the tent set up on the lawn in front of the main building—tables with white tablecloths and glittering crystal, servants everywhere. We had the football players come by in their jerseys to meet the couples in attendance, and we had athletes from various other sports wear their uniforms. Volleyball and basketball, baseball and track and tennis: most of our athletes were there.

Walter had won the regional championship in tennis the year before as well as putting in a good season at second base. He attended in his baseball uniform, duly shook hands and answered questions. Really, he was exemplary, just what we would want—classically handsome, clean-limbed, articulate, smiling. After half an hour or so, several of the prettier ladies among our donors had surrounded him, and I drifted over to listen in. *What about Dylan Thomas?* said Hallie Calloway, the much younger wife of the CFO at the Medical Center. *Don't you just love him?* Walter quoted something from "Fern Hill" to Hallie's great satisfaction, and then Rebecca Lee, whose husband claimed descent from the General himself, touched Walter on the arm and proffered her highly competitive décolleté.

Sugar, I knew your mother, and she would be so proud of you.

Walter went still and stared at her. *You knew my mother? How did you know my mother?*

Mrs. Lee was visibly discomfited by his intensity and she stood back. I saw, if he did not, the flush spread up her bosom and neck. *Well, I was in the UDC with her. Lucinda knew more about the real South than—*

Walter gave a bark of contempt.

She wasn't my mother!

He turned and walked off. You can imagine the reaction. Luckily I was there to step in.

Please pardon the length of my explanation. I realize, writing it, that Walter has been a concern of mine for some time, perhaps since that ninth-grade encounter. I go too far in sharing a dream I had—let us call it my third example—but it says much.

In the dream, I was alone in my office at Cumbrian Academy working on a class schedule or some such task when Walter tapped on the doorframe. I told him to come in, and he came and sat across from me, full of the heat of some passion, his cheeks flushed, his clear blue eyes alight, his hair mussed, his tie askew. He talked about some issue—something to do with Ronald Reagan and Melvin Bradford and George Will and the National Endowment for the Humanities. You know how the young are capable of a more ardent engagement than those who have seen how the world goes. I nodded and murmured as one does. I thought of Keats's line about letting someone rave, and then, on a sudden impulse of warmth toward him, I leaned across the desk to straighten his tie; I think I may have touched his cheek.

He sat back in revulsion and his face went cold. I was nonplussed, of course. But it grew worse. Beneath his stare, I felt the chill of rejection—truly an ultimate rejection, as though at the Day of Judgment. I had been dismissed in an instant, as quickly as one might flip a light switch. Never with Walter Devereaux Lawton would there be those moments of affectionate recollection years or even decades later, that respect for a beloved teacher that might blossom into friendship. I was being erased. The sense of myself, the store of knowledge, the memories that constitute me, all my loves and hatreds, all were vanishing within me. The dream transposed us to different sides of the desk. *It was his office. He* was the judge. I heedlessly gathered a few things and left. The hallway ahead of me dwindled into darkness, into nothing, and I felt the first cold wind touch me. The walls vanished, and I found myself in the endless expanse of an Antarctic wasteland. Ice, nothing but ice, and I would be crossing it forever.

Of course, it didn't really happen, did it? It's just a dream. If he had erased me, he would never have asked me to recommend him. I know that rationally.

Yes, give him the scholarship, by all means! Who could be more deserving?

ATLANTA, GEORGIA

Judge Harold Lawton
Oct. 6, 1987

After a hurried lunch at his desk—a dry tuna sandwich with potato chips—Judge Lawton went to the corner of his office and sat in his favorite reading chair to review the files of the case scheduled for the next day. An Atlanta TV station had appealed their denial of a request for video of a convicted murderer's confession. The issues involved access to public information on one side and the right to a fair trial on the other. Sensational footage would get the station higher ratings and more advertising revenue, but the accused murderer deserved the scrupulous discipline of a court trial, no matter how guilty he might turn out to be. The media pretended to be full of high purpose, these righteous reporters with the inflections NPR made contagious, but a burr of irritation worked at him the more he read.

"Chief Justice?"

"Damn it!" he muttered. He heaved himself up and went over to his desk and pushed the intercom button. He thought she had better sense. "What is it, Marlana? I'm in the middle of preparation."

"I'm sorry to interrupt you. You have a call from Walter. Shall I tell him that you're busy?"

"No, no. I'm sorry to be so sharp with you. I'll talk to him."

He saw the blinking line and punched the adjacent button and sat down in the desk chair.

"Walter?"

"Yes sir. I'm sorry to bother you."

"Are you out of money already?" he asked in the ironic tone they had developed over the past decade.

"No sir. If I'm careful, I can probably make it for a couple more days."

Walter wasn't out of money. Aside from books, Walter's desire for things like clothes and cars and the other accoutrements of spirited and erotic youth hardly existed.

"So what's her name?" Another joke of theirs.

This time Walter startled him.

"Emily Stevens."

A girl coalesced in his imagination, and from something soft in

Walter's voice he could feel her watching from the bed in Walter's dorm room, quiet and alert, her hands crossed in her lap.

"Nice name. Where's she from?"

"Montgomery, Alabama."

"Okay."

He waited for the complication. It must be substantial to warrant Walter's second call from college. The first had come a year before when, still a freshman, he drank nearly a whole bottle of rum one night and had to be hospitalized with alcohol poisoning. At least it had warned him off alcohol.

He glanced at his watch. He was due back in court in less than an hour.

"Emily's adopted, too," Walter said.

"I see. Does she want me to help her find her birth parents?"

"No sir. She's met them. She's glad she was adopted. No sir, the thing is, I've realized I want my original name back. It wasn't my choice to be Walter Devereaux Lawton."

The request took Judge Lawton aback.

"Well, most of us are given our names, of course. I didn't realize the imposition had been festering all these years."

"Not festering exactly."

"Can you hang on for a second? Actually, let me call you right back."

"Sure."

He set the phone down in the receiver and turned to glance out the window. The gold dome of the Capitol rose a block away, surrounded now by skyscrapers. This was about Lucinda. Good Lord, *Lucinda*. Beautiful, brilliant, aristocratic, erotic, serenely racist Lucinda. Unlike the boy, the Judge had loved her. Like the boy, he had been comforted by Adara in the wake of her passing, and it was almost as though Lucinda had provided her for the both of them. Adara Loum she was now, married to a Nigerian, a French professor at Morehouse. And she was back in his life.

She had learned of his presence in Atlanta from the newspaper. She caught him by surprise one afternoon at work, introducing herself to his staff as an old friend from Macon. They showed her into his office. *I am so sorry* she said when they were alone. She was more refined now, even more beautiful, and when she came close, she put both palms on his chest and said *May I?* and kissed him on the mouth and caught his hand and leaned into him. Her skin, her scent. *You have no idea how I have missed you.* Strangely, he believed her. A few nights later, she came to his house, and from then on resumed her nocturnal visits—never announced, never certain until she came to him. She asked after Walter. She made no demands. He loved her, but he was not besotted with her, not foolish. Adara would not allow it. But, strangely, she caught him up in a different economy of thought, and his work in the courts reflected her influence, especially on issues of race.

Walter had loved Adara too. The judge felt almost selfish not sharing his knowledge of her. But Walter had also *hated* Lucinda—something he had never understood; within the polite forms which Lucinda enforced, the boy had been scrupulously cold to her. Not once had the boy violated her forms, even though she would have welcomed emotional departures, any real response to her, even overt contempt or anger. Anything. The self-control of his hatred tormented her, and the boy knew it. The judge could never condone such cruelty.

The boy's requested rejection of his name was a final rebuke to the woman who made him a Devereaux. It stung to see that a decade had not softened the boy's heart, and it stung to have someone of Walter's brilliance reject the Lawton surname along with her Devereaux. Now he would never pass it on.

He had Marlana dial Walter's number.

"Yes sir, Judge Lawton."

"I apologize for the interruption, Walter. Listen," he said, "it hurts, I admit, to have you reject the name we gave you. You should know that Rosemary's real name was not Peach."

"What do you mean? What was it?" Walter demanded, a new hostility in his voice.

"She made me swear never to tell you."

"Why would she do that?"

"You should ask her if she chooses to contact you."

"*She's alive?*"

"That she is."

"Why hasn't she tried to find me?"

"I don't know." He knew some things, and he would go to his grave with many secrets intact, but he did not know that.

"I guess it doesn't matter," Walter said at last.

"My point is that you could call yourself anything," answered the judge.

"No, I want to change my legal name to Walter Peach. Do I need your permission to do it?"

"It's called a deed poll," the judge said. "You could have done it when you were sixteen."

"Okay, thank you. Goodbye, Judge Lawton."

He hesitated.

ATHENS, GEORGIA

Walter Peach

January 28, 1988

"Turn off the light!" Emily mumbled.

She was facing away from him in the bed, and her hip made a comely curve beneath the covers. Bono and the rest of U2 watched over her from the poster on the wall of her bedroom in Creswell Hall, six floors above the occasional siren out on Baxter Street. The clock on her side table showed a few minutes before 3:00 am.

"Not yet," he said.

She twisted over to look at him, shielding her eyes, her face imprinted by a fold of the sheet.

"What are you *doing*?"

"Writing," he said.

"Go to sleep!" Then she relented, and her voice went childish. "Aw, come here, Elberta." She snuggled against him hot with sleep and slid her thigh over his, her arm coming across him, her hand seeking. He pushed her gently away, and a moment later she was snoring lightly, her lips mashed against his shoulder. He shifted her head back onto her pillow and adjusted the blanket to shade her eyes.

He had been Elberta to her ever since he changed his name to Walter Peach. It excited her—excited her sexually—that she had been the one to convince him to take back his original name, even though his adoptive father was Chief Justice of the Georgia Supreme Court. *My favoritest peach. My freestone man*, she had written in a poem for him. *My sweet Elberta.* George Kilgore himself had introduced Emily to him, the only freshman on the editorial staff of *The Fire and the Rose.* George had given Walter a wink over Emily's shoulder, gently urging her toward him. *Best poet his age I've ever seen.* He might as well have turned down the bedclothes for them. *Eager* did not quite describe young Emily's desire to please. After that meeting, Walter had taken her out for pizza. Her gaze was ardent, her pupils huge, when he read one of his poems to her, and she had led him by the hand to this very room, where she dismissed her roommate with a flick of her head and within minutes demonstrated skills that made him think differently about Alabama.

For a month or so, he was in love with her. She opened something in his heart that had been closed since Adara Watson left to go to Atlanta. She almost reminded him of Rosemary. At ease with her body, Emily would wander from his bedroom into the kitchen of the apartment he shared with Rob, a junior from South Carolina, and Edward, a psychology graduate student from Canada. *Holy shit!* he heard Rob exclaim one morning, and he came out in his shorts to find Emily beside the open refrigerator, naked except for one sock, with her forefinger pressed—*uh-oh*—against her lips in a Betty Boop pose. Rob had dropped his coffee.

Such things always excited her, and she had hurried him back to the bedroom. Many things excited her, but, as he gradually discovered, sentimental things gave her a pleasure that she regarded as spiritual. Especially photographs of herself.

Before Emily woke up, surrounded by her photographs, he had been thinking about pictures and time. He had no photographs of Rosemary, and something about photography itself unnerved him. *Jotting in emulsions/ these notes from the history of light.* A strange, viscous word, *emulsions.* Milky, clotted. Curds of light, metaphysically troubling. He owned a few photographs of himself and Judge Lawton and Mrs. Lawton, all formal, and even one of Adara Watson and her daughter Hermia, but no Rosemary. Emily had been adopted at birth, and she had dozens of pictures of herself all over her desk, her kitchen counter, her bulletin board. Beside him on the bedside table was one of her favorites—a stilled instant when the light fell upon this little girl looking back over her shoulder, worriedly, fearful upon her tricycle: her Easter dress, plastic tassels dangling from the ends of the handlebars, a little furrow in her brow, as though she were being reprimanded. She was under a blossoming dogwood tree; her adoptive mother gazed slightly aside, as if struck by the recognition, just in that moment, that this was not really her child.

Emily at four. Uncanny. All of her life at that moment surging innocently into the mousetrap of the camera—but she herself was gone an instant later, the moment already disappearing. The imprint of light stayed on the film—the trace, the capture—but time was already and always and instantly growing away from it, changing from it in every succeeding second, day after day, year after year. And yet there in the photograph was Emily, as she was then, held forever in an image at hand always. You could pick it up and stare at it and meditate upon who that was, that girl long gone, but also here in the bed, ready at the least hint. Now, or ten years from now, or in her old age, or after her death, the same moment would be there. A kind of immortal childhood, illusory despite its literal truth. Long after her death, curious grandchildren or great-grandchildren would find it and wonder at the worried-face, the arcane and ancient clothes. *Oh, that's your great-great-grandmother when she was little.* On and on until time itself would forget the immortal girl.

Suppose a whole life were made into photographs, moment by moment. Not a movie but an infinite sequence of stills. Emily, Emily, Emily, Emily continuously generated, spilling out of time into space. *This. This. This. This. This. This. Thisthisthisthisthis.* Every instant preserved.

Emily at nineteen, in the sexual humidity of her body, stirred beside him, mumbling something in her sleep, a little drool coming from her open mouth. What was it he wanted? Love? She would love him. But the movement of departure had already begun within him. He did not quite know what it meant, but it was definite and already irreversible. She had a certain beauty, but marred by graceless liberty, both in her gestures and in her poems. She lacked the charm of restraint, that testament to real amplitude and freedom, and her affectation of cuteness increasingly repelled him. Her pouty faux childlikeness—*Oooo my most favoritest peach*—as she looked up from gorging her ardor on him.

He had changed his name at her urging. But he owed his name to Rosemary, not to her. His lost and beloved Rosemary.

No. Not Emily. Emily no more. In a kind of flash on his inward eye, he saw the face of the woman he would marry, a face he did not recognize, the one, his destiny. Strange, the conviction that accompanied it.

Carefully he got up from the bed and replaced the covers. She was snoring lightly. He put on his clothes and gathered up his wallet and then keys, lightly, clasping them quiet, and put on his coat against the January cold. He turned the picture of little Easter Emily face down on the side table to spare her. He turned off the light and stepped out into the long hallway of the dorm.

It would puzzle her when she woke. She would pout about him for a while, but she would soon find someone else, and he would fade from her bed, a faint and then fainter trace in her body's memory. A pattern of words.

SUITORS

Part IV

She found me roots of relish sweet,
 And honey wild, and manna-dew,
And sure in language strange she said—
 'I love thee true'.

She took me to her Elfin grot,
 And there she wept and sighed full sore,
And there I shut her wild wild eyes
 With kisses four.

 John Keats, "La Belle Dame Sans Merci"

Ed Watkins

June 23, 2014

He was just pulling in to park his usual spot for lunch, safe in his own driveway, when his rearview mirror filled with Dexter's red Jeep, which came skidding up in a spray of dust and gravel. It loomed behind him, gunning up to him and threatening his bumper.

"What the hell?" he murmured. He couldn't believe how sour an ordinary Monday had gone. He watched in the side mirror as his brother flung open the door of the Jeep. In two steps Dexter was yanking open the F-150's door and hauling Ed off his seat and backing him against the truck.

"You," he said, poking him hard in the sternum. "Piece," poking again. "Of," poke—and two big tattooed fingers for the last word: "Shit." Dexter stood towering over his little brother, his dirty blond hair braided in dreadlocks, tied together in back with some kind of slinky leather snake. Five or six rings pierced both of his eyebrows.

"You called the goddamned sheriff on me," Dexter said.

"Why would I do that?" Ed said weakly. He could see Betty in the glass door with her hand over her mouth. He tried to get past, but Dexter stepped in front of him with his hands wedged in his back pockets. His black t-shirt had the sleeves torn off, and the ugly tattoos that he called his "boys" looked like they wanted a fresh heart to eat. Ed's own heart was acting up.

"Ellen told me you called and said I got some kid doped up." Dexter poked him hard again, moving around to block his view of Betty.

"Whoa, whoa, whoa," Ed said. "I never said that. Here was this boy didn't know who he was. Calling the sheriff was Bill Sharpe's idea. Hell, I didn't know what to do with him. Nobody said word one about him being doped up."

"What do you mean he didn't know who he was?"

"Big knot on his head."

"Who was he?"

"Well, *see*," Ed said, trying to sound scornful, "*that's* what I had to find out. He was sitting there in the store eating pickled eggs and moon pies and talking about the creek—"

"He talked about the creek?"

"He told Bill Sharpe he was coming up from the creek and his mama was in the kitchen making breakfast and all of a sudden she was gone, and the house was covered with kudzu."

"Coming up from the creek."

"That's what he said."

"So why in the hell," Dexter said, spitting to the side and leaning so close that Ed could see the shreds of tobacco in his teeth, "did you call the sheriff if this little shit was down at the creek? We're talking four million bucks of street value."

"Oh Ed?" Betty called in an unnaturally sweet voice from the side door. "Y'all come on in now and get a turkey sandwich. Dexter, I got us some fresh tomatoes sliced."

Dexter stood back from Ed, glowering, and raised a hand over his shoulder to acknowledge Betty without turning to look at her. Ed met Betty's eyes and shook his head before he looked back up at Dexter.

"They can't pin it on you," he said. "Nobody saw you down there."

"What if that boy saw me?"

"You were down there this morning? Seriously?" Ed almost shouted. *"God damn it!"*

"Checking on pipes, doing some weeding," Dexter said. "What I figure is Peach got scared."

"Peach?"

"Listen," Dexter said, applying his forefinger to Ed's sternum, "if it was just me, it'd be one thing, but I got people I made a deal with. If I get put away, I'm just saying, they'll come after you."

"*Me!* What people?"

Just then, Dexter's head lifted like a dog's, wary, and Ed heard a car slowing on the road. A second later, a Gallatin County Sheriff Ford Bronco eased up the driveway past the mimosas and the little metal storage shed he'd bought for his riding mower.

Deputy Matt Casper was driving, and he pointed at Dexter and spoke to Red Scott, who rode shotgun. Casper parked the Bronco to block Dexter's Jeep, close to Betty's flower bed. She'd spent half of June fixing it the way she wanted it, with her purple irises and day lilies and the big rocks she'd made Ed heave from one spot to another while she stood on the porch like General Patton. Every day she went out to Walmart and brought home flowers and bags of mulch, cedar chips, whatever the hell else her garden shows said to buy. And now, after several months of irritating Ed, her flowerbed curved up neatly from the driveway, flanking the brick walk to the front steps.

Matt Casper dropped his foot in the mulch before he saw where he was stepping. He winced and tipped his hat at Betty, who guarded the open door with her arms crossed. Red Scott stepped out the opposite door, and the two officers started up the driveway.

"Everything all right?" she called.

"Just came out to speak to Ed," Casper called back.

"Y'all want some ice tea or something?" she asked.

They all shook their heads, and Ed frowned at Betty to get her away from the door. Her mouth tightened at him, but she turned, and he heard her calling Phoebe.

"So Ed," Casper said, leaning back against the hood of the Bronco. "Hudson found out who that boy was."

"Is that right? Somebody in town know him?"

"Lady at the library. She called his mama and she came and got him. He didn't recognize her."

Nobody spoke at first.

"Who's his mama?" Ed finally asked.

"Teresa Peach. Husband runs the newspaper."

Dexter's eyebrows went up and he scratched the back of his neck.

"Turns out that piece of land the boy was on belongs to Peach," said Red. Matt had taken his hat off and he was turning it by the brim while he looked at Dexter.

"What piece of land would this be?" Dexter said.

Red grinned and looked at the ground, shaking his head.

"Up here next to Jimmy Proctor," said Matt. "The old folks call it Missy's Garden. You drive by, looks like ain't nobody been on it since the Civil War. Kudzu everywhere. But do you know there was quite a crop of marijuana growing down by the creek? It took me and Red and several other boys half the morning to chop it down. How many plants was it?"

"I lost count," said Red, looking straight at Dexter. "Three thousand? Four thousand?"

Dexter reddened as the two deputies stared at him. Ed saw a flinch in the crow's feet around his eyes.

"So you're saying," Dexter said, "Mr. *Gallatin Tribune* was growing bud on his property. Ain't that some shit."

"*Somebody* was growing it," Matt said mildly. "I ain't saying—we don't know if it was Peach."

"Why don't you ask him? How come you're over here talking to me?"

"He's out of town, turns out," said Red. "Besides, we're here to see Ed, not you."

"Could be Mexicans," said Dexter. "Cartels. They're all over the place, according to Mr. *Gallatin Tribune*."

"Could be, I guess," said Matt. "Could just be some local boys." He and Red both turned when they heard the radio crackle in their car. Red stuck his head inside the Bronco. "Well, listen, Ed," Matt said, striking his hat against his thigh. "Just wanted to let you know about that boy. Dr. Fletcher says his name's Buford Peach. It's a strange business."

"Good luck finding out who planted that doobie," said Dexter, faking a grin. "Hey, if y'all was to want to cut some out, I might be in the market."

"Is that right?" said Matt blandly. He was standing in the open door of the dusty Bronco with his boot crushing one of Betty's peonies.

Red made a mouth. "I expect we'll get lucky. We got the tire tracks on Jimmy Proctor's field road." Ed instinctively glanced at Dexter's Jeep. "We got boot prints. Some ATV tracks back in the woods. Fresh fingerprints on that PVC pipe he was using to irrigate."

When they left, Ed and Dexter waved and then stood looking after them.

"You leave any fingerprints down there?" Ed asked at last.

"Oh hell yeah," Dexter said stonily. There was a long silence. The boys on Dexter's shoulders were grim. "Peach must of got scared and tipped them off," he said. "Why else would his boy scout be out there this morning? We had a sweet deal, me and him."

"What do you mean, a deal?" Ed asked. A longer silence.

"We understood each other," Dexter said.

"What was the deal?"

"I leave the girl alone, he lets me use the land."

"What girl?"

"The teacher. Nora O'Hearn."

"The one who stayed with Miss Emma?"

"Miss Emma never did like me."

"Whose idea was this deal?"

"This foreign dandy-man. English or something." Dexter imitated his accent. "'Walter Peach has a property on Hopewell Road that would be suitable for an experiment in agriculture.' Just like that. He said it was five acres with a creek going through it. I said is that right. He told me I ought to talk to Peach about it, but I didn't have any leverage until I saw Peach trying to hit on the girl."

"The schoolteacher?"

"His niece. You believe that? I mean, I wanted this girl bad. But I thought about her and how much work she would be, not that I couldn't have got her, and I told Peach I would give her up for the use of his land. We shook hands on it."

"You told him what you were going to do? You shook hands?"

"Not exactly, but we understood each other."

Ed thought about it. "So he knows you're the one growing marijuana?"

"Well, yeah."

"Look, no offense, brother, but you call that a deal? All he has to do is say he didn't know about it."

"You don't understand Uncle Walter and Niece Nora. I'm telling you, the man would sell his soul to break into that honeytree—but now he seen the weed down there. Now he's scared and skipped town, but not before he sent that boy out to get me caught."

Ed thought about the boy who had sat in his store.

"Listen, Dexter, that boy don't even know what his name is."

"Then what the hell," Dexter exploded, poking him again in the sternum, "was he doing out there?"

Ed glanced toward the house and saw Betty appear at the door with Phoebe beside her, both of them big-eyed.

"How am I supposed to know?" he said.

"That little dipshit knows something," his brother said. Dexter rolled his head to stretch his neck and started toward his Jeep. He stopped and looked back at Ed. "And I tell you what, Brother Ed, you help me pin this on Peach or my ass is fried."

"I don't even know him."

"You want me to tell those people my brother tipped off the sheriff?"

"I swear to God, I—"

Dexter held up a hand to cut him off.

"They're big into family. You hear what I'm saying?" He looked at Ed's house and waved to Betty and Phoebe, whose fingers barely curled in reply, then leaped into his Jeep like Errol Flynn would have done it.

Betty always liked Errol Flynn.

Teresa Peach

June 23, 2014

On the front porch of Stonewall Hill, Teresa held her cell phone to her head and listened as it rang on the other end...one...two...three...four. Halfway through the fifth ring it went into voicemail and there it was, the cool, ironic voice: *You have reached the absence of Walter Peach. Please leave a message in it. The rest is silence.*

"Shit!" She jabbed End, ready to hurl the phone away.

Breathe. She inhaled slowly *Lord Jesus Christ, son of God,* and exhaled *have mercy on me, a sinner.* Above the trees along Lee Street, she could read the clock in the cupola of the courthouse: almost two o'clock. *Lord Jesus Christ, son of God, have mercy on me, a sinner.* The irresponsible bastard hadn't just abandoned her and his children, he hadn't done this week's paper, which was supposed to go to the printer that night and come out on Thursday, and Braxton Forrest had just called her.

She had a growing conviction about where he was and why he was there. He had been edging toward it ever since Nora left. She knew him too well. She had seen too much of his self-squandering, the way he would blame anything else for his chronic unhappiness—herself, teaching, the children, the newspaper, the weather, the world, anything at all. For years, almost since their wedding night, she was visited by the feeling that he might just do what he had obviously just done—get in the car and drive away. He said her rules for the children were pharisaical, which meant he wanted moral leeway for himself, and he could get the children on his side by being easy and friendly with them. He thought she still blamed him for Lydia Downs. He was right. She had never forgiven him, not fully. But their marriage survived the death of their son, and she had forgiven him as much as she could with Belen's help, Belen who had seen a deep goodness in Walter, who had said that Our Lady would take up his lost cause. Walter had never taken to the idea, even from Belen, that he could be forgiven. Back when he was Walter Devereaux Lawton, Lucinda had insisted on his baptism, but he said it "didn't work," and sometimes he told Teresa she was just like Lucinda, all about form and appearance. After their son's death, he had gone to confession, but he told Teresa that didn't work, either, as though the sacrament were some kind of home remedy he had been forced to try.

Now he wanted to avoid her altogether, especially now that he was pursuing another pretty girl who gave him an importance no wife with children and real responsibilities could possibly bestow. The grotesque triteness of it. Once she had been all he needed. The man she married was a young, exciting, melancholy, edgy poet who loved the textures of the real world the same way she did. She had grown up on a farm outside Demopolis, Alabama, tending chickens and growing flowers and raising calves to show in the county fair, and yet she could move easily in sophisticated intellectual circles. She had loved her father, who died of a heart attack at about Walter's age, days before her high school graduation—a plain, good, loving man driven into overextending himself by her mother, who was ambitious and discontent, always defensive with her Birmingham family about marrying a farmer. Bridget made friends more easily, but Teresa was the prize. She made the best grades in her school, year after year, more to appease her mother than for herself.

She had broken free to see who she was after her junior year in high school in a two-month summer program for gifted students. In Tuscaloosa, she had fallen in love with James Barron—tall, brilliant boy from Mobile—who made the world so alive and full of wonder that she gave him her virginity one hot July night in a pine grove on the border of the Alabama campus. She loved him without reserve. They left the program with tearful goodbyes, and then in the weeks that followed he never answered her unguarded letters. He abandoned her as though she had never existed. His sudden and unexplained rejection made her think she bore some deep flaw, something ugly and unlovable, that sent her into years of intemperate self-contempt. It still hurt to think of it. Afterward, she had never been willing to risk herself wholly again.

But he had awakened her mind. The next year she won a National Merit Scholarship to Auburn. In her senior year there, forsaking the boyfriend of the season—or maybe of the week—she converted to Catholicism under the influence of Annie Lee, the one friend who had not given up on her. Those late, tearful nights of miserable confession, which opened the way at last to her conversion, changed everything about her life. The easy friends of her first college years, the boyfriends, the sex, all dropped away almost unnoticed. She read St. Teresa of Avila, St. Therese of Lisieux, Flannery O'Connor, St. Thomas Aquinas, St. Augustine—everything she could. She took up contemplative practices, an hour or more of silence a day. After she graduated, she had a full ride at Duquesne in existential phenomenology. During the years of her course work, she turned down all dates, spending two hours a day in silent prayer, distinguishing herself in her classes, praying the Jesus prayer every waking minute.

She was seriously planning to spend the summer with the Nashville Dominicans until Walter gave a poetry reading at Duquesne. He was already rising in national reputation. *The Small Gnats Mourn* had been nominated for various prizes, and she remembered with a rush of warmth the way he read and the way his face changed when he saw her in the crowd—as though he recognized her. He sought her out afterward. She had been immensely flattered when he asked her to join him for a late dinner. They talked for hours about Heidegger and Jean-Luc Marion, phenomenology and poetry. *What are poets for in a destitute time?* Rilke, Hölderlin. Late that night, that very first night, he told her the story of his abandonment, the central, searing moment of childhood loss. Already then they were in love. He said he loved the intelligence in her eyes, her reality, her warmth, her soul, her beauty. What moved her most was what he said first: *I recognize you.* He had seen her in a glimpse of inward vision when he was still twenty in a Georgia dorm.

Most girls she knew would have taken him straight to bed, but she had felt such a burning that she took him to the chapel, moved by the conviction that this unique man should be under the protection of the Mother of God. *You believe in that stuff?* he asked. He said he was allergic to it—he suspected his wicked stepmother had secretly been an ultra-something.

Ultramontanist?

Maybe that's it. Hell, I don't know. I know she didn't like shaking hands with people in church.

The sign of peace?

I guess.

He had not been inside a church since his teens. But he did not mock her when she knelt and prayed for Rosemary.

He was the best poet of his generation before Lydia Downs and the death of their son. She still could not admit how much she had then hated him. Her faith—and Belen—had barely sustained her through the questions of justice and ravaging self-doubt. And now he was doing it again? The shallowness of it. And he was not a rising poet now, but a small-town journalist whose little awards she had to pretend to admire. And all he had seen of the faith that had kept her from killing him was judgmental moralism. *You're God's own private ferret*, he once said with a sneer when she chided his heavy drinking.

What was ironic, what hurt the most, was that the poet she'd married was coming back—but not to her. To *Nora*, niece Nora, painless Nora. Painless? More than painless. An opiate, a pure sunny rush of adulation.

She stared unseeing across the property. She had left him only once, the summer her mother died. Six years after the tragedy. Walter had come in drunk and randy one night several months earlier, and she was pregnant. June of 2003. Pregnant and loathing everything about it when she got the call that her mother was dying.

From the start her mother had scorned her for marrying him, all those years ago. She would never forget the contemptuous intonation her mother gave to the word *poet* when Teresa announced who her fiancé was. And then, all those years later, sitting there pregnant beside her mother's bed in the University of Alabama Hospital in Birmingham, looking down into the wasted features, the hand beckoning her close.

Davis Harkins asked you to marry him when you were in college, she whispered. *Now he's the richest man in Alabama. But you had to marry that drunk.*

He's more than a drunk, she said. You're dying, Mother. You should make your peace with God instead of criticizing me.

Not that she was praying herself that summer.

You could have been somebody. You were pretty and smart. But you married that drunk and he ran over your baby. Probably sleeping around when he did it. That's what poets do. Drink and sleep around and pretend they're important. If you at least had money, you could do for yourself.

She did her duty and sat there listening to the same thing, day after day, until her mother's last breath. She was the executor, so she stayed on to close up the farmhouse—all her responsibility, since Bridget was too busy with her children Duane and Nora. Teresa had let it go, but she wanted her sister to at least lend her Nora, who was eleven or twelve at the time, who could have helped. Meanwhile Rose was just eight years old, by herself with Walter in Waycross, and her poet husband was probably getting drunk every night once their daughter was in bed.

Her mother had a little money, not much, that she and Bridget inherited equally, and they also split the proceeds for the furniture from an estate sale company out of Tuscaloosa. Neither of them wanted a single thing their mother owned. Not a lamp, not a single silver spoon. But Teresa took away a further bitterness. Cleaning out her mother's desk, she found a small bundle of letters, all opened, paper-clipped together. With a dark heave of her heart, she saw the name *James Barron* on the return address. James had written her after all. She pulled out the first one and looked at it blankly. *Dearest Teresa,* and she shoved it back down unread. The meanness of her mother stunned her a decade later. Not only had she hidden the letters when they came, but she had then *kept* them so one day Teresa would find them and know what she had done.

The last thing she wanted to do was call the O'Hearns. *That's what poets do. Drink and sleep around.* But she punched in the number and her sister answered after the second ring.

"Teresa," Bridget said, "I swear to God I had no idea."

She could picture her sister's posture—high-shouldered and defensive, head thrust forward on her neck, her free hand at chest level, palm upward.

"No idea about what?" Teresa said.

"That you didn't know where he was. He told me he was working on a story. When he got here, he acted upset that you hadn't called about letting him stay here. I just put him in Duane's old room."

"Well, that's Walter, not you," she said. No use driving her further into evasions and excuses. "Did he say what he was working on?"

"He did, but ..." Bridget said vaguely. "You know I don't understand the stuff Walter does. Oh, shoot, something about—maybe Mexico? He's been getting Nora to help him."

She breathed in slowly through her nose. *Lord Jesus Christ, son of God, have mercy on me, a sinner.*

"How is Nora? What happened to her in March?"

"She told me some man in town was bothering her."

"Well, I wish you'd called to let me know." Immediately, she regretted the note of accusation. "I kept wondering if I'd offended her."

"She didn't tell *me* anything for a month." Bridget's voice was hesitant and concerned, not defensive. "But she said she told Walter before she left."

Teresa didn't answer at first. *Walter.* What else had they hidden? *Lord Jesus Christ, son of God, have mercy on me, a sinner.* She had found out about Nora's departure one night at supper back in March. For three dinners straight Buford complained about a substitute. On Wednesday at suppertime—it was St. Joseph's Day—Buford said that Miss Nora was gone, that the principal himself had come in to tell them. It was obvious that Walter already knew it.

"*Teresa?*" Bridget said. "Are you there?"

Her head jerked. "I'm here."

"Did he not tell you?"

"I guess he forgot."

"You know how men are," Bridget said. "Terry forgets to tell me about invitations to parties and then gets mad if I'm not ready when it's time to go."

She did not welcome the conciliatory comparison to Terry O'Hearn: Fox News on the TV, pot-belly sprinkled with cracker crumbs, beer in hand, big forearms and elbows driving down into the armrests of his recliner as he heaved himself forward and struggled vainly to get up, freckled face aflame with simulated welcome.

"Bridget, I can't get Walter to answer his cell phone. Is he there? Can

I talk to him?"

"I think so."

She heard her sister calling him. Moments passed. Then murmurs, footsteps.

"Hello? Aunt Teresa?"

It took her a second to speak.

"Yes," she said. "How are you, Nora?" Too clipped, too formal. *Lord Jesus Christ, son of God, have mercy on me, a sinner.*

"I know you're upset with me," Nora said, and her voice was as soft as magnolia petals.

Teresa glanced over her shoulder at the closed front door of the house and went down a step. Her heart was hammering as though *she* were at fault.

"Well, I *am* upset," she said, trying to sound as though she were mocking herself for it. "You left town without saying goodbye, and now it's been three months, and I haven't heard a word from you."

"I should have called you, but I was so scared I just wanted to hide, Aunt Teresa. I almost went to stay with Daddy's parents in Oregon."

"Scared of what?"

"I just—" Nora started to say and then faltered. "It's just so complicated."

"Is Walter there now?" she asked.

"Yes ma'am, he's right here."

Ma'am to her, *Walter* to him. She pictured the girl's look as she handed him the phone.

"Teresa," Walter said.

"Walter," she said back. She heard him excuse himself to Bridget and Nora. After a moment, a door closed and she could hear outdoor noises—a kind of windiness, a dog's desultory barking, a car going by, as if on a soundtrack.

"Has anybody come by the house?" he said.

She cocked her head, as if listening for the sense of what he was saying. He was worried that somebody might come by the house—the photographs at Christmas she had almost forgotten—and yet had fled to Nora O'Hearn, leaving her and his children unprotected? Good God. She changed hands with the phone.

"If you're worried about that, Walter, why aren't you here? I'm calling to tell you they found Buford today out at Missy's Garden. Rose took him early this morning. She said he wouldn't tell her why. Something happened to him out there."

"Oh my God," he said. His voice was full of dread. "You said somebody *found* him. Who found him?"

"A man named Bill Sharpe. Buford didn't know who he was. He hit his head on something. Bill Sharpe took him to the store out there. They called the sheriff to come get him because nobody recognized him."

"Slow down. What do you mean *found* him?"

She paused before she answered, staring down across the lawn. Two squirrels burst into view, chasing each other up the trunk of a pecan tree. She raised her eyes to the courthouse clock when she heard it strike two.

"Your son Buford was standing in the middle of the kudzu. Are you listening? He had hit his head on something. He couldn't remember his name. He kept asking for his mama. He says he was on the way up from the creek for breakfast and everything changed."

"I told him that story. I don't know what he's doing, Teresa, but I told him that the other day. Listen, did the sheriff go on the property?"

"The sheriff?" Just then the door opened behind her, and she went down another step. "Just a second," she said into the phone. Rose led Buford out. The boy gazed over the lawn and then glanced at her with the kind of recognition he would give a hostess but not his mother. Rose caught her eye and shook her head as she shepherded him back into the house.

"Walter?" she said into the phone, shaken afresh by the boy's behavior. "Nobody's pretending, do you understand? *I'm* certainly not pretending. If you don't come home—"

"I'm almost done up here."

"Almost done. Really? Well, I'm almost done down here."

The Boy

Now it was night. He lay on the bed listening. A cat howled in some kind of frenzy somewhere in the distance. A man's voice rose somewhere outside, calling, not angry, and some other man answered him. The tones came through, ask and answer, a little funny. He didn't know what they were talking about. They had been there a while after he and Mrs. Peach got back from the doctor. Dr. Fletcher said Buford just needed rest. They kept calling him Buford, but it didn't mean anything to him.

Take him upstairs. I'll come up in a few minutes Mrs. Peach told the redheaded girl.

Rose.

Roses are red, violets are blue. Rose is red-headed and so are

Not the same red as a flower. Redheaded Rose said this room was Mr. Forrest's. An old room with heavy, dark furniture.

I'm just right over here, if you get scared.

He wasn't scared. What would he be scared of? Around the edge of the ceiling were hunters carved into the wood, large men on horses chasing hounds and foxes. He knew other things, but not who he was. He knew what horses and hounds and foxes were. He knew about supervolcanoes and Yellowstone. He was like a circle without a center. A circle had to have a center to be a circle. He knew that too. All the points on the circumference of the circle were equidistant from the center. Except in him the center was missing. That one point was missing. Everything was equidistant from whatever wasn't there.

Still, it was peaceful if he just let it be and didn't get upset about it. Here he was, listening, breathing. Whoever he was. He was okay, just lying here.

He remembered a voice. A huge voice that filled up all the space there was or could ever be, a presence that was here now, always here, and spoke his real name.

"So who am I?" he asked aloud.

After a few seconds he heard the other door open and the redheaded girl stood in the doorway, wearing an old shirt with paint splattered on it.

"Did you call me?"

"No."

"I heard you say something."

"I just asked who I am."

"You're Buford Peach. Buford Augustine Peach."

"I don't feel that name."

The girl stared at him and then turned. She saw something out the window. When Rose looked back at him, she said, "There's somebody down there in the driveway."

He listened as she left. He heard the screen door slam. He heard her scream "I know who you are!"

But he didn't know who he was.

Dexter Watkins

Peach wasn't home. Didn't expect him to be home, didn't know exactly what he'd gone to find. He couldn't put it in words, get it up in his head, he didn't think in words all the time. People didn't understand that about him, how he just went with instinct, like a mountain lion or a god. Ed, Ellen, Emily, they didn't understand him.

Maybe he'd wanted to find the boy outside by himself. Put a scare in him. Show him his knife. Hold up the big blade right in front of his face, test his thumb on it. Put a good scare in him, tell him to keep his mouth shut.

Hell, too late for that.

He glanced in the rearview to see if the sister had followed him down the driveway. Came running out the back door at him, made him have to drive off. Peach's daughter. Redheaded piece of work. Hot-tempered, the way she'd come at his Jeep. Pale skin, hot eyes, a lot of sweet jiggle in that t-shirt. *I know who you are!* Wouldn't mind it if she'd followed him, but she hadn't. Probably inside calling the police.

He waited at the end of the gravel drive beside the big mailbox, glancing both ways on Johnson's Mill Road for a car. *Knew who he was.* Felt like that's what he wanted, for her to know him. She'd remember him. Be even better if somebody else saw him coming out of Peach's driveway. Get people thinking about him and Peach.

He reached under the dashboard and pulled out a joint and lit it with a flick of his lighter. Huge waste of weed that morning. The Gomez brothers were pissed, gave him shit, but got over it. Got over it too quick to suit him.

That's your problem, hombre.

Happens all the time, you don't know how to hide your crop. We ain't counting on one hillbilly, hermano. You got to worry about El Mocasín.

Dexter hated the way he said *hillbilly.* The younger one, Enrique. Sarcastic. Greasy little mustache. He wasn't worried about them anyway. It was the other one who scared the living shit out of him, just like they said. The Moccasin. The one who found him to start with. Before Peach even made the deal.

That smell that came off him. A long shudder went up his spine, and he shook himself to make it stop.

And Peach put that kid out there like a billboard.

He held his breath and then blew a long, perfect plume for his boys. The sweet buzz came.

So maybe show his knife to that redheaded girl. Get her by herself like he did the schoolteacher. Back her up against a wall, arms full of books. Say something to her to show he knew her, how he's been thinking about her t-shirt. Get her lip trembling, get her eyes to water, get her breathing, her neck and cheeks red. Put his hand on her, just a little. Get her scared and then put his hand on her. Just barely touch her. Sweet, her earlobe or the soft of her arm. Like he's marking her, like he already owns her. *Mine.* Her fingers will keep going back to where he touched her. She'll remember how she was trembling, the way her knees gave when he touched her. How dangerous he was. The little give and melt deep up inside her like fate. The exact feel of wanting him in there.

Fun to do that to this one, Peach's daughter. Like he did it to Nora O'Hearn.

Nora O'Hearn. The feel of her earlobe in his fingers, the way her eyes opened at him as she shied away, angry, but also wondering. Worried. Worried about what? About who he was, what they told her, what he'd done. What he'd just said to her.

Wondering about what it would be like with him.

The image of her shivered through him. Holy shit. He'd never be right until he had her. His insides turned over just thinking about her. He told Ed he'd given her up, the deal with Peach put her out of his hands, but you couldn't tell Ed the truth or it would always come back to bite you. Shouldn't have mentioned her.

He took another hit of the joint and held it, a really fine buzz starting to work, then let out the breath and pinched the fire out the window and crimped the end of the joint and tucked it back into its place under the dash. He wondered if Peach knew he had called her, if that was why he put his boy out there. Why Bill Sharpe found him. Sharpe had been taking her out before she left.

Some other deal Peach was working? Use Sharpe to get Dexter arrested?

Fury came surging up into his buzz.

Not now. Let it pass. Blow it away. Feather of Quetzalcoatl. Later. He'd be up in that honeycomb when the time was right.

He pulled out into the road, turned left and slowed at the yield sign. Still nobody coming. He followed Lee Street up the hill, and just as he got to the courthouse square, he saw blue lights flashing in his mirror. He sat there like a good, concerned citizen. A block behind him, a police car came out, swung onto Lee Street beside the bank, and turned the other way, just booking it down the hill toward where he'd just been.

Bill Sharpe

June 23, 2014

Rinsing the toothpaste from his mouth with a cupped palmful of water, Bill spat it out, rinsed again, and stooped to look in the mirror. The long face settling into what expression? Droll bitterness? Not exactly. He rolled his shoulders, did a head fake. Thirty-four years old. He had lived through the Jesus year, as his Atlanta friends called it. He guessed he looked okay, not that it mattered. Most of his old teammates from the Blue Devils championship team of 1998 were fat and bald, but Sharpe kept in shape. Weekends spent riding his big Cannondale road bike all over the county, doing some weights at the school gym. Still, a few strands of gray showed in his sideburns, as Chick Lee had announced with the news of his birthday to the whole Lee Ford showroom that morning. "But you know what?" Chick had said, gripping Sharpe's arm above the elbow. "Gray gives you gravitas, man. And a good car salesman needs a little gravitas."

Gravitas. Like that boy this morning calling him *sir.* Walter Peach's son, according to Hudson Bennett. Apparently the conk on his head had knocked the memory out of him. Maybe Dexter Watkins had caught him down at the creek and hit him in a rage over what the boy could find. Hudson said there was a huge crop of marijuana growing down there on Peach's property. Didn't sound like Dexter to hit a boy, sorry as he was, but maybe the boy had scared him. Or maybe the boy had fallen on his own and hit his head. Maybe he had run into a tree limb.

As he came out into the upstairs hallway, he could hear Martin saying his prayers in his room. The little guy would turn thirty in two weeks.

"I kingdom come, I will be done," his brother announced, "on earth as it is in heaven. Give us our trespasses."

"Forgive us our trespasses," his mother said quietly. Now in her late sixties, she still went in there every night to pray with him.

"That's what I said," Martin insisted. Stubborn. He could be standing there barefoot and swear he had his shoes on. He could say "I didn't eat that cake" when there was a big chunk missing and chocolate all over his face and hands. The mere, obvious truth, exposed and evident, might cow most liars, but not Martin. He saw words as good and useful tools for altering any objective circumstance that put him in a bad light. Politicians should study Martin. He could make facts ashamed of themselves.

At prayer time, Martin would take off the headset of his iPad and sit cross-legged on his bed in a t-shirt, thick-hipped and a little overweight. He would pray for Jerry, his boss at the senior center, where Martin called out bingo numbers and helped distribute newspapers to the old folks before commandeering their old folks' great room TV every afternoon for his favorite shows. At night, instead of praying for the sick and dying at Hilltop, he prayed for Chuck Norris or Disney characters like Zach and Cody and Good Luck Charlie. The Atlanta Braves, Selena Gomez.

"And I want to pray for Bill to marry Takesha," Sharpe heard him say, "and I can be best man."

Takesha? Who was Takesha?

"And she can bring Moose Tracks."

Sharpe remembered her now. The name plate glinting on the breast of the immense black girl with the huge smile in the frozen yogurt shop off I-75. *Takesha.* She always added Martin's favorite sprinkles without asking or charging.

Sharpe went down the hall and stepped into his bed room and there it was, without warning, the black wing, the memory that would not heal. He'd been in Atlanta working for Spartan Dog, the startup he launched with his friends from Georgia Tech. He was in his apartment on Ponce de Leon, packing his belongings to come home for the wedding: the feel of the mismatched socks in his hand when his cell phone rang. Slight, wispy-bearded, brilliant Dan Brinker glancing up at him from his desk across the room as Sharpe answered and then stood there silent, turned to stone, listening to his father.

Son, I hate to be the one to tell you.

Oh God. Is it Mama?

No, son. It's Deirdre. It's Deirdre. She—

The broken sob, the phone going dead.

Sharpe sat down on the bed as the story replayed itself: Deirdre and her mother driving back northbound on the interstate from Macon toward Gallatin after having some alterations done to the wedding dress, Mrs. Harper at the wheel. They must have been talking and laughing, their eyes half on the road when a square of sheet metal blew loose from a truck going the other direction—a light sheet of metal flying across the median. They might have noticed a peripheral glare or little flicker as it caught the wind and sailed up and up at seventy miles an hour. And who but God could have expected that it would turn as it did, deflected sharply downward by the stiff wall of air a passing tractor-trailer left in its wake?

The whirling metal dove through the windshield. He had pictured it a thousand times—Mrs. Harper screaming at the burst of glass, but Deirdre not moving, staring straight ahead with a strange look fixed on her face. Her head rested on the metal sheet like some kind of illusionist's trick, the corner of the square embedded in the back of her seat. When

Mrs. Harper hit the brakes, Deirdre's head tilted forward, rolled loose, bounced off the dashboard, onto the seat, into her lap, face upward, the eyes still open, still seeing.

A long shudder went through him.

He stood up and went to the window and stared out blindly over the yard. June 8, 2003, a week before the wedding. Already eleven years ago. Martin had wept inconsolably over Deirdre, who had always been kind and funny with him. She'd called him Moose, her own private nickname. *Mooth?* he'd say with feigned outrage. Moose Tracks yogurt reminded him of Deirdre. For years afterward, he had kept talking about the tux he had been about to wear when she was going to be his sister and he was going to be the Best Man. Bill Sharpe's Best Man Ever.

From June to December of that year, Sharpe had sat in this room, unaltered since high school, the same old basketball schedules and trophies and vintage movie posters. *Rio Bravo, Star Wars, Some Like It Hot.* His father, still several years away from the heart attack that would kill him, treated him kindly, but by October his patience with Sharpe's inaction had begun to wear thin, especially when days would go by with work to be done and Sharpe would not even get out of bed. Those six months had ruined the easy charm he had once had as the scholarship basketball player, the top student, the rising entrepreneur. His mother had fed him and tended him. She had gotten their pastor, Rev. Carl Hill—squarish, earnest, gregarious—to come to see him three or four times. *Bill,* he would say, *sometimes things just happen. An accident is just an accident. God didn't kill Deirdre. You can't ask why, because there's no answer. It doesn't mean anything about you. It's just what the Lord has given you to suffer.* On and on. Sharpe hadn't argued with him, but his whole soul had rebelled then and still squirmed at the idea that something so momentous, precise as a guillotine, could be a mere accident. How could the omniscient God have given it to him to suffer if He hadn't allowed it? And to allow it, He had to foresee it and therefore to intend it since He let it happen, in which case it had to *mean* something as part of His intention. What he felt most intensely was precisely the intention of it.

He heard a voice and walked out into the hallway again. His mother's light was still on. She liked to read the paper at night before going to sleep.

"Mama, did you call me?"

"No, it must be Martin talking to himself."

Martin's lights were off, but he was probably watching a show on his iPad and talking to the screen. Sharpe went back to the window in his room. The moon was a tiny waning sliver above the pecan trees. He still didn't feel like undressing for bed. His friends in Atlanta had kept telling him to shake off the religious brooding—as though considering Deirdre's death pure chance in a meaningless universe would somehow relieve him of the misery. No, he believed in God more than he ever had as a Sunday-school Methodist, but there was an abyss between God and his belief. He couldn't think of God without the dark intimacy of that pain of loss, which took him into the mystery of Providence. He couldn't pray to the goodness of God without thinking he had been singled out and known.

But it was this new failure that made him bitter. If he was honest with himself, he'd never felt about Deirdre what he felt for Nora. Now, with such a grief behind him, his emotions had a maturity that she respected, and at twenty-three, Nora had a poise and completeness, but more than that, a kind of brimming over that moved him deeply.

At least he had gravitas. Chick Lee said so.

When he first met her, back in the winter, he hadn't had any gravitas to speak of. He had seen her at a few football games in the fall, once or twice at basketball games, but this time she had been coming out of her regular Saturday breakfast at the Left Bank with some of the other teachers, and he had just swerved into a parking spot right in front of them and slammed on the brakes. They started back like a flock of pigeons.

Bill Sharpe, you scared me to death, tearing in here like that!

I'm sorry, Miss Emma. I just remembered I was supposed to pick up something for Mama, he said, lying as easily as Martin did. He had stared at the new girl. Great God, who was this?

What? Miss Emma said.

Ma'am?

What did you forget?

He stood there a moment looking at Nora. *I forgot again,* he said. Miss Emma sighed.

Well, let me introduce you. This is Nora O'Hearn. She's teaching fifth grade and living out at my place.

Pleased to meet you, he said, and Nora O'Hearn smiled at him with a little sideways hitch of her body as she held out her hand. It felt like kingdom come.

You couldn't do better than this one, Ginger Robertson whispered to him. *Listen,* she said out loud, *y'all want to ride a fifty-mile loop with several of us this weekend?*

A day or two after first meeting her in town, there was a warm spell, and he went fishing on the Ikahalpi, hitting some of the less accessible pools, working his way upstream. When he stopped to eat his lunch, he climbed up to a granite outcrop fifty feet or so above the river. Looking out, he saw the rapids downstream calming into a long bend, dark and smooth where it disappeared into the National Forest. There wasn't a house in sight for miles, and there never would be. Behind the outcrop, the land was flat for a good hundred feet all around before dropping off down the slope into mixed hardwoods and pines. It was plenty big enough for the log house that sprang into his mind, its broad porches and picture windows.

He went home, looked up the property, and called the owner, an old man in Macon named Roscoe Shillingsworth who had bought it cheap not a few years earlier and who could hardly contain his delight that someone finally wanted it. The old man named his price, which he must have considered exorbitant.

I reckon you have to talk to the bank, he said.

No sir. I can just write you a check.

That gave the old man pause.

You don't sound old enough to be rich. You don't sell drugs, do you?

No sir. When I got out of college, I started a company with some friends of mine.

What's it called?

Spartan Dog. We do internet security.

I don't mess with that stuff.

He had closed on the property within a month as he began his campaign to win Nora. He sent flowers to her out at Miss Emma's house, and the messages in the envelope included his caricatures of people in town—the mayor blithely imagining the town's adulation, Coach Lincoln throwing down his headset, Miss Emma as queen pigeon surrounded by other birds. He thought his talent for drawing had died with Deirdre, but here it was.

On their first date, they had spent the whole day in Atlanta: lunch at a place he knew on Highland Street; a foreign film whose name he couldn't remember—a Palestinian man and an Israeli girl in love—at an art cinema near Piedmont Park; a long walk through downtown.

So where'd you learn to draw like that? She said during a pause at a traffic light, standing back from him as though to see him better. *Your pictures are so funny they're a little wicked.*

She had never mentioned them before. He had supposed she didn't like them and he had stopped including them with the flowers.

I picked it up in high school. I did them for the school paper, and then at Tech I edited an underground magazine called Junebug.

Why was it underground?

What we did was a little wicked.

I had to hide the one of Miss Emma from her. It would have hurt her feelings!

But it was just too funny.

By Five Points, they were holding hands. He took her to dinner at a sushi restaurant, and they sat as close to the court as he could afford at a Hawks game against the Bulls that night, like a Spike Lee or Jack Nicholson. He called her daily after that. He wanted to take her up to the place he had bought. He wanted to propose on the spot if she liked it.

That would have been March 16, a Sunday afternoon.

But that Saturday, the day before, she had texted him. *Had to leave suddenly. So sorry about tomorrow! Nora.* He texted her back; she did not answer. He called, over and over, but always got her voicemail. After leaving the fourth or fifth message, he heard something plaintive in his voice and stopped trying. Pride, he supposed. His mother, who knew nothing of his feelings, had casually mentioned that the new teacher he had been interested in had gone home to Athens. She had picked up the story from somebody at church. There were whispers she was pregnant. He had exploded at her and then had to apologize. Later that night he looked up "O'Hearn" online and found what had to be her parents' address and drove to Athens to see her.

But he had ended up sitting in his car outside the house in the dark, talking himself out of whatever he would have done. He had given her enough chances to answer him if she had wanted to. What could her silence mean except one thing? He was unwilling to risk seeing her face if she were not pleased to see him, so, after an hour, he just drove away. The road home from Athens was long.

In some ways, it was worse than losing Deirdre. That at least was a pure grief—profound, metaphysical. This made him feel adolescent, full of self-scrutiny and anxious longing. He couldn't give up the image of her, the way she laughed up at him, the way she leaned against him, the feel of her breast against his arm, the way she would—

His head came up. Tires on the gravel in the driveway.

The crunching stopped and then started again, as if the driver were looking for something, not seeing it, rolling a little closer, exploratory and furtive. He glanced at the clock—10:11—and edged up to the window. Car without its lights on: the wild thought came to him that it was Nora, that she had come down to see him, that she was shy but here.

Then a door opened, the interior light flashed, and a big man got out, quietly shut the door behind him, and stepped out onto the lawn. The front porch light was off. The man came to a halt and stood there, a thicker shadow among shadows, visible only by the glimmering whites of his eyes. He stared up as though he could see Sharpe in the dark.

Sharpe got the pistol from the back of the drawer in his bedside table, grabbed the clip from another drawer where he had hidden it from Martin, and pressed it in as he walked into the hall and down the stairs.

"Bill?" He heard the alarm in his mother's voice.

He flipped on the porch light, threw open the front door, and banged the screen door against the outside wall, already leveling the pistol at Dexter.

"What do you want?"

"Whoa, whoa, whoa," Watkins said, backing up.

"What are you doing here?" Sharpe asked, cocking the pistol. He walked steadily toward him, aiming at his head. "You're trespassing."

Watkins raised both hands.

"Jesus, hold on, now. I just want to ask you something."

"Why are you standing in my yard in the dark?"

He heard his mother behind him at the door. Martin would be with her. He lowered the gun to his thigh.

"I didn't see your lights on," Watkins said. "I wanted to talk to you, but I didn't want to wake anybody up."

"Well, you've got everybody up now."

"Who is that, Bill?" his mother called.

"It's just me, Mrs. Sharpe," Watkins called. "Dexter. Dexter Watkins." She did not answer.

Watkins tried again, this time with Martin. "Not-Too, my man. What's shaking?"

"I'm calling the sheriff," his mother said. He heard the screen door bang shut.

Sharpe raised the gun again and pointed it at Watkins' face. "Mama doesn't much like that nickname," he said.

"God Almighty," Watkins said, taking another backward step. "I just wanted to ask you about that boy this morning."

"What about him?"

"Put the goddamn—put the gun down," he said. Sharpe aimed it at Watkins' knee.

"Come on, man," said Watkins. "They're trying to pin something on me. I just wanted to know what you said to the sheriff. If you said you thought that kid was high or—"

"Something hurt that boy."

"Hey, I heard they found something in the back of that old place," Watkins said uneasily, backing toward his car, "and now everybody's on my case."

"They found the marijuana you planted," Sharpe said.

"That I planted? I mean, why does everybody . . . " His voice trailed off. "Hey, whatever happened to that schoolteacher? For a while there I thought maybe you were trying to beat my time with her."

"What are you talking about?"

"Me and her we had us a little thing going—"

Sharpe fired between Watkins' feet.

Watkins yelled "Jesus Christ!" and jumped backward.

"Did you get him?" his mother called.

"No ma'am. I missed."

"Hurry up and shoot him. The sheriff might be here in a minute."

Watkins broke for his car. Sharpe kept the gun on him until he had backed to the end of the driveway and turned onto Hopewell Road. As he turned, Sharpe aimed carefully and shot his right taillight out. Martin whooped behind him.

Josiah Simms

He had his men find a girl and bring her to his room at the motel in Macon. A young one, he told them. When they knocked, Simms opened the door, and Gomez pushed the girl a little too roughly into the room and onto the bed.

Easy, he said. Don't hurt her.

A black girl, sullen and cute, just budding. Tight shorts and a tank top and an attitude that vanished when she saw his face and her fear began. She scrambled back against the headboard.

What you going to do to me?

How old are you, darling?

Twelve.

That's old enough, don't you think?

What you gon do?

Talk to you just like this.

Jesus Lord. Please don't hurt me.

Have I hurt you? No, sweetheart. I just want you to remember me. I bet you know some bad people.

Yes sir.

She was telling the truth.

And bad things have happened to you?

Yes sir.

I'm sorry about those things. But no matter how bad the people who did them were, I'm worse. I am the worst of all.

She stared at him, her eyes huge.

What you gone do?

Remember me. That's all I ask.

Yes sir, I will. I promise.

Will you tell the police?

No sir! Please, I won't tell nobody. Just please let me go. Please don't hurt me.

Oh, but you've seen me, darling. Nobody who sees me lives long.

She was crying and whimpering now, pulling into herself, clutching the pillows against her.

Please don't kill me. I ain't done nothing.

But I *want* you to live. I *want* you to tell the police exactly what you see. Tell them my name is Walter Peach.

With one elegant gesture he came out of his robe, stood before her as he was, and opened wide his mouth. The girl gaped and gagged. She suddenly convulsed, her eyes rolled back into her head, she lost her urine. A very faint suffusion of pleasure went through him. After a moment more, he closed his mouth and put his robe back on and went over and opened the door. The other Gomez was standing there guarding the room.

Take her back where you found her, Simms told him, and let her go. Don't touch her, do you understand?

Si, Moccasin.

Bill Sharpe

June 24, 2014

The morning news was about Iran, rising seas, the warmest May on record, Mexican tequila—no mention of a marijuana crop in Gallatin County. Sharpe turned off the radio and slowed as he passed Vernon Jenkins' corn fields and approached Missy's Garden. No one was there now, just the tide of kudzu, the sun in the dew, mosquitos, gnats, wasps, the mayflies here for a moment and gone. Missy's Garden—abandoned, haunted by stories—and now thick with Nora O'Hearn and her Aunt Teresa and Nora's stories about the two Peach children and the poetic genius of her misunderstood Uncle.

Walter Peach. Good God, he was just the editor of the *Gallatin Tribune* and she had talked about him like he was Shakespeare. An old buddy of Braxton Forrest's, decent enough, intelligent, knowledgeable, but a little too sardonic and edgy for the locals. Good for a joke at breakfast from Hiram Walker and his buddies. *How them cartels treating you?*

So the kid was Peach's son. According to Nora, he was full of ideas you would never expect from an eleven-year-old. But the boy he'd picked up yesterday was a zombie. Something worse than a knock on the head had happened to him.

He stopped at the corner of the property and got out where Sheriff Bennett had parked the day before. He walked up the rise, glancing to his right down Vernon Jenkins' long rows of tasseling corn. A quarter-mile or more away was Vernon's two-story farmhouse, where Vernon's wife was taking down sheets from the clothesline in back. Not a breath of wind blew to make them belly out. Yesterday, he had seen the path cut through the kudzu to the house, but Bennett and his deputies were more interested in the big stand of marijuana by the creek. Who had gone over to the house? The path had been cut recently—recently, but not yesterday, because the kudzu had shriveled and started to turn brown. Peach? Had to be Peach—but why? He knew in his gut it had something to do with the boy being there the day before.

He saw a small, crimped butt under the shade of the oak. That would be Dexter's. He picked it up, sniffed it, and put it in his pocket. The path turned at the closest corner of the house and he followed it along the side to a door in back. Kudzu had been roughly cleared from the entrance and the screen wrenched from the frame and propped back against the door. The door was not locked. He opened it a crack. There were footprints in the dust near the door and several others disappearing down a hallway.

He could go in, but instead he stood with his head bent for a few seconds, listening, hearing small scurrying sounds, and a strong conviction came over him, a kind of terror. Nobody had used this place for a meth lab or anything else, but something was in there, and he recognized the effluvium he had smelled on the boy's clothes the day before. Whatever was in there had scared that boy out of his mind.

The sheriff needed to find it, not Bill Sharpe. He set the screen back into its frame, glanced at his watch—7:21—and turned to leave. All the way back to his truck, he kept slapping the back of his neck, but it still felt like he had a spider crawling up it.

When Sharpe went inside the Country Corner, Ed Watkins turned around from the shelves where he was restocking the cigarettes and jumped.

"God Almighty. You ain't found another boy?"

Sharpe took the roach from his pocket and set it down on the counter.

"Dexter must have left this."

"The hell's that?"

"Don't act like you don't know."

"Looks like a cigarette to me."

Sharpe was leaning toward Ed Watkins when a long black Lincoln pulled up in front of the store and stopped very close to the building. A big black man quickly got out of the back seat on the other side and a Hispanic just as big from the front seat closest to the store. As the second one got out, Sharpe got a quick glimpse of the driver, also Hispanic. The closer man opened the car's back door, and a short man got out, broad-shouldered, low-slung, with a pocked, sour face. When he saw Sharpe and Watkins through the window, he hitched up the trousers of his black suit and limped toward the door. As he came inside, jangling the bell, he took off his sunglasses, nodded at Sharpe, and then fixed his gaze on Ed Watkins, taking him in, scratching the hollow of his neck with one finger where it showed through his open-collared purple silk shirt.

He smiled as if Ed was funny and then turned to look around the store, rubbing his right thumb against a knuckle. He reached in his jacket pocket and took out a roll of bills. Thousand-dollar bills, Sharpe saw, as he put one on the counter. Grover Cleveland. Why were the most obscure presidents on the largest denominations? The man counted out ten Grovers onto the counter, made a face, waved his hand at the interior of the store, waggling his head slightly, and counted out ten more.

"What the hell?" Ed said.

The man held up a bill toward Sharpe, offering it to him. Sharpe shook his head. The man shrugged and smiled and put it back on the roll, which he put back in his pocket. He looked back at Ed.

"I give you this long," he said, holding up two fingers.

One of the big men came in the door holding a gallon can of gasoline he had just filled at the pump in front.

"This long for what?" asked Ed. "Hey, buddy, let's don't bring the gas in the store."

The Mexican touched Sharpe's arm again and tilted his head toward the door. Sharpe started to protest, but he found himself gripped from behind. One of the men must have gone around back to come inside. Strong as he was, Sharpe could not move his arms. Meanwhile, the other one started splashing gasoline along the walls, between the shelves, over the magazine racks.

"What the fuck?" Ed said, his voice rising. "What the hell are you—"

"You are Ed?" said the short man, pushing the bills toward him. "You call the sheriff? Take your money. And take what you have in register. All this, yes? My gift to you." He put another bill on the counter as if it were nothing. Another. "No problem. You go home to Betty—tell her Carlos is sorry about scaring her. And driving on her garden. Hurry, amigo. Tell her I said *buenos dias*. Tell Phoebe not to get fat like her mama. You have one minute now."

Ed was ashen. He grabbed at the money and stuffed it in his pockets, then opened the register and scooped out everything he could hold. Coins spattered out of the slots in the drawer and clattered onto the counter and rolled across the floor.

"I swear to sweet Jesus Christ, I didn't do a—"

"Eduardo, *calma*. You need more money?"

He put down another thousand, caught the eye of Sharpe's captor, and flicked his head toward the door. The man propelled Sharpe through the screen door and out into the parking lot and walked him over the gravel to his pickup, holding both wrists in one of his huge hands. He opened the door and pushed Sharpe behind the wheel. Before Sharpe could move, he took his pistol from behind his back and pointed it in Sharpe's face, backing up and waving with the barrel to tell him to leave. Sharpe slammed the door.

As he started the engine and edged forward, he saw Ed stumble from the store. The short man glanced up at Sharpe before putting his sunglasses back on. One of the guards opened the car door for the short man, and the other escorted Ed over to the gasoline pump before getting in the passenger's seat. Sharpe's captor stood in the doorway of the store and carefully threw a match inside. When the flames erupted to his satisfaction—a great sucking whoosh that backed him up—he turned and got into the car, taking his time, paying no attention to Sharpe. Pulling forward, the car eased out of the lot onto County 73 and headed off, not hurrying, toward the Interstate.

Ed had backed up against the gas pump. He was staring, slack-mouthed, as the store burned. Sharpe pulled up behind him and opened his window.

"You better get away from that pump. I'll call the sheriff as soon as I can get a signal. You want a ride home?"

Ed squeezed money in both hands; bills spilled from his pockets. If he heard Sharpe, it did not register.

"Ed!" Sharpe said.

Ed turned stupidly. When he recognized Sharpe, he seemed to remember all the money that he was clutching. He began trying to stuff even more into his bulging pockets—ones, fives, twenties. When a bill fell loose and gusted away across the lot, Ed awkwardly ran after it, stomping at it with his right foot and trying to keep all the other money intact. He had almost managed to trap it under his right foot when the updraft of the fire took hold of it. It rose up and drifted—Grover Cleveland gazing benignly at poor Ed—directly into the flame that had just burst upward through the store. Ed cursed and suddenly began to weep.

"Do you see this shit?" he cried, gesturing at the fire.

By now, three or four other passing cars had slowed and pulled onto the lot. Sharpe recognized the black preacher Ed had insulted the morning before; the old gentleman watched with pursed lips, shaking his head. An SUV eased off of 73, followed by a big van full of Bible school kids; a white F-150 stopped on Hopewell Road, and Sharpe recognized Jimmy Proctor's wife in the driver's seat. And then, swerving around her, tearing into the lot, almost skidding into the burning building, came Dexter Watkins himself.

He leapt from the Jeep.

"What happened?" he shouted at Ed, giving Sharpe one furious glance.

Ed turned on his brother furiously. "It's your fault. Thought you were going to be some kind of drug lord. You goddamn fool!"

"Shut up, Ed. You peed in your pants."

Ed looked down and cursed and swiped at himself with a handful of money.

"Those fucking Mexicans burned my store down!"

Dexter stood in front of the flaming building, his fingers buried in his dreadlocks, shaking his head.

"This ain't on me," he said. "It's that goddamn Moccasin."

Bennett

Hudson Bennett was on his way north on I-75 when the news came in from Ellen Wolf that Mexicans had burned down Ed Watkins' store.

"Bill Sharpe just called me. Says they pulled up right in front of the door and came in and doused everything with gasoline. This short Mexican in a suit made a big deal of giving Ed thousand-dollar bills. They got Bill and Ed out and then threw a match in there and burned it down."

"How many of them?"

"Four. The driver, two big men like movie bodyguards, Bill says, and this short one. Scarred face, short and broad, walks with a limp. Bill took a picture of the car with his phone and I'm running the plates now."

Bennett slowed and pulled off on the left shoulder as the traffic sped around him.

"Give me the description."

When she did, he drove up to the cut-through and paused there to call Gary Beamer, the Butts County sheriff. Bennett had been on his way to breakfast with Beamer and Wendell Longfellow from Spalding County to talk about coordinating their efforts now that the cartels seemed to be making inroads into middle Georgia. The scale of the bust the day before had alarmed them all: the street value of all that marijuana would have been closer to four million dollars than the two Bennett had thought. When Beamer answered, Bennett described what had happened and gave him a description of the car and the license plate number.

He pulled out into traffic. It used to amuse him to see the traffic slow down when they saw his car; now it gave him a sour feeling about human nature. He gunned it south toward County 73, lights flashing, as cars dodged into the right lane. He was scanning the northbound traffic for the black car.

"You sure this was Mexicans?" Beamer asked.

"I ain't seen their passports," he said to Beamer.

"Okay, Hudson."

"Whoever it is, they burned down Ed Watkins' store. And it turns out they'd already been to his house."

"They burned his house down?"

"No. Just went in. Scared his wife. Found his daughter still in bed."

"Jesus. Raped her?"

"No, she's just ten. Took some of her things. Drove all over the garden in the front yard on their way out."

"Not Dexter's house but his brother's?"

"That's right."

"So the brother knew something? They're trying to keep the brother quiet?"

"That's what I figure."

But Bennett didn't really think so. Going after Ed Watkins didn't make any sense unless it was aimed at everybody surrounding Dexter. Letting them know how things were going to be.

He told Beamer he'd call him back later. When he got to the exit at County 73, he still had not seen a car fitting Ellen's description of it, but as soon as he turned left and started toward Watkins' store, he saw the car in the entrance to the new development, Phoenix Estates.

Just sitting there, all four doors open. Nobody around it.

Just then Ellen Wolf radioed him.

"What'd you find out?" he asked her.

"Stolen from a funeral home in McDonough this morning."

"I'm pulling up behind it now in the entrance to Phoenix Estates. Nobody here. They must have had another car, which is why they didn't care if everybody saw them in this one."

"So you'll check it for prints," Ellen said.

"How about you call the state patrol to do that? Maybe get the GBI in on it. Get Matt or Red to come out here and stay with the car until they show up."

"Yes sir."

Bennett got out and walked around the abandoned car. The warning chime was going. They hadn't even bothered to take the keys. Up the hill, a bulldozer slowed and stopped. They still had a lot of grading to do on the subdivision, not to mention the infrastructure, but nobody was working. The driver stepped from the cab onto the treads, took off his cap, and wiped his face, shading his eyes and staring downhill at Bennett. When Bennett waved the man toward him, the man jumped from the treads and started down the graveled drive that the construction company used. Bennett walked a few yards up to the gates, turning sideways to keep the car in sight.

The bulldozer operator was a big man in his thirties, bearded. Bennett did not recognize him. Coach Fitzgerald would have had him on the defensive line if he had lived in Gallatin. His beer belly swayed and strained his t-shirt out as he stepped over clumps of sod and stray rocks with the heaving gait of a man getting used to the stomach he had put on himself.

"Morning," said Bennett, offering his hand. "Hudson Bennett. Gallatin County."

"Gimme a second," the man said after shaking his hand. He raked a wad of chewing tobacco from his cheek and spat off to the side. "Wasn't expecting to have to talk this morning." He was breathing hard even from the downhill walk. "Jeremy Chestnut," he said. He spoke with a whicker that reminded Bennett of Andy Devine in the old Westerns.

"Wondering if you saw what happened to the men in this car, Mr. Chestnut," Bennett said.

"I's looking the other way when they pulled up," he said, pointing up at his bulldozer. He adjusted an Atlanta Braves cap on his sweating forehead. "But when I turned around to back up, I seen four men get in an old car. Mexicans, looked like, dressed up like businessmen. We got a bunch of them work out here, but they don't dress like that. Which I ain't supposed to say they're out here."

Bennett nodded and raised his eyebrows.

"They hid soon as they seen you," said Chestnut. "They're back yonder in the woods."

Bennett had to smile.

"Was the other car already here?"

"No sir. Pulled up while them men was getting out. Brown. It come from over toward the Interstate and they got in it. Didn't even close the doors of the other one. How do you figure that? I mean how hard is it to close the doors?"

"Brown, you said?"

"Old brown four-door. Seventies. Buick, maybe."

"What about the men?"

"Two big ones. Big as me. Hell, bigger. A short guy with a limp. Wide shoulders. He was taking off a suit and tie, it looked like. Threw 'em back in the black car. The fourth one I didn't notice much. Medium height."

"Who was driving?"

"Too far away to tell."

"So five of them in this one car. Which way did they go?"

"Toward the Interstate. Strange thing was the way the Mexicans acted."

"The ones who got in the car?"

"I'm talking about the ones up here before you come up. When they seen them men in the car, they all threw down whatever they was doing. They was looking at each other and saying things to each other in Spanish. When one of them did that crossing thing, they all did it."

"Crossed themselves?"

"I guess. Where they end up kissing their fingers?"

Bennett nodded and thanked Chestnut, who was already stuffing his cheek with tobacco.

"You was already looking for them men?" he said.

Bennett nodded. "They burned down Ed Watkins' store right up the road here."

"Sweet Jesus! I been in there. Burned it down! How come?" Chestnut spat and tilted his head, waiting for some explanation. When Bennett shrugged, he nodded and turned and started lumbering back uphill toward his bulldozer. A few yards up, he stopped.

"They ain't killed nobody?" he called.

"Not so far as I know," Bennett said.

Back at his car, Bennett found some yellow crime scene tape in the glove compartment. He was starting to put it in a broad circle around the car when Red Scott pulled in behind him.

"Find anything?" Red asked him.

"I'm leaving it for the state."

"What, you think they booby-trapped it or something?"

"Red, just let them do this."

Red held up both hands.

"Sheriff?" he heard from the radio. Ellen's voice was urgent. "Come in, please!" He reached in for the radio.

"I'm here."

Raïssa

Sitting very still and upright at the old vanity in the front bedroom upstairs, she had her knees turned to the left and her torso to the right while she gazed straight ahead into the mirror. She sank one hand in the thick of her hair and admired the lift of her breasts in the knit top. Suppose Andrew Perkins happened to pass the doorway just then, if somehow he happened to be in the house because her father had hired him, say, to help with some repairs.

A metallic RAP! RAP! RAP!—so loud it resonated through the floor—interrupted her reverie. Somebody at the front door. Nobody used the front door. Her mother would handle it.

So, okay, Andrew would be passing the doorway in his t-shirt with cut-off sleeves showing his big, smooth muscles, and he would be wearing a low-slung tool belt, and he would glance in and see her and do a double-take—*Raïssa?*—like he had never seen her before. But he would know her real name, which meant he had been thinking about her. She would see him in the mirror and their eyes would meet and she would wait just a moment to turn. *Andrew!* she would say, quietly, as though she'd been expecting him for ages. Or *Andrew?* touching her neck as though she were totally surprised and a little scared.

RAP! RAP! RAP! She started.

It was the great brass lion's-head knocker on the front door. She winced in irritation, suddenly seeing herself as the exiled Princess Raïssa in a cheesy Disney movie. Why didn't her mother answer it? What idiot would be knocking at the front door, anyway? Nobody had done that since the man with the creepy card at Christmas.

And then she remembered that her mother had taken the boy—she couldn't think of him as Buford—to see Dr. Fletcher again.

What if something had happened to her father?

Barefoot, she ran down the front stairs, touching the split place in the newel at the bottom and glancing over the large open foyer nobody had used since Christmas. Whoever it was would see the old Forrest family furniture—a faded Queen Anne sofa that faced the fireplace, a spindly end table with an original Tiffany lamp, and matching ornamental chairs with lion armrests staring at each other across an expensive Afghan rug.

She unlocked the massive door. It squeaked as she opened it. Standing there was a heavy-set Hispanic man with a broad, pitted face. She was a head taller than he was. He smiled humbly, turning a baseball cap in his hands. He wore a clean white t-shirt, but also, weirdly, good slacks and dress shoes. Behind him in the drive, several men in an old brown car glanced up at her, and she saw one of them say something to the others, who smiled and nodded. She wondered how they had opened the front gate. Had they broken the lock?

"*Buenas dias. ¿Tu papá está aquí?*" the short man said.

She stiffened with fear. She had studied Spanish since fifth grade— she had even been to the Cathedral of Our Lady of Guadalupe in Mexico City with a youth group in Waycross before they moved to Gallatin— but she instinctively played dumb. They seemed to want work. The man mimed hoeing and trimming.

She tilted her head, uncertain.

"You want yard work?" she guessed. "I'm sorry, but we already have a yard service." She shook her head to make the point, waiting for him to react. His head gave a sideways twitch, as if he felt a mosquito hovering next to his ear, but he didn't make a move to leave.

"*Tu papá tiene muchas plantas.*"

She added, "Thank you very much, though. *Muchas gracias.*"

Too girlish. She smiled as politely as possible and started to close the door when he casually put out his hand and stopped it.

She met his eyes with a dark inward quailing.

"Walter Peach, he is your father?" he said. "*El escribe?* He writes the newspaper?"

"Yes sir," she said. Those photographs. Her mother had pleaded with her father to stop writing about cartels. Even Mr. Forrest had told him it was dangerous, especially after the controversy around the Tate County football game and the threats at the *Tribune* office. He had reluctantly stopped.

The man nodded knowingly at her.

"Your father, he write things not simpatico, *pelirroja*," he said. One of his front teeth was broken. "A man with many plants should be simpatico. You understand? *Muchas plantas.*"

"Many plants?" she said, glancing at the front slope of Stonewall Hill with its azaleas and boxwood hedges and ancient crepe myrtles, its shaded lawn under the oaks and elms. "*Muchas gracias,*" she repeated firmly.

Before she could draw back, he caught her with his left hand and pulled her toward him. With his right he held her chin. She tried to twist free, but he easily overpowered her, and she went still and stared at his pocked face, the thick hairs coming from his nostrils, the pits in his cheeks, the broken and uneven teeth of his grin. His breath smelled of coffee and garlic as he pulled her, trying to kiss her, and she twisted aside. He laughed and his grip relaxed, and she ducked and jerked away, almost falling, and tried to force the door closed, but again he stopped it with one hand. She heard one of the car's doors slam shut, then another.

Her heart pounded painfully. Behind her was the emptiness of the house. The kitchen, the knives in the block on the counter if she ran.

Too far.

The short man's small eyes lingered on her breasts, which were heaving with her breath. Insolently, he looked down her body. Her tight shorts, her bare legs. She shrank back, thinking about the foyer and anything she could use to protect herself. *The fireplace tools.* When the short man turned and said something—*eh, premio?*—to the huge black man coming up the steps behind him, she turned and ran around the couch, bumping the end table. The Tiffany lamp tottered—she grabbed at it—and then it fell and shattered. Oh God. She felt the short man behind her. The brittle old cord caught at her foot and tripped her, and she fell against the rack with a clatter and another scream.

As she straightened up, turning, she grabbed behind her and caught the poker from the rack and hid it behind her as she faced the short man. He kicked the broken lamp out of the way and stood grinning at her. His tongue came out as if he were about to lick an ice cream cone, and he stepped closer and then reached for her, but she stepped aside and whipped the poker down as hard as she could. The steel smashed hard into his face—blood burst from his nose, he howled, he cursed, he snatched at the poker, but she kept her grip on it and thrust the sharp tip at his eyes and he backed away, holding the bridge of his nose, cursing her.

The other men clapped from the doorway and called things to him. He spat on the floor as he limped out onto the porch. "Leave a message for *Walter*," the short man told them. "*Follar a su pelirroja.*"

"Get out of my house!" she screamed. One of the big men smiled and averted his eyes; he was almost handsome. The other one looked at her as the short man had and lifted an eyebrow and took a pistol from the back of his pants, gesturing with it for her to drop the poker. Her knees went weak. After a moment, she dropped the poker and it clanged on the floor. He gestured again, jerking the pistol barrel upward and plucking at his own shirt. *Mostrenos tus tetas*, he said. She backed up, bumped against the couch, blood rushing in her ears.

And just then, from the kitchen side, she heard her mother.

"*Rose!* What was that? Where are you?"

"Stay in the kitchen! Call the police!"

"Come here! I need help with the groceries."

The two men, who had separated to approach her from different sides, stopped. The one with the gun lifted it in the direction of the kitchen and looked a question at the short man on the porch, who stood still for a moment, considering, and then shrugged and shook his head and beckoned them out. He looked at her, touching his nose, glaring like a maddened animal. He said something and made a gesture so obscene she felt the shame of it pour through her like hot oil. He stopped and looked back at her. *Dile a tu padre que cambiaré a su familia por la pelirroja. ¿Lo entiendes?*

She nodded. He disappeared. She heard the car start.

"Rose!" her mother called. She came through the door from the sitting room into the front foyer and glanced at the open door, the poker on the floor.

"Oh my God! The Tiffany lamp!"

"Call the police!"

"The police?"

"Hurry!" Raïssa waved toward the door. "Hurry!"

Her mother rushed to the threshold, and a moment later, the brown car went slowly out the front gate, crossed Lee Street, and turned left onto King.

"What happened to the lamp?" her mother demanded. "Your foot is bleeding! There's blood all over the rug!"

Sudden nausea sent Raïssa through the door and over to the railing on the porch, where she leaned over and vomited into the azaleas. Her mother followed her, fumbling in her purse for the phone. Raïssa heard her make the call.

"What do I tell them?" she asked, holding it away from her mouth.

"Some men just came here. Mexicans, I think. They were about to— Oh my God." She vomited again, shuddering uncontrollably.

"The police will be here in a minute," her mother said.

"I feel so dirty."

Her mother took her face in her hands and looked into her eyes.

"They were—they threatened you?"

"Three of them. It was about Dad. They tried—I hurt one of them with the poker."

"Oh my God, Rose. I'm so sorry, sweetheart. I'm so sorry."

Her mother embraced her, squeezing her hard, but Raïssa could not give herself to the embrace. She stood stiffly. She felt as if the men's eyes on her body had left her covered with a viscid slime that would soil her mother too. She could smell it on herself more strongly than the vomit. She wanted a hot shower. Soap and soap and soap. Over her mother's shoulder, Raïssa saw Buford come into the foyer from the kitchen side and stare up curiously at the two of them. When they heard the sirens, the boy went to the door and looked out at the driveway. Impassively, he stared toward town, abstracted from the scene, an alien.

Within seconds, two police cars, lights flashing, pulled up through the broken gate into the front driveway. As policemen on walkie-talkies spread out through the grounds, one of the officers, a big man with a blond crew cut, came bounding up the front steps two at a time.

"Ma'am," he said to her mother, and to her, "Miss Peach. Can you describe them?"

Raïssa looked up at him. His face was pleasant, earnest, urgent. SGT. BILLY REEVES said his metal name tag.

She crossed her arms on her chest. "The one who came to the door was a short man with a scarred face." She felt her mother's arm around her. "And two big men," said Raïssa, "one black and one Hispanic. Somebody else driving the car."

"So four men?"

"I think so."

"What scared them off?"

"Maybe my mom coming in."

Billy Reeves looked at her mother.

"Or they just wanted to leave a message. Did you get the license plate?"

"No, but it's an old brown car."

"And they threatened you?"

She could not answer.

"They came in the house," her mother said. "I think they would have raped her."

Sgt. Reeves nodded and walked along the porch talking into his radio before shutting it off. He hurried down the steps, shouting. Two policemen ran to his car; doors slammed; they accelerated down the driveway, paused at the gate, and a second later sped into town, not onto Sharp Street. The other police car stayed, and two men, both just a few years older than she was, stood near it with their backs to her, hands crossed in front of them, scanning the grounds.

"We'll be here, ma'am," one of them said to her mother. When another car came roaring up the driveway, one of the men went around to the back of the house.

"Don't you want to go inside, sweetheart?" her mother asked. Raïssa shook her head. "Rose, you said it was about your father?" She shook her head. "You have to tell me, Rose. What else did they say to you?"

A shudder went through her. She would never repeat some of it. And the other part would terrify her mother.

"Teresa?" someone called.

Sheriff Bennett was coming around the side of the house. He paused to say something to the policemen. He nodded, asked something, nodded again, and came up the steps toward them, holding his hat.

"You folks need to know these same men burned down Ed Watkins' store out on Hopewell Road about an hour ago."

Her mother gasped. "You mean where Buford was yesterday?"

"Yes ma'am."

"Oh my God, who are they?"

"Cartel men, we figure. Walter was right. They said something to you?"

"To Rose."

The sheriff looked at Raïssa. His face was sober and compassionate. He was not a handsome man, not as big as Billy Reeves, but more authoritative. His demeanor of respect and courtesy made her trust him.

"What did they say, Rose?" her mother asked.

Raïssa sighed and looked up at the sheriff. Already she felt the blush rising up her neck and into her face.

"He said for me to tell Walter Peach that he'd trade his family for the *pelirroja*. The redhead, meaning me."

Sheriff Bennett glanced at her mother and then back at her. A pained expression tightened his eyes. He shook his head.

"Trade?" her mother said.

"The rest of you. The rest of you for me."

"*Trade you?*"

"Maybe in Mexico," said the sheriff after a moment, and the look that came onto his eyes startled her, it was so murderous and cold. "Not in my country."

Walter

June 24, 2014

Nora wore a sleeveless yellow cotton dress. She sat with her legs crossed, knees slightly angled toward the window, her right hand encircling her coffee cup, her left wrist just on the edge of the table. The middle finger unconsciously tapped the tabletop in time with the reggae playing in the background. Outside, it was a bright, humid, summer day, thunderstorms coming. Inside the Starbucks it was just cool enough, and she was lovely and casual, her hair pulled back in a ponytail like his, her shape so precise that a singing bliss suffused his limbs just to see her.

He closed his hand over hers, stilling it. She met his gaze, not moving her hand except to lift one knuckle against his palm, and, when she smiled, something in his heart gave way. Like what? Like a creek high in the mountains when the last ice gives way to coming summer. Something happened in her, too, and she saw him see it. She pulled her hand from under his and smoothed her dress down her thigh.

"What do you think possessed Buford?" she said.

"Nora, listen—"

"Walter, no, don't say anything!" she broke in. She uncrossed her legs and leaned toward him. "Please," she said, putting one fingertip on his lips, as she might on a child's. "Please don't."

His phone buzzed and skittered on the tabletop. He had to check his impulse to sweep the goddamn thing crashing into the front window as he sat back from her. His blood was pounding dangerously in his neck. Men his age had died of heart attacks over less.

"You know it's about Buford," she said.

He sighed and picked up the phone, glancing at the display.

"What is it, Teresa?"

"Walter, where are you?"

She sounded breathless and scared, which alarmed him.

"At a Starbucks," he said.

There was a small pause. "You and Nora?"

"That's right."

"So you haven't even started home yet."

"Not yet," he said defensively, irritated that he was being put on the spot. "Don't you think Buford's just playing at—"

"Listen to me. A car full of Mexican men came to our house this morning, and if I hadn't come home, they would have raped Rose."

"Sweet Jesus," he said. He stood up, his hand gripping his ponytail.

"Sheriff Bennett says they burned down Ed Watkins' store."

"Bennett's there?"

"Yes, thank God."

He looked across the table at Nora, shaking his head.

"Rose answered the door," Teresa went on, "and the one in charge told her he was looking for you."

"Looking for me?"

"They would have raped her, Walter. She said . . . not that you seem to care . . . she's never been looked at like that. That man told her he would trade her for the rest of us."

Walter stopped breathing. "*Trade* her? Meaning what?"

"He said he would trade the redhead for the rest of us."

He went outside onto the sidewalk, but the traffic noise made it hard to hear and he cupped his left hand over his ear.

"What do you mean 'trade her for the rest of us'?"

"*You know what he means!*" she cried. "It's what you've been saying all along."

"They want us to give them Rose?"

"Everybody warned you to leave them alone, Walter. Even Braxton. Speaking of Braxton, he's called twice about the paper. The printer wants to know when he's getting it. Did you forget you have a job? That boy who takes pictures has been trying to cobble something together. Braxton's flying down here right now. Picking up after your mess."

People stepped around him on the sidewalk.

"I'm coming, I'm coming."

"You did something because of Nora. I know you did. Otherwise you wouldn't be there instead of protecting your family."

"Dexter Watkins did this, not me."

A chorus of horns on Broad Street deafened him. He turned to look back through the glass at Nora. It was not her fault. He was the unclean one, not Nora.

"Walter?" Teresa said. "Are you still there?"

"Let me talk to the sheriff."

"I'll find him and call you back."

He caught Nora's eye and beckoned her toward him. She gathered up her things and tilted her head inquisitively as she pushed open the door and stepped into the outer noise.

"Is Buford okay?"

"Mexicans from the cartel came to Stonewall Hill."

"Oh my god!" she cried.

"They burned down Ed Watkins' store, and now they're coming for me. They say they won't kill the rest of us if we give them Rose."

"Give them—"

His phone buzzed. Bennett. He answered it roughly.

"Sheriff. What do you know about these people?"

"Same ones who burned down the store. Bill Sharpe saw the whole thing. Before that they went over to Ed's house and scared his wife and daughter."

"Bill Sharpe? The one who found Buford?"

He saw Nora's reaction to the name.

"He said a short Mexican with a scarred face kept putting thousand-dollar bills on the counter—even offered Sharpe one—but then they doused the place with gasoline and burned it down. Ed's scared to death to say anything. He claims the store caught fire all by itself."

"Where's Dexter?"

"Good question."

Across Broad Street, a young mother and her little children were playing on the North Campus lawn. A little girl tried out a somersault and rolled over sideways and lay there for a moment unmoving and a terrible abyss opened inside him.

"Is my family safe?"

Nora kept her hand on his arm, looking into his face and waiting for Bennett's answer to register. A tall student walking past did a double-take when he saw her and ran into a bicycle chained to a tree, but then spun around gracefully, giving her a small bow.

"The police have two men here for the time being," Bennett said. "We've got the State Patrol and the GBI on it with a description of the car. As for Dexter, I hear from your daughter he came by your house last night, but I wouldn't worry about him. We've got his prints from the PVC and some other prints they're running now, so as soon as we find him, we'll arrest him. The Feds will be coming in soon if there's a cartel involved."

"What should I do right now?" he asked Bennett.

There was a pause.

"How about get your dumb ass home?"

Peach held the phone away from his ear for a second, furious.

"What if Watkins is on his way up here?"

"Good God, we'll catch Watkins. I always heard there was no fool like an old fool, but you're going out of your way to prove it to me."

"Screw you, Bennett."

"Your daughter was almost raped. Your wife thinks her family's about to be murdered. Your boy's lost his goddamn mind. They're down here scared to death and you're sitting up there playing patty-cake with trouble."

"Is Teresa standing there next to you? Is she enjoying this?"

"She's got more discretion than that."

"That's a pretty big word for you to use, Hudson."

"Fuck you, Peach."

The phone went dead.

Nora, knowing that she must be under discussion, had turned away. She was strolling under the trees between the Starbucks awning and the rows of newspaper boxes along the sidewalk on College Avenue. She stopped and bent over to brush something off her ankle and her sandal dangled loose below the arch of her foot as she lifted it.

What he would give.

What Watkins would give, who had traded Nora for the marijuana crop and who would trade her again to protect himself now from the men who had burned his brother's store.

She heard him approaching her and turned.

"If Watkins knows where you live," he said, "he might give you to them."

"He wouldn't—"

"You don't know what he might do," he interrupted. "He'll use anybody he has to use. He's not as scared of the law as he is of the cartel."

Backed against the newspaper box, she stared at him.

"Call your mother. Tell her you're just going to Gallatin for the day. Just come with me. I can't leave you."

"Walter, she'll call Aunt Teresa."

He knew what Bridget would think. He took his phone from his pocket and found the number.

"Bridget?" he said when she answered. "You remember that man who scared Nora back in March? Dexter Watkins? He was mixed up with a drug cartel."

"Well, that's terrible. I'm glad she left."

"Listen to me," he said. "They go after families. They've already gone after Dexter Watkins' brother, and he wasn't any more involved than you are. I'm telling you, Bridget. They know where you live, so you need to leave. Check into a motel or something. I'll take care of Nora."

"Oh my god! Why would they come after us?"

"Pure terror. You need to get out of there."

"Oh my god, oh my god. I'll call Terry."

He took Nora's arm and steered her to his car.

Dexter

After he left Ed's store, he drove northeast on 73 for a mile or so to make it look like he was headed to Jackson. He thought he would throw them all off. Take his time. Let his boys Q and H do their stuff.

He checked his mirrors—nobody there—and turned left onto old Hiram's Ferry Road and followed it until the pavement ran out.

He slowed down, looking for a pine tree with a big burl in the trunk. Found it. Just past it, overgrown with saplings, an old woods road ran through the back of the property his family used to own. Nobody had used it for years, and the ruts were soft with pine needles and old grass. The youngest trees bent under the bumper and scraped along the underside. He eased forward until the Jeep was hidden from the road and then got out and went back to cover his tracks. Anybody see him? Nobody.

He smoothed out the tread marks in the loose dirt and kicked the bent grass upright and pulled in far enough under the bigger pines so nobody could see him from overhead. A helicopter kept chopping back and forth somewhere nearby but never right above him. Reminded him of being in the sand box. He crossed his arms and squeezed his boys and listened to the sirens. Be looking for the Jeep. He broke a few branches to put over the chrome parts in case they glared.

He found a big pine tree and leaned back against the trunk in the heat, pulling a joint from the pocket of his shirt and his old Zippo from his jeans. He fired up and took a long drag, sucking it down in his lungs and holding it and holding it until he felt his boys warming up with the THC. Nobody could catch him. He was smarter than anybody else, anyway, and besides that he had his boys. He let the smoke out in a long stream that he split in two with his tongue and adjusted his crotch, stirred by the thought of himself. His upper boys he showed everybody, Huitzilopochtli and Quetzalcoatl, but his lower boys, his special premium idols, Dexzilopochtli and Dexzalcoatl—they were going to bring him Nora when the time was right. They always brought him who he wanted.

A big black ant crawled onto his left hand, crossed his wrist, and started up his forearm. When it reached the crook, Dexter quickly flexed and crushed it with his biceps, opening his arm again to see the thing struggling sideways with its broken body. He picked it up and put it on his tongue, smiling as it writhed there, thinking of Bill Sharpe as he spat it away. He wanted a curse working on the man. He gripped his lower boys left-handed and said some dark words. Too bad he couldn't bend Sharpe back on a stone altar and cut him open and hold his heart up to the sun and then feed it to a god with a mouth like a furnace. Now that was some

267

old-time religion. Loved that stuff ever since he heard about it back at Fort Huachuca.

Two or three more hours should do it. Nobody would think he would hide this close, especially after the Mexicans scared the living shit out of Ed. It wasn't the Gomez brothers he was dealing with. One of them had mentioned the Moccasin, which was the name they used for that strange English dandy-man. Burned-looking. Eyes with no feeling in them. The way he covered his mouth and said *Welcome, Walter.* Peach getting one look and busting it up through the kudzu like a track star.

Wasn't the Moccasin who went in the store. Short guy, stumpy and muscled-up, Ed said, like the Swearingen boys from the mill village. Limping, face all eaten up with smallpox. Twenty-nine $1000 bills dropped on the counter. Supposed to be thirty, but one of them got caught in the updraft of the fire. Dex told him it was his money anyway, since Ed had cost him the whole crop of bud. That worried Ed. Fat-assed Ed. And Ed was worried because Sharpe wouldn't take any money—like Sharpe had something on him. Ed thought taking the money meant you would keep quiet. You took the money, you protected Betty and Phoebe. But Sharpe didn't take the money, so that meant they would come back and kill Ed anyway. Ed's hands trembling like he had come down with the Parkinson's their daddy got. He would sell out Dexter in a heartbeat, so Dexter made sure to tell him he was going to Jackson, to Juanita's house, said it several times—not that Ed was taking much in, but it might stick in his mind if the police asked him. He also said it to Jimmy Proctor's wife.

But here he was, right on their old land. His father had sold the hardwoods on the back acres to help pay the taxes, but the taxes kept going up, so he had finally sold the land itself, including the old house (which they tore down the first week) to some people from Atlanta. *Taxes is how the government lets you know who really owns your land,* his daddy had said. That was about the same time Dex came back from Afghanistan, wanting to go home and get over what the government had done to him, and found out he didn't have a home to go to.

Time just sat there. He listened to the sirens fade and the heat of the summer day settle in. It had to be almost noon. They would all be over in Jackson looking for him, so he got up and stretched and started the Jeep, loud as hell after so much quiet. He backed out from under the trees and eased forward in the ruts, squeezing past half-grown pines, bouncing over rocks and crushing fire-ant beds and bending springy saplings.

It was just a quarter mile or so behind the house those Atlanta people had built to the back of the old barn on Ed's property. When he got there, he stopped and sat idling, staring at the gray, half-rotten wood that had crumbled away at the bottom. He could see daylight all along the base. Virginia creeper had spread up the right side toward an opening high up in the wall. On the left side were stacks of lumber his father had left. The old man had wanted to build a tree house for the grandchildren he was expecting. Ellen was still in the picture, then, and it still looked like Dexter might have kids and hold down a regular job at Plant Ocmulgee and be a normal citizen. That was before Afghanistan and being awake three days straight on amphetamines and finding that family with weapons wrapped in goat hides under their house.

He thought about those months in the stockade in Bagram and the time in jail in Macon after he got busted for selling some pills to an undercover officer. He thought about what it would have been like to live in a trailer with Ellen, year after year, watching her get fat, pretending to be happy but knowing the truth: a couple of beers after work and a few TV shows and kids and the same old thing in bed. What was *that* for a life? Hell, jail was better—do your time, get out with that bad-ass aura women liked. Have more fun than fifty husbands. And more fun to come if he didn't get caught too soon. He knew right where Nora O'Hearn lived in Athens. She wouldn't be expecting him. Surprise her. Get her in his car. Break into that honeycomb.

And after her, Peach's hot-tempered strawberry daughter. Check off another one for Dexzalcoatl.

He rolled his head on his neck, feeling his blood start to stir where it counted. Serve Peach right. But that's if he didn't get caught.

So not this car. Not this hair. Not these rings in his eyebrows.

Had to look like a husband to get all the things husbands couldn't get.

First thing was to get rid of the Jeep.

If he pulled around to the front, Ed or Betty might see him. If he left the Jeep behind the barn, a helicopter might spot it. He got out and walked around to the front of the barn and went in the opening, stepping over loose fence posts, bales of flattened chicken wire, an old hoe, part of a tractor fender, the engine from a mower—all Ed's junk. Smell of mildew and spilled oil. He spat in a doodlebug hole in the fine dust, and up in the hayloft a pigeon suddenly broke for the light and startled him. Probably bats hanging up in there.

He went all the way to the back wall looking for a spot wide enough for his Jeep. He'd have to bring it through without hitting a beam. He found one that would be tight but ought to work. A rotten crossbeam sagged from nails on both sides, so he pulled off the pieces and threw them aside. He paced off the distance between uprights—wide enough—and then paced over to the barn's side wall. He pushed what he could out of the way and then went out to the entrance, standing in the shadows and staring down toward Ed's house.

If they were gone, he could get in there and cut his hair, shave, pull out the rings. Nobody was outside, but that didn't mean shit. Betty's car sat in the driveway. Maybe he could tell her the Mexicans were coming back. See Betty go still as a doe and open her mouth like she used to, back when she was pretty at fifteen or sixteen and he would grin and show her his chewing gum and chew it real slow. Passed her off to Ed after a few months, a long time ago now. She remembered even if Ed didn't want to.

He could get Betty to give him her car if Ed wasn't there. Get her to do anything.

He slipped around the far side to the back of the barn, paced off the distance from the side wall, and marked it by leaning an old one-by-four just where he thought the upright would be on the inside. He paced off the width again and leaned another one where the other upright would be. All the boards were vertical, so it ought to work. He started the Jeep, lined it up, and pushed through the back of the barn just fast enough to splinter the wood without making too much noise or knocking over the whole building. Boards snapped above the windshield and scraped across the roof. When a nail shrieked above him, he hit the gas irritably, pushing loose junk ahead of him until he had cleared the side. Ruining his Jeep. He shut off the engine and pocketed the key and stood looking at the jagged hole he'd made, the broken planks hanging there. He went back outside to the old stack of boards—there could be yellow jackets and snakes in there—and flinched when a wasp floated up, but the nest didn't seem to be in the stack, so he quickly pulled out enough lumber to lean against the back wall like somebody had something in mind. They would notice the hole if they were looking, but they wouldn't be looking.

Almost done. He went around the side of the barn closest to Ed's house, peering down toward it for signs that anyone was around. If he knew Ed, they would be long gone—but why hadn't they taken Betty's car? He tripped over a rusty harrow hidden in the weeds and caught himself with both hands against a young pine oozing resin. They came away sticky and smelling like turpentine. Nothing to do about it. Inside the barn, he scooped up dust and hay from the floor and threw it all over his car; it fused to his palms and got his jeans gummy when he tried to wipe them off. Have to find some steel wool later. A rusty bike with two flat tires leaned against the front of the barn. He propped it against the left front fender of the Jeep and examined the effect. He dragged an old tarp over the other side of the Jeep and scattered more dust over it, instinctively wiping the gunk off his hands by rubbing his jeans.

He backed away, looking it all over from the entrance. Nobody would think to look here, and if they did, they wouldn't think this wreck was his fine red Jeep. Not dented and scratched and filthy. Everybody knew he loved his Jeep.

A burn of blame settled onto Peach. And Peach's boy. And his redheaded bitch of a daughter.

Save them for later. He turned to look at his brother's house.

Nothing was moving. Whatever the sheriff and the FBI had done looking for evidence was over now, so Watkins decided to risk it. He jumped the chain link fence, crossed the lawn, and opened the back door. As soon as he stepped into the kitchen, he knew the house was empty. Two chairs had been turned over in the living room, and the coffee table was shoved to one side. Standing for a second at the front door, he saw tire tracks all over Betty's garden. That would be the Moccasin's boys. He guessed Ed had taken Betty and Phoebe to her parents' house in town. In the bathroom, he washed his hands to try to get off the resin, but without much luck, and he couldn't find any steel wool. He rifled through the drawers until he found a pair of scissors. From the trash he shook a sheet of newspaper loose from the rest of the paper and spread it over the immaculate sink. More shit about ISIS cutting off people's heads. Whole row of boys. Jesus.

His hands started to shake. He met his eyes in the mirror.

First his fine crop of weed and then his Jeep and now the famous dreadlocks that took years to grow and loving care to keep alive. He shook his hair forward and pulled one of the dreads out and tried cutting it at the base, but it was so tough and thick he couldn't get the scissors through, so he went to the kitchen, checking all the windows to make sure no one was coming. Beside the stove he found a knife block set. He pulled one of the knives out and tested it on his thumb.

Back in the bathroom, he cut through them savagely, one by one chopping the dreads, feeling his way carefully along the top of his head and down the back, dropping them one by one into yesterday's news until a nest of beheaded blond snakes looked up at him. In the mirror was a staring stranger. He would need a barber's clippers to even out all the idiotic tufts.

What looked especially stupid now were the rings in his eyebrows, so he started working them out. It was hard to unscrew the balls on the rings with his big fingers and impossible to do in a hurry. Little Vietnamese girl had put them in. Tiny little fingers, leaning her sweet petite body into him, putting her knee on his thigh, saying things in that cute accent. He thought about just yanking the rings through his eyebrows, but that would leave them ragged and bloody, and the last thing he wanted was anyone's attention. Finally, he teased one out, then another. That left four more, and by now he could hear another helicopter off in the distance coming toward him. He had to get out of here. Leave the goddamn things. He scrabbled through the drawers and found an old trimmer Ed must have used when he tried growing a beard several years ago. It was dead, but the charging cord was next to it, and it came on when he plugged it in. Pushing the blade into the roots of his dreads, he smoothed out the tufts and checked the length of the back ones with his fingertips as well as he could, feeling his way, blowing hair out of the blades when they choked.

He still didn't look like a husband. More like a poster for the Aryan Brotherhood. But what the hell. Nobody would recognize him. He could work out the rings on the road.

He wadded the newspaper around the springy hair and dropped in the two eyebrow rings. Cleaning around the sink with one of Betty's washrags, he put back the scissors, and took the wad of newspaper out to the big trashcan they kept in the backyard, where he stuffed it under the white kitchen bags that stank in the summer heat.

He could hear the bird hovering somewhere off to the south. They would be looking for Dexter Watkins in his red Jeep, not some tame goober in a blue Corolla. When he went back in, he took the knife to the kitchen, rinsed it off, and replaced it in the block. The clock said 11:47. He realized he was starving, so he opened the refrigerator and took a loaf of whole wheat bread, a package of sliced turkey, a package of ham, a pound of cheddar cheese, a jar of mayonnaise, and three apples. In a drawer, he found a paring knife they wouldn't miss. He was thinking he would have to hot-wire the car, but when he opened the pantry door to take to look for a plastic bag, he saw Betty's the big pink feathery keyring that held the keys to Betty's car and on a hook next to it was Ed's Braves baseball cap, which he put on over the damage. Sweet lord, it was almost too easy. His boys were watching over him. He put the food in a plastic Ingles bag, added a package of pita chips, and headed out the back door to the driveway.

Maybe when he got to Macon he could look up that sweet little Vietnamese thing and she could get the other rings out. He got into the driver's seat of Betty's car, pushed the seat all the way back, and adjusted the mirrors until he could see. The important thing was to act like a husband. He thought of Ed and arranged his face in what seemed to him a suitable expression, pussy-whipped and sour.

The look was still fixed on his face when he backed to the end of Ed's driveway and put on his blinker like a good citizen.

And then Red Scott, just standing there in plain sight, stepped out from beside the mailbox. He was pointing at Dexter a pistol while he talked on his radio in the other hand. Dexter ducked and started to gun it, but before he got five feet, the sheriff's Bronco roared up and blocked him in front. Two other cars came from both directions on Hopewell Road. Just when he thought about getting out and running for it, Red opened his door. While Dexter stared into the unsteady muzzle, Red reached over left-handed and took the keys from the ignition.

"Hey Hudson," Red called in a high voice. He held up the pink feathers for everybody to see. All of them were grinning. "And look here— you were right," he said, pulling Dexter from the car and lifting off the Braves cap.

Dexter lunged at Red, who jumped back out of reach, and then two or three other men he didn't know surrounded him. It was over. He was going back to jail, and when the reality of it hit him, another desperate impulse rose up in him. He would rather die than face it again. But he was scared to die, too, scared to see what he knew he would see when he did, and suddenly all the fight left him, the old trembling took over, and he stared at the ground, his teeth chattering in the afternoon heat.

He thought about sitting on the floor of the cell, a shitty hole over in Bagram, trembling, trying not to sleep, because when he slept he kept seeing the look on the father's face when the man saw him shoot his wife and then the children because they had come out of the other room and scared him. Shot them and shot them. The little girl's arms and legs flailing as she took the bullets. The blood everywhere and then the awful silence after he shot them all. His ears ringing. The cries coming from elsewhere, other houses. The feeling he had then, staring down at them, that he was damned, that nothing he could ever do, nothing, nothing, nothing, could ever make up for this, nothing the government could do to him, only the Hell that had already started and would go on forever and ever. Standing there trembling like he was trembling now. Look. Look at this. The corporal coming in from the street a minute later and saying *Jesus Christ, Watkins*, and Dexter knowing that Jesus Christ looked like a family of dead Muslims.

"Jesus," he said out loud.

"Dexter," Hudson Bennett said. "Hey Dexter."

He looked up at the sheriff, who took his arm kindly. The other men around him seemed different now, too, not mocking. Maybe a little embarrassed.

They put him in the back of the sheriff's Bronco.

Walter

A few miles south of Madison, the road came around a curve and down a hill with woods on the left and long stretches of pasture to the right. As they came over the rise, the vista spread out before them, and there, larger and greener than ever, just where the road flattened out at the bottom of the hill, stood the tree Walter had loved since he first saw it decades before. Grand, perfectly shaped, it overshadowed the road and part of the pasture. Now as he and Nora came down the long hill, a line of black cows ambled toward it, heavy and slow. A creek ran through the far part of the pasture, and a farmhouse sat back at the edge of the woods. Often his hand had risen from the wheel in salutation to this presiding presence, but now the enchantment of it was gone.

Just as they passed through its shadow, Nora said his name, and he looked at her.

"It's impossible, Walter."

He looked back at the road.

"I would have ruined my life for you. I would have ruined your life and Aunt Teresa's. Rose's, Buford's. Just an hour ago, I would have."

"I know that."

"So I need to know what happened to you," she said. "I think it's what I've needed to find out this year, what's been compelling me to be near you. After your first two books, something happened, didn't it?"

"My son died," he said. "My oldest son."

"No, I knew that. How could I not know that? I mean something happened to your gift. Your son's death wouldn't have destroyed what you had before. Not by itself. You were already a poet of loss."

"God damn it!" he shouted.

She shrank against the door.

"Just take me back home," she said, her eyes starting with tears.

"He *died*, I said, but *died* isn't the word. I'm lying to say he died. He was two years old. It was just after Rose was born."

"My God, what do you mean?"

"I killed him."

"Oh no. Oh my God. Not on purpose?"

"Of course not. Jesus Christ."

Second by second, he felt himself more distant from her, like a swimmer trying to reach the shore but borne out and away on the riptide. His colleagues in Athens had known some of it, of course—the death of his son—but neither they nor the greater world had known the whole story. Even Teresa had never known it all. Braxton Forrest had come closest, he realized, the night he had told Walter his own story in Waycross, the time he sought out Walter for the job in Gallatin.

But where did it start? Not in the driveway in Athens. The child's body curled beneath the tire. Teresa's rising and endless scream.

Not even with Lydia Downs and her necklace.

No, many years before that. The day he came up from the creek and his mother was gone.

They rode in silence. They had the road almost to themselves. Occasionally cars would pass on the other side, pickup trucks, tractor-trailers laboring up the hills. After a mile of farms and pastures, they came over the crest of a hill and down into woods that crowded up to the right of way on both sides of the road. Around a turn, up another long hill, still forested, another crest, and out to their right an opening, a field overwhelmed by kudzu.

Walter let out a long breath.

"When I was little, I made a necklace for my mother," he said. "I had this friend named Cletus McBride, and once when we put pennies on the railroad tracks, the train wheels just smashed part of mine. Lincoln's head was smashed flat, but on the bottom you could read the date, 1967, with a D under it and see part of Lincoln's shoulder and his clothes. On the back it said ONE CENT along the bottom curve. I took the penny to Cletus's house and punched a hole through the top with a nail and threaded a leather cord through it and gave it to my mother for her birthday. It was pretty in a simple kind of way, and I thought she might like it because I was born in 1967. She loved it because I had made it for her. She wore it all that week after I gave it to her, the week before she disappeared. She made sure I saw it every day, dangling there from her neck."

He glanced at Nora. She nodded, waiting.

"And then she was gone," he said. He lifted his fingers from the top of the steering wheel rose and dropped them again. "I never saw her again. I forgot all about that necklace until I saw it on one of my students in the spring of 1997."

A hundred yards or so ahead of them, a tractor pulling a flatbed trailer loaded with hay bales did not pause at the stop sign on a side road.

"Don't do it!" Walter cried.

But the thick-necked old farmer ignored the car barreling down upon him and pulled out onto the highway. Walter had to hit the brakes and almost skid to a halt behind the trailer. Two cars—three, four, five—shot by close together on the other side, followed by a slow truck hauling logs that projected far beyond the bed and dangled a red warning flag from their tapering ends.

Hay blew back at them from the bales swaying slowly in front of them. As soon as the lane cleared, Walter passed, blasting his horn and leaning across to glare out Nora's window. The old man paid no attention, as though traffic on the road never merited his notice. Walter accelerated so violently that it thrust Nora back against her seat, and almost immediately they came around a curve into a small crossroads town he had forgotten, where the speed limit suddenly dropped from sixty-five to thirty. Another truck pulled out of a lumberyard beside the railroad tracks and crossed into their lane.

"God *damn* it!" Walter shouted, pounding the steering wheel again with the palm of his hand.

Nora glanced away out the side window. A few moments later, she turned back to look at him.

"Who was the girl wearing the necklace?"

When the truck turned at the intersection and the road cleared ahead of them, he took a deep breath.

"She took a class I taught on the Romantic poets. One of my friends on the faculty told me that she was a talented sculptor, so I went to her show that semester, and she saw me there, and we talked for a long time. I was almost famous in those days. Over the break, she got rid of her boyfriend and signed up for the creative writing class I did in the spring."

She dreaded hearing what he was going to tell her.

"She fell in love with you?" she ventured.

At first he did not answer.

"After her fashion," he said at last.

"And how old were you then?"

Another pause.

"Thirty-four, thirty-five, somewhere in there."

For a long time he did not speak.

"Her name was Lydia Downs. Girls in my classes were always flirting with me, but I had a two-year-old son, we'd just had Rose. I was happy with Teresa."

Nora bent her head at the mention of her aunt.

"Lydia had a kind of insistence, though," he said, "and a kind of genius, not just in sculpture, and she was beautiful in a way completely different from the sorority girls. Of course I was flattered. She wrote me a poem. We found occasions. And then one afternoon she had on that necklace."

When he said it, he forgot Nora was there. It startled him when she spoke.

277

"What did you say to her?"

"Where did you get that necklace?"

"What did she say?"

"She said *It was my stepmother's*."

"Oh my God," Nora said. "Oh Walter."

"So I said *Tell me about your stepmother*."

He drove in silence.

"Walter?" Nora said.

"Lydia grew up in Seattle. Her father taught something—politics or history—at the University of Washington. Her mother died of cancer when she was five or six, and her father remarried a couple of years after his wife's death. A painter."

"Did your mother paint?"

He did not answer.

"Walter, please."

"Lydia said her stepmother had always worn that necklace."

He did not say any more, and she did not press him. Finally, he spoke again.

"I asked Lydia *So why do you have the necklace? Did something happen to your stepmother?* And Lydia said that she had found the necklace on her dresser one morning two years before. Her stepmother had disappeared. Her father was able to trace her to Atlanta, where she rented a car at the airport and drove it all the way to Tampa, Florida."

"What did you do then?"

"With Lydia? I held the necklace and looked at it."

"She gave it to you?"

"No," he said softly. "No," as if he were admitting something.

"What did you say to her?"

"I said I made one for my mother once that looked like this. And she asked me what had happened to my mother, and I said *She died*."

"Why did you say that?"

They came over a hill, and the muddy Ocmulgee River lay at the bottom, crossed by a long bridge. The light from the water hurt his eyes.

"She gave me back Rosemary." He went silent, and then he said, "Her smell and her touch."

Nora turned her head as they crossed the river. A large bird was flying away upstream above the water. She wiped her eyes.

"I had found her again," he said. "I didn't want to lose her."

"As though Lydia was your mother," Nora said in a strange, flat voice.

"I went home that afternoon," he said. "Teresa and I had bought a little house in a subdivision north of Athens off Jefferson Road—a plain little place with one tree in front and a mimosa in the backyard. It was a sunny day in April, a beautiful soft day, and I was full of the strangest elation, as if all the old laws had been canceled and the world was new. When I got there, Teresa was sitting on the front steps.

"From the moment I pulled in the driveway, she stared at me. Walter wasn't quite three. He was playing in the grass, running after a soccer ball that he would keep kicking by accident. Rose was asleep in one of those folding canvas strollers. Teresa was pushing the stroller back and forth and staring at me. Her eyes looked so dark and full of accusation that I almost left before even getting out of the car. But I did get out. I slung the strap of my bag over my shoulder and took my books out of the back seat and started toward her.

"Walter saw me and said *Daddy!* and ran toward me. I picked him up with my free arm and walked toward Teresa. I remember neighbors out in their yards, somebody down the street mowing, kids on bikes. Standard Americana. Teresa just sat there and stared at me, pushing the stroller back and forth. I said *What's the matter?* and put down the boy, but she didn't answer, just stared at me, and I saw in her eyes everything that I had been with her and all that I had betrayed. Her hand pushed the stroller back and forth.

"*I called her* she said, and I said *What are you talking about?* And she said *Lydia Downs* and I felt my heart go cold and I said *What do you mean you called her?* And then my rage rose as I thought about what some busybody must have told her, somebody who must have seen me.

"*What are you doing calling her?* I said, and she said *You're my husband. I told her she was just a stupid, infatuated girl but you were my husband and we had children and you had made a solemn vow before God Almighty in the sacrament of marriage—I asked her if she had any idea what that meant—that you would love and honor me.*

"And I shouted *You called her?*

"I was so furious I just hurled my books in the bushes and went back to the car and started it. I heard Teresa shout *Wait! Oh my God!*—and she tripped over the stroller starting up, pointing and screaming. I thought she just wanted to keep me from going back to Lydia, so I slammed the car into reverse and backed up."

"No," Nora said.

"Walter had chased his ball behind the car. I backed over my son. He was crushed up under the tire."

"Walter, that's—

"Within an hour, all on the same day. I found my mother and I killed my son."

"Oh God."

"Was it? Was it the all-good, all-merciful God? He took my son, He took my talent, He took my dignity."

"Stop it."

"And Teresa wants me to *worship* Him? She wants me to go confess to some priest in a booth, some middle-aged queer with a soul like a mealy apple, sitting behind his curtain fantasizing about his altar boys and smirking at the so-called faithful who are needy enough to tell him their humid little sins, and she wants *me* to confess as though that will *save* me, as though—"

"Stop it!" she cried.

They slowed at the intersection of the highway between Macon and Jackson. It was exactly thirteen more miles to Stonewall Hill.

Thirteen more miles.

Teresa

She was on the front porch when the Subaru at last came down Lee Street from the courthouse square. Her heart was a great dull burning, an unclean immolation. Walter had been gone since Friday with Nora O'Hearn. All morning, thinking of Walter back in Athens, she had been full of dread. Knowing what he felt for Nora stirred up the story of Lydia Downs. All morning she had been feeling again what she felt that black April day. Their child crushed and unmoving beneath the back tire, that terrible moment that would never leave either of them, never. Perhaps in heaven it would be transfigured by divine meaning and redeemed into joy, but the very thought of the transformation made her bitter.

She went back through the house to the kitchen and stepped out the back door. Two policemen stopped Walter and checked his ID as he was coming around the front of the car. Walkie-talkies crackled from elsewhere in the yard.

"Seriously?" he said.

"Seriously," Teresa said. "At least you're home."

Nora O'Hearn opened her car door and stood uncertainly, smoothing her yellow dress. Teresa glanced at her but did not speak.

"How's Rose?" Walter asked.

"Terrified."

His eyes moved past her. Buford came down the steps beside her.

"What's going on, son?" Walter said. "What are you playing at?"

The boy looked confused and a little frightened.

"I'm not playing," he said.

Nora came close now and held out her hands to him.

"Buford?" she said.

"No ma'am," he said. He did not recognize her, and Teresa's heart yielded a little, a very little.

The Boy

After Mr. Peach stopped asking him questions, the boy went back inside the house and up to the room. Rose came in and sat beside him on the bed.

"Can I show you something?" she said. "Look at your right elbow."

She lifted his right arm and bent it at the elbow and twisted it a little to show him the side that was hard to see.

"You see that scar? That's from a bike crash. Feel that."

With his left hand, he felt the ripples and ridges of it.

"You were riding with no hands and a car pulled out in front of you and you used the brakes before you grabbed the handlebars. You came home with your elbow looking like a smashed jar of salsa. And people say you're smart."

"I don't remember riding a bike," he said.

But he remembered what bikes were. Two wheels. Two circles with centers. What was the center called? The axis? No, the *earth* had an axis. A bicycle had *axles*. A bicycle worked by connecting two wheels, two axles. The axles let the circles spin. The axles, the spokes, the rims of the wheels, the tires on the rims. Air in the tires. He remembered that. You pushed air into the tires.

What was that called?

Pumping. He smiled to remember the word.

You took ordinary air and squeezed it. You pumped it into a tire with both hands on the pump, squeezing air into the tire until the tire was hard. *Pumping.*

She gently turned his arm over and touched a spot near his right wrist on the inside of his forearm. He looked up at her and smiled. He liked the way it felt when she touched his skin. Soft, careful. Gazing at him with her green eyes, a slight scowl, the eyebrows, her intense mouth. She touched the spot again.

"You burned it here when you were pouring popcorn from the big pot Dad pops it in."

"Popcorn," he said. All those p's. *P*ouring *p*o*p*corn from the big *p*ot Dad *p*o*p*s it in. A mosaic of yellow kernels in hot oil simmering and stirring and hissing and then—one! ONE!—suddenly exploding in white pops. Popcorn. Noisy, steaming.

He remembered that.

Excited, he looked at the girl Rose and as she looked back at him, he saw the skin around her eyes begin to quiver. Her lids flooded.

"Buford?" she said.

He waited to see if anything would happen inside him. Nothing happened.

"No," he said.

The tears spilled out of her eyes and she wiped them roughly away. She shook her head and in two steps she was gone from his room.

He looked at the undersides of his forearms. She had missed a spot. There was a small blank reddish circle exactly halfway between the base of his hand and the inside of his elbow on his left arm. He pressed the tip of his forefinger into it: it felt like the exact middle. He turned his arm over, spread his fingers, examined the backs of both hands, and then turned them back over and stared at the lines in his palms, the long ones that looked like rivers, the other ones crisscrossing them. It was strange that people looked at you and judged you because of your body. It wasn't like you got to *pick* it. You just showed up in it, the way he had showed up in this one, with somebody else's scars on it. It had already been going when he arrived in it. People called him "Buford." How long would he have to be in it before he could say *This is my body*? So what was he? Where was he before he arrived?

A mockingbird sang close by outside. *Gone* again *gone* again WHEAT! WHEAT! WHEAT! *gone* again.

Maybe your body was your fate. Did God just throw a blank soul into one body or another and see what happened? He pictured a girl born ugly—huge nose, broad hips, shoulders like a lumberjack. Did she *decide* to look like that? Everybody snickering when she went to the board. Or Law Crater who could outrun everybody in their grade from kindergarten on, and everybody praised him for it, but he didn't have anything to do with it. No matter how hard you tried, you would never be fast if you weren't born fast. The things you could do something about—the things you could work at—didn't seem to make any difference to people.

FAST! FAST! FAST! *nobody* nobody *up* and then *up* and then *over over over* said the mockingbird.

So what should you do? Go to God with a list of complaints? How did you do that, exactly? What about people who decided they were born the wrong sex? They're inside this body already their whole lives when one day they say *Good Lord! I'm in this girl's body, but I'm supposed to be a boy!* He smiled at the idea. He had complaints about his body, but nothing major. What if he looked like Janice Knowlton? Maybe *she* should have been a boy. But there you were; you just came that way, like Tim Withers, who was six inches shorter than everybody else and had asthma and blew his nose all the time. Jesse Bullfinch, the catcher, was massive, broad-faced as a steer with thick lips and huge hands that made the bat look small, but he couldn't play in the infield like Buford. Mr. Chambliss had put Buford at shortstop because he was *quick as a wink* and *sharp as a tack.*

Something inside him, some watcher, shifted, as though settling on the other foot. The mockingbird sang close by, and he glanced through the window, trying to see it.

Sang, sang, up through rills and slow soft notes and then on a *skip* of a LOST BEAT climbing *up up up* and off on *another run! another run! another run! Run! Run!* He saw the bird now, on top of the gable, hopping, turning, frantic. When he looked back at the spot on his arm, he remembered that a wart had been there. Dr. Fletcher had touched it with something very cold to freeze it off.

He sat very still.

He felt the center come quietly back into the circle, like the choir director resuming his place after an intermission.

The mockingbird sang. He flowed back into himself. He was Buford Peach. Buford Peach was his name. His name, but not *the* name. He was Buford again, but he was not entirely Buford, and he knew now that he had never been entirely Buford and would never be.

Sometimes, even as a small child, he had felt this body, even this mind, as something else than what he really was, as if it were a dream he had been born into and would one day awaken from. He had just now, minutes ago, inhabited this body with its scars and its history when he had not been Buford. He had been in this body, but it was not *his.* Or his but not Buford. Not knowing who he was, he had been a person, maybe as much a person as Buford Peach was.

He could still feel and remember how he could think and feel and know things even though he did not know who he was. Knowing who he was had not mattered as much as he had thought it would. When it had not mattered, he had even felt a peace. He had been simply been the boy, deeper and quieter than Buford Peach, but without a name, without that thing teachers called a "personality."

How could he remember not knowing who he was? The name that the voice spoke—something like a verb, but quiet, perfectly quiet, beneath hearing—had exploded who he was, and yet now he brimmed over with himself, he streamed into his body and *was.* He could not say it to himself, but he felt it, this *going* he could give himself to. It broke from something deep inside and *gave* him and was him and would never be lost. Silent, motionless, eternally welling into time. He felt it for less than an instant: a pulse of conviction, quick and stunning as the strike of a bullet, and it was gone.

He waited for a moment to see if anything would change.

And then he remembered the smell of the house in Missy's Garden. He remembered going in there with his father when the door was still locked. He remembered going in there by himself and kicking it open.

Tremors ran over him, almost convulsions. He ran from the room.

"Rose?" he cried. "Mama! Rose!"

Bill Sharpe

All day he had been interrogated by officers from the State Patrol and the GBI who would borrow Chick Lee's office and ask Sharpe for descriptions of the men who had burned down Ed Watkins' store. He left the back door of the dealership at five.

"You hear they locked up Dexter Watkins?" Chick Lee called from across the pavement, holding up his smartphone. Chick had lost weight lately—some kind of diet that put him in ketosis and kept him irritable—and Sharpe always had to look twice to recognize his profile.

"About time," Sharpe said. Hudson Bennett had told him earlier. Bennett almost felt sorry for Dexter, who was reliving the whole thing in Afghanistan. PTSD stuff. Sharpe had nodded, but it would take a while before he could forgive Watkins. *For a while there I thought you were trying to beat my time with her.* Rage rose in his throat just thinking about it.

In his pickup, driving up toward the courthouse square, he turned off the news and called his mother on his cell phone to see if she needed anything in town.

"Can you talk to Martin?"

"Put him on."

As he got into downtown, he turned right onto Lee Street and stopped at the red light at Johnston Street, putting on his left blinker, and held the phone to his ear. His brother probably wanted him to bring home some frozen yogurt or—his favorite—mango sorbet, which he claimed didn't give him diarrhea. Out of the corner of his eye, he saw people descending the courthouse steps, and he turned to see who they were. Harold Melton, his classmate all through school, now the district attorney. Buddy Fingal, the county coroner, with his stiff-legged limp. Some other men he didn't know.

"Bill!" his brother said into the phone. "They burned down the store!"

The light turned green, and he eased forward, waiting for the oncoming traffic to get through the intersection.

"I saw it."

He turned left as soon as it cleared.

"You saw it! Are you coming home?" said Martin. "What if they burn down our house?"

"I'm coming," he said, and he glanced at the people on the sidewalk in front of the *Tribune* office. Braxton Forrest was going into the building. Teresa Peach was outside with her daughter and Hudson Bennett. And then his heart blazed. There she was. Before he could think he pulled into the open parking space closest to them and got out.

"I'll bring you something," he said into the phone and pushed the end button.

Nora glanced up and saw him. To his amazement, her face lit up and she broke away from the others and ran to him and put her arms around him. He held her in astonishment and terror. His hand rose to the back of her neck.

"Oh my God," she said, standing back and looking up at him, her eyes wet. She touched his cheek with her hand. "Oh my God. I am so glad to see you."

He did not know what to say. His phone buzzed, and he glanced at it.

"Martin," he explained, and she nodded, looking into his eyes. He listened to his brother's careful explanation.

"How is he?" she smiled. She looked very tired.

"Scared. I told him I'd bring him something. He wants Moose Tracks with cookie dough sprinkles."

"Can I see him?" she said.

"Come have dinner with us."

She was good with Martin—teasing him, pretending she was going to eat his Moose Tracks, holding his hand until he was spellbound. She was bright and thoughtful with his mother during dinner.

"Why don't you marry that one?" she whispered in his ear as Nora went down the front steps ahead of him. "Do you want me to ask her or will you?"

"Ask me what?" Nora said, turning.

Out in the driveway, he held the door for Nora and she watched him as he went around to the driver's side and got in and started the truck.

"Ask me what?" she said.

"You know what I want to ask you," he said.

She met his eyes in the half-dark. After a moment, her eyes dropped. "Can you wait a little?"

"I've waited since March."

"I've been confused," she said.

"Was it something I did?"

"No, don't ever think that."

"I didn't know what to think."

"I'll tell you, but not yet."

He wanted to kiss her, but instead he backed up and turned around and drove down Hopewell Road, pointing out Missy's Garden, where he had found the boy.

"Buford didn't know me today," she said.

"I'm not surprised."

At the corner of County 73, he slowed to show her the burned store.

"They know I'm a witness," he said. "So why haven't they come after me?"

"I don't know. They only seem interested in Walter."

For a long time, she did not speak. He drove past Phoenix Estates and took the interstate toward Gallatin. Halfway to town, she lightly took his hand. Her left hand, small-boned, live, soft. She held his hand all the way into town, past the courthouse and down Lee Street and up the driveway behind Stonewall Hill, and all the way his heart floated in a spell he never wanted to break. He knew how Martin felt.

"I'll walk you up," he said when they stopped.

"Don't," she said, but she leaned across the seat and pulled his head toward her and kissed him, holding his lips against hers a moment longer when he started to pull back, the pressure of her wanting hand on the back of his neck, a moment more, and a soft parting. After a few seconds outside of time, she broke free and opened her door and ran across the gravel and up the steps and inside.

Shouldn't he punish her? Would he simply forgive her for all the pain she had caused him? Right now, with the feeling of her hand still haunting his, the touch of her tongue like flaming cognac, it all evaporated. Hell yes, he'd forgive her.

He sat there for a moment. He was backing up his truck to leave, looking for any hint of her in the great old house, when he saw a still shape in a window halfway up the near side.

Someone looking down at him. It had to be Walter Peach. But Sharpe was past Peach now. All the way through town, he drove with the windows down, waving to everyone he saw.

Buford

Once during the night, he woke up and saw a shelf of photographs, a mirror reflecting unfamiliar angles, a lamp shade he did not recognize. It was happening again. For several seconds, he stared in bewilderment, until his mind came back to him and he remembered that he was in Professor Forrest's room. He turned over and went back to sleep.

When he woke again, the first light was in the room, but the sun was not up. He trembled, still half in his dream. He had been cutting through kudzu that got deeper and deeper until great walls of it stood on both sides of him like the Red Sea, all of it growing and curling upward. Ahead of him the house was sinking and drawing him with it. He felt the undertow take him and sweep him downward

And he woke up. But who was he?

Just before the first wave of panic reached him, he remembered. *Buford Peach.*

Buford Augustine Peach. He looked at the scars on his forearms, and the night before came back to him. Things were better. He knew who he was, and his father was not going to run away with Miss Nora. But none of them were safe. And that wasn't the worst thing, because of who was in the room at Missy's Garden. He saw his foot rise, he saw himself kick the door, kick it again, saw the door slam back against the wall in a swirl of dust and tiny squeals.

He scrambled out of the bed and stood panting. Nobody knew but him. He had to show them.

ALISON

Part V

We are stardust
Billion year old carbon
We are golden
Caught in the devil's bargain
And we've got to get ourselves
Back to the garden

Joni Mitchell, "Woodstock"

Bennett

Stabbing his scrambled eggs distractedly, Bennett looked at the *Macon Telegraph*, where a picture of Watkins' burned store had made the front page. **Cartel Suspected in Gallatin County Arson**. He found his name, read the statement attributed to him, read what the State Patrol spokesman said, read what the GBI said, and what the FBI said. It was the third day. He could not shake off the feeling that had hung over him since he woke up in the dark and could not go back to sleep. Something else was coming. The Gallatin police had stationed men to watch the house, and the FBI was bringing in more, but he feared for the Peach family.

He got up to pour himself some more coffee, and he had the carafe in his hand when his landline rang, which startled him so much he spilled the coffee on himself. No one except his mother called him on that phone, and she would never call before seven in the morning unless there was something wrong. He grabbed a dishtowel to swab at his leg and went out into the hallway to answer it.

"Mama?"

"Hudson?" the caller said. Male, definitely not his mother.

"That's right."

"Walter Peach. Sorry to call so early."

Bennett set down the coffee, remembering the last thing he'd said to him.

"What's happened?"

"Nothing new, thank God."

"Your daughter's okay?"

"It's Buford," Peach said. "He knows who he is again. He says we have to go out to the property and go inside the house. He wants you to be there."

"He remembers what happened to him?"

"I took him inside there last Friday, and he went back in by himself on Monday morning when Bill Sharpe found him outside."

Bennett took in this news. He remembered the boy sitting there on Monday—two days ago—at the table in the front of Ed Watkins' store, traumatized by something. And the smell that lingered in his car.

"So you went in there Friday morning? You were out there and you didn't see what Dexter was doing?"

Peach was silent for a moment before answering.

"I saw Dexter and a stranger down there on the creek. I think they saw me."

Bennett held the phone, breathing out slowly.

"How come you didn't call me?"

"It's complicated, Hudson."

"Is that right?" The only thing that would keep Peach from calling, Bennett thought, was that he was an accessory. Bennett just didn't quite see how.

"So you cut that path we saw."

"That's right."

"So what's in there?"

"There's a door in the house locked from the inside. There's a copy of my first book, and until Friday, I hadn't been in there since my mother left in 1974."

"Okay," Bennett said, beginning to feel a crawling in his spine. The idea of going inside that house. He supposed this was what they elected him for.

"Buford says she's in there."

"Says who is in there?"

Peach did not answer at first. When he did, his voice sounded thin and distant.

"My mother."

"Your *mother*?"

"He wants to show us."

Bennett shook his head and dabbed at his thigh with the towel. He sighed. "I'll be out there in twenty minutes."

"Make it half an hour."

He hung up and went back into the kitchen. The eggs were cold, and he thought about microwaving them, but instead he dumped them into the trash can and rinsed off the plate in the sink. He could get something out at Ed Watkins' store.

But no, he couldn't do that, could he? He stood there for a moment staring at the floor. Just then his cell phone rang, and he saw the office number. Too early.

"Ellen? What's up?"

"You need to go out to Ed Watkins' store," she said with a climbing hysteria. "They found a body that's—oh my god, Hudson! What's happening to us?"

He could hear her crying.

"A body that's what?"

"*Beheaded!* It's the short Mexican from yesterday."

"Sweet Jesus!"

"You'd better get out there."

"On my way."

He had to steady himself by putting a hand on the table. *Beheaded.* By God, Peach was right about these cartel people. But who would have beheaded their own man? Was this some kind of rival gang?

No need to call Peach. He would see him out there.

All day yesterday they had been looking for the short man with a pocked face who had thrown money at Ed Watkins and threatened Rose Peach. Well, there he was. Red and Walter had noticed a yellow ribbon around the gas pump when they drove back past Ed Watkins' store, and they had pulled in out of curiosity. The head, propped upright, sat at the base of the gasoline pump, mouth gaping, eyes vacant. The concrete base of the pump was stained with his dried blood. His body lay nearby in the ashes of the store, hands bound behind his back with zip ties. Beside the head, there was a small envelope of the size that people use for personal correspondence, and neatly typed across it were the words **To Sheriff Hudson Bennett.**

"You want to open it?" he said to Red.

"Addressed to you." The deputy handed it to him.

He slit it open cautiously with his pocketknife. All that stuff about white powder years back. No powder in this one.

Inside the envelope was a neatly printed sheet folded in thirds:

> To understand this sight, my friend, examine the digression in Chapter Seven of <u>The Prince</u>, where my motives might be guessed (or where perhaps you and the others reading it might be cleverly misled). A speculation: suppose that rival interests within the Sinaloa cartel have been vying for this section of new expansion, and each has been told—by whom, I will leave to your surmises—that the other is trying to destroy it. My own local designs (after one little matter of revenge) are legal and broad, ultimately pacific. But how to make lawmakers see the light? Once it was tobacco, once it was cotton, and now this opportunity comes for a new exploitation of lotos eaters when marijuana is legalized. Is this the region, this the soil, the clime? Investment today, both in real estate and enlightened agriculture, leads on to fortune—or to death!
>
> Luke O. Stoma

Luke O. Stoma? Whoever the hell it was, it was no Mexican. *The Prince?* Educated. That's where a little more college could have helped Bennett. He could ask Peach.

Bennett gave his deputies the rest of the day off. They were too rattled to be any good to him anyway. He was rattled himself, but he stood there and looked at the head and the body. Then, fighting down his nausea, he got back in his truck, leaving it running to keep the air conditioner going while he made the calls to the State Patrol and the GBI. He put the envelope on the passenger's seat and sat there staring out through the windshield while he waited.

"Sheriff," Ellen said over the radio.

He picked it up.

"Any luck?" he asked.

"I got Ed at Betty's sister's. Ed's on the way back now to ID the man. I told him you'd wait at the store."

"Okay, I'll stay put. How's Dexter? ... Ellen, you still there?"

"He keeps talking about that family he shot. It's funny, Hudson. He sounds like the man I married. This is the wrong time to say it, but I . . . kind of love him again."

Twenty minutes later, the GBI van sat near the store entrance, and men stepped carefully around the site, photographing everything and tweezing up evidence into sealed plastic bags, just like on TV. They looked up when Ed Watkins' pickup swerved into the lot and Ed leapt out and left it running with the door open and hurried toward the store. Bennett got out of his Bronco and intercepted him. When he explained what had happened, Ed stared over at the covered body.

"They cut his head off?" he said, his voice rising.

"Somebody did. Excuse me," he said to one of the GBI men. "This is Ed Watkins. They burned his store yesterday. He might be able to ID the body."

"Special Agent Porch," a GBI man said, shaking Watkins' hand. He took him over. "Are you ready, sir?"

Ed nodded, and the agent removed the cloth covering the head. Ed blanched and stumbled backward. He turned and rushed away to vomit into the ashes of his store. He stayed bent over for a few seconds before noticing the body a few feet away and swearing. The uniformed agent took his arm.

"Steady now, sir," said the agent. "We just need you to confirm his identity."

Ed walked back and stared down at the head.

"That's the one who gave me the money," he said.

"You're sure?" they said.

"He acted like he was in charge. And a day later he ends up like this. Who the hell did this?"

"Whoever was really in charge," Bennett said, touching the letter in his pocket. He would have to show it to the GBI, but first he wanted to see what Peach could tell him. "Maybe a rival cartel working the same territory."

"Jesus, Hudson," Ed said helplessly. He walked in a circle and ended by looking toward his ruined store and the body, clasping his hands on top of his head.

"You knew that crop was down there," Bennett said.

"Dexter told me. He thought he was going to get rich. He came after me yesterday thinking I'd called you on him, and maybe the cartel thought the same thing. But I don't get this," he said, waving over at the head. "What's this supposed to tell me?"

"Might not be for you," Bennett said.

Ed looked about as defeated as a man could look. Bennett watched him climb back in the pickup and bump slowly out of the lot and onto the road. He watched the GBI men do their work. The FBI would arrive soon. Over the next few hours, the whole thing would be like September when they had found the heroin in the wrecked truck on I-75. News teams would be prying into everybody's business. Accusations would start.

He thought about Gallatin when he was growing up. All the clichés—safe and sleepy, nobody locked their doors. But for years he had felt the community beginning to fall apart, maybe because the town sat beside the interstate, like an overhang of grass and trees slowly being washed away by a creek until a flood comes—of course a flood was coming—and it collapses into the water and disappears. Peach was always writing about invasive ideas and the effects of modern global economy. But damned if he didn't turn out to be right about the cartels. It wasn't just crime. People didn't talk to each other in person anymore because they were always on their smartphones. They felt like they were connected to the whole world—all the news, all the information you used to have to ask somebody about or go look up in the library. Even pornography, right there on your computer or your phone. No risk of shame. It used to be a little town could be its own place, but now the sick world reached right inside it.

He got back into the Bronco to think. He first saw the change coming with Janet Brownlee. Beautiful Janet, senior year. After the prom and the parties, they had gone out with a few other couples out to Dixon's Mill on the Ikahalpi River at daybreak. Coffee and donuts and licking the sugar off her fingers and her kissing the flakes of it off his lips and sitting there with their arms around each other watching the red ball of the sun rise through the pines, the other couples scattered on other rocks out in the river. The warmth of her body pressed against him in the cool of the morning, the smell of her perfume, her arm coming down to block his hand when it strayed up toward her breast.

He shifted in his seat, remembering how she had left to spend the summer working at a resort her rich aunt knew about on Long Island. They had lingered and lingered the night before she left. He had had his arms around her from behind when they were standing on the empty campus of the old college, out by the pond, watching the moon, and his hands rose up her body and she sighed and let him and he cupped her breasts in his palms and his heart rode in bliss, his body pressed into hers. *I want you to marry me* he had whispered into her ear and she had turned around and looked at him, her whole soul in her face, her eyes dilated. *Oh, Hudson.*

Not yes. Just *Oh Hudson.*

An EMT ambulance pulled up, lights flashing, and the paramedics got out. Ezra Carson, Hart Joseph—good boys he had watched grow up. Somebody had to pick up the body, he supposed. He lifted a hand to them as they went over to the ashes and lifted the sheet the GBI had put over the corpse. Hart stepped back, almost stumbling. Bennett could read his lips: *Sweet Jesus.*

Montauk. That was where it was. He had looked it up later—a place on Long Island for rich people. When she had gotten back in late August, he had gone to pick her up, and as soon as they were out of sight of her house he had pulled over and kissed her, and she was ready. His first encounter with the Sexual Revolution.

Here came her tongue, live and exciting, and she flowed against him eager with her breasts. Her hand went up his thigh and he went cold as knowledge broke over him. He pushed her away, heartsick, and when she tried again, he pushed her away again and turned the car around and drove her home without a word. *What's the matter?* she kept saying. And then she said *I know you must have been with other girls.* And when they got to her driveway, he went around the car and opened the door for her. She got out and touched him on the cheek with her palm. He wouldn't look at her.

Nope he said.

Nope what?

I haven't been with other girls.

And then she said it again, and it was different this time. The last thing she said to him. *Oh, Hudson.*

She was married now to some big financial guy in Atlanta.

A tap at his window startled him. He looked up, expecting it to be a GBI man, but it was Walter Peach. The man looked gaunt, drained. Done with his tomcatting. Bennett turned off the Bronco and got out to stand beside him.

"Didn't get over to your place yet." He gestured at the scene by way of explanation.

"They told me somebody cut off his head?" Peach said under his voice. "This is the man who came to the door of my house?"

"Ed Watkins ID'd him. I wouldn't want to ask your daughter to."

Peach nodded.

"Listen," Bennett said tentatively, shy about saying it, after their sharp exchange. He shouldn't have said *Fuck you*, he thought. Just popped out of his mouth after Peach's criticism of him. "He left me a note. Whoever did it. It's a little above my pay grade."

"What kind of note?"

Bennett had given the note and the envelope to the GBI officer in charge, Lieutenant Ames, and now he walked Peach over to meet him.

"Walter Peach. *Gallatin Tribune*," Peach said, extending his hand. Lt. Ames shook it and half-turned to Bennett for an explanation.

"He's not here for the newspaper," Bennett said. "We found the marijuana on his property. I want to show him the note, see what he can figure out about it."

Ames eyed Peach with suspicion, but he went to the van and called inside, and a young woman wearing disposable rubber gloves brought the letter over in a Ziploc bag. She extracted it and held it up for Peach to read.

"Sweet Lord," Peach murmured. "Luke O. Stoma? That sounds like a joke. *Stoma* is mouth in Greek. Luke O. would be *leuko*, which is white, as in leukemia. So *white mouth*? Does that mean anything to you?"

"Not a thing," Bennett said. "What's *The Prince*?"

"A famous sixteenth-century book by an Italian named Niccolo Machiavelli. It's about how to get power and keep it, sort of like a Mafia handbook. My adoptive mother made me read it a long time ago. This man named Cesare Borgia takes over a lawless area and puts a harsh governor in charge to clean things up. The people hate this governor, so after a while, Borgia beheads the governor and leaves the body in a public square to make a statement."

"What kind of statement?" Bennett said.

"He liberates the people from this tyrant, but he also makes them more afraid of him than they were of the governor."

"So we're supposed to be scared of Luke O. Stoma."

"Exactly. Can I use this for the paper?"

"No sir," said Lt. Ames. "Valuable evidence."

"You see what it means?" Peach said. "This 'White Mouth' is playing cartels against each other and using the fear of their violence to show that the legalization of marijuana is the best solution."

Bennett pursed his lips and shook his head. He saw it now, but he would never have understood that on his own.

They watched Ezra and Hart roll the stretcher with the body on it up to the ambulance and then inside. A moment later the EMT men approached the pump, where two GBI men were standing above the Mexican's head.

Bennett and Peach drifted over to join them. Somebody had put a sheet over it earlier, and now one of the GBI men reached down and lifted it away. The men stirred, several of them cursing. Bennett knew the dead man's look would haunt him, because there was nothing in it like regret or some last longing for life, just a kind of stupid surprise, a dull, criminal resignation.

They put the head in a plastic bag inside an Igloo ice chest. Peach was still there, taking notes for the paper, Bennett imagined, seeing that he was right all along, not that it could be any satisfaction to him. Bennett could see the boy through the windshield of the car watching them solemnly. Waiting them out, so they could go over to the old house to see another dead body.

Bennett sighed. He'd had about enough for one day looking at the beheaded Mexican. He just wanted to take a long hot shower and then drink some bourbon and sit in his chair and stream a few episodes of *Longmire*.

Peach came up beside him.

"I know you're busy," he said. "But do you mind? It won't take long to show you what's there."

Bennett nodded. "I'll meet you in a minute."

Back in the Bronco, he radioed Ellen and told her where he was going.

Walter Peach

The sheriff was just pulling up behind them when Buford opened the door of the Subaru and got out and started up along the fence line.

"Buford!" Walter got out and called over the top of the car. "Wait a second!"

The boy stopped and turned. His face was working as though he were about to cry. Walter went around to the back of the car and got out the bush hook he had used on Friday and nodded to Bennett and they started up toward the big live oak.

"You're in a mighty big hurry," Bennett said to Buford kindly. "So you think somebody's inside there?"

"Yes sir, there is."

"So you've already been in there?"

"Yes sir."

"That's what you did Monday?"

"Yes sir."

"By yourself," Bennett repeated.

"Yes sir."

Bennett glanced around at the kudzu and then down at Vernon Jenkins' corn field and smoothed his hand down the back of his neck. Steeling himself, just like Walter.

"Okay," Bennet said. "Show me what you found."

Walter led the way along the barbed wire and up the rise to the path they had cut across from the live oak to the house. The vines they had cut on Friday were brown and dry, but already new tendrils of kudzu uncurled on both sides. A foot a day, they said—so five feet of new growth since Friday, grasping and growing. Off to his left, a wasp rose languidly from the green mass of leaves.

He led Buford and the sheriff down the path and around the side of the house to the back. The screen had fallen flat beneath the overhang. The door stood slightly ajar.

"I locked that door," Peach said to Buford.

"You gave me the key when you were looking for the machete. I found it in my pocket when I put my jeans back on."

"So why didn't you give it back?"

"Because you were gone."

Walter nodded and glanced at Bennett. Gone to Athens, toying with the affections of Nora O'Hearn. Sick self-loathing came over him.

When he pushed the door open, dust floated out into the sunlight, and he stepped into the close, dank, organic smell that oppressed him. He waved a spiderweb out of his face, and the sheriff stepped up beside him in the kitchen, glancing at the pans abandoned on the stove, the mealy dust. There was a scurry somewhere close by and a dark shape fled across the floor.

"Hold on," Bennett said, taking a step backward as a shudder went through him, his hand going to his pistol. "I hate rats."

"I'm with you," Walter said as the sheriff gathered himself.

"Where's this room, buddy?" Bennett said to Buford.

Buford led them now. He went to the other side of the kitchen and pointed down the hallway and stepped back beside Peach. They followed as Bennett made his way through the underwater light from the window at the end of the hall. The door to Peach's childhood room was open, and now so was the other door, just a crack, as though someone were peeking out. His mother's door. She would get up in the summer morning naked as Eve except for the light shorts she slept in and she would stretch, arms straining high above her head, breasts rising, and then suddenly drop her hands and shiver and smile at him.

Bennett backed into Walter when they heard another scurry inside. The boy took Walter's hand.

"Don't you want to wait outside?" he said.

Buford shook his head. Walter nodded to the sheriff, whose hand instinctively went to his pistol again as he took a step into the gloom and pushed against the door. It squeaked inward on its stiffened hinges and the old dust rose around it. The smell overwhelmed them.

Bennett

Not wanting to see what was there, he looked at the room itself to give himself a little time. No furniture to speak of. A plain chest of drawers on the opposite wall with the top drawer a little open. Drawings, it looked like. Beside the bed was a cardboard box with a square of plywood on top of it supporting an empty glass. On its back in the middle of the floor, a straight-backed chair. Bennett righted it and set it against the wall beside the window, where a few feelers of kudzu had squeezed in past the sash and died.

He had actually *wanted* this job, back in the day—his way of serving God and the Constitution, establishing justice, ensuring domestic tranquility. He had run for office three times now. But was Gallatin County supposed to pay for the knowledge of human nature that kept settling in him, silting up in him, year by year?

He had to look. He went and stood beside the bed, fighting down his nausea. Her gray hair had fallen from the grinning skull. The mattress had absorbed her as she decomposed to her skeleton. A thin book covered with dust lay on the bed to the left of her. The closed room, kudzu a foot deep outside the window, no way to get fresh air without violence.

And by God, fresh air was what it needed.

"Let's go outside," Bennett said.

When they came out through the kitchen and the back door of the house, Peach stood looking downhill through the kudzu behind the house, his hands on top of his head.

"You think it's your mother?" Bennett said.

"God knows. It might be. It must be."

"Any idea why she'd come back here to die?"

"Not a clue."

"Something was in that glass," said the boy.

"Why do you say that?" Peach said.

They both stared down at the boy. When the boy did not answer, Bennett intervened.

"We need to get the coroner out here, see what he thinks. We need a death certificate, for one thing. You okay?" he asked Peach.

"I guess. My God."

Bennett walked back out the cut path and down the fence to his Bronco and radioed Ellen in the office.

"Where've you been?" she exclaimed. "I've been trying to get you for half an hour."

"I told you I was headed out to—what did you call it?"

"Missy's Garden. All this time? Listen, they just found two more bodies at that new development. Big men, we think the ones from yesterday. Both of them shot through the chest. They were sitting up inside the blade of the bulldozer when the Chesnutt fellow started it up this morning."

Bennett's heart hurt. He closed his eyes and leaned his head back on the headrest of the Bronco.

"Okay," he said.

"Chesnutt says he didn't see them at first," Ellen said. "He was turning the bulldozer around when all the Mexican workers started pointing and crossing themselves. Every one of them quit."

"I'll drive over there in a minute," he said. "We need to get Buddy Fingal out here to Missy's Garden."

"Oh my Lord. Who is it?"

"Peach's mother, it looks like. Locked herself in and died all alone and nobody to miss her or find her body for almost twenty years—"

She went silent for several seconds.

"Walter Peach's mother?"

"That's what we think. She's been here long enough for kudzu to grow a foot deep over the whole house."

"Oh Lord, don't even tell me."

"The boy found her Monday. I figure he panicked and hit his head when he saw the body." He pictured the boy's blind panic—screaming and turning and running full speed into the door's edge as it rebounded from the wall. He pictured the boy coming to in that room, the rats scurrying from him. Wandering down the hallway into the light and the yard. "You imagine going in there by yourself and finding that? You better call his mother and tell her what's going on out here."

"I'll call her."

After she signed off, he sat staring back down Hopewell Road toward the lights still flashing outside the burned store. Even the thought of Teresa Peach softened him. Why couldn't he have found a woman like her? Janet Brownlee had come to the twenty-year class reunion looking better than ever. Some kind of Arab name now. Her husband was an investment hotshot in Atlanta, and he gave Sybil Forrest High School enough money to build a new fine arts building. *Because it meant so much to Janet*, he told everybody, which Bennett thought was bullshit. Nice guy, though, lean and tall. Modest about his superiority.

Janet had pretended not to remember Hudson at first. The little flicker of her eyes over his uniform. And then

Oh, Hudson! You're the sheriff?
Just like Andy Griffith.

The radio crackled.

"Hudson?" Ellen said.

"I'm here." He stared down Hopewell Road.

"Teresa says she's coming out."

"Make sure there's a police car with her. I want those people protected. You call Buddy?"

"He's with those other two bodies."

"I better run over there to take a look."

He got out of the Bronco and walked quickly back up to let Peach and the boy know he was leaving. They had come out to the oak tree, which had to be a hundred years old or more. Peach was leaning at arm's length against the trunk, his head hanging. He stood up straight as Bennett came up to him.

"Why would she do this?" Peach asked.

"It's hard to know why people do things."

"Dad!" the boy said. "Look at this." With a stick he raked the cigarette butts out of a small tray embedded in the bark. "It's a hand!"

For a second, Bennett thought he meant another dead body. But it was the hand of a sculpture, a woman's hand, palm upward, covered past the wrist by the bark that had grown over it. They stood staring down at it.

"Something going on?" They all glanced up at the same time and saw Vernon Jenkins at the fence peering in at them from the edge of the shade. He raked a plug of tobacco from his jaw and dropped it in the dirt and spat after it and wiped his wet fingertips on the leg of his overalls. Bennett walked over to him and Jenkins held out the same hand over the top strand of barbed wire. He was a big man who always had something a little sardonic in his expression.

"Hudson," Jenkins said. "Good to see you. And who's this?"

"Walter Peach," Bennett said. "His son Buford."

"By God, Walter Peach," said Jenkins. "Ain't seen you to speak to since you was mighty little."

Walter took the boy's hand and walked past the old man without answering. They went down the path toward the car.

"The matter with him?" Jenkins asked.

"Just upset, I imagine. We found his mother in there."

Jenkins reared like a horse that sees a rattlesnake.

"*Rosemary?* In there?"

"You knew her?"

The old man's mouth opened and closed again. He met Bennett's eyes momentarily and nodded. His voice was low, his eyes suddenly rimmed with red. "Sweet Jesus help me. Help me, Jesus."

"Sounds like you knew her pretty well."

Jenkins turned and started off down the field road to his house. A few yards off, he stopped and spoke over his shoulder.

"People don't know a goddamn thing about Rosemary. Not a goddamn thing."

Bennett watched him walk off and called after him. "It might help to hear what you know."

Jenkins turned around. "Not in my house. You call me. I'll come out to talk to you."

Bennett was almost down the path to his Bronco when the coroner's SUV pulled up behind Peach's Subaru. Peach and his son met Buddy Fingal and two men with him. Bennett waited for them. Round-faced, his red complexion as smooth and clear as a child's above his Santa Claus beard, Buddy Fingal labored up along the fence. With each step he swung out the stiff left leg he had injured in Vietnam and planted it beside him, moving with a kind of ungainly momentum. As always, he wore an old, sweat-stained white cowboy hat and an oversized black t-shirt with CORONER printed in big white stenciled letters. The two younger men were Elroy Gibbs, a skinny white boy, and short, square Bobby Gant, a sober young black man.

As he reached the small gathering, Fingal grabbed at a fence post, missed, grabbed again and stood panting.

"Praise God," he wheezed. "Praise God."

After a moment, he nodded at Bennett.

"You been a busy man here lately," Bennett said.

"The Lord corrects his chosen," Fingal said, taking a breath that heaved his stomach upward. "But it's way worse on them He ain't chosen. Bobby, y'all go on check it out." He tilted his head sideways and the two other men immediately went down the path toward the house.

Fingal turned to Bennett.

"What we got?"

"Might be a suicide. A long time ago now. I'm guessing fifteen or twenty years."

Fingal's eyes had no levity in them. The darkness there, wounded and hard, must have come from his acquaintance with all the forms of death. Bennett's mother said that Fingal had been a hellion and clown all through high school. He was drafted and went to Vietnam, where a spell of drinking and doping had landed him in lock-up. Afterwards, he told people he had met Jesus in the stockade. He had come out a changed man and earned a Silver Star before the injury to his leg sent him home. Back in Gallatin County, he became a living reproach to his dissolute old friends. He preached at revivals out in the country churches, and he could conjure such a convincing description of hell, he could get a congregation of tough old farmers like Vernon Jenkins to open up to Jesus. The county elected him coroner decade after decade.

"You over at that new subdivision?" Bennett asked. "Ellen says they found more bodies."

Fingal nodded. "Black one and a Mexican. Propped up inside the blade of the bulldozer. Holes in their chests. Didn't need me. GBI, FBI all over the place. So I come on over when Ellen called me." He looked down and spat in the flattened leaves between his feet in their old work boots, then glanced out over Jenkins' field and up at Bennett. "You remember three days like this?"

"Not in my time," Bennett said.

"Cartels in Gallatin County, just like Peach said."

"Looks like it."

Fingal blew out a breath and took a long look at the kudzu-covered house.

"Ellen said this might be Peach's mama."

"Could be."

Fingal met Bennett's eyes and held them.

"They went after Peach's girl?"

Bennett nodded. "They were after Peach. She answered the door."

"Something like this happens for two days," Fingal said, "it won't end till the third. This here is the third. You know what I'm saying?"

"Sure do. I was thinking the same thing this morning."

"I tell you what," Fingal said. "I bet you Dexter Watkins is glad to be in jail."

Bennett smiled. "You want to convert him, I think he's ready."

"That's the Lord's doing," said Fingal seriously. "Ain't none of mine." He gazed at the shrouded house. "I remember plenty of stories about the woman lived out here. Some kind of hippie. I didn't know she was Peach's mama. So in there under all that kudzu?"

"It was a foot deep over the back door. Peach hadn't been in the house since he was a boy, but she must have come back and not told anybody. Door of the room was locked from the inside and the boy busted it open Monday."

"Went in there by himself and found the body?"

"That's right. And then hit his head. Forgot who he was."

"Probably glad to after seeing that. Where's Peach?"

"Went over toward the house with the boy a few minutes ago."

Fingal nodded and blew out his breath. "I reckon I better go see how we're doing." He heaved himself away from the fence and made his way up the cut path.

Bennett glanced at his watch. A little after nine o'clock. He wished he still smoked. It would be a good time to tear off the plastic and the strip of foil of a new pack, tap it against the side of his hand to start out a cigarette, take it with his lips, slide the pack in his pocket. Pull out his Daddy's old Zippo and flick the wheel with his thumb and hold the blue flame there just long enough to light it, whiff of butane and then the first good drag. Snap the lighter shut and pocket it. Let out the smoke.

Too bad it killed you.

He thought about the hand projecting from the trunk of the oak tree, full of cigarette butts. He had heard from somebody—maybe Miss Emma—that there were statues in Missy's Garden. Statues swallowed up by living trees. He rolled his head on his neck to fend off the shiver.

Buddy Fingal was coming back from the house. Behind him, Gibbs carried the cardboard box, and Bobby Gant had the glass from the bedside in a clear plastic bag. Fingal himself held a book closed around the forefinger of his left hand and he was tossing something else in the palm of his right hand as he limped toward them. Peach and the boy followed. When Fingal noticed them behind him, he held up the large paperback book. "On the bed beside her. Facedown. You recognize it?"

He handed it to Peach, who opened it to the page Fingal's finger kept and stared down at it, shaking his head.

"What is it?" Bennett asked. Peach gave it to him. It was a painting of an angel hovering over the body of a woman with a huge, highly satisfied-looking snake coiled around her whole body with its head resting across her breasts. There were flames in the background, maybe Hell, and the angel's face looked out toward the viewer, sick with regret, like he was too late to help her. He looked at the cover. William Blake. A piece of paper fell from the book, and he stooped to pick it up from the ground. It was a handwritten note. Bennett read it out loud. "At the end of my suffering there was a door. Hear me out: that which you call death I remember."

"The hell's that?" Fingal said.

"It's from a poem," Peach said bleakly.

"Listen," Fingal said, "this thing was in her hand."

He held out to Peach what looked like a necklace—a flattened penny on a leather cord. Peach took and stared down at it. He made a noise in his throat and turned away and walked a few steps into the shadow of the oak and dropped to his knees.

Teresa

She stood in the butler's pantry, her hand still on the landline phone, bent over with an almost unbearable pity. Ellen Wolf said they had found Rosemary Peach's body in that kudzu-covered house. For months now, her stiffening pride had estranged her from Walter, but something had begun to change just last night after she had seen Nora O'Hearn and Bill Sharpe outside the newspaper office. She had felt her heart begin to soften, and now, in a flood of guilt, she realized how much malice she had harbored toward her husband—what curses she might half-consciously have laid upon him, what summonings of the Furies who held Stonewall Hill in their dark might, this place with its past of impossible wrongs. She could hardly imagine what Walter must be feeling.

She decided to take Rose with her to Missy's Garden and let her drive the Subaru back while she brought Walter home in her Focus. Braxton Forrest had hired two off-duty policemen to patrol the grounds at Stonewall Hill, and Hudson Bennett made sure that a deputy (not one she recognized) accompanied them when they drove.

As soon as they pulled out of the driveway, the deputy stayed almost on their bumper, prompting a steady, sarcastic commentary from Rose. *Do you think he can smell my perfume? He's so close it's probably got carbon monoxide in it.*

Finally, Teresa hushed her.

"Just imagine, before we get there, what your father must be feeling. After all this time, he finds his mother, and Ellen Wolf says it was suicide."

Rose fell silent.

"He's sure it's his mother?" Rose asked.

"She had the necklace in her hand that he gave her."

Rose shuddered. Teresa shuddered in response, thinking what Walter's mother must have been like when she first arrived at Missy's Garden in the 1970s. Radical ideas and good looks. Alone with a young son. Half wild, careless of clothing, not sending Walter to school.

And then after several years she had simply abandoned her son, whose whole world she was, who knew almost no one else, except Vernon Jenkins and his pinched wife. Abandoned him without a word of goodbye. What had she been doing there in the first place?

And what could have moved her, after disappearing for decades, to return to the old house without even telling him? She had never tried to find him or explain or make amends. To hide away, close herself in, and die alone?

And her Buford had gone in there by himself, into that house covered with kudzu, full of rats. *He* had been the one to find her, shocked out of himself by the horror of it. She pitied him, but then her heart rose in pride at his bravery. She had known from the first moment of his life that he was called to extraordinary things, and she had always feared him a little.

She took the exit and turned onto County 73. Every variety of law enforcement vehicle surrounded the entrance of a development called Phoenix Estates, and an EMT vehicle pulled out from the drive, headed toward the interstate. Up the slope, a puff of smoke burst from a bulldozer as it started up. Down the road half a mile or so, they turned onto Hopewell Road, where the blackened ruins of the Country Corner still smoldered. A woman was standing under the trees with her hands in her hair, and a state patrolman stood nearby writing things down.

A moment later, they came to the old property. Sheriff Bennett's Bronco was parked on the right of way, facing the other direction, with Walter's Outback, Buddy Fingal's coroner truck, and an EMT vehicle behind it.

Hudson was waiting. He had been very attentive to her after the incident with Rose, and she felt a warm friendship toward him.

"Teresa," he said, opening the door for her and offering his hand to help her from the car. "Thanks for coming out. It's been a pretty rough morning."

She stood beside him, looking over the kudzu at the shrouded house. "In there? Oh my God."

Buddy Fingal's men came down the path with a covered stretcher. She crossed herself and whispered a Memorare as they put the body in the back of the vehicle. Its lights flashed steadily as it drove away, as though there were some emergency.

A moment later, Walter and Buford came down a path beside the fence. Walter looked ravaged—and Buford, as soon as he saw her, leapt over the ditch and ran to her. He hugged her convulsively, the way he had when he was little and woken from nightmares.

"You're so brave," she whispered to him. He hugged her tighter, so tight it hurt, and when she lifted his face, his eyes terrified her.

"She drank something," he said.

Teresa looked at Walter, who shook his head.

"Let's wait for Buddy's report," Hudson said.

Walter opened the door of the Focus and slumped into the passenger's seat. His left hand kept balling into a fist so tight she could hear his knuckles crack. A drop of sweat ran down between his eyebrows and into his left eye, and he swiped at it unconsciously.

"I'm so sorry, Walter." Teresa put her hand on his arm, and he glanced up as if he were startled to find her there.

"I don't understand a goddamned thing," he said.

She waited a moment. *Lord Jesus Christ, Son of God, have mercy on me, a sinner.* Something came to her, an insight out of her own darkness.

"Do you think Mrs. Jenkins had anything to do with her disappearance?" she asked. "You said Vernon used to visit your mother."

His eyes rose to hers, full of speculation.

"My God," he said. "Maybe so."

"She would have had a reason."

"That's right."

He stared up Hopewell Road and stirred in his seat.

"I should have taken pictures. Jesus, I have to write this story."

"You just found your mother's body!"

"It's my newspaper. I already missed last week."

"The Macon news people will cover it before you can get out another paper. You know the Atlanta TV stations will pick this up."

"*I'm* the one who said there were cartels in Gallatin County. It's my story. It's even my *property*," he said, waving at the kudzu and the abandoned house.

In through the nose *Lord Jesus Christ, Son of God* out slowly through the mouth *Have mercy on me, a sinner.*

"What are you doing, praying?" he said irritably.

She sighed and honked her horn. Rose got out of the Subaru and walked over to her window.

"You and Buford go on," Teresa said. "We'll be a few minutes after you."

Raïssa

The same deputy who had followed them from home tracked them past the burned store and out to the interstate. Raïssa accelerated down the entrance ramp and put on the blinker to merge onto I-75. She checked her side mirror and pulled in behind a big truck with a yellow sign on the back instructing her how to complain about the driver. She met the deputy's eyes in the rearview mirror—she was pretty sure he was in love with her—and then glanced over at Buford, who was staring straight ahead like a zombie.

"So you found her on Monday? You went in there by yourself?"

A violent shudder went through him.

"Do you remember not knowing who you were?"

He nodded.

"What was it like?"

"My name didn't mean anything."

Buford turned his head to watch as they passed a school bus from Mount Bethel Holiness Church. It seemed to be full of rioting first-graders, several of whom mashed their faces against the windows for their benefit. Rose sighed and gripped the steering wheel with both hands.

"Do you remember when Mr. Sharpe found you out in the middle of the kudzu?"

He nodded.

"Why did you make me take you out there? Mom was furious with me when she found out."

"I knew there was somebody there. Dad took me out there early Friday morning and he's the one who wanted to go inside. Once we got in there, he went into his old room and found a copy of his book—"

"One of his old childhood books?"

"No, *his* book. *The Small Gnats Mourn.*"

"That wasn't published until 1992," Raïssa said, "before he even met Mom, right?"

"Right," Buford said. "So."

"So *she* had it." A long shudder went through her as she thought about it.

"And there was a door locked from the inside," he said. "I knew she was there."

"Right, who else could it be?" she said. She nodded and wiped her eyes. "That was Friday? Why didn't you say something that next morning?"

"Because I had this dream," Buford said. "I was in there by myself in that house at Missy's Garden. I was going down the hallway toward the locked room, and there was an open trap door and steps going down. I could see light down there. I heard this sound... kind of tock...tock... kind of random and spaced out. I was supposed to go down there, so I did."

Déjà vu overwhelmed Raïssa. "I had that dream! Were you scared?"

"I expected to be, but I wasn't."

"Was it like wind chimes?"

"Bones," he said. "Big bones like you'd get from a butcher."

Recognition dazzled up her spine.

"There were cloister walks around a courtyard," she said, "and bones hanging in clusters like chimes in the colonnades among the bougainvillea. Breezes stirring the blossoms and the bones. Blue sky. Did you see the women?"

"Huge women with snakes for hair," he said.

"In purple robes?"

"They sat on the ground around the tall fountain with the goldfish."

"Did they say anything to you?"

"They were going to, but the Lady came."

"The Lady," she said.

A deafening blast startled Raïssa from her reverie. The grille of a massive truck filled the rearview mirror. Dazed, she glanced at the speedometer. *35!* She put on her blinker and veered onto the shoulder as the truck roared past, followed by a line of cars. Angry faces, gesturing men. A teenaged girl in the passenger's seat of a minivan gave her a prolonged finger, her mouth open in feigned disbelief; the embarrassed mother talked angrily to the back of the girl's head. The deputy pulled up close behind her again, shaking his head. She would have pulled farther off, she would have stopped and abandoned the car, she would have fled into the fields beyond the access road, but Buford pointed ahead, and she saw that the first exit for Gallatin was only a few hundred yards away. She rolled toward it on the shoulder. Now in the rearview mirror she saw the lights go on. A siren whooped, and the deputy gestured. She stopped on the far right of the shoulder. A few seconds passed before he got out of his car, as though he were calling in her license plate.

She lowered the window as he stepped up beside her.

"Are you okay, Miss Peach?"

She read his nametag. Sage Perkins. Andrew Perkins' brother. She smiled and then started to sob.

Walter

A few days ago, he would have seen this evidence of cartel violence as his vindication, but now it was just a distraction—and Teresa was right. It would be very old news by next week. He took a few pictures with his iPhone.

"You're sure it was your mother?" she asked him when he got back in the car.

"She had a necklace," he said. "I made it for her the week before she disappeared back in 1974."

"Oh sweetheart, that must have been devastating."

"The last time I saw that necklace—."

He could not say it.

"Was the day she left. The day your life changed."

"No."

She glanced at him, confused. "Really? Well, when?"

He looked across at her—the clear lines of her profile, the strength and purity of her face. She seemed to have been born to suffer whatever he would do to hurt her. No, that was wrong. She never asked for suffering, like some kind of masochist. She just believed marriage was a *sacrament*, that strange word, which meant she believed in *him* despite everything he did to her, and she believed that God meant something in joining her life to the unhappy mess that was Walter Peach.

There was no point in hiding it.

"It was around the neck of Lydia Downs the day I ran over our son."

They were just turning left onto the entrance ramp for the interstate. She swerved over on the shoulder and slammed on the brakes and turned off the car and got out. She walked over into the grass at the side and bent over, hugging herself, down on her haunches all the way to the ground. She stood, then, tottering, and walked aimlessly. When he got out and went to her, she looked up at him, her face full of the whole misery they had endured. She was shaking her head, as though she were trying to negate everything, every thought that surged up within her.

"How did she get the necklace?"

"Her stepmother gave it to her."

Teresa stared at him. Her whole body convulsed, and she bent over again.

"Oh my God, oh my God…"

He embraced her, but she was stiff in his arms.

"Let me go," she said.

She turned away from him, staring distractedly out over the ceaseless traffic.

"I've known for a long time that I'm damned," he said.

"Good God, Walter! Turn up the self-pity!" she cried with instant ferocity. She got into the passenger's seat. "You drive."

He got in and adjusted the driver's seat.

"You are *not damned*," she said.

"You don't feel the design?" he said. "This morning I found my mother's body, and she had on the necklace I saw on Lydia Downs the day I ran over my son. You don't understand that? What is it you don't fucking understand?"

"Do not curse or I will get out of this car and walk home."

"All this." He waved his hand back toward 73, toward the store, Missy's Garden, the dead bodies of the Mexicans. "All this is my fault. What but design of darkness to appall?"

"Why is it all *your fault*, Walter?" she asked scathingly.

"Because I said something several months ago that Dexter Watkins took as permission to plant that marijuana."

It took her aback. Her eyes flooded with recognition.

"Something about Nora," she said.

"Yes."

"You slept with her."

"No, I did not."

"Thank God. Thank God for that." A sudden surge of old fury blazed through her. *"But you slept with Lydia Downs."*

The old darkness. He gazed through the windshield, seeing nothing, letting the fury and dread fade until the interstate traffic came into focus. What had brought Lydia Downs into his classroom and him into her bed? It was like Frost's "Design," the dark sonnet he used to deploy against the witlessly optimistic Baptist coeds in his classes in Waycross. Three white things come together in the night—*a white heal-all flower, a white spider,* and *a white moth.* Lydia was the white heal-all, he was the white moth somehow steered toward her in the night, and God was the dimpled white spider that ran to him delighted and bound him and held him up as the prize of damnation.

> *What but design of darkness to appall?*
> *If design govern in a thing so small.*

He turned on the car.

"Walter," she said. "Don't drive yet. Look at me."

He met her eyes.

"You could have been faithful to me," she said.

"I think it was fated," he said.

318

"I don't believe that."

He could not hold her gaze.

"I know you don't." He checked the mirrors and put the car in gear. "You know what I have to do now, don't you?" he said.

"What?"

"Find her."

"Find who?" she asked, her face white with apprehension.

"Lydia Downs. I have to tell her about Rosemary. I have to find out how she got that necklace."

"For God's sake, what are you *talking* about? How can you—*Good God*, Walter. *Please* Walter," she said as she saw his face. "I'm begging you. Don't bring it all back up. *Please*."

Bill Sharpe

Just as Bill turned onto Lee Street on his way to see Nora, an old woman in an ancient green Buick pulled out of the Gallatin County Bank parking lot in front of him. Tiny as a child, she gripped the steering wheel grimly and strained to see through it as she crept down the street at ten miles an hour. He would have passed her, but a regular stream of cars kept coming up Lee Street off Johnson's Mill Road, probably after something at the high school.

He bumped the heel of his hand on the steering wheel. His mother always told him to be patient with old people. *What you need to remember is that they used to be as young as you are.* This particular old sweetheart could have been Marlene Dietrich back during the Great Depression, but now she was keeping him from Nora. She slowed and slowed, put on her blinker, stopped dead, and then, at the pace of someone in a walker, made a right turn onto Ewell Street where the funeral home was.

Now the way opened before him, and Bill's heart opened with it. He hit the accelerator. Big, columned Stonewall Hill rose between Lee Street and Johnson's Mill Road. Braxton Forrest's place. That very afternoon, Forrest had come into Lee Ford to talk to him.

Listen, Bill, I just want to tell you one thing. God doesn't single us out for no reason.

Bill didn't know what to say back, so Forrest shook his hand and patted his shoulder and left with a wave at Chick Lee. Bill's hands were big enough to palm a basketball, but an hour later he could still feel Forrest's legendary grip in the small bones. They said he had snapped Dutrelle Jones's forearm with one twist, and Jones had been an NFL linebacker.

Chick came over to him later.

Why did Cump want to meet you?

Who's Cump?

Braxton Forrest. He asked to see you.

Me? I don't know.

What did he say to you?

He said God doesn't single us out for no reason.

Chick was eating a piece of beef jerky—part of the diet he was on, apparently. His breath had the distinctive hot smell of voluntary starvation.

You think he was talking about Deirdre? Chick asked.

That was a long time ago.

Chick pointed the jerky at him.

Maybe he meant finding the Peach boy. Well, listen to him. He ought to know.

Forrest had been singled out himself, no question about that. All those deaths, all the rumors.

Bill turned left onto Johnson's Mill Road and then swerved happily into the back driveway. When he pulled up behind the house, two men ran around the sides, both of them armed. He recognized Willie Devers, who had been the point guard for the Blue Devils a few years after Bill graduated. The other was a slight white man in his thirties with an unpleasant triangular face. Willie recognized him and said something to the other man and waved Bill in.

He met them on the walk into the back door of the house and shook their hands.

"Any trouble?" he asked.

"Tell you what, I was happy to get this work, but Mr. Forrest ain't paying us enough," Willie explained. "You hear what happened to them men out at Ed Watkins' store? One of 'em beheaded?"

"Seriously," Bill said. He nodded at the house. "I'll say this. Walter Peach was right about the cartels."

"Ain't that the damn truth?" said the white man, whose mouth seemed to have too much juice in it. "Bobby Oldroyd," he said, offering his hand. "Any word on them goddamned wetbacks?"

"Come on, man," said Willie.

"Listen," Bill said. "Is Miss O'Hearn here?"

"Whoo, that your girl?" asked Willie with a wink. He nodded out to the back garden.

Bill walked over to a wooden gate, taking in the large garden at a glance. A trellis on the left side of the garden supported a mass of bean plants, and all along the back border nearest the old barn were a dozen or more tomato plants that had outgrown their cages. In between, divided by rows of marigolds, were beds of flowering squash and cucumber plants and watermelon vines. Back in the far right corner was a huge fig tree.

Nora was leaning over a raised bed of herbs that Teresa Peach must have tended. He recognized basil, parsley, oregano, sage, rosemary, and lemon balm. She still had not heard him. She crouched down, pinched the leaves of the lemon balm, and lifted her fingers to her nose. When he cleared his throat, she turned and saw him and rose quickly.

"You scared me." She looked serious. "Were you watching me?"

"Just for a minute. Want to go somewhere and get a glass of wine?"

"I just got a call from my aunt that Buford found Walter's mother out in that house."

The smell of the boy, the blank dismay. "That's what it was on Monday, wasn't it? Oh my God, no wonder."

"Come inside for a minute," she said.

Walter

Bill Sharpe's pickup sat in the driveway when Walter and Teresa got back to Stonewall Hill. Rose and Buford were close behind them, and he heard the Outback on the driveway.

"I'm going up to the study," Peach said.

"Walter," Teresa said, touching his forearm. "Please don't do it."

He cut through the screen porch to the back stairs to avoid seeing Sharpe and then went up to the landing and into the study. It was still just late morning. Still the same day. He opened his laptop, got on the Internet, and typed **Lydia Downs** in the search bar. For seventeen years, since the day he ran over his son, he had avoided any mention of her. Even when he was drunk and maudlin, he had never once gone online to search for her. Never once. There was no flicker of interest, no lingering temptation there. But twice in two days now, the name had returned.

After all the Facebook profiles was **Lydia Downs Contemporary Glass and Metal. Yuma, Arizona.**

He clicked on the website, and there she was. Older but still young, hardly seeming past her mid-thirties even now. Sunlit, she wore jean shorts and a skimpy tank top that showed the shape of her breasts—tanned arms akimbo, head tilted. She looked calculating, intelligent, frankly sexual. Behind her was a metal-sided building, on the ground around her a scatter of large undulant metal forms. In the distance loomed saguaro cacti and dry mountains.

Across the right of the screen at the top were options:

Home • Portfolio • Blog • Videos • Info

He clicked the videos and watched the first of them, his heart yawing strangely: Lydia painting metal for an outdoor installation. He clicked on another: Lydia installing a large blue-glass form, floral and thalassic, inside a high-end restaurant in Phoenix—one of a number of these of different sizes that alternated with brilliantly colored flat metal disks along a high adobe wall. *This one is exactly forty-seven inches across,* she explained in the video as her smile flashed over her shoulder. *They're all based on prime numbers.*

At the bottom of the screen he found a phone and an email address to contact. He called the number and waited, full of dread. When it went to voice mail, he hesitated for a second.

"Lydia," he said. "This is Walter Peach. I found the penny necklace today. You remember it. That was my mother's necklace." He faltered to a stop. He knew that Teresa would be coming up the stairs. "Rosemary was inside the house I own outside Gallatin," he said. "She's been dead a long time. The whole house was covered with kudzu." That wouldn't mean anything to her. "I know you had it. I just want to know how she got the necklace back. Can you call me?"

He gave her his number and ended the call just as Teresa came up beside him and looked over his shoulder at the website. He put his hand on the laptop to close it.

"You did it anyway," she said bitterly, blocking his hand and leaning in to look. For a long moment, she did not say anything. "So that's Lydia Downs."

"I have to know how Rosemary got the necklace."

"Lydia must have given it back to her."

"She said her stepmother had disappeared."

He put his arms around her waist and pulled her against him and pressed the side of his face against her breasts. After a moment, she put her arms around him.

"Oh, Walter. I don't know what you're doing. God help you." She pushed him away. "You're home, but you're not here. I don't know how long I can stand this." She started toward the door to the landing on the stairs. "You might want to spend a little time with your children, don't you think?"

He nodded but did not answer.

When she was gone, the clock on the desk said 11:40, and he checked online to see what time it would be in Yuma. Mountain Time, two hours earlier, so 9:40. She'd be working, she probably wouldn't get the message until—

His phone rang, and he saw the 928 number he had just called.

"Walter, my God, is that you?" Lydia said when he answered it.

"It's Walter."

She did not speak for a moment.

"I got your message. I'm just trying to process—"

"How did she get the necklace?"

"I can't do this on the phone. Can I see you?"

"God, no. Please just tell me."

He was aware of being rude, and he fought down his impatience. He could hear a high-pitched whine in the background—drilling or sanding.

"Just a minute," she said. "Let me go outside."

A moment later, she came back on.

"Walter, are you telling me you are her son?" Lydia said.

His heart beat heavily in his throat. He realized that he was standing. He saw Rose looking up at the house from the driveway and held up a hand to her.

"You knew, though, didn't you?" she said. "You already knew who my stepmother was that day. You had to." He did not answer. "Walter, why didn't—"

"How did she get the necklace back?" Walter interrupted. "It must have meant something to her. I must have meant something."

There was a long pause, as though Lydia were hesitating to answer him.

"You don't know who she was."

"What do you mean? She was my mother. She was Rosemary."

Hearing the door onto the landing open, he looked up. "Hold on," he said. Buford came in with a cup of coffee Teresa must have sent up to him. He thanked his son, and after Buford left, Walter said, "What do you mean *who she was*?"

"Are you near your computer?" Lydia said.

"That's how I found you."

"Well, Google 'Alison Graves.' A-l-i-s-o-n."

A dark qualm went through him. "Alison?"

"Yes, Alison Graves."

"There must be lots of women named Alison Graves."

He typed in the name. There were. But in a box on the right side of the screen was the name *Alison Graves* and a black-and-white photograph of his mother as he remembered her. His heart heaved. Across the bottom of the box, under **People also search for**, he saw more names: **Sara Jane Olson, Katherine Power, Kathy Boudin, Bill Ayers, Harris Akers, and Bernadine Dohrn**. Terrorist bombers from the 1960s and 1970s.

"Good God," he said into the phone.

"Go to her Wikipedia page and read it to me," Lydia said.

He clicked on the link and read aloud the first paragraph, which was riddled with hyperlinks.

"Alison Graves (1948—), with Harris Akers, was a founding member of a 1960s radical group called Nouveau Émile. Its principles of radical equality and 'organic anarchism,' including free love, spilled over into violence after the Kent State shootings on May 4, 1970. The group's targets were public schools, which they saw as perpetuating a system of incarceration and indoctrination. In the fall of 1970, Nouveau Émile members peacefully occupied a small elementary school in Glenview, Illinois, and "liberated" the students. Graves later expressed outrage at the psychological effectiveness of the educational system, because the children began crying and none of them would leave their classrooms.

"Graves and Akers later turned to violence. They were indicted in the Christmas Eve 1972 bombing of Rosecrans Elementary School in Chicago that killed a janitor and a second-grade teacher and left the teacher's young son severely burned. Harris Akers was captured in 1973 and convicted of manslaughter in 1974, but Graves was never found. In 1998 police in Chicago received a written confession from her, postmarked from Florida."

After he finished reading, he held the phone and said nothing.

"Are you there?" said Lydia.

"Florida," he said.

"She wrote me about the same time she sent that confession. She was working for an old woman in Naples, Florida."

"She knew you," he said numbly. "She didn't know me."

"I'll make a copy of her letter and overnight it to you. Give me your address." He hesitated, fearing that she might try to come in person, but he then gave her the address.

"Call me after you have a chance to read it," she said. "Will you do that at least?"

"I will," he said. "And I'll email you now so you'll know how to get in touch with me."

He ended the call, emailed her, putting **Graves** in the subject line.

He clicked on Harris Akers (1946–1998). A long entry. Akers was apprehended in 1973 and served eight years in prison after his conviction in 1974. In prison, he wrote a book about education called *The Cultivation of Idiocy*. After his release, he finished his doctorate at New York University and took a post-doc in philosophy at his alma mater, the University of Chicago, where he taught courses in Heidegger, the Frankfurt school, and Foucault until his death by asphyxiation in 1998.

He stared at the picture of Akers as a boy with his parents and put both hands on the desk to steady himself. Buford looked exactly like him.

Teresa

On Thursday morning, Teresa called Fr. Corrigan at St. Joseph's in Macon to request a funeral Mass. They had brought Fr. Corrigan to dinner at Stonewall Hill twice since their move to Gallatin, and he wanted to help her, but her insistence on a Mass for Alison Graves confused him so much that he called his young assistant priest to the phone.

No, she told Fr. Andrzejewski, Alison Graves was not a Catholic. Fr. Andrzejewski referred her to the diocesan office in Savannah, where the person first given her request transferred her call to an expert in canon law. Dr. Melissa Fullerton listened patiently and then asked why Teresa wanted the funeral to be Catholic if the deceased was not Catholic. Feeling foolish by now, Teresa said that their family was Catholic, and they wanted Walter's mother—his children's grandmother—to be buried in the Church, even though she had not been in the Church herself and might have taken her own life.

"Well, you see," Mrs. Fullerton said to her, "if she had the chance to be Catholic while she was alive and did not choose to be, then the Church has no right to make her Catholic after her death. A funeral Mass for a non-Catholic might give scandal."

"*Scandal?* Really?"

"As if the Church were overstepping its bounds and infringing on the free will of the person who could have chosen the Church and did not. Especially if—so."

Especially if she killed herself. This argument silenced Teresa for a moment; it sounded like a veiled judgment about the salvation of Alison Graves. Walter did not care about a Catholic funeral, she knew, but he would still scorn the Church's reasons for not allowing her one. She herself had lost the visceral sense of obedience that she had felt before the scandals about sexual abuse, but she did not want Walter to have occasion to criticize the Roman Catholic Church for damning his mother.

"Well, what if we had a requiem Mass to pray for her soul? It doesn't really need to be a funeral Mass, because there won't be a regular burial. She's been dead for sixteen years, and her body was just discovered."

"Sixteen years!"

"She was in an old house overgrown with kudzu."

"Oh my Lord. So she had—I mean—"

"Her body had decomposed. My husband wants to have her remains cremated."

"The Church does *allow* cremation," she said, "but doesn't really approve of it. Christ didn't rise from His ashes, if you see what I mean. He wasn't a phoenix, I tell people."

"I do see," said Teresa.

"If you do cremate the remains, you should respect the doctrine of the Resurrection and treat her ashes as you would treat her body. You should reverently inter the ashes. You should not keep them in a shrine in your home. You wouldn't keep her dead body in your home, would you? And you shouldn't scatter her as though you were releasing her entrapped spirit into the elements, despite all those sentimental scenes in the movies. You wouldn't cut up her body and throw it into San Francisco Bay or the Grand Canyon, would you?"

Dr. Fullerton must have had to use these arguments before.

"Dr. Fullerton," Teresa said, "I fully embrace your position."

This information gave Dr. Fullerton pause.

"Oh, I see," she said.

"But since she was not Catholic..."

"Oh, that's right. I forgot that she—so all right, the Church has no authority to prescribe your treatment of her ashes. All we can do is make the recommendation to *you* as a professing Catholic. I mean, if you want to take her to Sea Island and—"

"I *said* I embrace your position," Teresa said with involuntary asperity. "Can there be any objection to praying for her in the intercessions at Mass?"

"Are you asking whether the act of suicide means that she is damned?"

Dr. Fullerton didn't mince words.

"Of course I am."

"Suicide is a violation of the Fifth Commandment, but the Catechism says that certain conditions may extenuate responsibility for the act."

"Yes, I have the passage here," Teresa said. "It says, 'We should not despair of the eternal salvation of persons who have taken their own lives. By ways known to him alone, God can provide the opportunity for salutary repentance. The Church prays for persons who have taken their own lives.' So as I understand it, there can be no objection to praying for her in Mass."

"No, of course not," she said, sounding pleased that someone cared about the Catechism. "You may certainly pray for her at Mass."

"Should I tell Fr. Corrigan in Macon?"

"I'll have the bishop call him and ask Fr. Corrigan to remember her in the intentions at the 9:30 a.m. Sunday Mass." She sounded increasingly sympathetic.

"Thank you," Teresa said. "I will email you his mother's name."

Walter

He went to the office and tried to write something about the murders, which had already been all over the Macon news, the Atlanta news, the *Macon Telegraph*—everything Teresa had said. What was the point of even writing it up? It was Thursday, and this week's *Gallatin Tribune* sat on his desk, largely written by Rob Waldrop, the Southern Studies major at Mercer, and stitched together remotely by Braxton Forrest. It was the best issue in weeks—a great headline, "Heaven's alleged killers have first day in court." That was about a white woman accused of murdering her five-year-old daughter with her black lover. Also on the front page was the capture of an escaped criminal, two train wrecks, and a fatal accident on I-75.

All this was going on? *Heaven's alleged killers.*

The story nobody knew about was his mother, but how could he write that?

He stayed at the office all afternoon, accomplishing exactly nothing, and went home after five, raging for whiskey. He went up to the study and looked up more about Alison Graves and Harris Akers. He was on his third drink when he saw the FedEx truck come up the back drive. He went down and signed for the white envelope just as Teresa called him to dinner, so he took the envelope to the dinner table. When she saw it, Teresa stood and went into the kitchen.

"What *is* that?" Rose asked after a tense moment.

He cut into his meat loaf and looked at her. Rose had been subdued and weepy since the attack on Tuesday. It was hard to remember now those nights of poetry—he and Rose and Nora reading aloud, sounding out lines, finding the pleasures in the play of language.

"Something about my mother," he said.

"Who's it from?"

"A woman who knew her."

"Who?"

He did not want to say the name of Lydia Downs in front of his children.

"A lot of people knew her."

"So that's from a lot of people?" Rose said.

"Leave it alone, Rose," he snapped.

When Nora came into the dining room to say that she was going out with Bill Sharpe, he took advantage of the interruption to excuse himself. He took the envelope up to the office and opened it and found the letter inside, a photocopy of a neat, legible typescript on pages torn from a white legal pad.

Naples, Florida
April 12, 1998

Don't be too alarmed to hear from me. You must have thought by now that I was dead, whatever it means to be dead—pure absence? lingering ghostly presence? (I intend to find out soon)—but I'm paradoxically just fine. As far as anybody here knows, I'm a simple, never-married, middle-aged woman earning my keep by tending the houses and pets of rich old people who pay for Florida to be the earthly paradise. If I'm noteworthy, as I had hoped never to be in Seattle, it's for my amazing humility in dealing with the demands of haughty old women from New York City. I overheard one of them say to her friend on the phone, "I swear to God it's better than going to my analyst. You can say anything to Griselda" (I've named myself Griselda Walters), "and she just stands there and takes it."

If they only knew: there's a cliché for you. But then you don't know, do you? And your father doesn't know.

The only man who knew, the only man I truly loved, died a week ago, and now I'm so alone in the vast wreckage of the world I'd hoped for that I'm writing you for a favor, you, the only daughter I have. Daughter and lover of the lie named Sarah, now the lie named Griselda.

But you're not a lie. I'm proud of how free you are of everything that stifled me. I'm prouder than I can say of your art and your boldness.

Where to start?

My real name is Alison Elizabeth Graves. What does that mean, a real name? The one that makes you a relative, that relates you to the dead past and its web of unasked-for kinship—such as, in my case and therefore (alas) in Knecht's, descent from old Senator Graves of Georgia, first Secretary of State in the Confederacy, a slaveholder who, five years before the Civil War, defended the permanence of slavery—in Boston of all places!—"based upon the idea of the superiority by nature of the white race over the African."

There's a passage I have never managed to forget.

My father was an internist, my mother the owner of a public relations business. I grew up an only child in Atlanta. I had a standard white-bread-and-Cheerios childhood with piano lessons and a tampons-and-senior-prom adolescence in the football South. I went to schools that rewarded me for being just exactly what they thought I was supposed to be. I was pretty and well-to-do and smart enough to get a full-tuition scholarship to the University of Chicago and canny enough to take it.

And so, in the fall of 1966, in an English class on Romantic poetry, I met Harris Akers, the most brilliant and radically engaging man of his generation. I liked what he said. I liked his boldness in disagreeing with the stuffy professor. When we talked afterwards in the hallway, he told me to forget Wordsworth, who had been headed toward the "Ode to Duty" and the Anglican Church all along. He said to read Blake's Marriage of Heaven and Hell.

I went back to my room and read it and then reread it and read it again. "Energy is the only life and is from the Body; and Reason is the bound or outward circumference of Energy." I loved it. The next day, we talked for hours—over coffee, over beer and then pot (my first time) deep into the night. We made love (also my first time), and by morning, he had pulled the veil from the world of institutions that oppressed me. As Blake says, "For man has closed himself up, till he sees all things thro' narrow chinks of his cavern." That morning I saw a world of such liberty, such shining possibility, such Eden—"it was all/Shining, it was Adam and maiden" (to switch poets)—that I have never quite lost that vision, and yet all around me I saw and still see the "mind-forged manacles" Harris revealed to me.

Harris and I read together constantly, and I drifted away from classes, from classrooms, from systems. When I discovered that I was pregnant, we went to live in a commune near Madison, Wisconsin, and read Rousseau—Émile especially—and my son was born in the summer of 1967 among the organically grown beans and tomatoes and zucchini, the pot smoke and laughter, the easy nakedness, the sweet edenic dream. We all took care of each other. I remember a woman named Holly patiently brushing my hair while I sat outside nursing the baby and everyone else was swimming in the lake, young and naked and beautiful, and I can still feel the brush in my hair, the trance of that wonderful, smooth, repeated, gently tugging stroke and the way Holly said "I just love your hair" and pulled my head back into her with her breasts against my shoulders and pulled my face up and kissed me on the forehead and the baby let go of my nipple and reached up for Holly, his lips shining with my milk. We were bacchae. To be young was very heaven.

It has been so worthwhile being alive. I would never say it hasn't.

But elsewhere there were terrible race riots—Detroit that summer. The more Harris thought about it, the less he felt that we could make a separate peace as we'd been doing. He'd almost been drafted in 1964, but when they examined him, they discovered that he had heart damage from the rheumatic fever he had as a child, but he didn't think his exemption exempted him from fighting the system. We needed to do something, and so by the spring of 1968 after a bad winter at the commune (some squabbling over duties) we were back in Chicago—which meant back in the world of needing money. Harris had to get jobs doing gardening or landscaping or pizza delivery or factory work, whatever he could find. I had the baby to tend. There we were, the ironically typical family.

Harris was arrested during the protests at the Democratic convention, and I remember those days without him and the anxiety I felt. Whatever he did, I wanted to be a part of it. I hated being away from him. That next winter we were terribly poor, destitute, living in a tiny apartment in a black neighborhood on the South Side, subsisting on ramen noodles and brown lentils, using torn-up old sheets for diapers for little Knecht (our pet name for him after a character in Hermann Hesse's magnum opus). But despite all that, we were happier than we had been since the commune, and that's where we were when Harris had the idea for our movement, Nouveau Émile. He wanted to break away from any connection to economic ideologies like Marxism. He loathed the willingness of people like Lenin to sacrifice millions of people as though only <u>they</u> understood the secret workings of history. He just wanted freedom from institutions. His term was "organic anarchy"—the idea that things would develop rightly with respect to each other if they were unimpeded in unfolding their own natures. He would quote proverbs from Blake: "The apple tree never asks the beech how he shall grow; nor the lion, the horse, how he shall take his prey." Several of us would sit huddled together in blankets and I'd be feeding Knecht some horrible mash from a jar and we'd be talking happily about how liberation would begin with this child. Knecht was the new Émile, the one we named our movement after. The promised future began with him.

We saw Lyndon Johnson as the face of everything we hated. Then Nixon—where did America come up with Richard Nixon? Woodstock in 1969 was a respite. We made it there, Knecht and all, in a VW bus (pardon another cliché) driven by friends from the commune. Harris said Woodstock was the vindication of our generation. Sometime during the fall after Woodstock, my parents died in a car crash in Atlanta. I didn't know they had died. Nobody knew how to get in touch with me. I didn't find out for a month or more—and now I don't remember how I did find out.

Despite their disappointment in me, I was the sole heir, and they had money and property. I called our family lawyer, an old man named J.C. Lawton who had known my grandparents, and got him to take care of selling their property, everything but a place outside Gallatin, Georgia, that could never be sold because of an agreement made when it was first purchased after the Civil War. I remembered it vaguely, because my parents had driven by it once, and my father told me it had been the home of his beautiful grandmother, Zilpha Graves. Mr. Lawton said it was mine now since I was the survivor in the Graves line, and he sent me a map and his number to call if I ever needed help with the property. He took care of getting money to me. Harris preferred barter and trade; he thought of value arising from "the thinging of the thing"—he was reading Heidegger by now—so there's considerable irony in the fact that we made it through those next years living on the money my parents left me. So many ironies. Harris didn't like ironies and wouldn't acknowledge them.

You can read on your own about what Nouveau Émile did. For several years, we were just activists—protestors at school board hearings, loud presences outside administration buildings. Harris wrote a pamphlet called "Recess as Revolution" that we'd pass out. And finally, when all we got was groans and scorn and dismissals, we became terrorists. Even then, when we took over an elementary school, our group was a joke, because the children wouldn't leave. The Sun-Times headline was "No Deal, Émile." Harris couldn't stand that. We bombed the other school just before Christmas of 1972. Harris wanted the bombing to be the breaking story that would attract camera crews and hordes of reporters, which was why we'd timed the bombing for 9:00 p.m., thinking everybody would be long gone from the school on Christmas Eve. And there it was: the lead story on Channel 2, Channel 5, Channel 7. We sat on the floor in Warren Peterson's apartment since he had a TV. We were excited to see what kind of commentary we'd stirred up. That's when we found out that we had killed two people, a Mexican janitor with seven children and a black second-grade teacher close to her due date; she was collecting a few things she'd forgotten to take home because she wouldn't be back after the Christmas break. Her little boy, Knecht's age, went in with her, and he was badly burned. There was a picture of the boy in his bandages and a bitterly ironic caption quoting the passage about Jesus being wrapped in "swaddling clothes."

We were no joke now. We were the cause of death and poverty and grief because we wanted to be on the late news and not be a joke. It was all amour propre. There was no point trying to pretend the bombing was a political statement for Nouveau Émile. Not with the killings. If it had just been the building—you see? If it had been the institutional structure, as we intended. . .

Warren got paranoid about our being in his place once he saw that people had died in the bombing. He was so edgy, we were sure he would turn us in himself, so we went back to our apartment. We thought we had just a few hours before the police would track us down. We sat at the table in our apartment, and Knecht was on the floor in his diaper, playing. Harris asked me if there was anywhere I could go with the baby.

Without you? I said. Split up? He told me we had to split up or we'd be caught. They'd be looking for us together. He had some friends in upstate New York. If we wanted to see each other again, we had to leave now. I told him about the property outside Gallatin. I said I'd go there if I had to go somewhere. I called Mr. Lawton, whose voice was very weak. I told him I needed to come there and nobody could know who I was. I remember the way he sighed. "Miss Graves, I'm a dying man, but I'll help you. The next time you call, it will have to be my son." He told me his son's name and gave me a phone number. So I told Harris where I was going and how to get there. Harris held both my hands and said not to write down the address anywhere, ever. He'd come as soon as he could. He knew people who could help give me a new identity.

In January of 1973, two weeks after the bombing, Knecht and I got to Gallatin with the help of friends along the way. When we had to take different names I became Rosemary Peach, Rosemary from Simon and Garfunkel's song and Peach from being in Georgia. I invented a violent husband I had escaped from, in case anybody asked, and little Knecht became Walter Peach—Walter because it reminded me of his father, who was acting like the tyrannical husband in one of the Canterbury Tales. Walter and I lived in that house in the country. When we got there, I was dismayed, because there were broken windows, a leaking roof, holes in the floor, rats and mice. The Jenkins neighbors saw us and came by, and I explained that I had the boy and no job. I said an aunt told me I could live there. But I didn't know it would be like this, I told them, and I sat there on the front steps and cried.

They acted like my story was reasonable. Vernon helped me fix it up. I told him I didn't want it to look like anybody lived there, at least from the road, because it might get back to my husband, and I was scared if he found me, he would kill me. I asked Vernon to help protect me. So we got through a cold month or so and then grew vegetables (and a little pot) and canned things as I'd learned to do on the commune. I had plenty of cash hidden in the house, and I was a mother. I brought up Knecht, my new Émile. Harris visited once that summer. He showed up in the middle of the night and left before dawn because he was too scared to stay with us, I think. Knecht wept to see him go. But then he was caught later in 1973 and put on trial in Chicago with lots of publicity and sent to jail. He never gave me up. He couldn't send me letters from jail because then the authorities would know the address. Friends from the radical days came by once or twice to bring me messages, at least in the first months, but it was too dangerous, and they stopped. After a while, I got to know Vernon Jenkins better. He was a big, good-looking man who brought me things and helped me clear away Zilpha Graves's old garden in the back and visited when his wife was gone. I was pretty open in those days.

Early one morning in June, Walter was down at the creek—he loved that creek—and I was making breakfast. There was a knock on the back door, and a woman said, "Alison Graves?" and my heart froze.

I turned off the stove where the bacon was about to burn and went to the screen, and there stood Minnie Jenkins. She was a grim sparrowy woman. Her mouth was tight as a beak. She opened the screen a crack and handed me a folded piece of newspaper. I unfolded it and saw my picture next to Harris's above a story about Harris's conviction for the school bombings in Chicago. There were pictures of the janitor and the teacher who died and the little boy who was burned.

"That ought to be your little boy," she said, touching the picture. I looked back up at her. She said, "Pretty boy's down at the creek. I waited till he was gone. I done called the law and told them who you was. Said I was scared you might commit suicide instead of be caught."

She yanked open the screen and came inside. She held a pistol, very big and wobbly in her hand, that I had seen Vernon use on snakes.

"I ain't had babies, which it's God's judgment. It hurts me with

Vernon but I guess it don't hurt a whore like you." She pointed at my stomach with the gun. "You got a baby ought to be mine up in that whore belly? Show me where you and Vernon go to do it. That's where I'm gon shoot you. Shoot you in the side of the head and then put the gun in your own hand. I'll tell the police I showed you that newspaper and this is what you done. And pretty boy will come up here and look at you with your brains blowed out."

She kept out of reach or I would have tried to overpower her. She backed me down the hallway toward my bedroom. All I could think about was Knecht coming in and finding me dead and what that would do to him. I began to plead with her. I told her they would find out she killed me. There would be a trial. Everybody would stare at her and think about why Vernon would—

"Don't you think everybody already knows why Vernon's done took up with a whore?" she said, and she raised the pistol to point at my head. "They call me little dry Minnie. It's the Lord God's reproach on the third and fourth generation."

I told her I would leave and never come back. I would never see Vernon again.

"Swear it," she said, "and I won't kill you. Swear it on that boy's life."

I swore on Knecht's life I would never come back.

"They'll be chasing you. Murderer and whore, too. Chasing you from now on. Soon as they catch you, that boy goes into foster care, don't he? They'll make sure he don't see you, won't they? A murderer and whore."

"Can I just say goodbye to him?"

"Is them sirens I hear? You take one step toward the creek, and I'll shoot you in the head."

She held the gun on me while I got my purse and got out my keys and got in the car, an old blue Fairlane, and just left my beautiful son behind. She was laughing. I cried all the way to the Atlanta airport. I imagined him coming into the house and not finding me and starting to panic. Calling "Rosemary? . . . Mama?"

I never saw a police car all the way to Atlanta. I left the car in the lot at the airport and nobody stopped me when I was buying a ticket to Portland, Oregon, where I had a friend in the old network. While I was waiting for the airplane, I got some change and called the number old Mr. Lawton had given me years before and told the woman who answered where Walter was.

In Portland, nobody arrested me. I cut my hair and changed the way I dressed and became Sarah Barnes. Minnie was right. I was pregnant with Vernon's baby, and I aborted it just to spite her. I was out of my head in those days. I wrote Judge Lawton and told him where I was. I was dying to talk to Walter, to see him. I gave the judge a number and a time to call. I waited by the phone in my friend's house, dying to talk to my son, dying. But when the call came, it was a woman.

"Rosemary?" she said with terrible sweetness. "I happened to intercept your letter, thank God. And thank God I know where you are! When they arrest you, I have a few charges of child abuse to add to the list. The federal authorities should be on their way as we speak. Never, never try to call my poor child again."

My friends told me later that I had escaped by five minutes. I changed my appearance again and made my way to Seattle and opened the art studio. The years went by, and the more they did, the more painful it became to think of disturbing his life with mine. I kept up with Walter as he was now through Judge Lawton. Halfway through those years you came into the studio, and I fell in love. You were the most talented child I had ever met, and I had met your parents. When your mother died, I married your father and loved him—but not the way I loved Harris. I was always hoping somehow Harris and I would find each other again. He had been out of prison and teaching for years, and all I had to do was fly to Chicago to see him, but I was scared, just as I was scared with Walter. All the complexity, all the deception.

It's hard to explain the kind of fear I felt, but it was more than just fear of being caught and sent to prison. I also thought of those decent people we had killed. I thought of the boy we burned and of how he would grow up scarred and how people would always look at him with morbid curiosity. A boy the same age as Walter—that poor dead woman's Walter. What would become of him? What would it be like to see him and know that what I did had ruined his life?

And then, four years ago, on the anniversary of the school bombing, my story was featured on a show about America's most wanted criminals. They had drawn all kinds of possible changes, aging me, framing my hair differently and so on. One of the pictures looked just exactly like me. It was uncanny. The show made earnest appeals to the public and offered a reward, the whole bit. They showed pictures of the teacher and the janitor and the burned boy.

Two days later, one afternoon before you came home from school, a man came to the door, a thin elegant man, beautifully dressed in a tailored suit and a broad cream-colored fedora.

"Is this the Rousseau home?" he asked. His voice sounded British, but he spoke with a slight speech defect. He kept his gloved hand over his mouth and his face. I told him politely we were not the Rousseaus and started to close the door.

And then he said, without excitement, as if ironically, "Not the Rousseaus, really? Oh my God, Alison, have you given all that up?"

"My name is Sarah," I said, and my voice was shaking. "I don't believe I know you."

"No," he said. "But I know you. Why, I think about you all the time."

He moved his hand. His face was hideously burned. He sent his regards to Walter. When he left a moment later, taking his time on the sidewalk, I stood there terrified. Once he was out of sight, I called an old friend in the network who knew my secret, and within two hours, I had left you the necklace, cut my hair very short and dyed it, and caught a flight from Seattle-Tacoma to Tampa.

Now please, Lydia, can you send the necklace back to me? Knecht made me that necklace. He has been just what I hoped he would be—a poet, a man who pulls the veil from the world. A poet in a destitute time.

I do not know why the world must be as it is, why we should be given such visionary hope and then see things ruined, but it is so. A force exists in the world, an exacting force, whether we call it karma or fate or tragedy or the wrath of God, and I <u>know</u> certain things. I <u>know</u> I had to leave Walter because I killed that woman and her baby and burned her little boy, who grew up and waited and found me in Seattle. I do not <u>guess</u> these connections: I <u>feel</u> them, I <u>know</u> them. If you have not felt this force of karma yet, you will come to feel it: a stern and precise intelligence of retribution, so precise that only those who suffer it can truly understand its inner personal bearing.

Just this week, I saw that Harris had died. Harris, my beloved Harris, is dead, the most intelligent, most beautiful, most vital man of my life. I cannot tell you what bottomless misery it causes me. I will never see him again. Not in time, not in eternity, which I can imagine only as a feeling of infinite loss.

The necklace Knecht made for me has come to mean more than I can easily say. Please use the address on the envelope and send it to me. Just the necklace—that's all I ask. You don't need to write. I will let you know when I have received it. Please forgive me for all the rest.

Alison

Walter

On the bottom of the last page, Lydia had written a note:

You can imagine what I felt, reading that letter, when I realized who you were and what we had done and how right she was about what she was saying. You must have felt it on that day I cannot bear to remember. But when I first read this, I understood <u>dread</u> for the first time. I didn't try to write her—my God, imagine telling her what we had done and what had happened afterwards—but I sent her the necklace and included my e-mail address, and a few days later, she wrote me an e-mail to say she had received the necklace. Here it is.

Walter read on:

> Harris went to jail for eight years, and when he came out, I was already married to your father. Harris just resumed his life after that. I don't know how he had thought it out. I don't see why he was willing to accept imprisonment, the symbol of everything we'd opposed. Was it to avoid the kind of deceit that was forced on me? Or was it penance for the people we killed and the little boy we burned? I don't know. I will never know. Harris is gone. Maybe he just didn't love me.
>
> I'm afraid that Walter's genius will be ruined by this dark fatality in the world, as mine has. Something makes me feel it.
>
> But not yours, Lydia. Not yours.
>
> This thing hasn't touched you. Go somewhere and be free and do what you love. I offer myself to you, Lydia—-I know that sounds too dramatic, but I do. I am the old lie from which you must be born again, the cave of shadows from which you ascend, the false origin you must renounce to find your own truth. I renounce myself. You have made a brilliant start. Let my life be the veil you tear aside to see the world as it ought to be.
>
> Goodbye, my darling.
> Alison

I've lived with this for sixteen years, Walter. I never said a word to my father. I've lived with the knowledge that somewhere she was dead. How strange, how fitting, that she went back to that house in Georgia. You know what I keep thinking? Somehow she sent me to you.

Sometime in the middle of the night, when Teresa came looking for him, he let her read it all. She wept through most of it.

"So I was supposed to be the new Émile," he said when he finished. "Knecht. I was supposed to be the beginning of the new age, and she just left me behind when she got scared."

Teresa nodded and fell silent. He gathered up the pages of the letter.

"Who is Hermann Hesse?" she asked.

"You never read him?" he said. "Rosemary had his books when I was little. He's a German novelist everybody read in the Sixties. *Beneath the Wheel, Narcissus and Goldmund, Steppenwolf.* Knecht is the main character in a book called *Magister Ludi.*"

"Are you coming to bed?"

"Not yet."

Dexter

Bars again. The toilet beside the stairs of the Gallatin County Jail needed flushing or maybe plunging, and nobody came when he complained about it. The smell took him back more than the bars. The bucket in the corner of the cell at Bagram. The ancient little Afghan who brought him his food would sometimes empty it, not very often. Sometimes he would trip—pretend to trip—and spill it over all the floor and grin. Beaver teeth, burn scar like the Moccasin's on the half of his face where the eye was missing. Grin that beaver grin and say *Shit!* Came out *sheet.* Only English word he knew.

Sometimes in Bagram Dexter would see the little girl he had shot. She would come and stand just outside the bars and act like the tiny Vietnamese whore he had known in Atlanta. *Dex-terrrr!* she would say in her whiny way. *Dex-terrrr, baby. Why you shoot me, Dexter? Hmm? You no like?* She would look at him and stick out her tongue and hike up her skirt.

Standing now in his cell on the second floor of the jail, he held the bars. In the other cell, a skinny white boy in a bloody t-shirt sat on the straight chair covering his face with his hands and rocking forward and back. *I fucked up man, I really fucked up. O Jesus O Jesus O Jesus.* Behind him, a black man lay slumped unconscious against the back wall.

"What happened?" Dexter asked the boy, who stopped rocking and looked up at him.

"If it wasn't my best friend hadn't said she slept with him—I might of just, you know? But the knife was right there on the counter and she had this bitchy look on her face, and I just grabbed it and stuck her. Is this big enough for you, bitch? Just, like, kept sticking her while she screamed and bled." He held his hands up and shook his fingers at the blood on his shirt. "And now—O Jesus. Jesus."

"You killed somebody?"

"My girlfriend! I loved her and I killed her!"

The boy looked up at him, and Watkins knew that look. More than the smell, that look brought him back into the trembling when he stood over the still bodies and the corporal came into the room. *Jesus Christ, Watkins.* And there was Jesus lying all over the room.

He let go of the bars and his hands went to his dreadlocks, but they were gone, and he felt around for a second and his hands went to his shoulders, to his boys Huitzilopochtli and Quetzalcoatl. Pyramids and stone altars and hearts torn, still beating, from the chests of human sacrifices—that was his kind of religion, hell yes. But then he remembered what a Mexican in his unit had told him. Four hundred Spaniards under

Cortez had burned their ships and marched inland and destroyed the whole Aztec empire in a few months. His boys Huitzilopochtli and Quetzalcoatl had wilted away like bad dreams before the name of Jesus Christ. Guy named Sanchez—wanted to be a priest after he got out, but he didn't make it—Sanchez would tell him you could say it was guns or disease that destroyed the Aztecs, you could say whatever you wanted to say, but everywhere Jesus Christ went, Sanchez said, the real power belonged to the God on the cross. You could tear his heart out, but his heart would sacrifice *you*. His whole body was rigged. He was an IED of mercy.

Watkins let his head drop back, his face to the cracked and spotted ceiling of the cell, and he bellowed, shaking the bars.

"Jesus!" he wailed. The boy in the other cell stopped moaning and stared at him, shaking. Watkins remembered his mother one morning when he was eight or nine and they had just come back from church. The choir director, an old lady named Julia Searcy, loved his voice, and she got him to sing "Just as I am, without one plea" in the adult choir. His mother was a young, pretty woman then, before she got unhappy and heavy. She hugged him right there in the kitchen for a long time. *I love you so much, Dexter! I'm so proud of you!* He remembered what it felt like to be up in the choir loft, standing behind the preacher with the preacher looking at him and everyone else in the choir and the church, staring at him when he sang solo, exalted looks and almost shock every time he opened his mouth. He remembered looking out over the congregation, just singing and watching women dig in their purses, pull out Kleenex. For a little while, for an hour a week, he was the angel Mrs. Searcy said he was.

"Jesus!" he bellowed again. He wanted to feel now the way he felt then. Just as he was, without one plea. He stumbled over to the window and looked out at the town in the dark, at the courthouse clock lit up, a few strong burning stars.

"Jesus!" he shouted.

There was a flicker from the dark and a burst of light. His mother came walking toward him in a blue gown full of stars.

Dexter, she said, holding out her arms.

Somebody was yelling. He watched his body fall backwards, but he was already standing outside it. He saw his heart torn out and burning on the floor like a coal.

Dexter, she said, quiet and lovely.

COTTONMOUTH

Part VI

Several of Nature's People
I know, and they know me
I feel for them a transport
Of Cordiality

But never met this Fellow
Attended or alone
Without a tighter Breathing
And Zero at the Bone.

Emily Dickinson, "A Narrow Fellow in the Grass"

Bennett

Yesterday, he had called Gary Beamer and Wendell Longfellow to see if the cartels had done anything else in the neighboring counties. Nothing since Tuesday, they said. Later, the GBI and the FBI called to ask him in detail about the past few days. Then that afternoon—this was still Thursday—the coroner's report came back on the woman in the old Peach place: traces of coniine, an alkaloid from hemlock, in the glass beside the bed. Definitely suicide. He called Peach and then went home and made himself a frozen pizza and sat out on his front porch after supper with a beer, waving to Coach Lincoln and his daughter as they jogged by. There was a new couple he didn't know—power-walkers, glancing at their watches, reluctantly friendly: probably from Atlanta.

He sat there dreading what would happen next. When it got dark, he went in and streamed an episode of *Longmire* and then went to bed and slept all night without waking up. His cell phone rang a little after 6:00 on Friday morning.

"Sorry to call you so early, sweetheart." LaCourvette Todd. Nobody else called him *sweetheart*. "I need to tell you they got Dexter Watkins."

"What do you mean?"

"They had a sniper waiting and he went to the window."

It took him a few seconds to clear his head. He sat up.

"You mean Dexter's dead?"

"Hollow point in the forehead."

"Lord have mercy."

"Amen," said LaCourvette. "Everybody ran him down, but Dexter wasn't so bad."

"I'll come by," he said and ended the call and slumped back on the pillow.

The three-day rule hadn't worked. They had shot Dexter on the fourth day. This was the fifth day since they had found the Peach boy in the kudzu, and all bets were off. New rules.

Ellen would be all busted up despite everything Dexter had done to her. He closed his eyes and imagined Dexter standing at a window looking out. A moment later, he was falling backward in a spray of blood. Dexter's ghost stood up from the body and walked out through the wall of the jail. The men in the other cell watched, calm as grazing cows. It didn't make sense that a ghost would set off the alarm system, but Dexter's did, and the Mexican stood there holding up his severed head with his hands over the ears—

Bennett woke up again. He fumbled with his phone until he saw the Stop button and turned the alarm off. Already 7:00? He must have been more tired than he knew. He got up in his t-shirt and boxer shorts, used the bathroom, and started for the kitchen. He had remembered to set the timer the night before, and the coffee maker was hissing and popping at the end of the brew. He got a mug down from the cabinet, poured a little cream in the bottom, filled it with hot coffee, took a sip—never hot enough—and set it in the microwave for thirty seconds. He would call LaCourvette back after he got the paper.

He opened the front door, glanced both ways to see if anybody was looking, and then stepped down in his shorts and picked up the yellow plastic bag from the bottom step. As he got back inside, he pulled out the *Telegraph* to see what had made it into the news this morning. **Cartel Strikes Business in Gallatin County**. A large manila envelope slipped from between the sections of the paper onto the floor and he picked it up. Blank on the outside, not sealed. Some kind of ad.

Back in the kitchen, he took his coffee from the microwave, sat down at the table, and casually slid out the contents of the envelope. His mug stopped halfway to his mouth.

In the first photograph, he was sitting on the front porch, turning to set down his beer, and his sour face was turned and slightly lowered; this would have been last night, when he saw the coach and remembered the new arts center and thought about Janet Brownlee. There was a small red cross neatly inscribed over his right temple. The next pictures were of the Peach family: Walter Peach at his desk in the *Tribune* office; Teresa Peach, her hands in the kitchen sink, her head turned to say something back into the room; the boy standing just inside the screen door. And there were three of Rose in her bedroom, half-dressed, taken from outside and below. He stared for a moment, and then turned them over, embarrassed for her and ashamed of himself. Except for Rose's, all the pictures were marked with red crosses like the one on his head. Little red hearts were drawn all over Rose, on all the places that smote whoever had made them.

His heart was pounding. Deep breaths, Dr. Fletcher had told him. He thought about his father dropping dead at forty-five.

Under the last photograph was a business envelope he did not open, not addressed to him, but to Braxton Forrest. He called LaCourvette.

"What I don't get," he said, "is why these people are making so much trouble over this one crop of marijuana. They must have growers all over the place."

"Something strange about all of it," said LaCourvette. "Killing they own people. Hold on a minute."

While he was still on the phone, he heard her dispatch two police cars to Stonewall Hill and put out an APB for a white Lincoln somebody had called in.

"Walter Peach told me he saw Dexter down there with a stranger in a sombrero," Bennett said.

"Did the boy see him?"

"I don't think so. Why?"

"How about the girl when they came to her house?"

"I don't think so. Who is it we're talking about?"

"Boss they call El Mocasín," LaCourvette told him. "Cottonmouth. Things he's done I don't even want to tell you, sweetheart. I'm gon call the FBI."

Walter

The sun woke him up in the armchair of the study. The new day felt like the rind of the day before. Alison Graves's letter slid from his lap onto the floor as he stood up. He stooped for it and sat at the desk and stared at the last page, bleary, his head aching. Rosemary Peach was Alison Graves. Alison Graves was Sarah Downs.

There was a light knock.

"Walter," Teresa said in a thin voice. She put a hand on his shoulder from behind him, and he felt her trembling.

"I fell asleep in the chair," he said defensively.

"Walter, listen," she said. "We just got a call from the FBI. I have to tell you something bad."

He stood up from the chair, dizzy, instantly dreading what she would say.

"Is it Rose?"

"No, thank God. Somebody shot Dexter Watkins last night through the window of the jail."

"Shot him," he said dully.

"Killed him, Walter. And this morning Hudson Bennett got an envelope with pictures of all of us—you, me, the children. *Do you hear me?* Somebody has been watching us again like at Christmas. Somebody has been taking pictures. But this time there were crosshairs on our heads— all except for Rose, because they seem to have different plans for her. And Hudson said there's a letter for Braxton."

In his field of vision, a flickering zigzag began to vibrate, just a little thing, as though the filament in an old light bulb had suddenly flickered on. There was another knock, and Rose came in, unusually tentative and vulnerable.

"Dad? The funeral home called asking about arrangements."

"Arrangements for what?"

As he looked at her, the zigzag grew and began to shimmer and cover the features of her face. Scotoma, they called it. The word did not describe this brilliant, multicolored, visionary construct of coming migraine, with its ramifying fortifications.

"A funeral for your mother," she said.

"A funeral?" he said, shading his eyes. Then the idea struck home. A funeral? "Good God, we can't have a funeral! For a Most Wanted terrorist? We'd have a national media circus here."

"I'm just telling you they called," she said before she left.

"Stay away from the windows!" he called after her. "And Rose! Bring me some aspirin or ibuprofen! I'm getting a migraine."

"I'm the one who called the funeral home," Teresa said quietly. "She's your mother, Walter."

"We'll just call attention to what she did," he said. "She killed people, and she got off scot-free and came down to Georgia and fucked good old Vernon Jenkins while her son listened and learned in the next room."

Teresa slapped him.

"Ever since I married you," she said fiercely, "it's been *Rosemary, Rosemary, Rosemary.* And now that you've found her and you know why she left, you turn on her?"

He waved at the air, holding his head. The pain began to pierce his eye socket with every heartbeat. He bent over in his chair.

"All that time she knew where I was," he said. "All she had to do was be standing there on the sidewalk somewhere. *Walter? Do you recognize me?* But she let my witch of a stepmother scare her off, and she never did it. All along Judge Lawton knew where she was. My whole life everyone has lied to me."

"They must have had their reasons," Teresa said.

"And that idiot Akers I've even *heard* of."

"He's your father."

"*My father.* Good God. What kind of father is that?" The idea settled on him strangely, and he waved the air again as if to scare it off. The migraine bore steadily inward, beat by beat. "You want me to have a *funeral* for this woman, seriously, who walked around naked and slept with Vernon Jenkins when I was right across the hall? I mean *loudly.*"

"Stop it, Walter."

"I see old Minnie's point—a whore who turns out to be a fugitive bomber. What kind of *mother* is that?"

When she moved to slap him again, he caught her hand and pulled her toward him. His field of vision shimmered with elaborate adornments already beginning to dissolve at the edges into a skull-deep pounding, as though the bones of his head were underground rock splitting along a fault line.

"Walter," Teresa said, pulling his head against her breast, "have a little mercy on your parents. Honor your father and your mother."

"They didn't even give me a name!" he said, pushing free of her. "*Knecht.* It sounds like you're clearing your throat."

He stood up and groped his way to the liquor cabinet and found a bottle.

"Great, Walter," Teresa said. "That's just great. You know what? Listen to me."

"What do you want?"

"People are trying to kill us. What are we going to do?"

Where her voice was, a crazily blurring medieval fortress of green, red, and yellow tessellations crumbled in successive tremors.

"Let them shoot us," he said. "What a relief, merely being dead. Here, I'll give them an easy shot."

He went to the big window and spread his arms.

"Oh good God!" she said disgustedly. "Just sit here and get drunk first thing in the morning and feel sorry for yourself."

He put the bottle back.

"Thank you." She left him, and he was grateful she was gone. Just a few days ago he had sat across from Nora O'Hearn. Nora. Now there was—

What? There was pure, taunting illusion. Like that poem Yeats wrote in his old age. *How can I, that girl standing there,/My attention fix/On Roman or on Russian/Or on Spanish politics?*

The oldest fantasy. Pleasure without consequences.

Wasn't that the whole dream of the woman he knew as "Rosemary Peach"—not *Mama*, but *Rosemary*? The whole dream of this woman named Alison Graves?

Alison.

With a pulse of his headache came the belated recognition that the man who had said the name *Alison* in the *Tribune* office a year ago, the one who had bought the ad in Spanish back in March, was the one in the creek bottom with Dexter.

He leaned back his beating head, trying to think. It was all there to think, but he could not think it. The man who found Alison in Seattle back almost twenty years ago? The burned face. They could not have Alison in common. How could they?

He thought of her, his *Rosemary*, all shining with nakedness as she weeded by the creek. Wearing her jean shorts, she would hold her arms up over her head, and mosquitos would light on her nipples, and she would brush them away and laugh, her skin agleam with a sheen of sweat. *Hurry up!* Alison would say, sticking her tongue out at him, and he would spray her naked torso with insect repellant while she squinched her eyes shut, joyful in the narrowing spaces of her liberty.

A scatter of bones molded into a rotting mattress, a stench of death.

Old death. Old, old death.

The memory of it deep in his nostrils, deeper than the migraine in his skull.

How did she get back into the house? Through a window? Or did she still have a key? The door had not been forced. And how long was she there? It could have been a day, a month, a few hours. Long enough to walk into his bedroom and drop *The Small Gnats Mourn.*

At the end of my suffering there was a door.

Why would she bother to lock the door?

The plant grew wild in Washington State, an invasive species. It took over whole fields, like kudzu. Socrates had drunk hemlock because the city had condemned him to death. Was that her commentary, that she was a victim of the state? Or was she saying that even the imperfect justice of the laws was better than Akers' organic anarchy? Or was it that—

"Dad?" said Rose, putting her hand on his shoulder. He shielded his eyes. He could not see her except in dim outline behind the brilliant scotoma and the beat of *Tyger! Tyger! Burning! Bright!* She took his hand and opened his palm.

Tell me my fortune. Who is it who can tell me who I am?

"Here's the ibuprofen." She was trembling like Teresa. She shook the pills into his palm. "Dad," she said, "just swallow them."

When he did, she took his hand again as though he were blind and put a glass of water in it. He drank, and when she took back the glass, he felt for her hand and kissed it.

"God, I'm so scared," she said.

Forrest

Marisa Forrest drove Braxton from Portsmouth down to Boston Logan for a flight to Atlanta. He and the Waldrop boy had already talked about the big marijuana bust, the arson, and the murders—the undeniable presence, just as Peach had said, of cartels in Middle Georgia—but all the way down to Logan, Marisa relayed what Teresa had told her about the discovery of Walter's mother. Dead for all those years in that old house covered with kudzu. He had seen it once on a trip down to Georgia—he and Peach touring the county.

All the way down on the flight, he thought about what it must have taken to go inside that place—the rats, the smell, the awful abiding interior deadness. And what it must be like to have a psyche where that place was the hidden image of one's inmost soul. Was that where Walter was, God help him? He thought about the psyches of houses, Bachelard's "poetics of space," Miss Havisham's house and Hester Prynne's cottage and Sutpen's Hundred.

That place in the country and Stonewall Hill had some kind of kinship he could not remember. Some deep, troubled history, like so much in the South.

The boy Buford had led them in after entering, earlier, all by himself. Forrest's heart warmed to think of him.

After renting a Toyota SUV at Hartsfield-Jackson, Forrest made it to the Red Roof Inn in Gallatin by midnight on Thursday. If he wanted the newspaper to keep going and if he really wanted to help Walter, he had little choice, just as he had thought earlier. Walter showed no inclination to resume his responsibilities. According to Teresa, the man was a mess after finding his mother's body and then discovering—through his old mistress, no less—that his parents were terrorists.

At the motel, he finally fell into a fitful sleep broken by trips to the bathroom. When it was daylight, he stopped trying and got up. He took a very hot shower and put on jeans and a t-shirt and sat down with his laptop to check his email before going to look for some breakfast. Just as the desktop came up, somebody knocked on the door.

Too early for the maid. 7:30? Who could it be? Nobody knew he was here, not even Marisa. Another knock. He sighed and got up and took a couple of steps over to open the door.

"Mr. Forrest? Sheriff Hudson Bennett. Can I come in for a minute?"

The sheriff stood there unsmiling in his hat and his short-sleeved khaki shirt with the sheriff's badge over his left pocket. They shook hands and Forrest stepped aside to let Bennett enter. The room was still humid from his shower. There was a table beside the front window, and he had draped clothes on one of the two chairs, so he threw them on the unmade bed and pulled one out for the sheriff.

"What's happened? How did you find me here?"

Bennett handed Forrest a pair of disposable latex gloves and a manila envelope. Solemn man, Forrest thought.

"You mind putting these on, keep from messing up any fingerprints?"

Forrest worked the gloves over his hands, opened the clasp, and tilted the envelope. Out slid a stack of big glossy photographs. His heart went strange in his chest—Bennett himself, Walter Peach, Teresa Peach, the boy, all marked with red crosses on their heads. Little red hearts for Rose.

And a sealed business envelope addressed to him: **Prof. Braxton Forrest, Room 214, Red Roof Inn.**

"What the hell? Who knew where I was? I didn't get here until midnight."

"No idea," Bennett said. "I got a message myself the other day. Mine was next to that Mexican's head out at Ed Watkins' store."

"You didn't open this?"

"No sir."

Forrest opened it and spread it out on the table so they could both see it.

Dear Prof. Forrest,

Some years ago, I came upon your first book, *The Subjunctive Abyss: Achilles in the Iliad*. Quite readable, I found, if a bit too broadly conceived to satisfy the nitpickery of a true classicist, which of course you are not. What struck me was your insistence that Achilles suffers the knowledge of having been denied supreme immortality, which his mother Thetis would happily have bestowed upon him had his father been a god instead of the mortal she was forced to marry. You do not back away, with fastidious scholarly scruples and doubts, from fully acknowledging that he has been *deprived in advance* of the divine life that would have made him whole and complete, instead of this welter of pain and lust for revenge and grief and momentary triumph and underlying dread.

Do I recognize myself in your Achilles? Of course. No one of genius can fail to be aware of a certain godlikeness. My sympathies lie with his deprivation. To take one relatively minor instance, *mon semblable*, think what it means to be born "black," as they call it. Would I choose as my "race" at birth this one labeled "black"? Well, it seems a bit complicated, full of grievance and accommodation and redress. So, hmm—I think not.

Oh, wait, I do not *get* to choose! *Really?* I am *assigned* "blackness"? By whom? And then I watch my mother die? And I am hideously scarred for life?

Simplest would be not to believe, I suppose, in the Assigner. But the sting is rather too personal, so how can one not? The Lurker, the Observer-from-within of one's existence, the Depriver who would not be satisfied without one's lifelong *awareness* of deprivation. All the *if, could, might have been* of one's deepest thwarted hope. What you call the subjunctive abyss.

Your Achilles could never strike at Zeus, his own Depriver. How could he? Hector, the god's substitute, had to absorb the wrath of Achilles' deprivation—the whole boundless absence, the negative of immortal supremacy denied. And readers object that Achilles dragged the body of Hector around! That little Trojan was a frustrating minim of the inaccessible giant corpse Achilles would have made of the god! Less beautiful but close in kinship was Ahab, striking through the mask of the White Whale, unable to reach the Jehovah who singled him out before birth for eternal damnation.

And I have to make do with Walter Peach! I know more about the fool than he knows about himself. Poor pwetty Walter's Wosemawy wan away, boohoo? I watched my mother bleed out a heartbeat at a time a foot away from me, crushed by a fallen beam in the explosion, her throat pierced by the splintered semicircular arm of the standing classroom globe she had just bought for her students. I lay pinned on the floor, helpless to escape the fire, screaming and screaming as it reached me.

You would be a worthier adversary than Walter Peach, Prof. Forrest, but I must accept what the Depriver has—*given*, isn't that what they say? Oh, goodness, let me lie down on your couch, Herr Doktor. (Is that what Hermia did, by the way?)

I am Lazarus, come from the dead, come back to tell you all, I shall tell you all.

Yes, all—someday. But in the meantime, I just *must* share this, because you will understand me: Like the heroes in your *Iliad*, I take solace in imagining the agony of the bereaved. It is so hard to appreciate such emotions these days.

And long ago I copied a sentence from your book: *Achilles cannot experience his life as other men can, even though all of them also have to die, but rather, superb as he is, he feels an unbounded metaphysical rage at his deprivation, and although killing others momentarily soothes it, like salve on a burn, even the slaughter of all the living could not ultimately fill the subjunctive abyss within him.*

Like salve on a burn: oh my. Too true, too true, dear Braxton, in literature as in life.

Until we meet,
Cottonmouth

Forrest rose and stood staring down at the letter, his heart pounding. Who knew about Hermia?

"Make any sense to you?" Bennett asked.

"He's pure evil."

"Apparently, 'Cottonmouth' is what he's called in English. The Mexicans call him The Moccasin. Some kind of crime boss."

"Maybe," Forrest said. "He's more than that." He touched the photographs and looked up at Bennett. "He's an emissary."

"What do you mean?" Bennett asked.

"I mean we'd better say our prayers."

Walter

He was lying in the bedroom with a wet cloth over his eyes, trying not to think. Heartbeats tore jaggedly into the sides of his head. He was just dozing off when he heard a gunshot, then another immediately after it—shouts, a flurry of shots. He slung the cloth aside and sprang up. Teresa and Rose stood tensely in the hallway, staring toward the garden.

"What was that?" he cried.

"I don't know," Teresa said.

"Is Buford okay?"

Rose and Teresa whirled toward him, already calling. "Buford! Buford?"

No answer.

Walter struggled down the back steps and into the pantry. Not there. Not in the kitchen. At the screen door was a man with FBI on his back in big yellow letters. The man was shouting to someone outside. As Peach came up beside him, another agent came running toward him in a crouch across the back yard. He was leading Buford back toward the house, guarding him with his body.

"What happened?" Peach demanded.

"Get back!" said the first FBI man, pushing him to the side as the other came in with Buford.

"They shot at your boy," said the second man. Buford's right ear was covered with blood that ran down the side of his neck and onto his shirt. His shirt front and jeans were flecked with bits of leaf and soil.

"Who did?" Peach demanded. Before he could think about it, he grabbed the pistol from an agent's holster and pushed open the screen door. The grip in his palm, his finger finding the trigger, the other hand feeling for the safety. An immense rage lifted him out of himself. As he stepped outside, something snatched at the back of his head and doorframe splintered beside him. Inside, one of the men yelled, almost screamed. Peach was away, he was down the steps, but then he was grabbed and hauled back, and he tried to hold up his head, cursing, struggling to fight free, but the man was too strong and he fell backward to the floor. Someone yanked away the pistol *Give it here goddamn it* and pulled Peach roughly into the kitchen next to Buford, who sat calmly staring up at him, his back against the old cabinets, a wet washcloth to his ear.

"Are you okay, Dad?"

As the rage drained out of him, the migraine came thundering back. He felt an infinite weariness.

"I'm okay. How about you?"

"Miss Nora saved me."

Walter stared at him. The boy must be in shock. Why the hell had he been outside at all? He put his hands to the sides of his head to try to still the pounding. Both of the FBI men were in the kitchen. One of them sat slumped on the floor holding his hand over his left eye and saying over and over, softly, *O Jesus, O Jesus*. Blood trickled down his cheek. Walter looked up at the one who still stood over him, a very big, coal-black man, still panting from the melee of exertion. He held his FBI identification card up to Walter. Special Agent Hezekiah Billings.

"The fuck you trying to do?" Billings said. His eyes were less hostile than disturbed and apprehensive.

"I guess I went crazy there for a minute," Walter said.

"You pretty damn lucky."

"What do you mean?"

"I mean an inch and you be dead. Sniper almost got you."

"Got me?" Peach said, incredulous.

Billings pointed across the room at the splintered frame of the screen door. "Clipped your whatever. Ponytail."

Peach's hand went to the back of his head. He felt the back of his collar, then his loose hair, and a belated terror came over him.

"Hawkins caught a splinter in his eye," Billings said. "Man just missed your boy out in the garden, too. Nicked the tip of his ear. Inch of difference, you hear what I'm saying?"

His heart gave strangely. That close?

"Thank your guardian angel," Teresa said as she and Rose bent over Buford, both of them weeping steadily.

Buford looked up with an odd placidity. Definitely in shock, Peach thought.

"Son," Peach said, "what were you doing out there?"

"I had to go out there." The boy's face showed no shame, no remorse.

"You had to."

"Yes sir."

Peach's head pounded painfully.

"Go upstairs with your mother and stay out of sight. Do you hear me?"

"Yes sir."

The boy obediently left and went up the back stairs. Teresa looked back at Walter, her eyes large and dark, the ampersand etched sharply between her accusatory eyes, like the day he had come home from seeing his mother's necklace between the bare breasts of Lydia Downs.

There was a great whoop from outside.

"*Got him!*" he heard someone shout. "Got the bastard!"

Men were cheering. A wave of denouement washed over him, and Walter lowered his head thanking God. He started to get up and was surprised to find Billings still there beside him, helping him to his feet. The man was half a foot taller than he was. When he was standing, Billings put a hand on his shoulder.

"What's that boy's name?" he asked kindly.

"Buford," Walter said.

"I never saw anything like it. I swear that boy went out there to draw fire," Billings said. "Not a lick of fear in him. Like he just wanted to show us where the shooter was."

Walter met Billings' eyes and nodded. Billings touched his back and went across the room to help Hawkins to his feet. Walter followed them onto the steps. Men were running toward the old barn. Already he could hear the sirens of approaching ambulances. Before they arrived, Hudson Bennett pulled up in his Bronco and got out, showing his badge. He saw Walter and walked across the gravel of the drive toward him.

The pain in Walter's head was returning, heartbeat by heartbeat, and the siren made it worse. The sound grew and grew and then died slowly as the EMS crew poured out and surrounded the two wounded men. He and Bennett stood for a moment watching two paramedics help Hawkins, two others lifting the other wounded man, who was in much worse shape. The crew got them into the ambulances and out of the driveway within a minute. Bennett stood just beneath him on the step.

"I gave that letter to Forrest," he said, turning toward Walter when the sound died down. "This Cottonmouth, he's not after you because of a patch of marijuana. He's known who you are a long time. You folks need to get the hell out of here. This man means to kill you all. Deserve it or not. Maybe you deserve it, I don't know, but I'll be damned if the girl does, or that boy. Or Teresa."

Peach waited a moment to answer, seeing in Bennett's eyes something Bennett himself would never acknowledge. Bennett dropped his eyes and nodded and went back to his car.

Bennett

He sat in the Bronco for a few minutes. The FBI men acted like it was all over, but whoever they had just shot, it sure as hell wasn't Cottonmouth. He would bet the house on that. He couldn't settle down. Finally, he got out and walked through the vegetable garden out to the collapsing barn and went in through the wagon entrance. Decades of undisturbed dust roiled up into the slanting sunlight from all the men tramping through it. He asked an FBI man where the sniper's body was, and the man nodded toward a wooden ladder. Bennett climbed it and pulled himself onto the unsteady boards of the hay loft, grabbing an angled two-by-four that supported the roof.

Two G-men stood over a body lying in its blood near the opening that faced the back of Stonewall Hill. Probably in his forties. Not Hispanic, but dark. Maybe Eastern European or Turkish. His heavy face was scarred from smallpox or acne. Next to him was a bag from Burger King and a large coffee, still upright. Still warm.

"Don't touch that, sir," an FBI man said.

Bennett shrugged. "I think you can figure out who touched it last," he said.

The shooter had missed the boy, then hit Bill Phipps, the Gallatin officer who tried to help Buford after the first shot. This piece of shit had tried to shoot the boy again. Who would shoot a boy for money?

Bennett stood looking toward the house—the garden, the screen door, Rose's room through the limbs of the big oak tree. He saw her walk to the window, looking back at the barn. He wanted to wave at her, tell her to stay down, stay out of sight. For a second, she seemed to see him looking at her, but he stepped back himself, embarrassed, remembering the pictures of her this dead scumbag had taken and what those people meant to do with her. He looked down at the body and spat on it.

"Jesus, Sheriff," one of the FBI men said.

"Did I shock you boys? Sorry. Do you know how many dead bodies this makes? I've kind of lost count. And this slimeball won't even point us to the main one."

"Sinaloa cartel, turns out, did those killings yesterday," said the older agent. "One faction went after the other one."

"This one here, he's got a German ID," said the younger man. "He's the one shot Dexter Watkins. We found his car back here a quarter-mile off on a wood road."

"White Lincoln?"

"Yes sir."

Bennett nodded. "Anything in it?"

"Yes sir. A notebook with some kind of writing looks like when you're on a heart monitor. Found his ID and the camera he used on his rifle scope. We'll go through the pictures."

"We're not any closer to the one behind all this?"

"No sir. We hear he's called the Moccasin."

"What I hear, too."

At four in the afternoon, he was at his desk, spent and yawning after talking to Ed Watkins. Through the window, he watched the heat shimmering above the cars in the parking lot. Beyond them was the interstate, where the great world poured through Gallatin. Once, long ago, it was a town without all the cars, the eighteen-wheelers laboring north and south twenty-four hours a day, full of who knows what? A hundred years ago. Way back when it was just the railroad. Dirt streets, barefoot children, dogfights over disputed territory between dogs that still had their goods, roosters crowing in people's backyards. And the girls in their simple dresses, women being helped up onto buggy seats that creaked on their leaf springs. Come Saturday morning the ladies of Gallatin would walk around the courthouse square, strolling on the sidewalks under the awnings, swirling their parasols, visiting, going into shops. There were shady porches and courteous greetings and the day fading and the house lights coming on, the sound of crickets. No TV, no radio, no air conditioning.

Was there ever such an America? Maybe not. Maybe it was all an illusion.

A great dark pang of despair went through him.

The phone rang. He sighed and lifted the receiver.

"Ed?"

"Sheriff Bennett? This is U.S. Marshal Aengus Dunne."

Bennett sat up. Dunne had been two years ahead of him all through school before he transferred to a military academy in Virginia in ninth grade. He had played defensive end for Army at West Point. After a decorated stint in Iraq, he joined the U.S. Marshals out of their Macon office.

"You know Ed Watkins identified the driver of the vehicle at his store," Dunne said.

"So he told me. He's scared to death."

"Pablo Rodriguez Alejandro from Culiacan, Mexico," Dunne said.

"Any chance of catching him?"

"We found him up in Gwinnett County. Shot through the back of his head while he was eating breakfast. Somebody thought he sold out the cartel men who were killed the other day. Apparently this was a reprisal."

Bennett stared out the window. Two fighting mockingbirds whirled up from a light post at the edge of the parking lot.

"It's hard to keep up."

"Right, well, we need to get the Peach family out of here. Now."

Bennett thought about the head sitting by the gasoline pump out at Ed Watkins' store. That wasn't a reprisal. That was a message from Cottonmouth. Message after message—but what was the real message? A shudder went through him. Then another, longer one. He was glad Dunne couldn't see him. He closed his eyes and let out his breath before he spoke.

"So you're talking about witness protection?"

"That's right. We'd already brought it up to them before the shooter tried to get the boy and Peach. You saw what happened out there today. The cartels are brutal, but there's a certain rationality to their brutality, or they couldn't do business. This man doesn't care about what they care about—money, power, beautiful women. They say he's asexual, *asexuado*, but I don't believe it. I think—well, I should keep my theories to myself. But he's brilliant, they say, and absolutely cold. Even men like El Chapo are afraid of him."

Bennett thought about Teresa Peach trying to manage her family with this man trying to kill them. That good woman. Why couldn't he have found a woman like that?

"You mind if I go with you? The family's pretty rattled, and they've gotten used to me these last few days."

"I don't mind. It will be good to see you, Hudson."

Raïssa

Her father sat hooding his eyes, his thumbs pressed into the sides of his head above his ears, fingers interlaced over his eyebrows. She looked across his ruffled hair—weird without the ponytail—to where, far above, like one of the angels in the Bible, U.S. Marshal Aengus Dunne looked down upon them. They sat in the front foyer where, days ago, men had invaded the house and backed her toward the fireplace. Buford perched on the ottoman, ear bandaged, looking up, and her mother sat tensely on the white Queen Anne sofa's very edge.

Marshal Dunne defied her usual ironic description of the male sex, an inventory of vanity and comical inadequacy she based on the high school pickings (except for Andrew Perkins). Marshal Dunne did not loom, unlike Will Amos in the school hallway, but he was just as tall—taller. Much taller than Andrew Perkins. And yet his proportions were perfect. He could have been Buford's size or her father's five-ten instead of six-eight or, good lord, however tall he was. His form was cleanly, if that was a word. He had a large, noble, close-shaved head. A captivating scar disappeared into his left eyebrow. His stomach was flat as a brick under his uniform. Great tanned forearms corded with veins came out of his short sleeves. His wrists flexed with power, and his hands moved with an ease and expressiveness that belied their immensity.

Hercules would have looked like this, she thought, when he was going around slaying monsters. She still felt her hand vanishing meekly into his, almost like when Mr. Forrest shook her hand. A kind of vertigo came over her at the sheer clifflike steepness of El Capitan, Marshal Aengus Dunne.

The feeling stayed. But what she also felt, other than this mesmerized physical fascination, was gratitude that made her whole body feel like melting wax. This huge, beautiful man stood between her and the evil that had come through the door across the room, where Sheriff Bennett leaned now against the doorjamb. She could still feel her hand grabbing behind her, finding the cool metal handle, the poker whipping overhead with all her strength against that short one.

The one they beheaded.

She winced back from the image—but should she feel worse about that man's death?

She thought about her terror, and another spill of hot relief spread across her abdomen. Looking at Marshal Dunne, she wanted to let him know just how intensely grateful she was, how much she felt—how much relief she found simply that he was standing there so potently between her and that memory. He was talking, and she watched him talk. He must have been making sense, and she must have been smiling and nodding, but she just wanted to say *Marshal Dunne* and have him turn his gaze on her. Just drop his eyes and let them settle totally on her, amazed at her comeliness, his great, noble attention with its tremendous wingspan folding into contentment and coming to rest on her. And she would answer his gaze with her absolute gratitude. She would smile the smile everyone said was beautiful, maybe because it was so infrequent, but whatever, and she would make the whole offer of herself with her eyes.

What was she thinking? *Offer of herself*? Stupid to think of an offer—*offer?*—to a man so old, already in his thirties. Who looked like Hercules.

Well, he wasn't looking at her anyway.

"I don't know where we'd be without this guy. Thanks, buddy." He pointed at Buford, and she was instantly jealous.

"Yes sir."

His glance went to her mother, who smiled up at him and shook her head unhappily, eyebrows creased together. He looked at her father, who nodded at the praise of Buford. But Marshal Dunne would not look at Raïssa. Would not look at her or meet her eyes, even though she glowed at him like a Japanese lantern. Why wouldn't he *look* at her? He didn't have any reason not to.

"We're doing everything we can. The fourth man in the car who came here"—he *almost* looked at her—"was a Mexican in the rival Sinaloa faction named Pablo Rodriguez Alejandro, apparently an infiltrator."

"He hired the sniper?"

"No, he was found dead earlier today. But there was originally a fifth man in the car that left Phoenix Estates that morning."

"That's right. Whoever did it," Raïssa said, "must have been the one who did that."

Everyone looked at her except Marshal Dunne. She could see in Buford's eyebrows that he was about to say something about the absolute incoherence of her remark, so she blurted, "I mean the one who hired the shooter man."

Shooter man? Her mother regarded her with pure, wide-eyed irony. Marshal Dunne merely nodded over at Sheriff Bennett as though it were time to go. Why wouldn't he look at her? She raced through possibilities.

Maybe Sheriff Bennett had said something to him.

Her breath left her. *The pictures.* Sheriff Bennett had told her mother, who had told her that the shooter had taken them through the window late yesterday afternoon with a camera on a rifle scope. Late yesterday afternoon, she had been in her room trying on the new, Neiman Marcus clothes that Mrs. Forrest had sent her after hearing about the men breaking into the house and threatening her. They were lovely. The department store boxes on her bed, the foil seals on the tissue paper, the fresh cloth underneath, shaken out and held up, the dress and camisole—cool somehow, as though the paper itself had cooled and scented them. She had been alone in the room, undressing, looking at herself in the mirror, putting on the new things. And all the time that camera on the sniper's scope had been taking pictures of her. She felt a flush begin to rise from her neck.

Sheriff Bennett had seen the pictures. That meant El Capitan had seen them.

Her mother glanced at her just at that moment.

"Rose?" she said with alarm. "Are you okay? You're red as a beet."

Her father shaded his eyes to look at her. She would not flee the room.

"I was just thinking," she said, "of that man taking pictures."

Marshal Dunne finally met her eyes. A slight smile, a very slight smile.

Despite herself, she burst out laughing—exploded with it. And fled. She bumped into the end table getting away, but she had already broken the Tiffany lamp. A moment later she was gasping in the kitchen, trembling with humiliation, wincing away from the window. She could hear her mother calling her from three rooms away. She started to sob.

Walter

Dulled by two ibuprofen and two extra-strength acetaminophen, the migraine still flared with every heartbeat. It felt like somebody driving a nail into the cushions on the sides of his head. He went up the back stairs and into the study and stood looking out the window before he remembered he should stay out of sight. He backed away and poured three fingers of Knob Creek in his glass—maybe that would help—and sat down in his favorite armchair.

So they couldn't stay at Stonewall Hill. They might go to a motel in town, but Aengus Dunne said there were Hispanic workers at all of them, and with enough money, they could be bought off as informers. A safe house somewhere? Cottonmouth's intelligence network had found every hiding place of the cartel with no trouble. If they were willing to stay put for another day or so, highly protected, the U.S. Marshals could make better arrangements. There was some risk, but being in one place might be safest. Somewhere out there was Cottonmouth, the man his mother had nearly burned to death. Or maybe, Walter thought, the man had eluded everyone and he was already in the house, waiting hidden in a closet or behind a door. Or standing right behind him. He stood up and walked the study. He thought back to that first time in the *Tribune* office, when the man picked up the newspaper with the headline asking whether there were cartels in Gallatin and made some sarcastic comment. What was it? Thanking Peach for the *suggestion*.

He had been played all along.

He stared at his reflection in the office window as darkness fell outside. *Old aristocracy*, wasn't it, that Forrest had called him? And suddenly the jawline of Asa Daniel Graves ghosted there in his reflection, the ardent old racist, the Confederate firebrand. He nodded at himself. He thought about Harris Akers staring insolently at the booking camera after his arrest at a demonstration in Chicago. *His father.* Walter didn't even know his true name, if there was such a thing. Akers? Graves? No names but the dead ones. Or the invented one, Peach, that he had actually gone through legal paperwork to change from Walter Devereaux Lawton. Or the little bastard named *Knecht*.

The thought of Rosemary flooded him. Not Alison, but Rosemary. What must have gone through her mind in that moment when Mrs. Jenkins came to the door and held up the newspaper to her? Despite his bitterness last night, he knew Rosemary loved him. Rosemary with her casual beauty and her huge smile. She loved him. That vivid certainty remained after forty years. She was too intimate, but he had not known it at the time. He would lie back at the end of a day and she would hold him unembarrassed against her nakedness and read him stories as she stroked the inside of his forearm with her fingertips and he listened, mesmerized.

No one else around to let him see himself as others saw him.

Not until Cletus McBride.

And then Vernon Jenkins.

And then Mrs. Jenkins.

Rosemary loved him. That was no illusion. She must have loved him so much that she gave up everything to protect him from her life of lies and hiding. Anything that put her at risk for capture would have meant scandal and imprisonment. Exposure. Separation from him in any case.

So that was it. It did not satisfy him, not entirely, but he let a long breath, long pent up, slowly trail out of him. If she had tried to come back for him later, she would have faced the same danger. Was there a statute of limitations on arson and manslaughter in such a famous attack? Would Judge Lawton have turned her in? Judge Lawton had never told him his mother was Alison Graves, surely to protect him, surely at legal risk to himself.

What about Harris Akers' parents? He opened his laptop and Googled this man who had become his father. The Wikipedia entry, just like that, gave him two more grandparents. William Akers (1919–1981) had been the CEO of an electric utility. Cecilia Akers (1924–): was she still alive? She would be ninety years old. He had no idea how to begin to find her, and even if he found her, would it be worth it to disturb her peace of mind with a lost grandson and great-grandchildren whose identities were about to be erased?

He had just started Googling Cecilia Akers when his phone buzzed. It was Forrest.

"Walter? How's everybody doing?"

As Peach filled him in, he listened to Forrest's steady commentary of sympathetic curses and outrage.

"I'm coming over there. You up in the sanctum?"

"I've started a bottle of Knob Creek."

"I better hurry."

Seconds later, the phone buzzed again. From a different number this time.

"Walter? Sheriff Bennett. Sorry to bother you, but Buddy Fingal said to tell you that box next to your mother's bed is full of papers. He said you might want them."

"What kind of papers?"

"Letters. Diaries, it looks like. Newspapers. A few old pictures. All kinds of stuff. Want me to drop it by?"

Walter's heart began pounding so hard, the headache broke through the whiskey and the analgesics.

"Right now?"

"Might as well," Bennett said.

Peach called Forrest back.

"Listen, let's put this off until tomorrow, okay? Hudson Bennett's coming over with a box of papers that were my mother's. I'm going to need to look through them."

"Save me some of the whiskey."

Nora

She got back late to Stonewall Hill—so late, everyone else had gone to bed. That morning, Bill had driven her out to have breakfast with Martin and his mother, and then he took her out to the Ikahalpi River with a picnic lunch his mother had made and a cold bottle of Sauvignon Blanc. They hiked in and climbed up to a hidden plateau that overlooked the river and miles of state forest and ate under a huge shade tree. Bill had brought Gruyère cheese with fresh baguettes that they had with the wine. Mrs. Sharpe had made deviled eggs, which Nora loved, along with ham sandwiches, freshly sliced homegrown tomatoes, her own homemade potato chips, and a bowl of blackberries.

"I want to build us a house up here," Bill said. "When you left in March, I was going to bring you up here and ask you to marry me."

"I know," she said. "I wasn't ready."

"Are you ready now? Will you marry me, Nora?"

"Hmm, maybe I will."

"Maybe?"

All day long, he had been as ardent as a man could be. She knew he felt his powers returning because of her. She saw his strong and canny intelligence coming back, almost moment by moment. They lay on a blanket and watched the clouds go over, and he talked about his ideas for Spartan Dog—he still had the majority interest—and how they could protect people on social media and also devise ways to get them offline more, out into the disappearing real. His ideas had a poetry to them.

The more he felt like himself, the more attracted she was and the more importunate he was with her. She had roused all this ambition in him, and she knew it. And roused was the word. *Marry me!* He would roll toward her, seize her, kiss her, unbutton her until she made him stop. He would stop, though, and she felt his restraint as a way of protecting her. How to put it? He was protecting her from what he might feel about her—surmise about her—if she gave in to her desire and did not stop him. When he finally took her back that night, she was flushed and laughing and still a little breathless when they got to the driveway of Stonewall Hill, and two policemen stopped them.

"What's happened?" she asked, suddenly alarmed.

"Could I see some identification?" one of them asked Bill.

They let him through, but when she got out of his truck, other policemen with flashlights came toward her. She called goodnight to Bill, and went to the back door still flustered with his kisses. She had to explain to a policeman who she was—*I'm Mrs. Peach's niece*—and he had turned toward the kitchen to see if anyone knew her. Sheriff Bennett was there.

"Pretty Miss Trouble," he said. "You missed all the excitement."

"What happened?"

He took her back to the screen door and pointed to the doorframe a few inches above her head, where the wood was splintered.

"Sniper almost got your Uncle Walter. Bullet missed his head by this much."

She gasped. He held up Walter's ponytail, severed just above the band that had held it together, and her heart rose with terror.

"Man shot at the boy twice, too. Nicked his ear. Both of them lucky to be alive."

Upstairs, she had seen Rose, subdued and sweeter to her now, who had gotten out of bed to tell her, all over again, everything that had happened.

It was a hot, close night. She lay on her back in the dark in Professor Forrest's room with all the covers thrown off, even the light sheet. The cotton nightgown her aunt had left on the bed flattened against her wet skin like convent flannel. Rose said the room would cool off with the window and the hallway door open, but it did not. She had a fan blowing on her, but she was dying of the heat. How had they stood it in the Old South before they even had electricity?

She pinched the gown up and lifted it off her legs and such a cool rush came that she stood and stripped it off her body entirely. It felt like plunging into cool water. Naked, she stood for a moment in front of the fan and then tiptoed over and peered out into the dark hallway. Through the window at the far end by the front stairs, she could see the distant light of the courthouse clock. Rose's door stood open to her left, fan going; across the hall to her right was Walter's and Aunt Teresa's open door. Buford was all the way in the front of the house. A snore rose from somewhere.

She felt like a wild creature. She stepped over the threshold into the hallway and just then heard the creak of steps down the stairway, Walter from the office, and at the same moment a car on the gravel in the back. Its lights cast her shadow onto the hallway wall, but the steps did not pause. A bed creaked.

"Walter?" Aunt Teresa whispered. She backed into the room, stooping to pick up the gown. She heard her aunt go down the stairs after Walter. The screen door below her rattled lightly in the frame, and the low voice startled her, it was so close.

"Sorry it's so late. Thought I might as well bring it. Everybody okay?"

She stood aside to look down through the screen. Walter held the screen door open, and Sheriff Bennett stood in a circle of light.

"Come on in," Walter said.

"No, I don't need to come in. Just wanted to drop this off." Sheriff Bennett was holding a cardboard box. Walter took it and set it inside. Her aunt came up beside him in her robe, her arms crossed over her chest, her head tilted to the side in inquiry.

"What's this?"

"Papers and such. I called Walter about it," the sheriff said. "Thought y'all might want them. No reason for us to have them."

"Aren't you exhausted, Hudson?"

"Well, a little bit, tell you the truth."

"You get some rest, Hudson. I mean it."

"Yes ma'am. Just so you know, we have four men watching the house."

"I'm talking about you. Get some rest."

"Me? Yes ma'am."

She heard Walter and Aunt Teresa come back inside. Walter walked with the weight of the box back up the stairs to his study. Aunt Teresa asked him how late he would be, and he said he did not know. Outside, Sheriff Bennett lingered a moment, looking at the house, and as he turned and walked back to his car, Nora thought about the difference between the way he spoke to her aunt and the way he spoke to her.

Pretty Miss Trouble.

Showing her the bullet in the doorframe and Walter's ponytail, as if it were her fault. Pretty Miss Trouble. Was that all she was? She felt the shadow of blame settling upon her.

Had it been a smitten girl's prolonged and selfish dalliance? *Your niece, not by blood but by all else that's fated.* Yes, she was at fault, but it was also more than that. The poetry of it, she knew, had brought his real life back to Walter. He had faced things bravely. At least, she hoped so. And they had not done what they might have done.

What she would have done.

She dropped the nightgown clenched in her hand and stood naked as Eve in the dark, thinking of Bill Sharpe and his hands on the small of her back, pulling her against him, and smoothing down, down, pressing her until she felt him and weakened before she pulled away. She moved across the floor slowly in a kind of dance, thinking of how it would be when she gave herself to him wholly. She wanted to see him right now. The best thing she could do for her aunt—and for Walter, who gazed at her so mournfully—was to get away from them.

Yes, surprise Bill with a call in the middle of the night. He would be thrilled. She would wait until they were all asleep again and slip past the guards outside. She would go to him.

In the cool of her skin, she burned, stepping lightly, nakedly, in the savor of danger, the deep desiring darkness.

Alison

All these blank pages you just flipped through mean something. They're not blank at all. Go back and look at them. Pressed leaves, a flattened mosquito, bits of tobacco or weed, traces of wet drops—rain or tears. They all stand for a moment in a day on the road away from Harris. That's how I was in those days.

And then we came to Missy's Garden, Knecht and I. I'm writing this—this part, right now—so much later, almost twenty-five years after I left Chicago in the old Fairlane that Leon Walther gave me for my escape. I'm like a paleontologist discovering a fossil self. Much of it I hardly remember. Where are all those bright and terrible days? Where do they go? Can you walk through God's great dusty warehouses of all your streams of consciousness, moment by moment, and find the transcripts somewhere?

Unremembered, you might as well never have happened. And you are lost, unless somewhere you are held, still alive, in an image or a script. And if not held so, then what is the point of ever having been? Oh, is there a Heaven? I long to believe in one, but I cannot.

And so I cannot wait not to be. But there is no canceling my having been. I have been, and I am in these pages and I cannot bring myself to destroy this trace of having been that I leave to you. Who's there? Is it Lydia? My Knecht? Or some stranger?

I would have been how old in 1973? Just twenty-four. A woman, but also just a girl.

Mar 19

Knecht's playing behind the house. Yesterday I showed him how morning glories unfurl.

Morning glories. I love the name.

Unfurl he kept saying. *Furl, unfurl.* He gets words between his fingertips. He said *f* was like tissue paper but softer, more like skin. *F.* I told him furl was roll up or scrunch up.

Easy like eyelids, he said. *And unfurl is the cloth over the tables. We used to eat where they unfurled?* he asks me. *Tablecloths?*

He gets confused.

In the city where we were, I say, but I do not say Chicago in case they ever come and find me. *I think you mean the awnings, not the tablecloths.*

Like umbrellas? like eyelids? he says, and I nod. *But morning glories are lips,* he says.

He kisses me. He puts his fingers on my lips. On my nipples. *Ps is*

fatter than fs, he said.
    Lips, nipples, is fat, but fs furls.

Now he's out there patiently watching the morning glories unfurl. Squatting down, naked, watching them be so so slow. I see him pee without even thinking about it. Jetting out strong and yellow. Sweet little savage.
    Still early. Warm enough not to wear clothes.
    We can be unfurled because we stay in back, I tell him.
    Why do we stay in back?
    Because we're a secret.
    Why are we a secret?
    Because they would make us wear clothes!
    Clothes furls us, he says. *Close us. Skin wants to unfurl. See?*
    Proud of his little pee-pee penis.

Mar 23
    A scare. He went around the corner of the house while a car was going by, and I thought I heard it slow down.

Mar 25
    The neighbor's wife saw me in the backyard. At least I had on my jeans and shirt because it was cool in the early morning. I sat in the kitchen with my heart pounding for an hour. We have to have a story.

    Later. It's noon. We're down by the creek.
    Knecht, I say. *Knecht, listen. Don't do that, okay. You're not a baby. I should have other babies by now, two or three babies, who would keep you from doing this. If your daddy came there would be more babies. You wouldn't do this.*
    Why not?
    Because you're big now. We eat at the table. When you were a baby, my milk was all you had to eat. But you're not a baby.
    Lips like nipples, he says. *You used to say nipples rhymes with lips.*
    Squeezing me between his fingers.
    Why should I stop him? It does feel good. Why should it be wrong?

He thinks I'm his. He goes to sleep next to me. He sticks out like a hitchhiker's thumb.

Mar 26
    Harris says evil begins with the first prohibition. He says that the

will is not a problem until the no of prohibition creates amour-propre. I always ask him what he would do if Knecht wanted to eat a poisonous mushroom.

Nature instructs us, he says. He says nature will show Knecht that the mushroom is poisonous.

How? I ask him. *Will you let him eat it? Will you eat it yourself? You would have to get sick and maybe die from it to show him.*

Harris says he will think of a way.

I say that he would have to prohibit him from eating the mushroom even to show him it was poisonous, and he would be the one showing him, not nature.

Harris says he is the conscious part of nature.

I say he is conscious because he knows the prohibition.

He says it is too late for him, but not for Knecht. He says that real liberation will be full consciousness without amour-propre.

If Harris knew how much I missed him, he would come. He would risk it.

March 27

She came to the door today. That woman. I did not answer it, but she knew I was inside.

Hello? she said. *Hello?*

The accuser.

Knecht, I say. *Listen. You can't be Knecht now. Now you have to be Walter.*

Who is Walter?

You are. We have to wear clothes.

I don't want to close my skin, he says. *I don't want to furl.*

You have to stop being Knecht, I say. *Alison can't be Alison now either. Alison is gone now. Knecht and Alison are gone. You are Walter and I am Rosemary. Walter and Rosemary wear clothes outside. I'm still here, but now I'm Rosemary like the herb. Smell this.*

I break it for him and hold it to his nose. *This is Rosemary.*

I don't want to be Walter. I'm Knecht.

He tries to touch my breast.

Not if you're Knecht, I say. *Only if you're Walter.*

He draws back from me angrily. And there it is. The prohibition.

I say, *You have to forget Knecht. You have to forget everything that Knecht knew. Knecht and Alison are a secret now. Then you can have Rosemary.*

Walter can have Rosemary?

Yes.

He weeps. I see his hurt and his anger. Having to bargain for what he wants, give up this to get that. Everything pure I hoped for is gone now.

And so tonight, when no one can see us, I take him out to the cornfield to see the stars the way he loves. I show him Cassiopeia and the box of stars in Pegasus and how to find the Andromeda galaxy.

This last time, I said, *we can be unfurled outside. Listen*, I say, *if you want to find Alison, look for Andromeda. Rosemary is here but Alison is up there now, up there. Do you see Andromeda?*
He says he does. He says he wants to go there.

Buford

The house was eerily quiet, as though something had just disturbed it, and now it was listening: all its rooms, all its hallways, still and attentive.

Maybe not a sound in his ear but his ear itself. The tip of it throbbed against the pillow. His fingers went to the bandage. Blood the color of strawberries. He thought of Miss Nora's earring. When she had come inside tonight and exclaimed over him, he had almost pulled it from his pocket to give to her, but his hand was sticky with blood and he had left it. Later he took it to the sink in the bathroom and turned on the warm water and used the soap to wash his blood from the golden leaflets that lay across his palm, each no bigger than a thumbnail. He was careful washing the thin gold between his fingers, the hair-thin links between them, the delicate hook that pierced her earlobes. They had swayed when her head moved, when she turned from the blackboard to the class, head poised for their answers, eyebrows raised, the October trees outside dropping leaves like gold.

Miss Nora had saved him. He would be dead if he hadn't reached for her earring among the strawberries just at that split-second.

That hollow point would have popped his head like a pumpkin dropped off the roof.

One of the men said that.

He hadn't seen Buford close by, and the other man had told him to shut up.

Hollow, popped, dropped, off, roof. Point, popped, pumpkin.

He had reached for her earring because she was Miss Nora and he loved her. He wanted to give Miss Nora these leaves that fell without falling and hung shimmering and golden against the hollow of her skin in the recesses of her hair. He wanted to see her carefully feel them and, not looking, fit the hook into her ear, and smile at him with her tilted head, giving her hair a soft shake just for him, the gold leaves gleaming and flashing

and say how brave he was

and heal him with her eyes.

Was he brave? He guessed maybe so. He could have been scared, pale and trembling, snot-nosed, running to his father or his mother. But he was not like that. His mother had waited for him to break down, Rose had expected him to collapse, his father was angry that he showed no emotion. He had felt his mother's curiosity turning into worry, as though he were again becoming the boy who could not remember his own name. *In shock*, she whispered. But he was not in shock. He did not feel fear. He felt instead a great peace, like the night he heard the Name.

When was that?

Before all this. Before he forgot who he was.

But not in a day, not in a night, not when he was asleep, not when he was awake.

Where had he been? Not *there*, but *Here*, in the deepest *Here*.

As he listened into the darkness, a sound came to him faintly. Was someone out there in the hallway watching him? Somebody hiding in the house, ready to take his picture? Cottonmouth, they said. He peered into the shadows, waiting for fear, but instead he felt an immense protection, like being deep inside a psalm his mother would read him. *Let them be put to shame and dishonor who seek after my life!* He thought about the man who had almost killed him. He was dead now. Buford did not hate him. A long time ago, something bad had happened to that man, and so he had become more evil than what hurt him. The man would have been different if he could have heard the Name inside him.

What was that? Startled, he sat up in bed. It sounded like sobbing, a long, low moan that rose from somewhere deep in the house.

That was what woke him. An animal?

He was scared but he got out of bed and went out into the hallway. It was a hot night; a light breeze came through the screen. Again, the moan rose. There was no movement, no murmur, not in his parents' room, not in Rose's room. His heart leapt when he remembered that Miss Nora was down the hall, and he tiptoed down to her door and listened and heard a soft breathing from where she was lying in the hot darkness in Professor Forrest's huge bed. But she was not the one making the sound. He heard it now again—something else, somewhere below.

He tiptoed down the back stairs, knowing by heart how to avoid all the places where the steps creaked. He touched the big round knob on the newel at the bottom. It was louder now—more than one voice, a chorus of moaning. *Mmmm-hmmm.* But where could it be? He went down the hallway, and there was a door that he did not remember. All these years he had lived here and never noticed it. It had a faceted glass doorknob, and when he turned it, the latch stuck a little and he had to turn it harder to get it to open. He turned on the light. Inside was a descending set of stairs.

He started down the old wooden steps, holding the railing affixed to the left wall, but then came a turn to the right, away from the wall, and the railing gave out. The light did not reach down this far. The steps dropped away into a cavernous blackness. He paused and listened—*Mmmm-hmmm*—and stepped down, feeling with his foot, terrified of falling. Carefully he sat down and felt out to each side with his palms, hardly more than a foot to the edge on his right and six inches on the left. It was cold stone now, and he felt the slight hollow in the center of each step. He did not dare turn around, so he lowered himself like a toddler, sitting, a step at a time.

Sometimes the sound seemed fainter, swallowed up, and sometimes stronger. He descended and descended. After a few minutes, the voices grew steadily louder, a moaning interspersed with low chanting. The light grew, and then he could see an arched stone opening. Through it down below was daylight. Now he could see the steps, and he stood and walked down the rest of the way. When he came to the opening, he waited in the threshold. The huge old women sat hooded on the flagstones, dark and moaning in a circle around the stone fountain, where the water welled and fell down tiers to the base. Goldfish swam in the sunlit pool. It was the courtyard. Bones hung in clusters like chimes in the colonnades among the bougainvillea. Breezes stirred the blossoms and the bones.

Blue sky.

Through the openings beyond the columns to his right he could see a rocky mountain ridge, boulders held in place by whispered gravity, immensely old and uncanny, like shapes from abandoned planets. To the left he saw the sea.

As he stepped into the courtyard, the old black women looked up at him, moaning, rocking slightly, their eyes heavy as rain, the snakes of their hair stirring slowly under their hoods.

Who he be? one of them asked.

Mmmm-hmmm they moaned *Help me now.*

Another one beckoned to him. *He my boy. Come here, sugar.*

She gestured for him to come and sit by her. Huge. He went and sat beside her in the smell of musty closets and kitchen labor, hot irons and childbirth and vegetable rot and leaf smoke and wet ashes.

Mmmm. Help me now Jesus they moaned.

Who he be, Mary Louise? one asked again.

The one heard the Name.

Mmmm-hmmm. Heard the Name.

Help me Jesus. And saw the Lady.

Saw the Lady?

Have mercy.

Somebody gone die one said.

Somebody got to said the one next to him.

A pile of rubble on one side of the courtyard became a crumpled body with a hole in its forehead.

What's coming? one said.

Need a good one. A sweet one.

Mmmm-hmmm they moaned. *Help me Jesus.*

And then Nora stepped into the courtyard. He saw the noose around her neck and the rope trailing behind her.

Naw now. Not this one. Naw now said Mary Louise beside him.

Mmmm. Help me now Jesus they moaned. *Got to be somebody.*

Buford cried out, but they frowned at him.

Hush now, honey. Hush now, baby.

And then the Lady stepped among them.

They fell silent. They went so quiet

So quiet

Nora

Just at dawn, after those hours in the car, they forced her up the pathway by the barbed wire fence and stopped beneath a great live oak and made her strip off her clothes. When the driver leered and touched her bare breast, El Mocasín pointed his pistol at the man's face and said something sharp in Spanish. They arranged a blue blanket around her head and tucked it around her shoulders and pulled it tight around her throat with a noose. They used plastic zip ties to hold her wrists together and then bound her hands in front of her as if in prayer, roped against her body as they tied her to the tree, her back and bottom and heels pressed painfully into the bark. When they stepped back and looked at her, the two men ducked their heads and crossed themselves, and El Mocasín very slowly crossed himself, meeting her eyes through his mask, and gestured them away.

No one sees me and lives, he whispered to her.

She thought he would kill her then, but he followed the men down the path toward the road. The two others walked ahead of him reluctantly, both looking back constantly and pleading in Spanish, stumbling, but he peremptorily ordered them forward. As they neared the road, the one who had touched her, the driver, broke madly to his right, leaping out with great strides into the kudzu. El Mocasín calmly raised his pistol, waited a moment, and shot him in the back of his head. The noose at her neck choked her when her knees went weak. She wet herself helplessly.

Trembling, she pushed herself back upright and watched as El Mocasín stooped over the dead man and a moment later stood back up, dangling the keys to the car from his fingers. The other man stood paralyzed, begging, but El Mocasín shrugged as if everything were fine, holding up the keys while he walked toward him, but then at the last moment he raised the pistol and shot him in the forehead.

She expected him to come back up the path and kill her. Already in the posture of prayer, she prayed *God help me, oh God. Please help me, Jesus.* Standing with his foot on the second man's neck, El Mocasín looked back up the path, met her eyes again and removed his mask. Just at that instant, the first full sunlight broke through the trees and blinded her. Even through her closed eyelids the light was unbearable, and she turned her head to avoid its full force. A terrible, slow minute passed. Was it the face of God and not the sun? Had she died without feeling it?

When something shaded her she was sure it was El Mocasín. She cried out, but nothing happened. She opened her eyes and could see all the way down the path. He was gone. The car was gone. A great sob broke from her. She would have collapsed if the ropes had not choked her. She pulled herself upright.

Within seconds, she was aware of the mosquitoes. Clouds of them hovered and alighted, so much of her skin was exposed to their needles. They must have been feasting on her all along, but now the sound of them around her ears maddened her, the needling feel of them. Eyelids, temples, lips, nipples, everywhere. Three times she went into a frenzy of thrashing, and when at last she saw it was useless, she went still and let them feed.

Time meant nothing. Flickers of poems went senselessly through her head. *Thirty thousand to the rest.* She was half-dreaming. *Thou know'st that this cannot be said / A sin, nor shame, nor loss of maidenhead.* Maidenhead, lovely word, once such a prize for girls, now such a shameful possession. She longed for her maidenhead, her unrecoverable maidenhead, no longer hers to give.

Each single second was endless.

She saw a pickup truck go by. If she cried out, someone might hear her—maybe the people in the farmhouse on the other side of the cornfield. But at first, even here, her pride prevented her. Not to be beautiful? The idea of someone she might know finding her humiliated like this, naked and soiled. She wanted a stranger to rescue her, someone she would never see again.

Her whole body ached. Every muscle screamed for relief.

But more than that, her soul hurt from the terrors of the night she relived and relived like a film always playing in the background.

She had hid in the shrubbery, watching one of the policemen, who was turned the other way as he played a game on his phone. She had made it down the drive, through the broken gate, and out onto the sidewalk along Lee Street. She had meant to walk through town past the courthouse and down the half-mile or so to the all-night Waffle House by the interstate, where she would call Bill to come and get her. She had made it halfway to the courthouse, walking quickly, when she saw the car slowing, the kind of big white SUV a large family might have. She had thought it was some father on vacation, driving his sleeping family, concerned about a girl walking alone at 3:00 a.m. When the SUV stopped beside her, she wanted to assure them—the kind, sleeping family—that she was okay.

She stepped carefully into the lantanas between the sidewalk and the curb. She leaned toward the window and tapped on the glass, expecting to speak to a tired mother. But as the glass descended, she saw a hard, male, Hispanic face. The door opened on the driver's side and the driver got out, but no interior lights came on. The man looked at her—the man El Mocasín would shoot in the forehead—with his fated, unreadable eyes. The driver grabbed her from behind, clamped one hand over her mouth, and pulled her back against him, his other hand free on her twisting body. They forced her into the back seat, and she then went still with terror. Even in the dark she could see the tight noseless Voldemort mask of the man on the far side of the seat. As soon as the driver took his hand off her mouth, she meant to say *I'll scream! Where are you taking me?* But she did not.

I love a pop culture reference, the man said. He took the mask off as they passed beneath a streetlight and her heart turned over painfully. Without the mask, she could not see him at all. She could hear his labored breathing. A smell like rotten fruit, sickly and fermenting.

I will call you 'Persephone' he said, *another pop culture reference–but so much older.* She knew then that none of it had anything to do with Mexicans or cartels. His voice was low and rich and cultivated—British with a subtle nose of peaty smoke, black rotting fruit, cappuccino, toasty wood—

She shook herself awake, pushing herself upright again to loosen the rope that had tightened at her throat. She gasped for breath. She could not see her feet, which were bound to the base of the tree. To her left, something projected from the trunk. *A woman's hand!* A woman's hand with the bark grown around it like the rolled cuff of a sweater.

Her mind reeled and she turned her head not to see it. She must be dreaming it all. El Mocasín had not said those things. He was not really here.

The men in the front seat called him El Mocasín.

They were moving up Lee Street toward the courthouse square, and El Mocasín held something up to her with a hieratic gesture. It gleamed darkly in the streetlight, the size of a small plum wrapped in foil. He unwrapped it for her and held it forward on his palm. She shook her head in refusal.

Strange, isn't it, he said, *how the archetypal stories of the fall in Greece and Israel depend on something a woman puts in her mouth? Pomegranate or apple, what could they have meant? Not mere gluttony. It could be sex, but my gracious– the mouth? And animals have sex. You know what I think? That they mean to symbolize something we now know well: removing the pleasures of sex from the responsibilities of generation.*

I don't know what you mean.

Oh. Yes. You. Do. Taste this, he said, and lightly, very lightly, he touched the chocolate to her lips. It filled her nostrils. *Already you want it more than anything you have ever eaten. It says right on the package—let me read it to you: Anticipate the soft inner cream released in a gush of pleasure from the delicate breaking chocolate shell.*

She felt its roundness and her saliva ran and she longed to yield her mouth, to have it. It would be so simple. It would taste so good and placate him at the same time and he would spare her life.

She drew her head back and turned her face away.

Eating it he said *will liberate you from all the constraints of your life as you have lived it. It will make you rich, and the wealth it brings will give you the power of mind and the beauty of body that others long to have, but cannot have. And since they cannot have it themselves, they demean themselves to serve it—serve* you, *imitate* you. *You know exactly what I mean. You have already tasted that power on your own. Look at your subjugation of the great Walter Peach, look at Dexter Watkins, that poor fool, and Bill Sharpe, but this, O taste this and—*

I know the story, she said, turning back to him. Taste this, and it will wed me forever to the king of the underworld.

He laughed out loud, a new inflection in his voice.

Oh, darling, I was teasing you. It's just cream and chocolate. And I'm only *a Prince.*

The Waffle House and the motels loomed like outposts on the border of some dark frontier encroaching upon the known world. They drove under the interstate with its spectral lights streaming through the distances of silence.

She jolted upright, choking again. *God help me, God help me.* She stared down the path toward the road. A car went by. Another. She should cry out.

Instead she was back reliving it, still answering him.

But suppose it's poison?

I can force you to eat it, he said tauntingly.

But if you force me, it means I didn't do it.

Oh, that's right! So, I have to leave you free to choose. Oh, golly. How about this: Either you eat my truffle, or I'll let them rape you, he said, tilting his head at the men in the front seat. *You get to choose.*

Coercion either way.

She felt his smile, even though she could not see his face.

You think that eating this means *something*, he said, and he opened his mouth wide and she shrank back. The whole inside of his mouth was a ghastly white. He put the truffle onto his white tongue in the face she could not see and closed his mouth on it and a gust of rot nauseated her. *Mmm, cream and chocolate. I just love it.*

He produced another one from his lap and stripped off the foil and put it to her mouth.

She turned her head away.

I know it means something, she said. I wish I had never given in before.

Given in—to eating a truffle? Oh, you mean to that boy who played football. I can almost see him. I can almost imagine his name. In a back seat like this one. But you did give in, and not only to him, darling Nora, and so your yielding now means nothing. 'Means.' Listen to me. What is 'meaning,' anyway? A property of words, which are mere conventions. Whole languages have vanished without a syllable left behind. All those songs, all those poems and the poets who labored to compose them. Already the words you treasure most are blurring and the paper they are written on is dissolving away, all those deeply felt words puddling and softening and crumbling away to atoms. Some cataclysm, and poof—Shakespeare disappears. And you think opening your mouth for a chocolate matters? What will it matter next week, much less in a hundred years? A hundred and fifty years ago in a hovel on the howling plains of North Dakota, some virgin gave up her so-called virtue, and what does it matter? Or the deflowering of a girl in some palace in Ecbatana a thousand years before Caesar, with the eunuchs who bathed her gossiping behind fans of ibis and parrot feathers?

There is always a story! she cried.

No one remembers the story. You invent it because you need the reassurance.

God remembers it, she said.

He sucked in his breath sharply and leaned toward her. She almost saw a face—or less a face than the expression upon an absence that drew her in like an undertow. Her own words sounded pious and silly, like the taunt of a child. *God remembers it.* But they also sounded like her Aunt Teresa, what she could say without being silly. And just then, in that instant, she felt the inner conviction that all her inner thoughts, even these, along with everything she did, good or bad, went into the great poem of the world, massive but always intimate, full of echoes and rhymes and measures and variations and returns, and always in the tension of good and evil.

God! he said with mock alarm. *The old bogey of surveillance, the Emperor of Damn-Your-Soul? The One watching you right now? Trust me, that power is not on,* NO-*body's watching. No, sweetheart. The word GOD is a useful place to project our own pathological hope and revenge, but luckily, it's just a word. It says so right in the beginning of the Gospel of John. In the beginning was the Word. The secret meaning is that it's just a word. Call it the signature on the bottom line of our most ambitious fictions. We make our nests of language and live inside our little local 'meanings' through some kind of useful genetic instinct, don't we, lovely Nora? There's a salutary tendency bent into the chemistry of our neurons and webbed into the structure of our cells. Our bodies are really just colonies of cells, groupings like bees or ants, and someday we will understand how the idea of a self arises from those group dynamics.*

But you aren't stupid. You know with conviction, deep down, you know that you and I are just accidents of matter. We coalesced into consciousness out of moiling strands of protein, and we are going to flicker for just a tiny moment in the history of the universe. We seem important and singular to ourselves, and we construct little meanings that are as intense as we can make them, but they are going to disappear with our bodies and go into graves or ashes and molder away. A few years and NO ONE will remember, certainly not so-called 'God,' and voilá— meanings no more. You know in the depth of your mind, under all the illusions, that I am telling you the truth.

No, I know in the depth of my soul, she said, that even if we just existed for a fraction of a second, there would be something good, because existing would be better than not existing. Even for you. I am something good to you, or you wouldn't want me to eat your evil pomegranate.

OOH, ouch, touché. No, sweetheart, it just amuses me that it means something to you not to eat it. Hmm? He pushed it lightly against her lips. *Just a bite?*

She turned her head.

It went on for hours. They drove out through the county. He spoke to her and she smelled the fruity rottenness of his presence. He never once touched her skin, but she felt his crawling touch on the inmost texture of her. Just before dawn, the driver parked the SUV at the edge of Walter Peach's property on Hopewell Road, where the kudzu spread from the right of way all the way over the old house it had consumed. They walked her up the path. At first light they tied her to the tree.

She had not yielded, thank God.

But why did it feel as though she had? Why did she feel so soiled, so full of guilt and darkness and shame?

Her limbs trembled with the effort not to let go, not to fall senseless into the noose that would choke off her breath.

Would she die here? Her head rolled on her neck. She stood in torment with quivering legs, quilted with bites, on fire with itching.

At last, she began to scream.

THE DEAD

Part VII

"There is an opening downward within each moment, an unconscious reverberation, like the thin thread of the dream that we awaken with in our hands each morning leading back and down into the images of the dark."

—James Hillman, *The Dream and the Underworld*

Walter Peach

Saturday Morning, June 28, 2014

He was in the Subaru with Dexter Watkins, who shook a small mound of marijuana into a tissuey petal he had just pulled from a morning glory and began carefully rolling a joint with it. *See, you got to do it just right. You tear it, it won't draw, but you get it right I'm talking about a buzz like a bee in honeysuckle. You know what I'm saying. Your mama, she rolled a sweet doobie.* He held up the joint, neatly crimped at both ends, a smooth bagworm. He lit it and inhaled, his eyes widening as a hole appeared in his forehead and the back of his head exploded in a red mist. *Whoa.* His steady hand proffered it to Walter. As it burned, the thing gave off a small, shrill, agonized cry. Dexter was still talking. *Be like getting that sweet Nora to—*

"Walter?"

He woke with a start. He was still in the office, where he had spent half the night immersed in the papers of Alison Graves—newspaper clippings, mimeographed manifestos, letters from her parents—and he had fallen asleep in the armchair over a journal from her years of hiding in Georgia, a green spiral-bound notebook full of her handwritten observations and drawings. Still unopened were an older journal bound in leather and a manila envelope addressed to Sarah Downs at a post office box in Portland. Sunlight glared from the mahogany surface of the desk.

Teresa came in with a mug of coffee for him.

"You were reading all night?" she said.

It was his black Georgia Press Association Award mug. Best Editorial. Back in the kitchen cabinet were General Excellence, Best Feature, Best Page One. He nodded and took a sip.

"This is your Yirgacheffe?"

"I miss you," she said, laying her hand on his shoulder.

He glanced up at her and nodded. He did not tell her his dream.

"Walter, I miss you," Teresa said again. She gave his shoulder a soft squeeze. The ampersand of worry and thoughtfulness between her brows, the mussed auburn hair lightly streaked with gray, her body in its loose gown, her fragrance. For the first time in many months, a pulse of desire went through him.

"It's going to take some time to get through these things."

"These are her journals? How old were you?" she said.

"Seven when she left me. Five, maybe six, when we got to Missy's Garden."

"Were you really still nursing? Do you remember that?"

He wagged his head ruefully.

"Her nakedness?" she asked. "That's what 'unfurled' means? You never told me any of this."

"I did what she said and forgot Knecht."

"She thought the first prohibition was the first sin."

"Akers did."

"A prohibition is a gift," Teresa said. "It gives you choice. It puts you in a free moral universe instead of an instinctual one."

"And freedom means wrong choices, and wrong choices mean misery."

"That's a real world."

They might have kept talking, but just then Rose came in.

"Where's Nora?" she said.

"Still sleeping, I guess. She got in pretty late."

"No, she's not in her room. And Mr. Sharpe just called asking to talk to her."

Bennett

He waited with them in the breakfast room of Stonewall Hill for bad news. Dread hung over them. They sat stiffly in the chairs. Teresa led the boy and Rose on their rosary beads. Sharpe was standing stiff and pale against the wall, his long face somber, lips almost moving to the *hour of our death.*

No cars were missing. None of the officers posted around the house had seen her. The yellow dress she'd worn from Athens was in the room she slept in, so she must have been wearing the clothes she'd borrowed from Rose—jeans, running shoes, some kind of dark top. Teresa said there was a way out of the house they hardly ever used, a door onto the side porch. She would have been walking toward town, they all thought. But what possessed her to leave in the middle of the night? The Gallatin police, Bennett's deputies, all the officers available were going street by street through all the neighborhoods.

They heard the screen door slam and Aengus Dunne came in.

"We've looked all over the grounds," he said. "No luck."

"You think it's *them?*" Rose asked.

They all thought it. No one would meet anyone else's eyes. No one wanted to think it.

The boy Buford stood up. The bandage on his ear was spotted with blood. He looked up at them with a wild look in his eyes.

"She's out there. She's at Missy's Garden."

What made them believe the boy was hard to say, but they all did, maybe because it made sense. Where else would the Moccasin go to make a message of her? Maybe the boy just thought faster than the rest of them.

Bennett thought he should go out there with his deputies, but Teresa Peach insisted on going, too, and so did Bill Sharpe and the boy. Bennett was happy to have the boy the same way he'd be happy to have a bloodhound. Bennett radioed Red Scott and took Teresa and Buford in his car. Sharpe followed in his truck. Peach and Rose would stay at the house to work with Marshal Dunne's people getting ready for their move while Marshal Dunne monitored the search for Nora.

It was a guilty pleasure for Bennett to have Teresa almost to himself in the front seat with the boy in the back. She had on gardening clothes, some old jeans and work shoes and a loose man's shirt. He thought she looked fine. When she looked at him, asking him if he had slept, that concerned little wrinkle between her eyes sweetened his heart.

"Yes ma'am, some."

Bennett eased down the driveway in the Bronco, Sharpe just behind him, and he was explaining the situation to the guards at the end of the driveway when Braxton Forrest drove up in a big Toyota SUV. He held up a stay-there hand to Bennett and got out of his car to cross the gravel, but the guards intercepted, demanding an ID.

"What the hell?" he complained, flicking his head back toward them as he leaned into Bennett's window.

"They don't know you," Bennett said.

"Braxton, they got Nora O'Hearn," Teresa said tensely across the seat. "We think they took her out to Missy's Garden. We have to hurry! Can you stay with Walter and Rose?"

"Go! Go!" He waved them on. Bennett turned on his siren and floored the Bronco up Lee Street and through the courthouse square and down the hill and onto the interstate, hitting 120 mph before they got to County Road 73. Sharpe stayed right with him. Teresa clutched the grab handle the whole way.

"Where do you think she'd be?" Bennett asked the boy as they skidded to a stop. "Inside?"

"No sir. I think at the big tree."

Right away, as they started up, Bennett saw the bodies of two men, one facedown off to the left, already grown over in the green steam of the kudzu, the other lying on his back across the path, mouth open, eyes open, a hole in his forehead. No time to stop. He expected the girl to be dead, too, but there was a chance.

He ran up the slope with Sharpe close behind. And there she was. They had bound her to the big tree, looking like one of those Mexican religious statues you saw all the time, Our Lady of something. She was stripped naked except for a blue blanket over her head and shoulders. Her hands were tied so she looked like she was praying, and her head was slumped over into the noose around her neck. A terrible, exhausting sorrow rose in Bennett.

But just then, maybe from hearing them running, she pushed herself upward just enough. Her swollen face, distorted by hundreds of bites, rose slightly as she gasped and tried to scream, a choked, gargling sound. Bennett sprinted over and helped lift her head from the noose. He cut the rope with his pocketknife and pulled the blue blanket around her to cover her body. The girl's face was terribly mottled and distorted, her eyelids swollen shut with bites, her lips distended. What else they had done to her, Bennett did not want to imagine.

Sharpe should not see her this way, nor the boy.

"Let Teresa help her!" he told Sharpe. "Teresa!" he shouted.

Blanched and shaken by seeing the bodies, she came hurrying up the path with the boy behind her. As soon as she saw Nora, she told the boy to stay back, and Buford stood with Sharpe while Teresa helped cut loose from the other ropes her gasping and incoherent niece. Her weight sagged against her aunt and Bennett had to help lower her from the tree.

"Help me get her to the car," he said to Sharpe. Bennett took her torso, his hands clasped high on her ribcage. "Cross her legs at the ankle and lift from the bottom one," Bennett told him. Teresa lightly hid her face with the blanket as they carried her down the path and put her in the backseat of Bennett's Bronco with her head in Teresa's lap. The boy sat in the front this time. Bennett felt a shock of pity seeing Sharpe's face. That was how you looked when the woman you loved was some other man's victim. As he started the Bronco, Bennett radioed Red Scott, who was just leaving town, to get in touch with Buddy Fingal and the other agencies, because there were two new bodies out at Missy's Garden.

"Looks like the Moccasin," he said and regretted saying the name, because the girl moaned in the back seat hearing it. Teresa murmured over her, smoothing her head, telling her she was safe now, she was okay.

"Bill," Bennett said, "call the hospital when you get a signal. I'll go straight to the ER."

Out on the interstate, lights flashing, siren blaring, he pushed the Bronco to 130 mph. Cars pulled over in a long ripple before him.

Josiah Simms

Disguise was so easy, deception so perfectly simple. He could change his appearance and his effect on others instantly. All it took at the Holiday Inn in Gallatin was a stiff limp and a little glimpse of his face and a bandana modestly pressed to his mouth. "Y'all got any military discounts?" he said with a stoical Texas flatness. The massive woman at the Holiday Inn desk had been so full of pity, he almost loved her. She gave him the room for free and solemnly thanked him for his service, not once, but several times. People did not expect disguise—why would they?—and their credulity was boundlessly useful. Despite all the warnings, they also never worried about how much information was readily accessible to those who knew how to find it. It had never occurred to Braxton Forrest, for example, that someone of Josiah's resources could monitor his flight bookings and hire informants in all the motels of Gallatin. The Guatemalan janitor cleaning the lobby of the Red Roof Inn had texted "Luke Stoma" the room number when Forrest arrived at midnight the night before, and, within seconds, young "Jaime Morales" had received $500 on Venmo. If Forrest had known he was under surveillance, he might have taken precautions—but why would he think such a thing?

Josiah stood before the mirror in his room and opened his mouth. Impressive. He needed a few such reflective moments, so to speak, in his journal. He had no confidants, none at all, but he was rarely lonely. "Loneliness," that puttering and vacant-eyed nursing-home word, did not denote the hot desire for critical appreciation he sometimes felt, like a lover who needs, for his own completion, the awed and slavish adulation of the person he has just driven mad with pleasure. Or perhaps he was like a poet whose work is fulfilled when he sees written evidence of the pleasure of his best and closest reader. He felt such desire now, because his masterwork with Walter Peach was unfolding toward its climax, and he needed a witness. None of them knew who he was, and their ignorance would eventually become a disappointment in his future recollection of what was about to happen. One wanted credit, did one not? Even the self-absorbed Walter knew by now that the man called El Mocasín, Leukostoma, Os Bombacio, Cottonmouth, was none other than the poor little colored boy so badly burned in the Christmas explosion, who had become a Monster of Revenge.

They had no idea just what a monster—another failure of recognition. His series of Moleskine journals, over two hundred of them now, started when he was sixteen in Chicago. It would make better reading than Knausgaard's version of *Mein Kampf*. The journals would secure his posthumous reputation in a culture that relished next-door serial killers, canonized gangsters, and idolized Pablo Escobar. But all that was extraneous to this family matter. None of them had any idea of the ironies that had shaped the life of Josiah Simms around that of Walter Peach.

His mother, who could easily have passed for white, had been caught up in the black consciousness-raising of the 1960s. Brilliant and ambitious, Deborah Simms earned a full ride at the University of Chicago, where she graduated in 1965, just about the time Alison Graves arrived on campus. Deborah did a senior thesis on what she called "shadow genealogies," uncovering the secret white progenitors in black families, including her own. Already pregnant with Josiah from one of the black radicals on campus (three or four possibilities, it seemed), Deborah refused an abortion and married a naïve but wealthy Nigerian graduate student who discovered his mistake when a healthy child nothing like him was born seven months into the marriage. Okonkwo gave her some money in the divorce, primarily to keep his name from being attached to the boy, and she named him Josiah after his grandfather.

His mother, supported by Okonkwo's money, completed her MA in elementary education, which she considered the fulcrum of real political influence, and taught for several years before she married again. She was teaching at Rosecrans Elementary School in Glenview to support Josiah and her new husband, Georges Macias, who was finishing his dissertation on the power structures of American education.

So what brought his mother, leading Josiah by the hand toward his immolation, in range of the terrorist Alison Graves? What drew them both to Rosecrans Elementary School on Christmas Eve of 1972? What but design of darkness to appall? He had considered *Design of Darkness* as the title for his journals. Josiah also remembered Thomas Hardy's poem about the Titanic and the iceberg: Alison Graves and Deborah Simms Macias approached each other slowly, year by year, lured into proximity on that Christmas Eve, "bent/By paths coincident/On being anon twin halves of one august event." *By Paths Coincident*: another possibility.

It was all in the journals—his long months in the hospital, his gradual discovery of what had happened to him. As he healed, he suffered the recurring illnesses of the badly burned. He developed a chronic leukoplakia unique in medical history. He came to understand and eventually to enjoy how the monstrousness of his appearance induced the recoil and revulsion of others. So poisonous was his intelligence that Georges Macias had to be restrained by neighbors from killing the boy.

Did Josiah have a heart, he wondered occasionally, or did it burn away, sick with desire, in the flames of Rosecrans Elementary as he watched his mother die? Released back into the world, he refused to let his condition make him weak. Without intending it, without steeling himself or overcoming a natural pity, he discovered coldness, lack of fear, clear-headedness in circumstances that made others fear death. He did not fear death in the least, so often had he longed for it. Never a victim himself, he cherished the original sense of the word *victim*, something warm and living that was killed and offered as a sacrifice to a god. He savored the emotional spectacle of a proper victim, preferably a female one, but boys as well. On the streets, in the gangs, those who tried to bully him soon discovered that he could inflict pain without remorse, maim without compunction, and kill with real pleasure. Those who tried to use him found themselves used. He began to dominate and terrify those who wanted mere power and pleasure and the tribal bond of belonging. He discovered the uses of money and began to acquire it early.

Counselors despaired and wept in his presence; all schools expelled him, but he discovered books, and his mind's true kindred. His research into Harris Akers and Alison Graves, who had killed his mother and maimed him for life, kept mentioning a son with whom Graves fled, fate unknown. He carried out what he called *interventions*—the unearthing of Alison in Seattle (he meant to find her again later), the death of Akers by induced anaphylactic shock—but he could find no trace of the son.

And then, just three years ago, almost by accident (as the ignorant called it), Josiah found him. It turned out to be extraordinarily simple. He read Hermia Watson's book, where the name Graves came up in a most promising way. There were allusions in the archives of the *Gallatin Tribune* to a showplace that the artist Zilpha Graves owned out in the county. Two years ago, a single afternoon searching for the Graves name in the records of the Gallatin County Courthouse had revealed a piece of entailed property off Hopewell Road inherited by a man named Walter Peach. Walter Peach was now—it was almost baroque in irony—the editor of the *Gallatin Tribune!* A little research into Walter Peach led back to the University of Georgia and his brief career as a poet, to Judge Lawton, and from Lawton to the boy's legal adoption, and thus to the disappearing mother who could be none other than Alison Graves.

And now came the consummation. He knew from his informants that there would be a small service for Alison Graves. As soon as a few more details emerged, he would place the call to the media. A new sniper was already in town, paid this time not to miss. In the confusion during the slayings at the funeral, he would kidnap the redheaded girl and give her to the Sinaloa people as a gesture of appeasement. The other one, the victim who had given him more pleasure than anyone in years, had died

401

Bill Sharpe

"Look, Bill, it's nine in the morning," Dr. Fletcher said outside Nora's room, glancing at his watch. "You don't need to be here. I've sedated her, and she won't wake up until late this afternoon. Hell, she might sleep all night after an ordeal like that one. You should go to work. Say hi to Chick. Go sell some cars so you can go to Italy on your honeymoon. I'll call if something changes. Look, this isn't like Deirdre. She's fine. She just needs rest, she'll be okay."

Dr. Fletcher had been the doctor for every Sybil Forrest High School athletic team since the 1970s. When Bill fell in basketball practice and broke his left hand half a lifetime ago, Dr. Fletcher's humor and his air of sharing gossip about Bill's injury got him through it. His serious advice about what kind of choices Bill needed to make had helped him all the way through college.

Now Dr. Fletcher was getting visibly old. He was the same age as Braxton Forrest, but the arthritis in his feet tormented him, and he seemed to be eroding, not just in his body. He had received every honor the town could give him for all his work in the community, but people said there was sometimes something almost frantic about the man. He was apologetic, but without any reason to apologize. Today, though, when Bill needed him, he was the same Dr. Fletcher.

"It feels worse than when Deirdre died," Bill said. He had not meant to say it. He looked up at Dr. Fletcher, who met his gaze and then dropped his eyes, nodding.

"It's what a man feels," he said, as he hobbled to the other side of the hallway. "She's your fiancée. The kind of feeling you have, the helplessness, you want revenge for that. Not being there, not being able to protect her. It's not your fault, God knows, but that doesn't matter. It's like it's aimed at you, what happened to her. And you feel like *she'll* blame you even though it wasn't your fault. So you want revenge, every stone-age cell in your body wants revenge—but what if you can't get to the man who did it? I've seen many a man take it out on the woman herself because of the humiliation he feels. You have to watch yourself. Just go to work and come back later."

"Was she sexually assaulted? Just tell me."

"Not sexually. In fact, she says this monster protected her from those two men he left dead out there. But he assaulted her in worse ways, from what she says. She's traumatized, Bill. He left her to die, no question. She's going to have lasting effects from the repeated pressure on her trachea. She had thousands of mosquito bites. When they attack the membranous

403

tissues and the eyelids, you almost immediately get infection, and she was out there for hours. She might not speak or see normally again, at least not for a while. Look at me, Bill."

Bill looked up into the old doctor's eyes.

"It's worse than that. She's mentally injured—I even want to say spiritually—and the things she says . . . just let somebody else stay with her. A woman, maybe her aunt. Give her some time. She won't forgive you for seeing her this way."

"The Moccasin will try to kill her," Bill said. "I need to be here. I want her to know I'm here."

"Sheriff Bennett posted guards. Anybody comes in, they'll stop him."

Bill did not move.

Dr. Fletcher sighed and put a hand on his shoulder.

"I'll get a chair for you," he said.

Teresa Peach

Back at Stonewall Hill, Teresa got off the phone with Bridget, who had taken Walter's advice—she and Terry had driven to Savannah, where they were staying at a cheap motel near the beach. Terry sat on the bed watching the news from Gallatin with his Colt Mustang .38 right next to him, Bridget said. He had already almost shot the Hispanic maid.

Bridget was horrified at what had happened to Nora.

"Oh my God, Teresa! We should be there for her. We'll start—"

"No, stay put. I'm absolutely serious. I'll talk to you later. There are things I can't say on the phone. We don't know who might be listening."

As Teresa hung up, she realized just how violated Stonewall Hill now seemed to her, how vulnerable her sense of privacy had become. Even with guards around the house, she feared almost to move from room to room. She feared for her children.

"Somebody's coming!" one of the guards called through the back door.

"Walter!" she called into the living room, where he sat now with Rose and Buford. "Somebody's coming."

Through the back screen door, she watched the big SUV Forrest had driven that morning come up the drive and park beside the Outback. As soon as it stopped, Marisa Forrest opened the passenger door, already looking for her. Teresa gasped and ran down the brick walkway to embrace her, a long, heartfelt embrace that melted something inside her.

"I had no idea you were in town!"

"We just got in. Are you okay, sweetheart?" Marisa said, holding her face with both hands.

"Cate and Bernadette are here too!" Teresa exclaimed as the girls got out of the back seat.

"They were worried about Rose."

The screen door banged, and Rose came out. The two Forrest girls ran to her with exclamations and hugs and went inside. By now, Walter had ambled out, warm with greetings for the Forrest girls and Marisa. Braxton Forrest came around the front of the car, and he and Walter shook hands and leaned on the hood of the SUV.

A police car sat in the driveway. Marisa nodded at it.

"You must be terrified. We heard about the girl. I'm glad you have somebody here. They checked us when we came in. IDs, the whole bit," said Marisa.

"Can Buford help you with your bags?" Teresa asked.

"We dropped them off at the motel."

405

"I don't blame you for not staying here, Marisa."

"It sounds like you're not staying here much longer, either."

Teresa gave Marisa's arm a squeeze. "I bet you could use a cup of coffee," she said. As they went in the door, she put her arm about Marisa's waist. "I'm so glad you're here."

Forrest

Peach looked twenty years older, a ravaged and weary man. On their way inside the house, Forrest got a glass of water in the kitchen and caught up with his friend on the landing of the stairs. Walter held the door and followed him into the study that Forrest always thought of as his grandfather's sanctum, the place where his grandfather's irascible wife Sybil was forbidden to come.

The big desk was covered with old newspapers, letters, photographs, journals.

"The sheriff brought the box last night," Peach said, handing him an old *Chicago Tribune* from the desk before he sat down. "Meet my parents."

BOMBING AT ELEMENTARY SCHOOL KILLS TWO, INJURES CHILD

Christmas Day, 1972.

Above the story were photographs that Forrest remembered seeing in the seventies. Akers was looking at the camera sardonically, hands in his pockets, head tilted, self-consciously quoting a famous photograph of the young James Joyce. And Good Lord, Alison Graves. At a commune, it looked like. She stood under an apple tree smiling at the baby on her hip—young Walter, he assumed. She wore a t-shirt cut off just under her breasts, jeans, simple sandals, a beaded headband. A thick braid of her long dark hair came over her shoulder. She reminded him of his first girlfriend at Georgia, Susan Robinson, open and soft and easy. He had not thought of her in decades. He remembered riding in the back seat of Jim Wood's old Chevrolet Impala on the Blue Ridge Parkway on their way to a festival somewhere in Virginia. Her head was against his shoulder, she was singing, he was gazing out, stoned to placidity. The wind moved through a meadow of blue mountain grasses, and the look of the waves in the grass, soft and metallic at the same time, gave him a piercing bliss that felt like a promise of heaven.

What had happened to Susan Robinson? No idea. Forty-five years ago—a whole lifetime. She might be dead by now. Like Alison Graves.

"You wonder what good it is knowing the past," Walter said. "Whether there's not a haze of illusion you need just to get you to the next day. Like the major gift of Prometheus, which wasn't fire but forgetfulness of death."

"Pour the Knob Creek," Forrest said.

Walter went to the liquor cabinet and got out the bourbon and poured two generous glasses and handed one to Forrest, who took a sip and held it in his mouth before swallowing it.

"Look at that," he said, pointing up to the distant ceiling of the study, which paralleled the whole height of the house. A broad, slow fan like something in a movie set in the tropics—Sidney Greenstreet as the villain—revolved there, drawing up the hot air of the afternoon and sending a faint but steady breeze down the sides of the room. "People thought out the nature of heat instead of just canceling it with air conditioning. They learned to live with it. They did the same thing when they found the stories they needed to tell themselves. They knew exactly where they were lying.

"But were they lying about love between those enslaved and those who enslaved them? Was that total fiction? I don't think so. Were they lying about courage and generosity and sacrifice?" Forrest said.

Walter took a swallow and looked out the window.

"Wow, Braxton. You must have started ahead of me. Cue the swelling music and the Nobel Prize. I'm talking about my terrorist parents."

Forrest looked at Walter and drank off the rest of the glass.

"Right," he said. He held out his glass, and Walter poured again. "We're cynical now. So fucking cynical. And do you know why?"

"Because we found out about the real past?"

"Well, some of it—the part about class struggle and race hatred. But what about people who knew each other inside out? We forgot that. And the problem is, the past holds you hostage until you know it, know it all, all sides of it," Forrest said. "You have to be brave enough to face it. Never think otherwise."

Peach grimaced and took a big swallow of bourbon.

"So what's this?" Forrest said.

He reached over and picked up a large brown envelope on the side of the desk closest to his armchair. It was addressed to Mrs. Sarah Downs, 36 Trautman Lane, Seattle, Washington. The return address was Harold Lawton's in Macon. It was postmarked January 1979. It was unopened.

"Who's Sarah Downs?"

"Another iteration of my mother," Peach said. "Whatever's in it, it's everything Judge Lawton knew that he never told me."

"Judge Lawton?"

"The one whose wife tried to rename me."

"I thought you were brought up by relatives in Macon. You always just waved it off when I asked. But we're talking about the man who was Chief Justice of the Georgia Supreme Court?"

Peach's face clouded, and he winced away from the question before he nodded. But Forrest knew that Judge Harold Lawton, with his equanimity and humor, had done more to bring about needed corrections in racial injustices during the volatile 1960s and 1970s than anybody else.

"Listen, if he hid anything from you, he had a good reason," Forrest said, half-standing to hand him the envelope. "Open it."

Peach undid the clasp and let the contents slide out into his lap. For a long moment, he stared at the document on top of the other papers, then shook his head and handed it to Forrest. It was a brittle old piece of paper the size of a business check.

The left side was covered with ornamental designs, and at the top was a printed dollar sign and a handwritten *2,000*. A bill of sale. On the same level, handwritten on a dotted line on the right, was *Gallatin Oct. 21*, and in print, **1855**. Then the body: **Received of** *Asa Daniel Graves two thousand* **Dollars, being in full for the purchase of a Negro Slave named** *Zilpha* **the right and title of said Slave I warrant and defend against the claims of all persons whatsoever as witness my hand and seal**. It was signed *Farquhar McIntosh* on a dotted line and stamped with a seal.

A wave of dread went through Forrest. His grandfather, T.J. Forrest, had bought Stonewall Hill from the heirs of Farquhar McIntosh a hundred years ago and built this house over the original construction from the 1830s.

"Any idea why this would be on top?" Forrest asked. "Or who Zilpha was?"

"I've seen her name just recently. But you know Graves, don't you?"

"Vaguely," Forrest said. "Big in Confederate politics."

"Asa Daniel Graves had had some kind of cabinet position in the Confederate government when it was first formed. Secretary of State at one point. So, Asa Daniel Graves," Walter said, "paid two thousand dollars to the owner of this property for a slave named Zilpha in 1855." He opened the laptop on the desk, typed, waited a second, and looked up at Forrest. "That's $50,000 in today's money. For one slave, and not a field hand—not somebody whose labor he'd expect to make money from. What do you make of it?"

"She was a concubine."

They stared at each other.

"You know who would know about her?" Forrest said. "Hermia Watson. She did a whole book on the slave families in this house."

Peach raised his eyebrows and looked at the floor. Forrest found Hermia's number on his phone and touched it to call her.

"Hermia," he said when she answered on the third ring. "This is Braxton." No response. Forrest looked over at Walter and shrugged.

"Well, hello, *Braxton*," Hermia said with quiet sarcasm. "I didn't expect to hear your voice again. Not in this lifetime, and maybe not in the one to come. Where are you?"

"Stonewall Hill. I'm with Walter Peach. There's been some trouble down here."

She laughed. "How unusual. I remember some disturbing pictures at Christmas. What kind of trouble this time?"

"It's complicated."

Her laugh, even richer. "Oh, is it complicated, Daddy? I mean *Braxton*."

He let it go. "Listen, I'm sorry to disturb you, but we need your help. What can you tell us about Zilpha Graves?"

There was a pause before she answered.

"You've read my book, right?"

He remembered paging through it a year or so back. Old pictures.

"It's been a while."

She laughed again, but more brittlely.

"I know what kind of answer that is. How's Marisa?"

"She's fine. She and the girls are down here too."

"I'm sure you're keeping up with John Bell. Half the country is keeping up with John Bell Hudson. You know John Bell, don't you?"

Their son, the football star. Something a little more than illegitimate.

"Hermia, listen," he said.

"Well, ask me a real question," she said bitterly. "The last third of my book is about Zilpha Graves, as you'd know if you'd even looked through it."

He stared at the floor.

"Listen, I'm sorry. Walter found an envelope of documents today. The first thing on top was a bill of sale for a slave named Zilpha. Farquhar McIntosh sold her to Asa Daniel Graves."

He heard her gasp.

"Oh my God! Oh Lord. I didn't know how she came to be in the household of Asa Daniel Graves. Oh my Lord. He *sold* her? That accomplished woman?"

"For two thousand dollars. Who was she?"

"You really didn't read it."

The hurt in her voice now stung him with real regret.

"I will now, sweetheart. I swear."

Sweetheart. What was he doing? He heard a kind of sigh.

"It's just humiliating," she said. "I read what *you* write."

"I swear I'll read it, Hermia. Can I put you on speaker so Walter can hear you?"

"Let me collect myself a minute. I'll call you right back."

"Thank you."

Sweetheart. A dark sense of sin welled up within him. He drifted over to the window and looked down over the immaculate grounds he had restored, the stone walls gleaming like sculpture, the lawn beautifully edged, the crepe myrtles pruned and shapely, the bench, the goldfish pond with its red flicker of underwater motion. He paid a crew of Hispanics, probably all illegal, to maintain the place. They arrived en masse, according to Walter, quick and efficient, spreading over the grounds with mowers and string trimmers and clippers and blowers.

When had they done this? Yesterday?

Good God. Maybe they were informers for The Moccasin. He was turning to ask Walter about them when the phone rang.

"Hermia?" he said. "May I put you on speaker?"

"Yes. I'm okay now."

Forrest pushed the speaker button.

"Hermia?" Walter said.

"Hi, Walter," she said. "I guess you haven't read it either."

He glanced at Forrest. "I'll read it now," he said. "I just found a letter from Farquhar McIntosh to Asa Daniel Graves. It's about Zilpha."

"My God, can you read it to me?" Hermia said.

"McIntosh to Graves, dated September 10, 1857. The salutation is 'Respected Brother,'" Walter said. "Half-brother, you think? Or was Graves his brother-in-law?"

"Graves didn't marry a McIntosh." Hermia said. "His wife had a French name—Guillory or Guadreau. But maybe McIntosh married Graves's sister."

"That would work," Walter said. "Okay, here it is. *Respected Brother, Felicitations on the birth of Asher. It heartens me to know of his robust health and fair complexion. Would it be amiss this early to speculate that his early rearing and education might better proceed in England or France, and very soon, dear brother, if our beloved Zilpha is so disposed? Or if the prospect of such a separation pains you, might you locate them in Baltimore, or, better still, in Philadelphia, so that your sojourn in Washington might be relieved by Zilpha's nearness? You know my sentiments, and I await your judgment. As always in this matter, my resources are at your disposal.*

Affectionately yours, F. McIntosh."

Walter stared at Forrest.

"My God," he said at last. "This is his daughter. McIntosh's daughter."

"I always suspected that!" Hermia cried. "And he *sold* her?"

"She was his child with a slave he loved," Forrest speculated. "A quadroon, maybe an octoroon. Maybe there's a New Orleans connection. Hermia, you say Graves's wife has a French name."

"Oh God," Hermia said. "I think I see it. Zilpha's mother was a gift to Graves's sister—the one married to Farquhar McIntosh—from Graves's wife."

"Say that again," said Walter.

"Okay, Asa Daniel Graves is married to a woman from New Orleans with a French name. Let's call her Marie. Marie decides to give Mrs. McIntosh, her husband's sister, one of her personal slaves as a housemaid."

"On what occasion?"

"Maybe the birth of the first McIntosh child," Hermia said. "Someone to help Mrs. McIntosh. Just a girl, eleven or twelve, modest and presentable. Let's say she's the daughter of Mrs. Graves's own personal maid from New Orleans, so she'll see her mother whenever the two families visit."

"McIntosh would be in his late twenties while this girl is growing up in front of him," Forrest said. "She's almost white. This would be early. The 1830s maybe. The daily sight of her, the proximity, works on McIntosh."

"So how can Mrs. McIntosh stand having her in the house?" Walter interrupted.

Forrest gazed out the window at the slant of light through the trees. They were silent for a long moment before Hermia spoke.

"Maybe the girl dies."

Forrest can almost hear the slave women summoning McIntosh to the slave quarters, the confusion and clamor—the cries suddenly cut short, McIntosh distraught.

"Giving birth to Zilpha," Forrest said.

"And then here's this living reproach for Mrs. McIntosh to endure," Walter said. "This evidence of her husband's infidelity. This white child of her personal servant. How does that work?"

They fell silent again.

"It works because it's her idea to start with," Forrest said, revising the scene in his mind. The girl would not have given birth in the slave quarters, but inside the house, inside the bedroom of Mrs. Graves. "Isn't Zilpha a biblical name? Walter, can you look it up?"

"You wouldn't need to look it up," Hermia said with asperity, "if you had read my book. Zilpha was the handmaid of Leah, presumably a slave. Leah gave her to Jacob when she wasn't able to conceive herself. Zilpha's sons are Gad and Asher."

"So what are we saying?" Walter asked. "I'm lost."

"That Mrs. McIntosh actually gave Zilpha's mother to McIntosh," Forrest said.

"Why would she do that?" Walter said. "I can't get it to work."

Forrest met his eyes for a moment. Walter was thinking of Teresa, Forrest of Marisa. What was it they didn't understand?

"I don't know," Hermia said. "I would say that McIntosh was so overbearing he just cowed her into submission, but Graves would never allow that behavior toward his sister."

"So we think that Zilpha is McIntosh's daughter with his wife's personal slave," Walter said. "We know he prizes her. She grows up beautiful and quick-witted. She's educated as though she were their own. Do you think Mrs. McIntosh wants a daughter so bad, she passes Zilpha off as her own?"

"Why name her Zilpha?" Hermia interjected. "These people are steeped in the Bible. They know everything pertaining to slavery. Look at how Graves talks about the 'practices of the patriarchs and the teachings of the apostles.' Her name must be a coded acknowledgement of her race."

"Let's say they raise her as their child," Forrest said. "But McIntosh's wife has to endure knowing her real origin," he mused. "And now McIntosh is in his mid-forties, heavier now, but still capable of fire. He loves this girl, but his feelings are complicated. She's his not just by blood but by actual ownership."

"What are you saying, Daddy?" Hermia said.

Forrest glanced at Walter.

"The devil gets into him. Mrs. McIntosh writes to her famous brother."

"Graves comes to Stonewall Hill," Walter said.

"He comes in thinking he's going to be reasoning with his brother-in-law," Forrest said. "But then he sees Zilpha."

"Fifteen, let's say. Maybe sixteen," Walter said. "The way she offers the tray with his glass and his bourbon and mint and meets his gaze without looking away. Her green eyes."

They fell silent.

"McIntosh can't stand the idea of losing her," Forrest said, again meeting Walter's gaze.

"So how does it happen that McIntosh *sells her* to one of the South's exemplary racists?" Hermia cried.

Forrest thought about it.

"Graves has the idea. He takes McIntosh aside and explains how they can assuage his sister. He'll buy the girl. He can tell his sister that McIntosh selling Zilpha will not only get her out of the house, but also humble her pride."

They thought again. Forrest needed some more whiskey.

"So McIntosh sells her to Graves," Walter said, "on the condition that her children will be brought up white in Europe or the North."

Forrest thought about it and shook his head.

"I don't know. When he sells her, he's telling everybody—including her—that she's chattel. Why would he do that and then try to pass her off as white?"

"What else could the letter mean? About educating Asher in England or Europe?"

"Look, you read Graves's theory of race slavery. Why would he try to nullify it by doing that?"

"I don't know," Hermia said. "Love?"

They fell silent again. Out in the yard, policemen and troopers came and went, and they heard women's laughter—unlikely in the circumstances.

"She might not have known she was sold," Forrest said.

He imagined the girl arriving in Graves's house. The initial frosty hauteur of Mrs. Graves and the house slaves, but then the softening, the increasingly intimate exchanges—maybe in French—between Mrs. Graves and the girl in the bedroom at the vanity. Quietly, kindly, Mrs. Graves tells Zilpha about her mother and grandmother. Graves himself is increasingly obsessed with her. Whenever his public duties release him, he haunts the boundaries of the female life. He insists that his wife join him in Washington, and she sees through his real reason—this girl not humbled by her race, but articulate and forthright, this girl whose side she increasingly takes against her husband.

"Zilpha understands her situation," Forrest said, and Walter looked up at him, nodding.

"She knows she can use what Graves wants," Hermia said.

"Exactly. Mrs. Graves even helps her see how to do it. Mrs. Graves can play Leah and give the girl to Graves, the way her sister-in-law gave the girl's mother to McIntosh. But the girl will agree only if he gives her what she wants."

"You think his wife would do that for a slave?"

"Maybe. If it's in her interest somehow. Maybe she has a little black blood herself. Or maybe she sees Zilpha's dream."

"So to have her," Walter said, "Graves promises Zilpha that her children will be raised in the North or in Europe. Raised white."

He looked up at Forrest with a strange smile.

"What?" Forrest said.

414

Peach held his hand over the papers on the desk. "What we're going to find is that I am the descendant of a slave born in this house."

He poured himself two more fingers of whiskey and did the same for Forrest.

"We're also going to find that McIntosh used the money from selling Zilpha to Graves to fund her move to Europe or the North," Forrest said. "Saved it for her children. Put it in trust. That's going to be how it ended up with Harold Lawton."

When Walter looked up at Forrest, his eyes were red. He put both hands over the top of his head.

"Hermia," Forrest said. "What did she do? What happened to Zilpha?"

"She called herself Zilpha Graves," Hermia said, "but she obviously wasn't married to Asa Graves. He sent her to Rome with their son Asher in 1860, and I suppose she was free to make her own connections. It was the kind of world Henry James writes about. Within a year or two, she was the mistress of an Italian nobleman named Alessandro Barberini who had a villa on the Amalfi coast built on old Roman ruins.

"This count had a sickly and very rich American wife considerably older than he was. She was one of those women who consider it socially advantageous to be married to a count, and she was willing to spend her money on him regardless of what he did in his romantic life. Zilpha was able to live in the villa undisturbed because his wife rarely came to Italy. Alessandro and Zilpha had a number of children together. Her son Asher—the one she had with Asa Graves—grew up with a private tutor until his eighteenth year. He came back to the States and enrolled at Princeton, but Zilpha remained in Europe with her other children until her nobleman died in the late 1870s. She was still in her thirties and still beautiful."

"How do you know all of this?" Walter asked.

"I tracked down several of her descendants in New York. One of them was an old widow in Sutton Place who wanted to impress me. She mentioned that Zilpha was an artist. One of Zilpha's friends was an American portrait painter she met in Paris in the early 1880s, Cecilia Beauregard. Princeton had Beauregard's correspondence in one of its special collections. So I went to the Firestone Library and asked to see it—and there among the letters from Mary Cassatt and Thomas Eakins and Charles Dana Gibson were dozens from Zilpha Graves-Barberini."

"Any idea why Judge Watson would send this to Walter's mother?" Forrest asked.

"No, unless—well, unless it has to do with inheritance. Count

415

Barberini left her money, and she had a trust from Graves, I think. She was still a beautiful woman. She lived in New York with Asher for some years after she left Paris. I've seen some of her paintings in New York. There's a portrait of her daughter, Emilia LeRoux Graves-Barberini. It's in my book—she was quite a beauty herself. But in her sixties, Zilpha moved back to Georgia and lived in a house out in the country."

Peach looked up.

"On Hopewell Road?"

"That sounds right," Hermia said. "I tried to find it once when I was living at Stonewall Hill, but all I saw was a place covered with kudzu."

"The locals call it Missy's Garden," Peach said.

"Short for Miss Zilpha, I imagine. She must have visited Stonewall Hill. Of course, it declined after the war when Farquhar McIntosh died. His sons suffered all the miseries of Southern men in the Reconstruction South, and by 1900 or so the house was in bad repair. When Braxton's grandfather bought it with money from his new cotton mill, he rebuilt it on top of the original—but I'm sure Braxton has told you all that."

"Some of it," Peach said, glancing at Forrest.

"I don't know as much about it as you do," Forrest said to Hermia.

"I think about Zilpha driving into Gallatin," she said. "I picture her in an elegant white dress and a great hat with feathers. You know, making her black driver pause at the gate while she gazes up at that fateful place. And McIntosh *sold* her?"

"I'm afraid so."

She whispered something they could not hear. Forrest held the phone close to his ear.

"I'm sorry?" he said. "Say that again."

"Could you turn off the speaker, please?" she whispered.

He did it and walked to the other side of the study.

"What is it?" he asked.

"You called me sweetheart. You meant it, but do you know *what* you meant?"

"Hermia," he said.

"Goodbye, *Daddy*. I'm coming down there."

"There's no need t—"

"I'm coming as soon as I can."

Walter

There was a notebook he did not show the others.

This is for you. I had forgotten it until now, turning those old pages. We were Rosemary and Walter. It was early in the morning in the summer. I made you get up and put on clothes because Vernon was coming to fix the refrigerator. You came from the kitchen down the hall. My room was full of morning light. As you came in you found me standing in the door of the closet, reading. You asked me what I was reading, and I showed it to you. A thick old book with a black ribbon in it. You asked me what it was.

A diary, I said.

What's a diary?

A book you write in just for yourself.

Why would you want a book just for yourself?

For your later self. When you're older. It's not my book. It's hers.

And I took from the book the picture of the lady whose book it was and showed it to you.

I found it in a wooden box under a board in the closet floor.

Who is she?

The lady who lived here.

What does it say in the book?

I showed it to you but it was cursive and you could not read it.

She says she was standing at the armoire polishing the silver when Mr. Graves came into the room and found her.

Why would she write that down?

Because that's the day her life changed.

Why did it change?

Because that day she let him hold her. When he came up behind her and put his arms around her, she did not turn away. This time she let him hold her. Because then she could be free.

What does that mean?

You did not understand it then, but you will understand it now.

There were several pages carefully cut from the old diary and paper-clipped into his mother's journal.

I told him what I was schooled to say: <u>Yes, Mr. Graves, but I want to see my father first.</u> What a child I was in those days, barely knowing myself or my own body, but Mrs. Graves, whom I knew to be my mother's cousin, had told me what I was to say. I was to tell him yes, but to hold him to his promise that I would be free and my children would be free. She told me that if he tried to force me, I was to say his name sternly, <u>Mr. Graves.</u> She taught me just how to say it.

I was to tell him yes but that I would give myself only on the land that would be my own land, this land, and only in a tent. I asked Mrs. Graves why it had to be a tent, and she told me that he was a Bible man and that if I told him that I was black but beautiful and that I wanted a tent like the tents of Kedar in the Song of Solomon, it would move him. I was to say that I would give myself, yes, but where I gave myself would be a covenant, and it would make that place my inheritance to be sealed in law for all the time to come. And if he told me that I was black and could not own it, I was to tell him that I would not be black when I was his and I was free.

I said the things she told me to say, and it moved him as she told me it would. He held himself from me and agreed to what I said because his desire was so strong. He brought me back to Stonewall Hill to see my father, who wept and embraced me and did not want to let me go when he saw me. And so on that Sunday in the spring of 1856, Mr. Graves drove me in his runabout out into the country. We passed cotton fields and wagons and saw the negroes walking to church; we met the carriages of men who tipped their hats to me and women who nodded pleasantly, thinking I was the daughter of the distinguished Senator.

We came to the place my father owned. Mr. Graves drove onto the grass and tied the horse where it would not be seen from the road and helped me down in my Sunday dress and my bonnet and parasol. We walked down through the dogwoods and then along the path by Caleb's Creek with the sunlight breaking through from above and the reflections from the water shimmering on the undersides of the leaves along the banks. It was lovely, and Mr. Graves was lovely in his manners, a Christian gentleman, tall and handsome and erect in the prime of life. I took his hand and told him that here he might pitch our tent, here beneath the oak trees. Here we could make our covenant.

I saw his heart flood into his face. And so he went back to the carriage and got his things, and here he pitched his tent while I wandered my land and imagined it and watched the bees in my honeysuckle and I sang "Hard Times Come Again No More." When the time came, I put away my clothes on the flat rock by the pool and bathed in the cool water and there was a mockingbird dancing from limb to limb above me and singing. Mr. Graves folded me in towels and dried me and I went in with him through the netting. He called me his bride and told me my eyes were like doves and kissed me with the kisses of his mouth. And when he came into me, I cried out but I did not stint on love. I gave myself and I owned myself and as his seed leapt into me, I took it into me, and we conceived our Asher and my freedom and the freedom of all my children to come forever.

And you said

> *He put a seed in her?*
>
> *Not like a seed we plant, I said. It's like that but not quite like that. She has an egg and he has a seed and his seed swims into her egg and makes a new person. Like you. That's how you became a person.*
>
> *An egg?*
>
> *Not like a chicken egg or a robin's egg. A tiny little egg you can't even see it's so small but it's round like a planet far up inside her. And he goes inside her and his seed comes swimming toward her like a comet from outer space that plunges right into Earth and suddenly the weather changes and the whole sky clouds over and the heart of the earth becomes something new, something so new that it never was before.*

You did not know what to say. I knelt and lifted a board and took out the wooden box and put the book inside it and closed the box and the put the board back and closed the door and smiled at you.

> *And do you know what else? I said.*

Walter

Her car was gone. She had left and had not told him. He did not find her at the stove. The bacon was smoking even though the frying pan was off the burner. He called and she did not answer. He went to the hallway and called. He went to her room and stood in it. All her things were there, her books and her bottles of oils and her candles and clothes. Her drawings and paintings of him. Her shoes. He picked up one of her sandals and smelled it—the leather smell and the smell of her foot. One of her shirts. He pressed his face into it, missing her body.

Rosemary? he called.
He waited and she did not answer. She was not in the house.
Mama? he called.
He knelt on her bed and looked through her window down the slope toward the creek. Baskets of herbs hung from the limbs. The woman stepped out of the tree.

On the old terraces on the slope, irises came up where she said no one would expect them. Zilpha's irises she called them.

She loved to go out early without her clothes
    and step down into the water of the creek
    early in the morning
    like today when he went down naked
    looking for where the tent once was
    when the creek still had the mist rising from it
    and it was cold in the pool where the fish were
    near the cedar tree and the flat rock

she would come back up sometimes not drying herself
    but letting the air dry her
    and sometimes the whitetail deer would come up the slope
    and stand close by her

she told him she would love to nurse a little fawn
    have its hard little head butt her breast and find her nipple
    and take her milk with its taking tongue
    just like he used to and still wanted to

and she would flow from herself and stroke its hard little head
and flow from herself right into its mouth and call it
little sister
little sister she would say *drink me*
drink my body little sister

He went to his room and she was not there.

From his window he could see the road. A pickup truck went by, going slow. He put on his clothes. Furled, he went to the front door and opened it and stepped outside. He never went out the front door. But she had left and had not told him.

With bacon smoking on the stove.

He went out to the path toward Hopewell Road through the waist-high wildflowers.

He looked back at the house, hoping she would come around the side of the house but

she was not there. And the car was gone.

Rosemary? he called louder. *Mama?*
Mama! He was louder now. There was nothing at all between his heart and being without her.
    Nothing but absence
    absence so huge it already made the night come
    with no stars and no moon

He went out into the ditch, he went through the ditch into the terrible and dangerous road, and he looked both ways, hoping to see her car returning. And then everything would be as it was before
    and she would hold him against her
    and he would have her to himself, the warm smell of her,
    close with no clothes and he would fall asleep against her
    dropping away with her so close
    like butter melting
    like warm honey

but the car was not coming back

she was gone

the road was a reaching emptiness of dust and sunlight
    not there
    not there
    not a word not a goodbye

and the world without her surrounded him
    and he stood and gave himself away
    until he was not even the sound of his wail
    not even the night of her infinite absence

Then the truck came back.
    A woman got out of it. Mrs. Jenkins, narrow and hard-faced.
    Well, pretty boy, she said. *Your mama's gone.*
    He saw that she was happy.
    You come with me. It's a good thing she's gone.
    He stared at her.
    Your mama was a wicked woman. A harlot.
    He did not say anything. He did not know that word.
    I'll take you to church, how about that?

Teresa

Sunday, June 29, 2014

When Teresa woke up on Sunday morning, Walter lay beside her, snoring lightly. In the night he had come to her hungrily for the first time in months, and his desire had disquieted her. She had responded slowly, worried about him, conscious of the shocks he had undergone, sickened a little by the sense that he was reliving something unrelated to her. But finally, pity had overcome her, he was so hungry—a melting pity, like the letting-down of milk to her babies. And it seemed that this would be all. But then she took fire. She could not have him soon enough, violently enough.

She could not remember anything like it since their early marriage—that April afternoon in the apartment in Athens when he had come in from teaching, and she was just leaning over, still unbuttoned, to put Rose in her crib for her nap and he came up behind her and his hands took her swollen breasts. A bout of sweet devouring madness. Afterward they had lain on the bed naked in that young languor with the breeze coming through the open window across their cooling bodies. He had propped himself on his elbow to admire her; she had fondly, absently, laid her hand on him. She remembered hearing a car door slam in the parking lot, voices, a neighbor girl, the classics major, calling her cat.

Aspasia! Here kitty! Aspasia!

And Walter's sardonic whisper when he rolled to her, lips to her ear: *Here kitty.*

She smiled and stretched, warmed again by the innocent memory. She felt ridiculously young.

She lifted her head to look at the clock. 8:09. She lay back and curled against Walter, her arm across him. What day was it?

Sunday!

She sat up, wide awake. They had to drive to Macon.

"Walter." She gave him a nudge and he stirred and looked up at her. "It's after 8:00. Mass is at 9:30."

"Let's go later."

"No! This is special."

"What do you mean, special? Why do we have to rush?"

"We have to go. Just come on."

She got up and put on her robe and went into the hallway.

"Everybody get up!" she shouted. "We need to leave at 9:00 for Mass. Everybody up! Rose! Buford!"

She went down the hall toward the bathroom, passing the room where Nora had stayed. The girl was still in the hospital, traumatized by an ordeal Teresa could hardly imagine. El Mocasín had arrayed her in a mocking imitation of Our Lady of Guadalupe. Hudson had asked Teresa to cut her loose, and when she did it, pity overwhelmed all the resentment she had built up against her. First the neck, then the zip ties holding her hands in place, then the ropes criss-crossed between her breasts that left livid marks on her skin. When she cut the ropes that held her tight against the big oak, the girl simply buckled, her ankles still bound. Teresa caught her, held her, supporting her weight, her wheezing and gasping body, and finally got the last ropes cut and the blanket wrapped around her. She had never seen a fatigue so profound.

They were only five minutes late when Walter dropped them off in front of the church. They started up the steps while he found a parking place. He joined them halfway through the first reading; they all shifted to their left to make room for him. Hurrying behind him came the Forrest family, who filed into a half-empty pew a few rows back.

It was the Solemnity of Saints Peter and Paul. A slim, lawyerly lector stood at the lectern on the epistle side and read with a slow emphasis that called attention to the text without calling attention to herself—a rare feat. The reading from Acts was about the angel that came to St. Peter in prison and waited for him to get dressed before leading him out past the jailers. She loved St. Peter's incredulity at being released, and the way the angel left him in an alley delighted her. She glanced at Walter when the choir sang the refrain of the Psalm, "The angel of the Lord will rescue those who fear Him," but his mind seemed to be elsewhere. But Buford was focused with an odd intensity.

The same woman read the Second Letter of St. Paul to Timothy. St. Paul spoke of his own rescue "from the lion's mouth." Teresa heard it as though for the first time. Had St. Paul been fed to lions and miraculously freed? Wasn't there another passage where he talked about fighting wild beasts at Ephesus? He must have faced a lion. It would be distasteful to say such a thing metaphorically in that age of martyrs.

The choir sang the Alleluia. When the priest announced the Gospel according to St. Matthew, they crossed their foreheads, lips, and hearts, and her children followed along in the Missalette when Fr. Corrigan stood at the pulpit reading about Christ's commission to St. Peter: "Upon this rock I will build my Church." Fr. Corrigan spoke in his homily about the papacy. Walter seemed altogether elsewhere, but when the priest mentioned the new threat to Christians in the Middle East, she felt her husband stir beside her.

"This is a new age of martyrs," said Fr. Corrigan, "and no one wants to admit it. Not the White House, not the media." He urged the congregation to pray for those in Africa and the Middle East. He told them to pray that they themselves not be put to the test. He emphasized the word *rescue* and ended with the assurance in the Gospel that the "gates of the Netherworld" would not prevail against the Church.

After the Profession of Faith, the same lector stood up to read the Prayers of the Faithful, and when she finished without any mention of Alison Graves, Teresa despaired of her request. But then Fr. Corrigan pulled a piece of paper from his sleeve and read in a firm voice, "And for the soul of Alison Graves, for whom this Mass is being offered."

Walter's head jerked up. He stared at Fr. Corrigan, who had already begun the prayers to close the Liturgy of the Word. And then he turned to look at Teresa, and his eyes brimmed, whether in gratitude or in anger, she did not know.

Bennett

Monday, June 30, 2014

U.S. Marshal Aengus Dunne loomed in the chair across from Bennett, reddening more by the second. It was barely 7:30 in the morning, and he was there to get Bennett's cooperation in the plan to take the Peach family—and now Nora O'Hearn as well—into witness protection later that morning. The whole process involved intensive planning and multiple levels of deception.

"What do you mean, a funeral?"

"For Peach's mother," Bennett said. "They had her cremated, and Teresa wants to do something quiet out at the cemetery. You know, down there at the bottom of the hill at Memorial Heights where people put the ashes in a box in a wall."

Marshal Dunne breathed out noisily through his nose. Dunne told him who Alison Graves was.

"My Lord," Bennett. "I had no idea."

"All of them out in the open? Can't do it, Hudson."

"Marshal," he said, glancing at his watch, "they're already out there."

"Damn it!" Dunne said, slamming a hand on Bennett's desk. "Who knows about it?"

"Funeral home. They just called to tell me about some woman coming in from Arizona. Said she would be the one I didn't recognize. I don't know who else."

Dunne's lips whitened and disappeared. "I can guarantee you who else." He smoothed his bare head with one huge hand and picked up his cell phone with the other, staring across the desk in the vicinity of Bennett as he tapped and swiped with his thumb.

"Sarah? Move everything up two hours.... No, I mean *right now*. I want a scan for at least one sniper—assume a Chris Kyle capacity—at or near Memorial Heights Cemetery just west of Gallatin.... That's right, U.S. 41. All vehicles should be in place within ten minutes. I want our people on the periphery. Now. Yes, I will be out there as soon as—say what? Yes, shoot to kill."

Bennett's phone rang. Usually, Ellen Wolf would have fielded calls, but she had taken the day off to help plan Dexter's funeral since there was nobody else to do it. Well, Ed, maybe, but Ed was scared to death.

"Hudson Bennett," he said into the phone, lifting a hand to Marshal Dunne, who was already heading out the door.

"What!" he yelled and put his hand over the mouthpiece. "Marshal, wait a second!... Say again," he said into the phone. "And when was this? Okay—the boy's dead? Not dead. I see, and they're okay? . . . Good. Good . . . I'll be out there in five minutes."

Marshal Dunne waited with a hand on the doorjamb, halfway out the door.

"Somebody tried to shoot Nora O'Hearn," Bennett said.

"God damn it! We had somebody out there."

"Some Hispanic kid, probably eighteen or nineteen. Got past your man and started down the hallway dressed like an orderly. Bill Sharpe was sitting outside the room. As soon as the kid looked up at the room number, Sharpe had him on the floor with his arm almost torn off. Sharpe said he felt it as soon as the kid came in the building. I'm headed out there. You'll call me?"

Dunne nodded. "We'll have the car there for her. Ten minutes." He started away and paused to look back. "Keep Sharpe out of the way."

"You think up in that section?" Ellen said, pointing up toward the weedy top corner of Memorial Heights. "You think Dex would like that?"

"I guess," Ed said. He could see Ellen felt something for Dexter even after all this time. Ellen had kept fit, he had to say. Kept the weight off. She looked a lot better than Betty, so he tried hard to feel something about Dexter, too, just for her sake. *Dexter, my brother, my own flesh and blood.* They had been almost friendly when they were boys, riding bikes, fishing in the Ikahalpi—but then he thought about how Dexter had passed Betty off to him in high school. *Broke her in,* he said. He soured again. Truth was, Dexter had humiliated him his whole life.

"Who's this, you reckon?" he said to Ellen from the corner of his mouth.

A tall man in camouflage gear came walking down out of the woods that bordered the top of the cemetery. He was carrying some kind of case.

"How you doing?" Ellen said to the man.

"Doing all right," the man said. "Y'all mind if I set up my equipment over here? Got to take some pictures of the folks down the hill there. Just looking for the best spot."

"Don't mind us," Ellen said. "You tell me if we're in your way."

"Yes ma'am, I will."

The man got out a low tripod and unfolded it. Ed glanced down the hill to see what folks he was talking about. By God. There was that little dimwit who stood out in the kudzu and started this whole goddamn thing and then ate up half his pickled eggs. And there was dumbass Walter Peach, who kept hollering about cartels in the newspaper until they showed up and burned down Ed's store and shot Dexter.

So what were they doing down there?

"Who's the service for?" Ellen asked the man in camouflage.

"Somebody's mother, sounds like," the man said. "I hear they found her in a house covered with kudzu."

"No!" Ellen said. "You don't mean . . . ."

She stood next to Ed and stared down the hill.

"Peach's mother," Ed said. "You believe this? Some kind of hippie from the 1960s, which it all came out on the news this morning."

"On the news? I didn't see it." Ellen shook her head. "I feel so bad for Walter, finding her like that."

"Well, listen, her and some other hippie blew up a school in Chicago and killed people, and she was on the run when she came down to Gallatin. She didn't mind showing herself off. Vernon Jenkins used to go over there. Smoke some pot with her. Said she was easy as wanting to."

"Hush your mouth."

"I'm just saying. Then ran off and left Peach and then came back and killed herself."

"Excuse me," the man said. "Y'all mind stepping aside a little so I can get my focus?"

They looked back at him.

"Sweet Jesus," Ed said.

"Oh my Lord," Ellen said.

The man had assembled a wicked-looking rifle with a scope and attached it to the tripod. He dropped to his knees and situated the tripod on the ground. Lying on his stomach, he adjusted the scope.

"I won't be here long," he said, looking up at them. "Y'all might want to forget you saw me. Maybe ride into town, get some coffee. I don't forget a face."

"Ed," Ellen said, "let's you and me go look at that plot."

Walter

June 30, 2014

Teresa insisted that they do something formal. They stood on the paving stones of the columbarium at the lower end of Memorial Heights. Two brick walls curved inward toward a mourner's bench in the middle. The brass door of a niche on the right stood open. Beside it waited a young man from the funeral home, who passed a handsome cedar box to Walter.

Good boxes always reminded Walter of what Yeats said about the difference between prose and poetry. You could go on correcting prose forever because it had no laws, but "a poem comes right with a click like a closing box."

Had she come right at last?

Rosemary.

He held the weight of his mother.

He stood for a moment facing his family and the Forrests and then turned blindly. The young man helped guide the box into the niche and then closed the door. Walter wiped his eyes and turned back. He pulled a piece of paper from his pocket and stood facing the others self-consciously.

"My mother—"

He cleared his throat and looked down at the paper.

"I'm not sure what to call the woman we're burying today," he said, "except *my mother.* Before she left, she was Rosemary, never Mama. That word had too many old expectations and roles built into it. During that time the two of us were living at Missy's Garden. She wrote many things in her journal, it turns out, and when she came back there to die in 1998, she wrote something new on the last page. She must have written it and then put her journal back in the box beside the bed. She must have brewed the hemlock and then drunk it and waited there on the bed. Or maybe she wrote it while she waited. I don't know. Let me just read it."

He looked down at the page.

"At the last—" he said.

He composed himself and started again, but he could not get past the first line.

"I'll read it," someone said.

She stepped through the others, who looked at her, confused. He saw Teresa stiffen. Good God. It was Lydia Downs. She wore jeans with pointed cowboy boots and a cowgirl shirt. She looked at Walter equably, with a slight smile, unashamed. The consolation he felt was the last thing he would have expected. She took the paper from him.

Her voice was clear and strong, and she gave each line the exact weight and pacing that made them hear it:

> at the last
> this is all I wanted
>
> to be standing outside
> the disguises of my body
>
> having shed my lies
> and all those names
>
> at last to unfurl
> to be nothing but origin
>
> to know nothing
> but the shape of going

Peach felt a bitter shock in his nostrils.

"Is this a poetry reading?" someone called. A tall, thin man in a white summer suit leaned against the Outback. "Some say the world will end in fire!" he cried. "Goodbye, Alison! I wish you joy of the eternal flames."

He lifted his panama hat toward the cemetery entrance and made a large beckoning gesture. Immediately, a CNN van bristling with broadcasting equipment roared up and skidded to a stop. A blonde woman jumped out, hurrying around the front, touching up her hair, smoothing her taut clothes over her little body as she ran toward them. The driver strapped on his camera gear and followed her. By now, other news vans had pulled up: Fox, ABC, NBC, CBS. Logos and numbers and call names. More reporters and cameras came rushing toward them.

"Mr. Peach! Who found the body of Alison Graves?" shouted the CNN reporter.

"Is it true that she killed herself when the police caught up with her?" someone else called.

Walter watched Cottonmouth, who turned with studied elegance, like the conductor of an orchestra, and lifted his right hand, palm upward, to someone up the hill. A strange cry came—a kind of high, sobbing laugh. Everyone stood paralyzed.

"No!" they heard a woman scream from the direction of the cry. They saw her leap forward like a shortstop diving for a hard grounder.

Her body jolted twice as she fell, and the sound of two shots reached them.

The newspeople scattered like a herd of startled deer. Up the hill, a man stood up, holding his rifle in his right hand and lifting his left, a gesture of almost comical denouement. As they watched, his head jerked sharply sideways, and a red mist of blood flowered in an angle of sunlight against the dark backdrop of woods. The body fell like a tree trunk as the crack of the shot came from the grove on the west side of the cemetery.

Screams, furious shouts. "Get down! Get down!" Walter dropped to his stomach on the grass and twisted to look around. Unmarked cars raced up both sides of the circular drive around the cemetery. Teresa and Rose were close by, Buford just to his left. Lydia Downs was behind a stone bench, and Forrest had moved Marisa and the girls behind the rented SUV. The news crews peeked out, weighing the possibility of instant death against the opportunity for a live shot on national news and a quick route to fame: *A sniper opened fire Monday morning at the funeral of 1970s fugitive Alison Graves . . .*

Walter felt strangely detached. Events unfolded through a consciousness he could not claim as his own. Somehow, he knew that the bullets that had hit the woman at the top of the hill were meant for him. More intensely than after the near-miss at Stonewall Hill, he felt a kind of otherness in being there, still alive, as though his body had been unexpectedly released from his own death. Radios were crackling. "All clear?" someone shouted. "All clear!" came the answer. People began standing up—cameras everywhere, reporters regrouping. Through the crowd of them, two women approached his wife and daughter and took them by their arms. "Who are you?" Teresa cried. She twisted back toward him, "Walter!" but they pushed her head down and hustled her to a car, with Rose bucking against another woman the whole way.

Cottonmouth had disappeared.

Then men came for Buford and for him.

Forrest

"No, I saw them!" Bernadette said. "These people came and like kidnapped the whole family. Did you see Rose?"

"They're being taken into witness protection," Forrest said.

"Are you sure?" Marisa asked. "I thought that was supposed to be later this morning."

"Did you see that man in the white suit?" Cate asked. "Was that like so weird?"

They sat in the SUV until one of the Gallatin Police waved them forward.

"We need the area clear. Follow the drive up and around, please, sir."

Forrest nodded and drove up and paused at the top to look back down the hill at the columbarium. The man in the white suit had to be Cottonmouth. The plan must have been to get the media to Gallatin to report the discovery of the notorious Alison Graves. The sniper's responsibility would have been to murder Walter Peach while the cameras were on him. It would be live, unforgettable, indelible, like Jack Ruby shooting Lee Harvey Oswald.

Everything would have worked if the woman had not jumped in front of the shot: Ellen Wolf, somebody had told him, a dispatcher for the Sheriff's Department.

He drove up Main Street into town. Clusters of people had gathered on the courthouse square. Media vans. Reporters asking locals about Alison Graves.

"Dad," Cate said. He glanced at her in the rearview mirror. "Who was that man, seriously? In the white suit?"

"Some kind of crime boss," he said. "The Mexicans call him The Moccasin."

"What was he doing?"

"Just thank God it didn't happen. If that woman hadn't jumped in front of the sniper, I think Walter Peach would be dead. Maybe Buford, too."

"I saw that!" Cate said. "Did she—is she okay?"

"She's alive."

"I need to speak to Teresa," Marisa said.

"They probably won't let you anytime soon," Forrest said, pulling up in front of the Red Roof Inn. "Where do y'all want to get breakfast?"

"Breakfast," said Marisa. "My Lord. We haven't even had breakfast."

"Give me about fifteen minutes," Forrest said. "I'm going to check by Stonewall Hill and see if I can find out what's going on with Walter's family."

Alone now, Forrest drove past the old college, now a state training facility for police. He bumped across the railroad tracks, remembering Marilyn Harkins and the summer of 1969. Everything was different now. On Johnston Street, all the stores were altered, all the people who used to run them dead or in nursing homes. On the corner of the courthouse square, the Confederate soldier looked so forlorn that nobody would even think to disturb him. Robert E. Lee was a different story elsewhere—now a villain, which was hard for him to fathom. He had a young colleague at Walcott College who got fiery on the topic, called Lee a traitor. Forrest had been so taken aback he just stared at him.

There was almost no traffic. He turned left and went slowly down Lee Street to the split in the road where Stonewall Hill sat at the top of the rise with its broad porch and its columns. He took the fork onto Johnson's Mill then turned into the back driveway. A Gallatin police car sat behind the house. He parked beside it and got out, calling to let them know he was here. He felt his pockets and realized he had left his iPhone in the holder that clamped to the air vent. He reached back in and released it, automatically checking it for messages.

A sound made him look up.

Billy Reeves, who had once arrested him, lay on his stomach on the brick sidewalk, his face turned toward Forrest, his eyes open. He looked like one of those bandits in the old Westerns who puts an ear to the railroad tracks to gauge when the train will be arriving for its ambush. Both hands were pressed against the bricks as if he were about to do a pushup.

Forrest tilted his head, starting to smile, but a second later, he saw the pool of blood spreading from beneath Reeves's body.

"Sweet Jesus," he prayed. Reeves's eyes closed and then slowly opened again. He was struggling to speak, to focus. Forrest knelt and leaned close to him.

"Surprised," Billy whispered and closed his eyes. "Surprised me," he said. He opened his eyes and focused on Forrest. "Inside."

Forrest scanned the windows of the house for movement but saw no one. He punched 9-1-1 into his phone and told the dispatcher where he was and what had happened. He patted Reeves's shoulder.

"They'll be here," he said. "Hang on, buddy."

A few seconds later, he heard a siren in town half a mile away. Moments after that, a second one. He waited until he heard the siren dying in the driveway and saw the EMT people leaping out. Then he started for the back screen door.

He went up the sidewalk, touched the splintered place in the doorjamb, and stepped into the house, where he smelled gasoline. Outside, another siren loudly died. He heard shouts and then a siren starting up again. He followed the splashes of gasoline cautiously—expecting a wall of fire at any moment—out into the back hallway, up the back stairs, where gasoline dripped down step by step and pooled at the bottom, and quietly onto the landing, where he followed the trail into the study.

Two policemen had started up the stairs behind him, but Forrest turned sharply and held up a hand and put his finger to his lips, shaking his head. They stopped, their hands going to their pistols.

He stepped inside the short hallway into the study. The smell here was stronger. He heard strange murmurs, almost like sobs. He quietly stepped into the light, and there was Cottonmouth, still in his white suit, bent over the desk with the folder open before him. His bald head was quilted and ridged with burn scars. Forrest took in all the details at once: the panama hat on the seat of the armchair, the pistol hanging in Cottonmouth's right hand, the gasoline can on the floor, an old metal Zippo lighter on the desk. The newspaper story about Akers and Graves lay open before the man, next to the bill of sale for Zilpha Graves. Whimpering noises broke from him, low moans. He was oblivious to Forrest.

"Why do they call you Cottonmouth?" Forrest whispered.

The man whirled toward him, his hand rising, and Forrest saw the cottony white obscenity of his open mouth as the gun fired. The bullet seared the side of Forrest's head. Staggered, Forrest grabbed left-handed at the pistol, and when the man's finger twisted in the trigger guard, the gun fired again into Forrest's leg as he snatched it away. And then his rage lifted him, a rage he had known only a few times in his life, high and lucid and merciless: he was beside himself, as he recognized later, strangely detached, watching himself become a thing of wrath. He took the man's hands and crushed them as though the bones were delicate models of balsa wood. The white mouth screamed into his face, and the broken hands dangled as the man's elbows pushed at him. Policemen were grabbing at Forrest from behind, but he shook them off, and his fingers closed on the bare head.

Smell of rotten fruit from the open white mouth, thick tongue white as a petal of magnolia lolling. The bone yielded slightly, cracked, gave inward, and his strength rose higher and he bellowed and after a moment the black staring eyes bulged out, lightless, and his strength rose and rose and then it was done. He threw the man down and took a step, trying to turn, but his leg yielded, and he fell against one of the men crowding the room and bore him down with him as he fell.

And then more hands were snatching at him. There were exclamations of horror. Shoes moved close to his face. He heard policemen shouting for help.

Bennett

At the hospital, Bennett waved at the receptionist when he came in, an old teacher of his named Edna Price.

"You back again?"

"Afraid so. How's Bill?"

"Still pretty upset when he left. I'm glad you talked to him."

"Listen, where's Ellen?"

"In the ICU. That is one brave woman."

"Can I see her?"

"I'll buzz you in. Lord, what a day!"

She pressed a button and found his way to Ellen's room. She lay there unconscious with her leg wrapped and elevated. IV, monitors. She looked pale and wasted. Her husband, whose name Bennett could never remember, sat faithfully near her. Bennett lifted a hand.

"I'll check back later," he whispered. "If she wakes up, tell her I came by."

He found LaCourvette Todd waiting in the lobby. She steered him over to a sofa beneath a huge photograph of the Great Smoky Mountains. Sgt. Billy Reeves had a punctured lung and a severed spinal cord, she said, that would leave him paralyzed from the waist down.

"What the hell happened?" he cried.

"You don't know what happened at Stonewall Hill while you were out here?"

Forrest was luckier than Reeves, even though the man had shot him twice—a furrow along the side of his head above the left ear and a bullet that went down through his right thigh and his heel. She said Forrest was out of his mind when he killed the man. After he collapsed, her men had brought him down from the office at Stonewall Hill, and it took four people to get him in the ambulance—the two biggest EMTs with a policeman lifting him and another EMT, a woman who said she knew Forrest, trying to stop the bleeding and get an IV going. LaCourvette had ridden with him in the ambulance.

"And you know who he was talking to?" she said.

"He was conscious?"

"He was talking to Miss Mary Louise the whole way."

"Your grandmother? She was—"

"Rest her soul, she went to Jesus last night, but here he was talking to her. And I swear she was right in there with him. Like I could hear her."

"Saying what?"

"Telling him what to do. Big old man half dead and him saying *Yes'm*

. . . Yes'm . . . like he was a little boy."

LaCourvette touched the device in her ear—Bennett was glad he didn't have one—and excused herself and went outside as Dr. Fletcher came through a door in his scrubs and headed toward ICU.

Bennett caught up with him.

"Can't talk. I need to check on Billy," Fletcher said.

"Is Ellen going to make it?"

"She'll make it. She lost a lot of blood."

"Who shot Billy?"

"I don't know his name, but he's dead now," Fletcher said.

"LaCourvette said Forrest killed him."

"Putting it politely," Fletcher said and excused himself.

Buddy Fingal in his white hat and black CORONER shirt was limping up the hallway Fletcher had come from.

"Sweet Lord help me," he wheezed when he saw Bennett. "This can't keep up."

"Who's dead?" Bennett asked. "Is this the one we've been after?"

"We'll have to get prints, if you can get prints off hands burned like that. Not much left of him to recognize. Head was crushed."

"Crushed?"

"Forrest did it," Fingal wheezed. "With his hands."

Bennett waited for him to qualify what he had said, but he did not.

"Come on, Buddy. That's impossible."

"Ought to be. But you remember what he did to Dutrelle Jones? Broke his arm with one hand? Bubba Ivey knew him back when they played football, says Forrest used to crack pecans between his fingertips—I mean index and thumb—like they was peanut shells."

"We're talking about a man's skull," Bennett said.

"Nothing hit him. I've seen every kind of blunt instrument trauma. No sir. The bone was crushed down into the brain from all sides at once. You think of another way to do that, you let me know."

"Good God."

"Amen. Righteous and mighty and ever to be praised," said Fingal.

Crushed his skull? He was about to leave when he got a call from Aengus Dunne.

"Marshal," Bennett said, "I guess you can call off the witness protection."

"Where are you?" Dunne asked. "That's exactly what I want to talk to you about."

"I'm out at the hospital about to see Braxton Forrest."

"I'll meet you there as soon as I can. In the meantime—Hudson, are you listening?"

"I'm listening."

"Not a word, you understand, not a hint that this was The Moccasin. As far as we know, this is somebody like the sniper hired to shoot Peach. Somebody hired to burn the house like they burned Ed Watkins' store."

"I hear you."

He spent fifteen minutes thumbing inattentively through the magazines on the table beside the sofa. Finally, a nurse he didn't know came and called him. Bennett followed her into ICU past Ellen's room. He found Forrest propped up in bed, huge, surrounded by IV stands and cords and monitors. One thick bandage wrapped his head and another his right thigh, which angled up from under the sheet. Forrest's eyes were closed, so Bennett sat down in the chair beside the bed and waited.

"I don't *know* his real name," Forrest said after a minute or so.

"I'm sorry?" Bennett said.

Forrest opened his eyes and focused.

"Hudson," he said slowly. "I thought it was Miss Mary Louise." Forrest started violently. "*Is it burning?*"

Bennett didn't smell anything, but he got up and looked around him.

"He meant to burn Stonewall Hill," Forrest said. "I stopped him."

"I hear you did. You think this is the one who wrote those letters?"

"What did he want in the study at Stonewall Hill?" Forrest sagged back, his big hands palm-upward beside his legs.

"I couldn't tell you, Mr. Forrest."

"Do you think he meant to die there? He had his lighter right on the desk."

"No sir, he had a ticket in his pocket to Lima, Peru."

Forrest did not speak for a while. He closed his eyes.

"Maybe it ought to burn," he nodded, after a moment.

"Sir?"

Forrest did not answer.

Not talking to me, Bennett realized.

"I know, God help me. . . . I ought to feel like a hero, but I crushed my own head. . . . Yes, Zilpha's child. A man already singled out to suffer. The chosen victim of the old one."

Again, Forrest fell silent. Bennett stood to leave, keenly embarrassed to be overhearing him.

"I know it's on me!" Forrest cried out. "God help me, Miss Mary Louise."

Bennett stood in the hallway for ten or fifteen minutes feeling like he should be doing something, but he did not know what to do. When Dunne finally arrived, one of the nurses coming around the desk, half-seeing him, instinctively shied away. The man was immense.

"How's he doing, Sheriff?" Dunne asked.

"Okay," said Bennett. "Kind of in and out. Maybe the painkillers he's on."

"We need to talk this out."

"You want Forrest in on it?"

Dunne tilted his head toward the room. "Let's get out of the hall, anyway."

Forrest was sleeping. Dunne pulled the visitors' chairs over next to the window that looked out over the front lawn of the Gallatin County Hospital campus. He sat down and looked at the floor for a long moment before raising his head.

"I want to do two things, and both of them could backfire. Either one could get me fired, and one of them could bring down a shitstorm of bad publicity on you."

"Sounds good," Bennett said.

Dunne leaned closer. "First, we keep it a secret, even from my own agency, that Cottonmouth isn't still alive. The witness protection process is already underway, so it goes on as planned. You with me?"

"The point being?" Bennett did not like the idea of deceiving the higher-ups. It took him aback that Dunne would suggest it.

"The point being that both factions of the cartels are so scared right now, they've abandoned this whole sector of their operational plans. They've ceded Georgia to Cottonmouth. The longer we can keep them thinking he's alive, the better chance we have of rooting them out."

"I don't know why your agency wouldn't see the logic of that," Bennett said.

Dunne waited until Bennett looked him in the eye. "Some of us are pretty sure we've been infiltrated by the Sinaloa cartel. We know who to watch for signs of nervousness, so to speak."

Bennett tilted his head. "Okay."

"So why keep the witness protection process going? Because it involves actual government money. That's what I could get fired over, but it earns us another level of believability both within the agency and with the media.

"And playing the media is the second thing I want to do. You need to hold a press conference while all the news agencies are still in town. Get your office to make a press release announcing it right now."

"Ellen Wolf would ordinarily do that. She's the one who took the bullets."

Dunne shook his head. "God bless her. Okay, look." He touched some numbers on his phone. "Sarah? Can you get some information out to the media for Sheriff Bennett? The one who would do it—right, okay, you heard . . . Courthouse square, I'd say." He glanced at his watch. "Say 11:30. Sheriff Bennett wants to make a statement. Okay?"

Dunne turned back to Bennett.

"Make a statement, take a few questions. Throw Peach under the bus for the time being. I'll coach you. You'll say just enough to mislead them without actually saying anything untrue."

"Why do we need to throw Peach under the bus?"

"So the media narrative is that he's escaping from the law. Meanwhile, to the cartels, who do that kind of thing all the time, it looks like Cottonmouth has disappeared the whole family. Either way, it gives us a chance to disseminate some useful misinformation and get these folks out of range. We don't know what kind of fail-safe measures Cottonmouth put in place if Peach and his family escaped today."

Bennett thought about it. *Out of range.* New names, new identities—it was too radical for his tastes. And maybe unnecessary. But Dunne was right. Who knew what else Cottonmouth might have planned? He thought about what Peach had gone through over the past week—discovering his mother dead, getting shot at, finding out his parents were terrorists, all of it. He thought about the traumatized boy, about the threat to the girl Rose, about Nora O'Hearn. His mind came to rest on Teresa, whose placid depths, even when she was most disturbed, had shown him things about himself he had not known, such as how much he needed a woman.

"What can I do?" Forrest said weakly.

Subtly, Aengus Dunne sighed and raised his eyes to Bennett.

"Thank God," he said quietly. "Mr. Forrest!" He stood and approached the bed, extending his hand. "I'm U.S. Marshal Aengus Dunne."

DIASPORA

Part VIII

Little soul, little perpetually undressed one,
do now as I bid you, climb
the shelf-like branches of the spruce tree;
wait at the top, attentive, like
a sentry or look-out. He will be home soon;
it behooves you to be
generous. You have not been completely
perfect either; with your troublesome body
you have done things you shouldn't
discuss in poems.

Louise Glück, "Penelope's Song"

Buford

Monday, June 30, 2014

The sun was low in the west, flashing between hardwoods and casting long shadows across the road. That meant they were going north. As they came around a curve, the woods ended and there was a field with black cows, a hazy mountain in the distance, and then another grove and the roadside fell away—a long valley bordered with mountains. Somewhere in the Blue Ridge? Or already in the Great Smoky Mountains? Tennessee, maybe, or North Carolina.

He must have slept all afternoon.

His father was watching him from the other side of the back seat. Buford couldn't get used to the ponytail being gone, the new short haircut. His father leaned forward to speak to the big men in the front seat.

"What about getting us in touch with my wife and daughter?"

"No sir. Not today," the driver said. "Probably not tomorrow."

"Seriously?"

"You need to understand something, Mr. Peach," said the black man, the one not driving, turning his head to speak over the seat. "No cell phones, no radios, you hear what I'm saying? Nothing any of these people could trace. I'm telling you, this man after you seem like he got more money than God Almighty, and he can whip our ass up and down the country with technology."

"You want to watch your language in front of my son?"

"Sorry. We just need you off the grid, you feel me?"

"You don't even have cell phones?"

"No sir. And that's why we're driving this old piece of shit. Sorry," said the driver. "No computer components."

"I guess the next step is to go Amish. Get a buggy and a pair of mules."

"Yes sir."

They drove in silence for a minute or so. Buford played with the window crank handle.

"You got any better ideas, sir, we're happy to hear them," the driver said. "You're the one they're shooting at."

In a few miles, the road started climbing into the mountains. At the top of a long northward curve was a scenic overlook on the right. The driver put on his blinker and turned in. There was one other car, an unwashed blue Chevrolet with rust around the wheel wells that must have been built when his father was little. One of its back lights had masking tape over it. Resting her behind against the front bumper was a middle-aged woman in a baggy orange Tennessee Vols sweatshirt and skinny jeans. She had a cigarette dangling from her right hand as she stared out at the view. She took a long drag, intense, as though she had to get the smoke through an English pea that was stuck in the filter. When they parked in the spot next to her, she turned to look at them with listless indifference. Smoke trailed from her mouth and nose.

"Son, you get out here," the driver said to Buford over his shoulder.

"You're kidding!" his father exclaimed. "You're splitting us up?"

"Just for a couple of hours."

"Dad," Buford said, panicked.

"Come on, guys," said his father.

"Sir!" said the other man, turning all the way around this time. "What we're doing takes a lot of coordination and manpower. The least you can do is cooperate. You'll be back together by twenty-three hundred hours."

"You want *me* to go with *her*?" Buford objected.

"She's your next ride," said the driver. "She's one of ours. I can't tell you who she is because that's part of your protection."

"Part of our protection," his father said scornfully after a moment. "Right."

The woman lazily scratched her neck and made a *hey-there* face and waved the hand with the cigarette at Buford. Sitting on the passenger's side of the Chevrolet was a short man in a NASCAR baseball cap and an undershirt. He got out and stretched his arms up over his head so the cloth rode up over his hairy stomach as far as his belly button. Then he shook himself, spat tobacco juice on the asphalt, and opened Buford's door.

"Let's go, bubba."

Buford stared up at him.

"Go on, son," the driver said.

Buford still hesitated.

"I guess they're helping us," said his father, and Buford heard his resignation and fear. "I'll see you in a few hours."

When he glanced at the woman, she met his gaze with a quick flash of intelligence and winked, and then he was suddenly not afraid. He got into the car. The back seat was dusty-smelling and had rips in the fabric with rubbery yellow stuff spilling out. He waved goodbye to his father, and the woman backed up and drove out onto the highway. She asked him how old he was and he told her eleven. The man did not try to make conversation with him but just stared out the windshield, occasionally lifting a cup and spitting into it. The sweetish smell of his tobacco filled the car.

After half an hour or so, when it was almost completely dark, they came out of the woods to the edge of a town—cheap prefab metal buildings, empty asphalt parking lots, signs for a Pentecostal Holiness Church, a Dairy Queen, a physical therapy clinic.

"You hungry, sugar?" the woman said over her shoulder.

"Yes ma'am," Buford said.

She pulled up at a place that advertised breakfast all day. He found the bathroom, and when he came back out, the woman was waiting for him. The booths had high backs and splitting red vinyl seats, and the menus were laminated sheets stuck between the ketchup bottle and the sugar shaker. Buford sat on the inside of the bench and the man slid in after him. The woman sat across from them and handed Buford a menu. She told him to get whatever he wanted.

"Yes ma'am."

"Calls me *ma'am*. Ain't that about the sweetest thing you ever heard?" she asked the man, who shrugged stoically and dug a thumb into an itch between his lip and nose.

"Sugarplum," the woman said, leaning over toward Buford, "you call me Pam, okay?" and the intelligence in her eyes burned a message into his.

"Yes ma'am," he said, involuntarily starting to smile.

The waitress was a fat, red-faced woman who walked with a hitch and wore an expression of long-suffering patience.

"How y'all doing?" she wheezed, putting the tips of her fingers on the table as though it had been an effort to get there.

"We gon be all right," Pam said, "once we all git where we're sposed to be going."

"I'm hoping for the good place myself," said the waitress. "Praise Jesus."

"Amen," said Pam. "What you want, sugar?" she said to Buford.

"Could I get me a stack of pancakes?" Buford said.

Pam shifted in her seat.

"Bacon on the side be all right?" said the waitress, noticing nothing.

"Yes'm."

"How 'bout you?" She looked at the man.

"Hash with eggs on it."

"You want to stay on the sunny side of life, sweetheart?"

"Over easy."

She nodded and looked at Pam.

"Me? I done ate," Pam explained. "But if you was to bring me some coffee, I bet you I could drink it."

"It don't keep you up, darlin'?"

"Well I hope it does. We need to get all the way to Roanoke."

"Tonight?"

"Else he's gone miss his mama's latest wedding."

The waitress looked at Buford sympathetically and started to say something, but then she sighed and pressed her lips together and shook her head. She squeezed the short man's shoulder as she limped away.

Forrest

June 30, 2014

Forrest's iPhone vibrated angrily. **Gal Co Sher**.

"Turn on CNN," Bennett said when he answered it.

The phone went dead.

Marisa and the girls were crowded into the hospital room where he had been moved after being released from the ICU. He found the remote on the side table and clicked it at the TV. There on CNN was a shot of a younger Forrest on a screen behind the speaking news anchor.

"—identified as Braxton Forrest, owner of a chain of papers including the *Gallatin Tribune* where Peach is the editor."

"A chain of papers," Forrest snorted.

"Police think that Graves, a fugitive since a 1970s bombing in Chicago [photograph of the bombed school, then the standard pictures of Alison Graves and Harris Akers], committed suicide when she was trapped in the hideout where she had been the mastermind of a drug operation recently uncovered in Gallatin County. Sheriff Hudson Bennett hinted that her son Walter Peach [photo from behind of a man—not Peach—at a newspaper desk] used his newspaper to divert attention from convicted war criminal Dexter Watkins [Dexter Watkins in uniform] while Watkins was using Peach's land to grow marijuana.

"Peach repeatedly blamed Mexican cartels"—the newscaster raised a thick, painted eyebrow as the Tribune's big headline CARTELS IN GALLATIN? filled the screen behind her—"for a locally based marijuana business. Meanwhile, for the past six months, Peach's newspaper has also been running classified ads in Spanish for 'marimba workers,' a coded appeal, according to DEA officials, to immigrants led to expect large profits from the marijuana trade. State police and FBI officials are investigating the death of Dexter Watkins and the shootings yesterday at the funeral of Graves. Authorities say that Walter Peach and his family [blurred photograph], who disappeared from their lavish home in Gallatin [picture of Stonewall Hill], are now being sought for collusion in the murders of several Mexican immigrants who—"

Forrest turned it off, smiling.

"What are you smiling about?" Marisa cried, her hands in her hair. "They have just vilified Walter. It's just—Teresa must be devastated . . . "

"No," Forrest said. "It's perfect. You'll see."

He picked up the iPhone and called Bennett.

"What'd you think?" Bennett answered.

"Couldn't be better," Forrest said.

"I had some help. What I'd guess," Bennett said, "is the *Gallatin Tribune* breaks the story about CNN's coverage."

"Huge headline," Forrest said.

Bennett

June 30, 2014

Lydia Downs shook her head in astonishment. She sat across from Bennett at the Left Bank, her bare legs crossed and angled toward the window. He was telling her about the press conference and the interview with CNN. Bennett could not remember ever being alone with such a beautiful woman, much less a beautiful woman who touched his hand when she said things and brought wit and playfulness out of him.

And he had just happened to meet her. He came in to get something to eat, and Mary Rose Ryburn got a scheming look on her face as soon as she saw him. She steered him across the dining room to Lydia, who was sitting alone and gazing out the front window, lightly tapping her wine glass with a fingernail. He would keep replaying the scene for a long time, he suspected. *Miss Downs*, Mary Rose said. Lydia had looked up at them pleasantly. *This is Sheriff Hudson Bennett. He's been in the middle of things, and he can help you understand what's going on better than anybody else. Hudson, this is Lydia Downs, Walter Peach's stepsister. She just got in this morning in time for the little service—and you know, now the whole Peach family is gone, so.* And then she had left them alone, gazing at each other across the table with interest and surprise. *May I join you?* Bennett had said.

Bennett had been at the hospital after the attempted murder of Nora O' Hearn, so he had missed meeting Lydia at the cemetery when the excitement broke out and the others were all whisked away. How had she known about the service? *Some Englishman called me in Yuma.*

Yuma?

Arizona. I flew into Atlanta yesterday and didn't get to bed until four this morning. And at six the funeral home called to give me the details.

Lydia told him that she had not seen Peach since 1997, two years after her stepmother disappeared. At the time, Lydia knew nothing about Peach except that he was a poet whose books her mother had around the house. And when she'd met him, it had nothing to do with her mother. *How did you meet him?* She had looked at him in the eyes, interested in his interest. *I took his poetry class.* He suspected there was more.

"So you deliberately misled them?" she asked, leaving her hand lightly on his.

"Not exactly. I acted official and speculated. A country sheriff not used to the spotlight. I had a little coaching."

"And they made this whole narrative about Walter out of it? You're not worried about losing your job?"

"Not much."

"Do you trust the people who took the Peach family? In Yuma half the police are on the payrolls of the cartels, they say."

"I trust Aengus Dunne. I didn't know the ones who took them. I shouldn't be telling you any of this."

"It's okay," she said. He believed her.

"Did you notice the boy?" Bennett asked.

There was a crash of shattering glass across the dining room.

"I'm so sorry!" Mary Rose said to the room. "I should look where I'm going." She had run into the busboy clearing tables.

Trying to eavesdrop, Bennett thought.

Lydia looked back at him. Her thumb rested between his knuckles.

"You were asking about a boy. Yes, I saw a boy. Walter's son, right?" she said. "You know they had an older son who died."

"I didn't know that," Bennett said.

"How old is this one?" she asked.

"I want to say eleven."

"He has a look to him," she said. "Like he's listening to something nobody else can hear. But not like he's distracted or elsewhere, you know?"

He nodded. "Interesting little guy."

"So, they're just—you know—*gone*?" she asked. She fitted her other fingers between his. Her eyes were gray-blue with a rim of purple. Good Lord. He was glad there was no reason to stand up just at that moment.

"The whole family," he said. "New names. No more Walter Peach. Or Rose or Teresa or Buford. They have no idea where they're going. Maybe they show up in a suburb in Connecticut or somewhere in Hawaii."

"So the U.S. Marshals just make up a new family?"

He raised his eyebrows and shrugged. "They're willing to do it because of the man Walter saw, the one who's been trying to kill them. Highly educated. The Mexicans call him the Moccasin. Why he's after Walter doesn't make much sense to me."

She pushed aside her plate, and he realized he had eaten his sandwich, too.

She put both her hands on his. "And you've been right in the thick of it. Protecting everybody."

"Just doing my job."

"Just doing my job, ma'am," she said with mild mockery. "Walter told me—this was last week—that you were the one who found my stepmother."

"The boy saw her first—"

He broke off, not wanting to describe it to her.

"It must have been awful. I could never tell Walter this, but I loved her very much. Nobody knew her as well as I did. When she married my dad, she pulled me out of public school and taught me herself, even though it meant less time with her own art. She always said that schools trained children not to see. She hated schools—which I guess is why she did what she did."

Bennett nodded. "I looked it up."

"Two dead," she said. "One was the janitor, the other a young teacher going on leave to have a baby. Her older son was so badly burned in the fire they didn't know if he would live."

"Anybody know what happened to him?"

"Not that I've heard. I know that Alison tried to find out. You know, from the time I was eight years old, I spent my childhood in the presence of this brilliant, beautiful, melancholy woman, and never suspected a thing. I didn't know her at all." She sighed and gazed at Bennett. "She took me in after my real mother died. She gave me confidence in my own perception. I loved her very much. But all that time, I didn't know who she was."

"It must be hard to find out," Bennett said.

"Harder for Walter, I think. She was a real person and a lie at the same time. I guess everybody's like that, really." She looked down at their hands and then back up at Bennett. "Is your mother still living?"

"She is."

"You're lucky to have her."

"You ain't getting me to talk about my mama."

She laughed out loud, and the waitress, a sweet-faced black girl Bennett didn't recognize, came by and refilled their water glasses. She set the check next to Bennett's hand.

"Let me get this," said Lydia, reaching for it, but Bennett captured the bill.

"My pleasure," he said, meaning it, meeting her eyes. She smiled at him with such genuineness that it felt like he didn't have to go to work for a month.

"How in the world did the media find out about her to start with?"

"My suspicion is Cottonmouth. The one trying to kill Walter," he said.

She glanced at the time on her smartphone and gathered her things—her purse, her rental car keys—and stood up. The fantasy of his charm vanished. He wondered what he had said to offend her. But then, her keys dangling, she leaned across the table toward him.

"I want to stay here a few more days, and I've got to go make some

457

calls to my clients. I want to go out to that house where you found her if you'll take me. But first I want to tell you the whole story. Can we start over breakfast tomorrow?"

"Yes ma'am."

"Maybe at your place? I'll cook."

He surveyed it in his imagination room by room and quailed from the prospect of her seeing it.

"It needs a little cleaning up."

"Well then I'll take you somewhere."

Good Lord, her eyes.

"Okay. But please don't tell my mama."

Walter

The Country Kitchen was popular with the locals, who greeted each other with the irony and forbearance of long acquaintance. Directly across from Peach in the booth sat the driver—thirties, medium height, with a receding crew cut and a bodybuilder's vanity. His upper arms bulged from the blue t-shirt as he forked the grilled chicken from his Caesar salad and speared the dark greens. He had an odd way of tightening his pectoral muscles so they would hop in his shirt.

"Man, that's just weird," said the other one. "I mean, you imagine a woman doing that?"

A head taller than the driver, he wore his hair in a tight fade with razored angles around his forehead and a line incised into one side. As if he were expecting someone to steal his food, he kept one hand at the side of his plate, guarding a chicken-fried steak, green beans, fried okra, and a massive baked potato that he had loaded with sour cream and shredded cheddar cheese.

The driver did it again and smiled.

"Unh-unh, man! It looks like a cow trying to flinch off a fly."

"Keeping myself loose. Part of my body awareness."

"The hell. You on a diet, too? You come to a place like this and order a salad?"

"You stayed away from carbs," the driver said, pointing his fork at the other's plate, "you wouldn't have them love handles."

"Girls got to hang on somehow. It's a wild ride. Like Goliath at Six Flags."

"Shit."

Goliath and Mr. Pecs. Walter smiled down at his own food. Fried catfish with hushpuppies, French fries, rolls, and coleslaw. Talk about carbs. He teased the tines of his fork along the dividing line of a fish's backbone and pushed the white meat off with the golden breading intact. He speared a piece and put it in his mouth.

"How do I know you guys aren't agents of the cartel?" he asked.

The men looked at each other and then back at Peach.

"Feeding you catfish and you still don't trust us?" said Goliath.

"Look, Mr. Peach, your family is fine," said Mr. Pecs. "You know you're on the government tab, right? Protecting you is what they call a quid pro quo. Right now, we're taking care of you so down the line you help us nail this guy."

"So, you work for the U.S. Marshals? The FBI?"

"Let's finish up. We'll take you to the motel."

"Is that where my son is?"

"Check your watch, sir," said Mr. Pecs. It was a little after nine. "Twenty-three hundred hours. Like I said."

"You gon eat all them hushpuppies?" asked Goliath, pointing to Peach's plate.

The Wild Turkey Motel was a rustic one-story place with a vintage 1950s sign. They pulled into the lot and passed the office and the row of identical doors and windows to park in front of room 119. A wizened couple sat in folding web chairs a few doors down, both of them smoking. A compromised bottle of Jack Daniels and an overused ashtray sat on the plastic table between them. Mr. Pecs nodded at them and fished a key from his pocket and opened the door. He must have already had the key when they left the cemetery in Gallatin many hours and hundreds of miles ago.

Peach got out of the back seat and stretched.

"Nice night, ain't it?" the old woman said, waving her cigarette at the view behind him.

Peach turned and saw the valley dropping away from the guardrail on the other side of the road. Lights showed from a few distant houses in the far depths, and he caught the gleam of a river. Above the dark mountains at the horizon rose a sliver of crescent moon.

"Yes ma'am," Peach said. A nice night—but where were his wife and daughter? Where was Buford?

"Rain tomorrow," said the man, stubbing out his cigarette and eyeing him. "Y'all traveling far? I see you ain't on no vacation since you ain't got no luggage."

Peach realized he had nothing with him—no toothbrush, no change of clothes, no book, no phone.

"A long way."

"Where you headed?"

"I've got a home in Glory Land," he said, and the woman looked up at him. By now his two keepers had come up behind him.

"Sir," Goliath said to Peach, touching his elbow.

"Y'all have a real good evening," Peach said.

"Planning on it," said the old man. "We on our honeymoon."

"Shut up, Dumont," the old woman said.

"Them's Feds," he heard the old man say sotto voce. "Poor bastard."

The room was empty except for two stacks of clothes on the dresser next to the TV.

"You need anything," Mr. Pecs said, "we'll be next door. For God's sake don't use the telephone."

The digital clock on the table between the double beds said 10:57. He went through the clothes—new jeans, boys' and men's; two sizes of underwear; plain t-shirts; a polo shirt for him and a Braves shirt for Buford; belts, shorts, sneakers in two sizes. In the bathroom were two plastic bags of toiletries. Walter's had a new toothbrush, baking soda toothpaste, unscented antiperspirant, and three disposable razors. Two hairbrushes sat next to the sink. Somebody had thought it all out—probably not Goliath and Mr. Pecs.

Just at 11:00, there was a tap on the door, and when he opened it, Mr. Pecs stood there awkwardly for a moment, and from behind him the woman waved to Buford. "Night." The boy smiled at her and raised his hand to wave as she closed the door behind him. Peach hugged his son, weak with relief.

The boy looked subdued but not scared.

"You okay?" asked Peach.

"Yes sir. She was nice to me."

"What did you eat?"

"Pancakes."

"Well, let's get to bed. They left us clothes and toothbrushes and such."

"I need to go to the bathroom."

When Buford came back, he poked through the clothes and found a pair of gym shorts and a t-shirt to put on. He took off the funeral clothes he had worn all day—the white shirt, the dark slacks—and dropped them in a pile on the floor.

"Why don't you hang those up?" Peach said.

"The lady told me I had to throw them away," he said. Without looking at Peach, he added, "Did they tell you where Mom and Rose are?"

"They said we'd see them in a day or two," Peach said.

Now the boy looked at him.

"We have to trust them," Walter said. "They didn't lie to us today."

"No sir."

"Are you tired? You want to go right to sleep?"

"Let's see what's on TV," Buford said.

Peach sat on the bed closest to the door and Buford sat on the other one. It was a new TV with a complicated remote, but they managed to get past the menu and find an old episode of *The Waltons*. John-Boy was teaching a woman how to read so she wouldn't be embarrassed around her daughter, who had just graduated from college. They watched the show without talking. When it was over, Walter turned off the TV and said they should go to sleep. Buford got under the covers of his bed. Walter got up to use the bathroom and brush his teeth and change into the shorts they had left him. When he came back, the boy watched him.

"Want to say prayers?" Walter said.

"Yes sir."

He sat on the boy's bed and they said the Our Father and Hail Mary and Glory Be and then prayed for Teresa and Rose and the soul of Alison Graves. For the first time in many years, Peach felt a purchase in his own prayer, a small access of real hope. It seemed incongruous in the circumstances, like the lightening of heart he had once felt when he lost control of his car on an icy road.

He pulled down the covers and got into his bed and turned off the lamp, but the curtains over the window let in a band of light from the parking lot that crossed Peach's pillow and bent up the wall. He got back up and adjusted the heavy cloth until it disappeared, adjusted the air conditioner, and got back into bed. An enormous weariness overwhelmed him, and he was just dropping into sleep when Buford spoke in the darkness.

"I've been having this dream."

"Go to sleep, son. You've got to be as tired as I am."

"Yes sir."

When Buford was little, when they had just moved to Stonewall Hill, the boy would wake up in terror from his nightmares and call Teresa—never Walter, always Teresa—and she would get up to comfort him until he went back to sleep.

He missed her now. As he drifted downward, a memory of his own mother came back to him. The bed they shared, the warmth of her body. She was his. So strange a childhood. No shame then but shameful now even to remember. And now she was standing as she stood then in the mornings, stretching her arms high over her heard, her breasts rising, the skin of the underside of one imprinted with the fold of the sheet. She was smiling at him like a bride. But was it Rosemary or was it Teresa whose happy body, moving off now, naked and sleepy and proud, the deer in the hallway parting for her, tentative in the tap of their light hooves on the wood floor, nuzzling their heads into her, sucking at the tips of her fingers

Raïssa

July 1, 2014

Raïssa crunched newspapers underfoot as she got up to go to the bathroom, where she was startled to discover in the mirror that she had on a pink gown with a picture of Justin Bieber on the front. She vaguely remembered accepting it the night before.

Were there three girls?

And then her memory reconnected.

The Bethlehem Baptist Girls' Choir from Valdosta, Georgia.

She and her mother had been separated at a roadside park in Oxford, Alabama, where she had stepped into the church van as instructed. Her mother, with a worried look over her shoulder, had climbed into the front seat of a minivan driven by a middle-aged man in a beige baseball cap. Behind him in the other two rows, as Raïssa saw before the door slid shut, were a bored-looking teenaged girl, two smaller boys, and an indeterminate kicking and squalling thing in an infant seat.

In her van, there were twelve other girls, an a cappella choir. She had listened to hours of practice led by the driver, a cheerful older woman who kept glancing back at the girls in the rearview mirror and opening her mouth in exaggerated ways as they sang. They had stopped to eat at a Denny's in Tupelo, Mississippi, and the girls in her booth were very polite to her and very curious, understanding her to be some kind of traumatized refugee. She had spoken only French and pretended not to understand them very well when they complimented her hair. She had spent the night in a room with three of them.

She remembered accepting the gown from a teary-eyed girl who told her that Justin Bieber was having a terrible year, just terrible, and she was so disappointed in him, and she would understand it if Raïssa didn't want to wear it. By then, she had been so tired she had just curled toward the window on her side of the queen bed while the other girls sang softly, their voices weaving surprisingly lovely harmonies.

In the bathroom mirror, she looked bleary with sleep. Her hair looked huge and turbulent after the standard chin-length cuts of the choir girls. As she washed her hands, she splashed water on her face and toweled it hard.

Why was there newspaper all over the floor?

There was a knock on the door.

"You need to get a move on, sweetheart."

She opened the door, irritated and suddenly shy. The supposed chaperone who had commandeered her the day before, a large florid woman, now wore a Holiday Inn uniform.

"Come on, sugar," the woman said. She was patting something on the desk. "Come over here and pick you out a style."

"A style of what?"

"You got to cut that hair, baby. It's like wearing a neon sign."

"You are NOT going to cut my hair!" she cried, her hands rising to protect it.

"Oh, hell yes I am, sweetheart, so get over here and sit your sassy butt down."

"You can't talk to me like that!"

The woman puckered her mouth and tilted her head, looking Raïssa up and down. Next to a stocky phone or radio on the desk was a pair of scissors and some haircut clippers a mother might use on her small sons.

"What I'm thinking is this one here." She held up a magazine and pointed to a picture of a girl with her hair cut short on one side and left long on the other. Raïssa backed away from her, but the woman was undeterred. "I know you don't want to cut that beautiful hair, darling. But those men know all about you, now don't they? They've got lots of pictures, I hear. So, we need to change you into somebody else."

Raïssa took in this information with growing horror.

"I got you some ripped jeans ought to fit. Here's a sleeveless shirt and how about this tattoo?" She pointed to an elaborate rose on a girl's shoulder in the magazine.

"You are *NOT* putting a tattoo on my body. That's hideous!"

"Well, okay, we'll just do a butterfly or something. And don't worry, princess," she said sarcastically, "it's temporary, not like mine." She showed Raïssa the rose on the side of her neck. "Maybe on your shoulder or maybe right here where it would kind of peek out of your shirt, like it was more of it, you know? Kind of pretty."

"Don't touch me!"

"Sit down, honey."

"I will not!"

The woman picked up the thing on the desk and said something into it. Two other women in poorly fitting Holiday Inn uniforms came into the room, one of them small and Asian and serious, the other tall and black.

"I am not your prisoner!" Rose protested.

But she was. They held her down and cut her hair and then took her into the bathroom and dyed the remnant black as she struggled and sobbed. She intended to prosecute them all. They held her still and applied a temporary blue butterfly tattoo to her right shoulder blade.

They made her put on jeans ripped at the knees and a worn tank top with a motorcycle on it, clothes she would never have worn in her life. And black cowboy boots that hurt her feet. When she saw herself in the mirror over the dresser, she looked like some kind of trashy biker woman.

"Whoa, honey," said the black cop, and even the Asian with the grip of steel looked her over with admiration. The white woman spoke into her radio. There was a knock at the door.

When they opened it, a big man in a black leather jacket and jeans with leather chaps over them stood there with two helmets dangling by their straps from his left hand. He looked impressed.

"Whoa. Want some breakfast, girlfriend?" he said, taking off his sunglasses.

Teresa

July 5, 2014

Her supposed husband of the day drove them across the Mississippi at Cape Girardeau and drove half an hour north to a state park, where they now stood at the railing of a viewing platform high on the western side of the swollen river. He solemnly, to her secret amusement, called himself Apollo Bowman.

He looked at his watch.

"They should be here soon."

She did not answer. Their alleged children, just three of them today, a mixed-race set this time, were racing each other up and down the walkway to the observation deck. They had appeared that morning in the lobby of the motel in Clarksville, Tennessee, where her husband of yesterday had left her the night before. Mr. Bowman had knocked on her door at 9:00 a.m. to introduce himself and their children.

Had she slept at all? She had spent the night worrying about where Walter and her real children were. Would these people—whoever they were, whoever was in charge—actually bring them all back together? Suppose she never saw her family again?

She excused herself and walked away from Bowman to the left side of the platform and leaned on the rail and looked upriver. Bowman had told her that St. Louis was a hundred and twelve miles north. *St. Louis.* A Catholic name, like so many in America. She said a prayer for her family. Last night, alone, in their immense absence, in her unknowing, she had experienced for the first time in many years the whole reality of loss. She had turned on the TV and stared at it, but the chatty vapidity and faux gravity irritated her.

She turned it back off. Last night and now, again, she found herself in the undertow of memory.

Little Walter's funeral. The priest's censer swinging its cloud of incense out over the tiny coffin. Her thesis on Jean-Luc Marion had died in the pew. How could this be a gift?

At least she was better now in the daylight. The great river moved beneath her, swift with flood, massive, spotted with flotsam. T.S. Eliot's "great brown god," Huckleberry Finn's river. She tried to stave off the thought.

Lord Jesus Christ, son of God, have mercy on me a sinner.

But it was too strong. It came back again. Again, she sat paralyzed in the house in Athens full of staring misery, bereft of mind, stripped of

467

feeling, her soul wandering some cold and featureless underworld. Again she watched Rose play with her dolls and the thought came into her mind: *Kill her.* Go in the kitchen and get a knife and come back and kill her. Leave her body for Walter to find when he comes home. Make him feel again what it means to have a dead child. One for you and one for me. Because he had killed her son. He had killed *her.* And for what? For what? For what?

For Lydia Downs.

Her hatred had been so full and black that when Walter came in she could taste the mud of the River Styx thick on her tongue, clogging her throat with loathing. She had watched him the way she watched Rose. *Kill him.* Get an ax from the garage and come up behind him and split his head. This man she loved who betrayed her. This man she had loved without reserve and who *gave her away*—as though she meant nothing. Gave away *everything about her*—and for what? For some trollop, some whore of a student, starry-eyed, as stupid as Nora O'Hearn.

No, not stupid. Otherwise, she would never have attracted him.

Not just some student. Lydia Downs.

Not stupid at all. No.

She had seen Lydia Downs on Monday. The very day her family had scattered in all directions.

Lord Jesus Christ, son of God, have mercy on me, a sinner.

Not stupid but brilliant and beautiful. Walter's stepsister. He said he had not known, could not have known until the very day, the very hour, when a black talon of black *lex talionis* curved up black out of Hell, dangling the necklace and gave him back his murderous whore of a mother through his whore of a stepsister.

Lord Jesus Christ, son of God, have mercy on me, a sinner.

And in that same hour he came home and ran over his son.

Lord Jesus Christ, son of God, have mercy on me, a sinner.

The image of his little body under the tire. His little body in the coffin.

In those days after the funeral she knew nothing. She asked over and over, asked herself, asked him, out of what impulse Walter had abandoned her to such meaninglessness and loss? She longed for him; she hated him with her whole soul; she believed him when he said how sorry he was; she believed nothing he said; she sorrowed for him; she wanted him in Hell. With satisfaction she watched his confidence fail. With despair she saw him fall into despair. She watched with mockery and followed with dark interest the classes missed, the papers ungraded, the phone calls and knocks on the door unheeded. She felt for him when she could not feel for herself.

Lord Jesus Christ, son of God, have mercy on me, a sinner.

It was years later when she conceived again. 2003, the year her mother died. And even by then she had not forgiven him. She remembered hoping the baby inside her would die. She bumped hard into corners as if by accident; she ran the bath too hot; she prayed to whatever demons listen to such prayers that the relentless little heart beating inside her womb would feel her utter rejection and simply stop beating and the alien thing would fall out of her body, the image of her own aborted love dried up and curled on itself and blind and dead.

Whatever was in her was Walter's and she wanted nothing of Walter. And the more she hated him the more she longed for who he had been.

How had they ever gotten through it? How had they stayed together? How had they survived at all?

The baby would not die. The baby made her eat and sleep. He pressed her forcefully all the way to term.

When she went into labor, she did not want Walter in the room as she had wanted him there for little Walter and Rose. No, she wanted to bear the whole pain alone. She was so full of malice, so bitter to the nurses who helped her, that they stopped speaking except to say what was absolutely necessary. She cursed God loudly, blasphemed his gifts with every wave of pain, every push, until the nurses feared to come close enough to help and the doctor himself murmured his horrified rebuke. But then as she pushed for the last time and screamed and they caught the baby from her womb, she heard the gasp and the squalling and something gave way in her heart.

A great sob, a boundless shame.

God forgive me! Oh God forgive me!

They had stared at her, uncertain how to act.

A boy, they said.

Ten on the Apgar she heard from nearby.

And after a moment, a black nurse with great kind eyes lifted the baby to her tentatively, protectively.

You want to hold him, honey?

Weeping, she nodded, and the woman had put the baby in her arms.

The boy looked at her. She had told no one this, certainly not Walter, but she had seen the baby—before a name, beyond any name—look her in the eyes and she had seen his eyes unmistakably come to focus. It was a look full of intelligence and care, profound care, as though his first and only and utmost concern was for her, and she felt her soul kick and stutter and sting back to life. She gave a long, anguished wail.

Great God Almighty, said one of the nurses. Another one crossed herself.

And then in the next instant the boy was a mere infant, utterly helpless and in her care, his eyes unfocused. She sobbed as she turned him and set his mouth to her swollen nipple and he clamped on as though he had been waiting these nine months just to get at her.

"Ma'am! Ma'am!"

Startled, she came to herself, and the river sweeping below her seemed to take away her footing. She grabbed the rail, dizzy. She watched a metal roof settle in the water under her, an uprooted tree rolling slowly over against it. She glanced at Bowman.

"I believe this must be one of yours," he said.

She looked down the walkway and saw a big biker approaching, followed by a slutty tattooed girl in cowboy boots and a tight tank top.

"That's not Walter," she said.

But the girl stopped, and with a strange yawing of her heart, Teresa saw recognition break across the girl's face, and then the hot rush of it in herself.

"Oh my God!" she cried. Rose's beautiful hair was all gone.

"No big scenes!" Bowman said sharply, looking away downriver. "Stop looking at her."

He quietly took Teresa's arm and steered her back toward the walkway. "Five minutes," he said, apparently to Teresa, as they passed the biker and the girl. "RV in number 14."

Summoning their faux children, he steered her up the walkway toward the minivan parked in the cul-de-sac. The children wanted to touch the big red Harley Davidson leaning on its kickstand next to them, but he warned them off. He drove them back out a winding road, turned left, and then wound back toward the river through the hilly terrain, turned left again, and followed the road around to where it split. To the left was camping. To the right was a railroad track and, beyond it, a parking lot and a view of the Mississippi.

Mr. Bowman eased along in the minivan. An Airstream trailer sat in the camping space at Number 14, hooked up to the water and electricity. Beside it was a big white SUV. As they passed, the door of the trailer opened, and Buford there wearing a green and gold jersey.

"That's my—"

"Wait!" Bowman said sharply as he drove on.

The camping area was not big, and looking back, she could see the trailer through the trees. She saw the motorcycle ease up to it. The man said something over his shoulder, and Rose got off and went up to the door and went inside without knocking. The motorcycle rumbled around the loop and passed the minivan without acknowledging its presence.

After a moment, Apollo Bowman turned back the other way and stopped at 14. His eyes met hers, and he bowed his head.

"Godspeed," he said.

Agnes of the Child Jesus

The first morning after taking her from the hospital, the women of the U.S. Marshals in charge of Nora cut her hair as short as a boy's in an apartment off I-85 near Greenville, South Carolina, where she had spent the night. The swelling from the mosquito bites had begun to subside, but the bruises from the ropes on her chest and neck had darkened. She looked hideous to herself in the mirror. When they approached her with duct tape, she panicked, but they talked her through it, flattening her breasts, careful to use lotions and pad the contusions, but she trembled now reliving the terror of it a week later. They dressed her in loose boys' clothes. For several days, they drove, apparently at random, through small towns in North and South Carolina. One day they drove over to Myrtle Beach, where they walked out on a fishing pier. *My God, can't you at least try to walk like a boy?*

This morning, they fed her breakfast at a Waffle House in Anderson, South Carolina, where she got in a blue Suburban with three sorority girls from Wofford headed to Atlanta.

She was supposed to be Alfred, the effeminate nephew of their sorority mother. The agent who drove pretended to be Alfred's other, less dignified aunt. All the way to Atlanta, Aunt May kept berating Alfred for taking hormones to turn himself into a girl. *Transgender, my sweet ass—pardon my French, girls. You never would have got such a dumbass, bizarro notion if it wasn't so much garbage out there on the internet. Even the kindergartens acting like the Lord God Almighty might have screwed up your assignment—I mean, sweet Jesus, Alfred, what you need is a stint in boot camp. Or some kind of real job where you don't have time to sit around wishing you could get rid of your little teeny weenie. Why can't you just be* gay—*I mean seriously, there are* real *girls. Don't you girls think so? Last time you looked? What do you think of this little fruitcake pretending he can actually turn himself into a girl? I mean, talk about* ridiculous.

I know I'm really a girl, Nora would murmur morosely. Or *I don't care what you say, I AM a girl* or *Mama used to let me wear a dress because she knew I was really a girl.* At first the sorority sisters were stiff, but by the time they got to Lawrenceville, where one of the girls was getting dropped off, she could feel their sympathies beginning to shift. *Bye, Alfred,* the petite brunette said sweetly, leaning back in through the door and squeezing Nora's hand. *I think you're gonna be real pretty. Remember Tri Delta when you get to college, okay?*

They cut across on I-285 north of Atlanta, dropped off the other two girls in Marietta, and headed north on I-75 to Red Top Mountain State Park. An outdoorsy woman named Patti Hendricks welcomed her to a big

473

RV situated at a nice spot overlooking Allatoona Lake. Patti had two boys, maybe seven and five, who came skidding across the pine needles to meet Alfred, glad to have an older boy around. Aunt May stayed, pretending now to be Patti's relative—or maybe not pretending—while Patti grilled some hamburgers, and then after they cleaned up and got the boys parked in front of a TV, the other women took Nora into bedroom she would share with Patti and helped pry the tape off her breasts. She got a shower and, afterwards, found a new pair of jeans and a new bra and a tank top and a pair of flip-flops. When she came out into the common room, the boys gaped like Buckwheat and Alfalfa.

Aunt May gave her a hug.

"Alfred," she said, "I was dead wrong. You might make it as a girl after all. And listen," she whispered, "we've got your back, sweetheart. I'll be close by just in case."

Just in case El Mocasín found her.

That night he did find her. He flowed soundlessly out of the lake and under the RV and into an opening in the floor under her room. He glided up the ladder of the bunk bed and between her legs and lay heavily upon her. *My darling*, he said, opening his white mouth. She smelled the rotten fruit and woke up screaming.

Something hit the ceiling with a bang and a second later the light came on. Patti was standing in the doorway, pistol held in both hands at her side. On top of Nora, wailing and holding his head, was five-year-old Blaine, his face distorted in terror.

"I'm so sorry!" she told him, hugging him to her. "It's okay, it's okay."

Earlier, he had snuggled against her while they watched three episodes of a Disney show called *The Suite Life of Zack and Cody* on DVD. He wanted to sleep with her, but Patti had told him Nora needed her rest. By now, Aunt May was behind Patti, also with a pistol, and Danny had come in rubbing his eyes, agog at the weapons.

"I had a nightmare," Nora said, hugging the trembling Blaine, who dug his face into her neck. She could smell the pee in his pajamas.

"We'll get that bastard," Aunt May said grimly.

The next night a new agent, a man named Jim, who pretended to be her father, left her in a dormitory at the University of the South in Sewanee, Tennessee, where she was supposed to be a prospective student. He gave her a prepaid phone with his number on it and said he would be nearby. She shared the room with Alice Huan, a girl from California who kept fingering an imaginary violin as she listened to her Bose headset with her eyes closed. When she opened them and saw Nora watching her, she said *You want to listen? It's Anne-Sophie Mutter performing Bach's Partita no. 2 in D minor.* She was reverent. *I love Anne-Sophie Mutter.*

Nora demurred, suddenly missing her books. When they turned off the lights and she closed her eyes, she could still hear the violin from Alice's headset, but after a moment it was playing in the vast dining hall where she was supposed to meet Bill Sharpe. When she went down the cafeteria line with her tray, the person at the counter turned around wearing a Voldemort mask. From the pan under the glass, he dipped onto her plate a slurry of whole apples, wormy and fermenting, collapsed on themselves like toothless cheeks. Yellow teeth grew from the cores. The smell filled her nostrils. She backed away in terror and bumped into the soft body of Aunt May, who was also Miss Emma. *Come on, sweetheart.* She took Nora back to a safe room. *I'll get you something special,* she said. When she came back in, she was peeling the foil from a chocolate truffle. *This will make you a real girl, Alfred,* but it was El Mocasín's voice.

Again, she woke up screaming. The terrified Alice summoned the resident assistant, who recommended a counseling center in town. Jim came within minutes when she called him. They drove through the short remainder of the night, and he left her early the next morning at the service entrance of the Dominican convent in Nashville, where she went in to be welcomed by two kind women in habits. She slept for most of the day.

They brought her to their common meal that evening. They were solicitous of her, but she dreamed of him again that night, waking the novices around her. They consoled her until she forgot the dream and the terror of the dream. She rose with them at 5:00 a.m. and spent the day dressed in a white habit and sat quietly listening to the community's prayer. She helped a little with their work. That night she dreamed that her boyfriend Mark from college was on top of her, and she was trying to get him to stop because they were in church—*someone was coming*—but he did not care, he forced her down violently. She pushed him away to look in his face, but he had no face, and El Mocasín tore her apart like a wet sack.

The novices consoled her again, but their confidence was fading. On the third night, after talking to the prioress and letting herself be called Agnes, after spending hours in the chapel trying to pray and feeling the warmth and love of the sisters around her, she did not dream of him. The next morning, she went to confession and talked about what had happened to her with El Mocasín and how she had felt she deserved it and how soiled she had felt afterward. The absolution eased her heart a little. At Mass that day, she went up with the nuns to receive communion. When it was her turn in line, the priest held up the host, and she began to tremble violently. The priest stared at her, then glanced around for help; the women behind her came up to ask what was wrong.

She closed her eyes and backed up a step.

"I'm okay," she said. She steeled herself and stepped forward. She opened her mouth and received the host lightly on her tongue and made her way back to the pew.

She sat quietly among the nuns in the sound of the other women breathing, the sound of pages being turned. The thought of Walter came to her, her aunt struggling with the ropes and holding up her weight, the wild look of Bill Sharpe when he stopped the boy in the hallway from shooting her. She wept a little, and then she prayed. After Mass, the other women looked at her with surprise, with real gratitude, and that day, she asked to stay, at least for a time.

Could she just stay?

She could, but she could not tell anyone where she was yet, perhaps for a long time. Her own parents might think she was dead. Her boyfriend could not know. She thought about Bill Sharpe. Would he wait for her? She thought he would, but he would be hurt so deeply. If only she could get a message to him somehow.

But if she could not, was she willing to be there under those circumstances?

It troubled her at first, but then she found herself willing to wait. A new peace overshadowed her. She set about the daily work they gave her.

Magdalena Guizac

In July, they learned to use their new names. She was not Rose and certainly not Raïssa, but Magdalena. Buford was Jacob, her father was Karl, her mother was Anna. Their last name was Guizac. They were from Green Bay, Wisconsin.

When he received his new driver's license and saw the name, her father looked at her mother and said, "That's got to be Braxton."

"What do you mean?"

"The name. It's from a story called 'The Displaced Person.'"

They laughed and kept laughing intermittently for five minutes. Magdalena thought they were unseemly, the way they flirted with each other.

They visited Green Bay just in case anybody asked them about it. They stayed in campgrounds on Lake Michigan and then later, driving as far north as Duluth, they went east and spent several nights in the Apostle Islands on Lake Superior. From then on, tending southward and westward, they went through Nebraska, where they visited Willa Cather's home in Red Cloud. They moved down into the Texas panhandle and over into New Mexico and Arizona, staying in random places whenever they got tired of driving.

They had their only real scare the day they left Tucson. They were having lunch at a rest stop picnic table, and a man on a motorcycle stared openly at Raïssa—Magdalena—when she walked back from the bathroom. He took in the four of them, but especially her.

"That man keeps staring at me," she said.

"You're his type," said Buford.

Not Buford. Jacob.

"Shut up," she said. Her hair had begun to grow out, at least enough to show red roots, and the tattoo had finally disappeared after a month of scrubbing. She liked the boots, though, and she happened to have on the ripped jeans that day.

Her father watched the man for a moment and then got up and approached him. The man took a cell phone from his pocket as though he were answering a call, turning his back. Her mother was watchfully putting condiments and cold cuts back into the ice chest.

"Don't go to the car," her father said as he walked back up. "Don't even look at it. I don't want him to see what we're driving."

He got out his own phone, which he never used except to get the maps and messages that were sometimes sent to them for the day. He scrolled through the contacts and held the phone to his head.

"Yes, a possible emergency . . . Okay." He walked over and stood about ten feet from the man on the motorcycle and took pictures of his license plate and then of him. Making sure the man and everybody else in earshot could hear him, he said, "Yes, a rest area on U.S. 60. We're headed northeast. The last town we went through was Globe. . . . A biker, maybe five-nine and I'd guess two hundred ten pounds or so. . . . Maybe forty, long greasy hair, receding hairline, beer belly, jowls. . . ."

"The hell are you doing?" the man snarled.

"Yes, he's confronting me right now."

Her father brought up the phone and took another picture.

"I'll send it, but here's a verbal description. Black t-shirt, black jeans, black boots with some kind of silver winged skull on the side. . . . Judging from the decals on his motorcycle, I'd say he was a minor agent of the principalities and powers. Very minor. Right, I'll send a picture of the license plate to this number . . . No, I don't see anybody with him, but you never know."

A siren went off nearby, and the man winced, but then he saw the State Patrol car pulling over somebody on the highway. Glaring steadily at her father, he strapped on his helmet, fired up his motorcycle a little too flamboyantly, and drove away.

"Wait for it," said the new Magdalena.

Right on cue, the man lifted his left hand in an obscene gesture.

Her father sent the pictures, and they waited another half hour until he heard back that the man was a registered sex offender, but not in the other database. Whatever the other database was.

"So Magdalena," said her brother. "What's this thing you've got for old guys on motorcycles? I remember when you used to be smart."

"I remember when you didn't—"

Didn't know your own name, she had started to say. Everything rushed upon her at once. She wailed. People all over the rest area stopped what they were doing and looked at her.

"Hush!" her mother said.

"My gosh, I'm sorry," Buford said. "I was just kidding."

She put one hand over her mouth and flapped the other in the air and bent over sobbing.

Karl Guizac

August 2014

They angled north through Santa Fe and up to Chimayo, where they visited El Santuario. Teresa, now Anna, wanted to pray for the Mexicans who had been killed, especially the ones terrified of El Mocasín. It was a strange pilgrimage church, famous for its holy dirt, and the whole place was decorated with tormented art. It prominently displayed abandoned crutches, evidence of the many miracles there. Also scattered about were large crosses that men had carried long distances in painful processions. Somehow, the authenticity moved the newly named Karl. There was something in this piety of suffering continuous with the obsessions of the Mayans and the Aztecs. Beauty and horror. They were heading back to the Sequoia when, on a sudden impulse, Karl excused himself from his wife and the children and went back around the church and into the newer building near it.

"Is there a priest here?" he asked a woman behind a desk, and she pointed at a hallway with her pencil. He saw a tall priest with a slight stoop leaving his office and caught up with him as he turned to go.

"Father, can you hear my confession?"

The priest, Hispanic and about his own age, glanced at his watch with a mild grimace and nodded toward the office he had just left. Karl followed him in, and the priest rummaged for his stole, nodded Karl toward a chair and then sat a little glumly, waiting for Karl to begin.

"Father, it's been—I don't know—a long time, maybe twelve years, maybe fifteen, since my last confession."

The priest raised his eyebrows and sighed through his nose.

"Go ahead," he said.

"Father, seventeen years ago I had an affair with my stepsister, and as a result of it, I accidentally killed my son. I was a drunk for years and failed my responsibility in every way. Last year, I fell in love with my wife's niece. Last month, I almost got my whole family murdered."

The priest glanced up at him.

An hour later, Karl thanked him and left the church. Anna was waiting by the car, the old worry lines between her eyes. Jacob watched him with interest.

"What were you *doing*?" Magdalena demanded, as if he had thwarted her plans for the day.

"I went to confession," Karl said.

This news silenced her. They got into the car, and he started it up.

"Let's get some dinner. Rancho de Chimayo is supposed to be good."

"Mexican again?" Magdalena said.

"It's New Mexico," said Jacob. "What do you want, lobster bisque?"

"Shut up, dimwit."

Teresa met Walter's eyes and tilted her head slightly to the side. He nodded at her, and a small smile started up.

MISS ZILPHA'S GARDEN

Part IX

For this perishable nature must put on the imperishable, and this mortal nature must put on immortality.

1 Corinthians 15:53

Gallatin

SPIN MACHINE, read the huge headline in the *Gallatin Tribune*. It was superimposed on a photograph of the CNN truck and the tight-skirted, avid reporter in the cemetery, microphone in hand. If the ROBBED! edition had garnered attention, this one found instant celebrity. The news stations in Atlanta leapt onto the story, and Fox News, supplying anchors' snarky quips, kept running video segments of Sheriff Hudson Bennett's carefully hedged actual remarks and then showed the editing done by CNN. Clips on YouTube went viral.

People in Nevada and South Dakota and Maine saw Sheriff Hudson Bennett, calm and bemused by all the misunderstanding, patiently answering questions. U.S. Marshal Aengus Dunne claimed to be searching for the missing Peach family, and he released composite photos of other people to keep the public from inadvertently finding them. Dunne himself received fan mail from across the country, the extremes being the selfie of a fifteen-year-old in a bikini on the beach in Coral Gables and a love poem by a seventy-four-year-old widow in Port Wing, Wisconsin. County Coroner Buddy Fingal gave a wheezing, detailed account of the long-decomposed body of Alison Graves that was widely quoted, and the next week, he was asked to speak on a Christian radio talk show with a national audience, where he talked about his conversion in Vietnam. Ellen Wolf received a special citation for conspicuous valor from the Governor of Georgia.

When had Gallatin ever been so famous? How could you top a most-wanted radical bomber who turned up dead in Gallatin County, buried beneath decades of kudzu? It was delicious—Alison Graves, Harris Akers, and their love-child, Walter Peach, once a poet, now the editor of the local paper. Dexter Watkins, war criminal. The almost-famous Forrest.

Hiram Walker, Chick Lee, LaCourvette Todd—they all had their moments. Vernon Jenkins and Ed Watkins avoided all media scrutiny. As CNN was forced into retractions, Anderson Cooper worried publicly about the extreme pressure put on young reporters in the age of social media. The network fired the reporter anyway.

It was an instant in history; it was Gallatin on stage beneath the spotlight of national curiosity that fell for a moment onto the town. Gallatin appeared on millions of screens—TVs, laptops, mobile phones—for a day, a second day, and then a mall shooting somewhere, there was a celebrity who abused little boys, there was another video of a beheading in the Middle East. Not for those distracted millions were the back pages of the *Gallatin Tribune*, founded by Josiah Graves in 1906, where there appeared the brief obituary of Mary Louise Gibson, a longtime member of the A.M.E. congregation, survived by her granddaughter LaCourvette Todd.

No one at all noticed the burial of a man named Josiah Simms, except the undertakers who grimaced over the body and lowered his casket into the old Gallatin cemetery. Rightly or wrongly, Aengus Dunne withheld the truth that Simms was El Mocasín—withheld it both from the man once known as Peach and also from the authorities, state and federal. He gave the story a very different spin: Braxton Forrest had intercepted a cartel assassin and arsonist at Stonewall Hill. In reality, Dunne and Forrest helped organize a network of federal agents in their off hours in an elaborate plan that Forrest funded. It would keep Peach and his family comfortable but also on the move, vigilant but free from actual danger. Forrest's wife Marisa considered the plan both cruel and sentimental. Who was he to manipulate their lives? Forrest defended himself by saying that Peach and his family had no ordinary life to resume in Gallatin. How could they simply return and take up residence? He quoted Allen Tate: "What shall we say who have knowledge/Carried to the heart?" They needed a new life, and it would be theirs to choose. It would be a rare gift. A nomadic time, a season in the wilderness. He suspected that they would be making *la vita nuova* already on the way.

Forrest himself went to confession repeatedly and was repeatedly absolved, but he knew no relief of soul. He underwent spiritual and psychological counseling, unable to stop reliving the moment his fingers broke through the skull and into the brain of Josiah Simms. Fr. Ingabire, a Rwandan priest who had lived through the genocide, was known for his healing powers. A placid man who seemed simultaneously inattentive and completely present, he told Forrest that evil could overcome people like flipping a light switch. Did he think evil had overcome him? Forrest said yes. Then Forrest said no, that he did not feel that he, Braxton Forrest, was doing it. What most grieved him was the idea that he had been "saving the plantation," killing a black man, revictimizing the old victim. Fr. Ingabire asked him if he killed the man in self-defense. Forrest said he did because the man shot at him twice. He had no doubt that the man would have killed him otherwise. Fr. Ingabire asked if Forrest killed the man because he was black. Forrest said he did not. Fr. Ingabire asked if there was anything about the man that he thought might have triggered his rage. Forrest thought about it for a long time and told him that it might be the whiteness of the man's mouth, because it terrified him. The priest asked him to pray about the meaning of "whiteness of mouth." What was that whiteness?

Meanwhile, Dunne accumulated more and more background information on Josiah Simms. The autopsy revealed that one of Simms's conditions was abnormal thinness of the parietal bones of the skull, perhaps related, like his leukoplakia, to the severity of his burns at a crucial stage of childhood growth. When they traced Simms back to a permanent compound outside Guadalajara, officials there found a set of notebooks detailing his life and crimes from the 1980s. Dunne, working with the FBI, had asked that they be sent to the FBI headquarters in Washington. In his youth, Simms had been Cottonmouth to the gangs in Chicago, where his peculiar sadistic ruthlessness marked him off from all other killers and gave him an unparalleled dominance from his teens. The peers of Josiah Simms in Classics and English in the 1990s at Oxford University, where he lived alone, always referred to him indirectly, as though he might overhear them anywhere they were—not an idle suspicion, given what he seemed to know. He never entertained. He never ate in front of others, and he always covered his mouth when he spoke. His intelligence impressed even the most accomplished, as did his wealth, which grew beyond bounds, it was rumored, through canny investments of funds he was assumed to have inherited. He seemed completely devoid of sexual interest, but he was suspected of sex crimes, though no one ever accused him. Children would sometimes be found physically unharmed but terrified to muteness within a few blocks of his flat.

In Jalisco, where he moved in the early 2000s, a nameless terror hung over whole towns. The mere whisper *El Mocasín* by a babysitter or housemaid could terrify the most recalcitrant children into obedience.

Karl Guizac

From Chimayo, they drove past Taos and up through the mountains into Colorado and then east to I-25. As they were pulling into Pueblo, Karl got a text from Braxton Forrest saying that he was emailing some scanned documents that needed to be signed in front of a notary public. They found an RV park on the Arkansas River, and as soon as they got the Airstream set up in a pleasant spot overlooking the water, he unhitched the Sequoia and drove it into town.

It was mid-afternoon on Tuesday. He followed the directions on his phone to an address on one of the downtown streets and took his laptop inside the building, hoping he could download and print out the documents and have his signature notarized all at once. The young Hispanic woman behind the counter—**Consuela Sanchez**, said her name tag—told him no problem, seated him at a table near a coffee machine, and set him up with wi-fi. An unopened email with many attachments from Lydia Downs that he would wait to read. He opened the one from Forrest first. Forrest said that he and a lawyer in Gallatin had done some work on the five acres on Hopewell Road, and he wanted to buy the place if they could get over a hurdle or two. He would pay Walter what it was worth, which ought to help him get settled somewhere.

Why not sell it? He would never go back to Gallatin. There was a nice piece of land under that kudzu, and it would probably appraise at $2500 an acre, given the growing demand out in the county. The money would give them a new life until Walter could locate new work.

He downloaded the attached files onto his flash drive and gave it to Consuela. She printed the documents out for him and quickly looked over them for places he needed to sign.

"Wow," she said.

"What's the matter?"

"It's just a lot of money."

He spun the paper toward him, and she put her fingertip on the line. Forrest was offering him $2.5 million—$500,000 an acre—for Missy's Garden.

He called from the parking lot outside, a hundred and fifteen degrees at least. He stared across the street at a stucco house with the bricks showing through, debris all around the back, a collapsed fence. Even Missy's Garden under the kudzu looked better than that. A bus, **911** hugely lettered down its side, sat abandoned in the bare lot next door.

Forrest answered him on the third ring.

"Braxton," Walter said. "What the hell?"

"Did you open the email from Lydia?"

"No, why?"

Forrest told him the land might be worth more than what he was offering, but he wanted to be fair, and he was willing to come up if need be.

"What are you talking about?"

Forrest told him to open the email from Lydia, so Peach went back inside, sleek with sweat and suddenly chilled in the overactive air conditioning. Other customers had come in, one of them wanting a summons served. He went back to his laptop and found the email from Lydia. ZILPHA was the subject line.

> You said you remember Alison reading from Zilpha Graves's diary? Well Alison left it where she found it—in a cedar box in a cubbyhole built beneath the floorboards of the closet. Braxton's daughter Hermia is beside herself. You know Hermia, I think. Interesting woman, to say the least. I'm a little sick of genealogy after being around Hermia for a few days.

It was too long to read now—page after page of the body of the email, pictures and scanned files that would take forever to download—so he skimmed ahead, trying to get the gist that Forrest needed him to understand.

In this little forgotten box, Lydia and Hermia had found letters, the first issues of the *Gallatin Tribune* from 1906, and a booklet called "After the Mysteries" about the statues on the grounds. No one had seen the statues for decades because they were embedded in growing trees, apparently on purpose. Lydia underscored one sentence from a letter Zilpha wrote to the sculptor: "Someday when we are all long dead and the tree itself has grown old and died, the statues will be released from their bondage, and for each one, the tree's own inner life will stand revealed as the mold of imperishable form, like our own bodies at the Judgment."

Forrest had hired crews to begin clearing the kudzu, and Lydia wrote that Hudson Bennett was helping her. Walter looked up from the laptop, bemused. *Hudson Bennett?* "Hudson has been out with me several times now, and so far we have found three statues. One of them is in a tree killed by the kudzu not far from the back of the house, just off the path down to the creek that we've started to clear—a woman stepping forward, her hand extended, her face uncannily calm."

He opened the picture with a tremor of recognition.

It was the statue he remembered from his childhood. Lydia had managed to preserve the tree and yet pry the trunk open to reveal the statue. The woman was stepping out from its bondage, as Zilpha had wanted, with her form molded in the wood behind her and her back foot still embedded in the trunk. The bronze was discolored but intact, the expression unchanged, just as he remembered it from his childhood. He had never seen anything like it.

Someone touched his hand. He started and looked up. The other customers were gone, and Consuela stood above him, her face full of solicitude.

"Did you want me to make some coffee?"

"No, that's okay. Thank you, though."

"So are you ready to sign those papers?"

"I guess so, sure. I don't want to turn down $500,000 an acre, I guess."

"I was going to say," she laughed.

"Could you print out a picture for me?"

"Absolutely."

He saved it to the flash drive and handed it to her. She went behind the counter and came back a minute later to hand him the image, looking at it as she came.

"Oh my God," she said. "That is, like—I mean—awesome. Okay, I just need to see your ID."

He took out his wallet and handed her the driver's license. As he did, his phone vibrated with a text message from Forrest, who had lately been growing disturbingly casual about their exchanges. CALL ME. Walter sighed and glanced at his watch. This whole thing was taking too long, and now he would have to go back outside to call Forrest in the heat. Consuela pressed the edge of Walter's ID against the signature line to compare the name on the card to the name on the document.

"Um, the document says Walter Peach," she said. "But your driver's license says Karl something. Goo-zac?"

He stared at her for a moment and then started to smile. There was no way to do this. That must be what Forrest had just recognized, too. In order for Forrest to change the document to read Karl Guizac, Peach would have to make an official name change, like the one in college when dear old Emily convinced him to kill off Walter Devereaux Lawton.

"Tell you what," he said, "let me give my friend another call."

He walked back out into the heat. Forrest answered and spoke hurriedly: "Walter, Hermia just reminded me about a legal document that goes back to McIntosh and Graves entailing this property. It can never be sold outside the family. I can't buy it from you, in other words, unless I'm your big brother. I wouldn't be surprised at this point."

Walter went back inside.

"Consuela, do you mind shredding those papers?" he asked.

"Okay," she said. "Everything's off?"

"I'm afraid so. Families are complicated."

Her eyes met his for a long moment, and unexpectedly, he read in them a history of misery.

"They're your blood," she said with a little too much resignation as she shredded the files. "What can you do? You have a nice day, Mr. Goozac."

The next day, at the rest stop on I-25 north of Denver, a young woman got something in her sandal as she stepped off the curb into the parking lot. She hopped on one foot and then put out a hand to balance herself on the Sierra, which was parked with the Airstream behind it. The materials from the information center that she was holding dropped through the open window onto Karl's lap, and she paused, irritated and apologetic, but she made no attempt to retrieve them. She scooped out the pebble from the sandal with the other hand and shouted "Connor!" and waved at someone across the lawn and ran away to meet whoever it was.

"Score?" said Jacob from the backseat.

"A perfect ten," said Anna. "I thought the balance of purpose and distraction could hardly have been better."

"Nine," said Magdalena. "Excellent overall, but she could have fumbled the papers a little instead of doing a straight drop through the window. Also, I thought she should have made a gesture to try to recover the papers—just a little something before she realized it wasn't worth it. What did you think, Jacob?"

"Nine point five. I agree with Magdalena, but I thought the pebble distraction plus the shout at Connor were terrific redirections of attention."

Karl Guizac shook his head

"What's the route today?" Jacob asked. He was holding open the massive, spiral-bound road atlas Walter—Karl, Karl—had bought him in Denver. Karl took the papers from his lap and leafed through them: a brochure about rafting on the Cache la Poudre River, a Wyoming map, a blank envelope. He unfolded the map and found Medicine Bow circled, a tiny numeral **1** beside it, then De Smet, **2**, and Yellowstone Park, **3**. In the envelope Karl found a scanned page of a clipping. No indication of who had sent it—Lydia Downs? Hermia Watson?

He glanced over it.

"Want to read this aloud?" he asked Magdalena, who started reading with sardonic asides.

"Just read it!" Jacob said.

"Give it to me," Anna said.

"A Connoisseur's Notes"
By Clemence Abbott, M.A.

Dear Faithful Lover of the Arts,

My proclivity, as *you* know all too well, is to reminisce about my glorious days in the cafes and museums of the Paris of my youth. Did I tell you about the time I met the tragic young Georges Seurat, a lovely man, who included my profile (near the water, beneath the hat) in his famous *Sunday Afternoon*? Perhaps I have mentioned *once or twice too often* the week I spent in Aix-en-Provence visiting the studio of my revered Paul Cezanne. How I treasured the small still life he gave me before someone stole it *en route* to New York. I should have remained in Le Havre! You must picture it on the inward eye: On a small square table, a black cat lies asleep on a fold of white cloth (a dinner napkin?) before a blue-gray stoneware pitcher. Two oranges vividly exert their color in the foreground, one upright, the other rolled over with its stem end pointing out of the frame at the viewer.

Always with Clemence Abbott, you must imagine, it is Europe, it is France, it is Paris and the privilege of the few. Reader, what will you *think* of me, what will you *say*, when I tell you that nearby, at this very moment, *not an hour's drive by carriage*, in a garden that is itself an achievement of the highest art, are the most stunning sculptures I have seen outside Italy or France? What will you *do* when I tell you what the *grande dame*, Mrs. Zilpha Graves, grandmother of our own esteemed publisher and editor Josiah, has created around her country cottage on Hopewell Road?

I cannot venture it in my own voice, dear reader! Imagine, if you would, a traveler from England, a man who wants to understand our America, happening upon "Miss Zilpha's" garden. His guide urges him to see the great houses along Cherokee Springs Drive, but our visitor has something of the reformer's zeal, and he insists on seeing "Niggertown," as our less enlightened brethren insist on calling it. They drive among the hovels of that unfortunate neighborhood and out thence into Gallatin County, where they see the Negroes in their head rags out in the cotton fields, they see briar patches and pine woods, red clay gullies and naked pickaninnies playing outside unpainted shacks on the dirt roads—our Southern romance. And then, behold! There stands a house, classic in its proportions, shaded by great oaks and elms, cool in the hot afternoon, with the garden spilling down the hillside behind it.

"Driver! Driver! Please stop here."

All the next day, as he travels by train to his hotel on one of General Oglethorpe's squares in Savannah, he muses upon his vision, and now, at the desk in his hotel room, he writes to his wife, who summers this year in Normandy with their two marriageable daughters.

My Dearest Eleanor,

I feel a bit like Bottom in the play. I have had a dream, and it is almost past the wit of man to say what dream it was. Five miles or so outside Gallatin, Georgia, lives Mrs. Zilpha Graves, a lady in her sixties, graceful and slender, of upright and elegant stature. Her face, like her bearing, retains something of the unmistakable beauty of her youth. Her eyes are a lovely olive; her smile is wonderful. When she met me at the door of her home, I must have appeared quite stupefied as I stood there, hat in hand, because the bun of white hair gathered at the back of her head was pierced by an elegant hairpin of gold and jade.

"Ming dynasty," I said, astonished.

"Not the usual greeting I receive," she said. "But yes. A gift from a dear friend."

She offered me tea beneath an umbrella on the flagstone patio behind the house. Helping serve were two lovely girls, one of them, LeRoux, thirteen or fourteen, and the other a younger Negro child named Ella. From my seat, I could see down the main path; there were great flowering trees and shrubs, recessed beds of iris and lily, a great spill of colors out of Eden all the way down to the gleaming twists of Caleb Creek.

It was a lovely conversation, touching often upon artists and authors we both knew but few do. After Miss Zilpha, as both the girls called her, had given me her adieu and retired to her afternoon rest, the girl LeRoux took me on a tour of the garden, and almost at once I recognized LeRoux's face in some of the statues—and such statues!—placed along the side paths, in the cool alcoves, each with a young tree growing behind it. Bees swarmed everywhere in the flowers. Oh, and the birds! When the girl and I sat on a stone bench, a cardinal came down to perch on the shoulder of her bronze image. Blue jays, little wrens and sparrows, goldfinches, a woodpecker high in a great elm, two gray-and-white mockingbirds flitting from limb to limb above us, descanting of—

Oh, I have overrun my space! And so much left to say!

Hermia Watson

Going over the contents of the folders retrieved from Stonewall Hill, Hermia sat each morning at the same table in a back corner of the Gallatin Library. All through July and into August, using letters, notebooks, wills, and long searches on ancestry websites, she gradually laid out the genealogical lines spreading out from Stonewall Hill, and she organized charts, partly by what she could confirm, partly by what she surmised.

Evenings she would take her work to her father as he recovered from everything. Forrest would not stay at Stonewall Hill. He had rented the old Hall house, now a bed-and-breakfast, for his family. Hermia would sit in the front room with him, and the two of them would muse over the names, generation by generation, which they would capitalize even in their conversation.

ZILPHA GRAVES had one son by Asa Graves, the man who bought her, ASHER, who was brought up in Italy and returned to study at Princeton. ASHER married an heiress in New York City and had two sons and three daughters, all of whom married and had children.

Do we know their names? Do we know what happened to them? Forrest would ask.

Not yet, she would answer.

All of them forgot, Forrest would say, what had happened in the generations before, in the dark days of the South, forgot as the diaspora spread to the Midwest or the Rocky Mountains, as far as Oregon or California, as far away as you could go.

Marisa attempted to be kind to Hermia. She would bring them coffee or glasses of wine. Cate and Bernadette would duck into the room, probably at their mother's urging. The exchanges were polite enough, and Cate was mesmerized by the complexities of this place called the Old South.

Forrest and Hermia would turn back to the children of Zilpha Graves.

ZILPHA also had a daughter EMILIA LEROUX GRAVES-BARBERINI and two more sons with the Italian nobleman BARBERINI whose companion she had been. The daughter we know, but the sons disappear into France or Germany or England, the trenches and the camps.

In 1878, ASA DANIEL GRAVES and FARQUHAR MCINTOSH, acting jointly, procured the legal services of CARTER DAVIS in Macon, who set up a trust for Graves's "nephew," ASHER GRAVES. Two years later, Davis married EMILIA LEROUX GRAVES-BARBERINI, the Italian beauty whose small watercolor portrait they found among the pages, along with a curious document swearing Davis and his professional heirs to "fealty" to the name and property of ZILPHA GRAVES in perpetuity.

The complexities dizzied Hermia—all these lives, all the stories whose inner quality she could not guess, all the characters whose exact sense of being in a particular moment she could not recover: an old man pausing at the bottom of the stairs at a sound from the bedroom and the smell of perfume, a child sitting in her grandmother's lap on Saturday evening skinning off her clothes, stepping into the wash tub beside the fire.

She could not reenter this name or that; she could not fathom the secret recesses of deep anxiety or still deeper love. Sometimes she would look through the library window at the Gallatin County Courthouse a block away, and her eyes would fill with tears because she could not sustain the tone of outrage that she wanted to feel at all these injustices unearthed at last. It was too complicated, too shot through with mere folly and actual kindness and undoubted love.

The days became habitual. She was always at the library when it opened at 10:00, but earlier in the morning, just after breakfast, she would drive out to Zilpha's Garden, watching the garden as it reemerged from under the kudzu. She would go inside the house and have coffee with Lydia Downs and read Zilpha's diaries. She would walk with Lydia to the sites of the statues and the freshly replanted flowerbeds and the newly trimmed hedges and the old stone benches. Little by little, the past rose up before her, thick as the present and sometimes thicker, and she saw little LeRoux and Ella as though they were living children.

I get so close, she told Lydia, breaking into tears, *but I can't really enter their world.* Lydia told her it was not the past that Zilpha wanted for her.

One night Lydia insisted that Hermia stay overnight.

You need to sleep in Zilpha's bedroom.

Where Alison Graves died? Where her body decomposed? I can't do that!

Lydia told her about the ancient practice called *incubatio,* when the supplicant or patient would undergo purification and then enter the inmost sacred space of the temple, perform a ritual, and sleep there to receive a healing dream. She gave Hermia a purification soap made of hyssop and lemongrass and essential oils. When Hermia came out of the bath, she put on the white linen gown that Lydia had left her and went into Zilpha's bedroom.

It was a hot night. A little breeze came through the screens. On the dresser flickered three candles before the small statue of the Virgin they had found in Zilpha's cedar box. *There's a prayer for this,* Lydia said. *You get in the bed and before you go to sleep you ask for the healing dream. You say the Our Father and three Hail Marys, and then you say this three times: 'Call to me and I will answer you, and will tell you great and hidden things which you have not known.'*

Lydia left her alone there. Hermia dutifully prayed, suspending her habitual irony—it all seemed so perfectly New Age—and got into the bed in Zilpha's room. Terrors came over her as she lay there waking, fingering the rose-smelling beads of Zilpha's rosary as she prayed for a healing dream and finally fell asleep. What came was as horrifying as it was healing.

In the depth of night Zilpha came to her, the young Zilpha, tall, with eyes the color of olive leaves, came gracefully to meet her, lovely and graceful, the secret daughter of Farquhar McIntosh and the secret bride of Asa Graves.

She held Hermia's face in her hands. *Dear child, you have to be born again out of everything that made you. Do you understand me? Born out of it, not overwhelmed, not suffocated by what you can never know.*

Yes ma'am.

They were in Stonewall Hill now. Hermia knew every inch of the place, but Zilpha led her to a door she did not remember.

May I show you?

The first steps were wooden; a few more steps and the treads were old stone. There were no railings, and it was completely dark. Hermia kept a hand on Zilpha's shoulder. They came to a place that smelled of hell.

Here there were chains, Zilpha said.

They did not stop their descent again until they saw a light far below, and as they drew closer, they passed into a stone archway, which revealed a courtyard with a central fountain. There were bougainvilleas in the colonnades. In the distance were mountains as old as the earth and opposite them, the surge and melancholy long withdrawing roar of the sea.

I was happy here, Zilpha said. *In the morning, I would watch the fishing boats go out. The seagulls would float the winds crying and diving and bobbing on the water. Asher was young here before he went off to Eton and on to Princeton. Here I could paint, here I could be loved. But the Old Ones found me. At midnight I would hear them gather and begin to moan, and I would come down to be among them. So huge, so hideous. I called them my girls. I would give them milk mixed with wine and honey, I would touch their heads with terrible hesitation, and those inside them would tell me their stories.*

The one you wrote about, your Eunice, told me how she refused to be silent when Mr. McIntosh took her oldest son from her and sold him to a slave trader.

She told me McIntosh needed the money because he wanted his daughter to have the finest clothes.

And I, Zilpha, I was that daughter.

When she had wailed and called on God for justice, the harsh sons of Farquhar bound her and took her down beneath the house and chained her there. Yes, she said, and did I know that the dress I laid aside for Mr. Graves had been paid for with her son? That time when I freed my children to come, when he first took me to my garden and laid me down in his tent. Did I know that the dress I took off was the sale of her son? Did I know what my brothers had done to her?

It could not be otherwise, Hermia said.

Oh, it was otherwise with me. Terribly otherwise. Oh, and the others besides Eunice, a dozen others, at least, in each of the Old Ones. At first, they came to accuse me like Eunice, but then they began to love me, the smell of me. Like massive bloodhounds, they would press their great faces hungrily to my body, snuffling and moaning, smelling the milk in my breasts and knowing all the children inside me, those who were born, those who were yet to come. They would protect my blood, they said, and my children's. I made them promise me that they would never take all their vengeance, that they would wait for a redeemer and someday be transfigured.

I would tell them about heaven, and they would raise their terrible, ancient faces, and their white mouths would open, their white, ghastly mouths, and they would howl, and their nostrils would spread wide, and they would shake themselves with longing.

And then Hermia was back at Miss Zilpha's Garden, in her room, not awake, but standing beside the bed where her own body lay in sleep. And the Old Ones were there around her. She stood in terror, and they smelled her and touched her. *This one?* Now Zilpha was among them, and behind her was Hermia's own mother, and down on the bed was Hermia herself, trying to get free, struggling to wake up, but caught in papery undergarments and heavy primeval swaddling. She saw that her hands were skeletal and moldy where they came out from the sheets, but they were already taking on flesh, digging their nails into the mattress as she reared up—

She broke free in the very early dawn. She was awake, but hardly healed. More like haunted. She rose and went out to the back of the house quietly. She meant to go down to the creek, but there, stepping toward her from a split-open tree, was Zilpha herself. Terrified, she watched for a long moment and then turned and went back to the bed. She lay as still as she could, sometimes trembling uncontrollably, until Lydia came at last to find her.

Sharpe

Late in the afternoon, Bill Sharpe pulled his pickup to the curb a block away from the convent in Nashville. He had heard through Miss Emma that Nora had *taken the veil,* she said, touching his arm, *up in Nashville. Temporarily. I don't think it will last.* But as soon as he heard the word *veil,* dread of loss dropped upon him more strongly than ever, more than with Deirdre, more even than when Nora had disappeared back in the spring or when he had thought she was dead, bound to the tree. Forever now she would be held just out of reach—a ghost like the dead in the old stories who would vanish into air if you tried to grasp them. If there were only some way he could see her, some way to make his case.

Early on the second Friday morning after she vanished, he stood in the showroom of Lee Ford trying to joke with the other salesmen, but nothing came to his lips. After a few minutes, the new girl in Parts touched his elbow, "Mr. Lee is asking for you."

Chick met him at the door of his office, solicitous.

"You look kind of lost out there, buddy."

He guided Sharpe to one of the leather chairs and asked his secretary to bring him a cup of coffee. Sharpe stared at the little bobblehead on Chick's desk. Barack Obama.

"My heart's not in it right now, Chick. I guess I need some time off."

Chick looked at him, distracted by something on his phone, until he turned it face down with a grimace and focused.

"You never had a spoiled daughter, did you?"

"Not that I know of."

"So," Chick said. "Let me guess. It's Walter Peach's niece?"

Sharpe nodded.

"I tell you what, that one's a prize."

"It might be a week. Maybe two weeks."

"Worth it." Chick waved him off as though he were a nuisance. "Right now, you couldn't sell free ice cream to a three-year-old. Take your time and bring her back with you."

Sharpe drove home and packed some clothes and said goodbye to his mother and Martin and left a little after noon. He decided to go straight through Atlanta. The traffic wasn't bad on I-75 or I-24, and he reached Nashville as rush hour began. He found the convent off the interstate and spent an hour circling the grounds, as though the walls and windows would yield clues of Nora. He parked where he could see if anything happened, and just after six, some nuns in white gowns and black things on their heads paced into their cemetery praying on big rosaries.

He followed the streets back toward downtown and took a room at a Best Western near Vanderbilt. At a bar and grill, he bought a hamburger and drank two double bourbons, listening to a young country singer from a small town in southern Alabama. The boy was good, just not good enough to make it—a little short of real talent. Sharpe could feel the boy's fate set, the failures and disappointments and forced revisions of his self-estimate after all the early praise. He would either take stock of himself and do something else altogether or pursue a dream he had no business having and end up a bitter old man carping at the TV and drinking by himself. The way Sharpe could picture himself in a life without Nora.

The black wing came over him.

Back at the motel, he watched two CSI shows in a row and went to bed. He woke early the next day. After some coffee and burritos at McDonald's, he went back and circled the convent grounds, parking in random spot after spot, until a security guard said "Move on, sir."

That night, a Saturday, he picked up a pint of Jack Daniels and drank. He walked for a long time along the Cumberland River and somehow found his way back to the convent, where he hung on the fence staring in at the lighted windows, wondering where she was. Where in all those rooms, behind all the prayers and rituals and religious clothes? He wanted her body lithe in his arms, warm against him; he wanted to kiss her and hear her laughter. He wanted to be the one drawing her smile. The next day, by God, he would go to the front entrance and *make* them let him see her. *Demand* to see the one they had stolen.

He got lost, stumbled through a bad neighborhood, where a prostitute crooked her little finger at him and a dealer flashed a skimpy dime bag. He asked a homeless man for directions and gave him the bottle. When he finally made it back to his motel at one in the morning, he remembered to take some ibuprofen before sleep, thanks to a roommate from college. It was past nine when he woke up. He made coffee in the little motel pot, took a shower, and drove blearily to the convent, trying to recapture the night's resolve. When he pulled into the convent parking lot, people dressed for church were entering so he blended in with them and sat in the back, vaguely intimidated, not knowing when to kneel or stand except by watching the families around him. The nuns were in rows buttressing the altar, lined up sideways, singing like angels. He could not find her face.

When everyone else went up for communion, he stayed put in the pew. After the people crossed themselves, he followed the crowd to the vestibule, where several nuns circulated, greeting couples, leaning to kiss children, laughing at things people said. He did not see Nora. He found a clear-eyed older nun who wore an air of authority, and when he started to explain himself, she politely led him aside.

"I don't even know what to call you," he said.

"'Sister' is fine," she said. "I am Sister Domenica."

"Sister, my fiancée—"

"Ah," she said, looking at him with such understanding that tears started to his eyes. Sister Domenica took him to a small visiting room and sat across at a decent distance, offering him her hands, which he took in his. "The young woman you are looking for," she said quietly, "has undergone a terrible shock, as I think you know. Here among us she has found safety and consolation and peace, not just in our company, but most of all in the presence of Our Lord Jesus Christ. It may be that in her healing, she comes to discern a vocation, which means she may remain with us, but often those who flee some danger eventually turn away, thanking us for the refuge we offer but choosing to return to their lives outside. You will have to be patient."

"Patient," he said bitterly. "I feel like a damned soul looking over into Paradise."

"Damned?" she said mildly, with a kind of astonishment. "*Damned?* No, you have been reserved for some high thing. I feel it with conviction. Go home and be patient, and if the time is right, she will come to you."

"Can I just see her?"

"Young man, we celebrate the Holy Sacrifice of the Mass every day of the week. Call for our schedule, yes. Come to our chapel. But please do not try to communicate with her. Not yet. This is a young woman more shaken and traumatized than most of us can imagine. You must be patient."

Magdalena

From the rest stop north of Denver, they drove up into Wyoming. They camped near Medicine Bow. Her father said their site was close to the setting that opened a novel called *The Virginian,* one of the books Judge Lawton had given him as a boy. Jacob spent an hour throwing rocks down the railroad track, left a penny on the rails that a passing train flattened into a perfect circle.

Early the next morning they kept going west, traveling briefly on I-80 and then heading north on U.S. 287 from Rawlins. At Muddy Gap, they went west on 287 and then drove another hour and a half to De Smet, where they stopped overnight at the city park. The Airstream was luxurious in its way, but she longed for Stonewall Hill and her room. She wanted privacy and permanence. She wanted to be there without being seen.

The next morning after breakfast, they unplugged and flushed the lines—routine by now—while her father went and bought gas. They went to Mass because it was the Feast of the Assumption, and when they exited St. Thomas, it was still just mid-morning. Her father wanted to follow a loop road west out of town toward the Wind River Mountains. A few miles out of De Smet, it twisted around the side of a hill and down to a creek, and as they came out of the curve, slowing now, they saw red cliffs on their right. To the left were great grassy meadows rising to a sweep of foothills stretching to the south as far as they could see. The hillsides were broken with ravines, crossed with occasional paths, spotted with groves and low shrubs the color of smoke. Beyond the foothills, towering all the way up into the clouds, were the Winds.

They passed a bank of mailboxes and a road to the left, then crossed a cattle guard. A sense of *déjà vu* visited her. When the road turned north and then started back east, her father pulled into a graveled overlook. Ahead of them a herd of mule deer was picking its way down a red cliff.

They left the Sequoia for the immense quiet of the day. From their left a huge bird—a great blue heron—came winging into sight, following the line of a stony creek around the curve of the cliff to their right, and they watched it disappear behind a grove of cottonwoods and aspens. A herd of horses galloped into sight, their manes tossing, and crossed a meadow in the middle distance.

"Can we stay here?" she asked. "I love it here."

"I hope so," he said.

"I love it too," her mother said. Her father smiled at her.

"You're Anna, right? You look pretty good in this habitat, Anna, if you ask me." He pulled her against him and put his arm around her waist and left his hand on her stomach and they looked up at high evergreens on the slopes, the last morning clouds lifting off the mountains.

Her mother had been sick now for several mornings in a row.

A sudden shocking thought went through her. Her mother's soft moony look. It couldn't be. It was too embarrassing to even think about.

"But today we go to Yellowstone, right, Dad?" Jacob said. *Jacob.* She was getting used to it. "You said we would."

"It's still early enough," her father said. He went over and retrieved the phone from the car. No signal.

But back in town, as they approached the park and their Airstream, the signal bars returned.

"Who would have thought? We already have a reservation."

There was also a text from Braxton Forrest: "The world is all before you, where to choose your place of rest, and Providence your guide."

A moment later another message came in.

"Pray for the soul of Josiah Simms."

And then a last one: "Cottonmouth."

Karl Guizac

Yellowstone was less than three hours away. Among the things he had been given was a yearlong family pass to any national park, and already they had worn down its laminated edges. After Dubois, where they stopped for lunch, they labored up to Togwotee Pass, and he had to brake most of the way down while the Tetons rose majestically before them. At Moran Junction, they turned right toward Yellowstone. He stopped at the booth and showed his pass—Karl Guizac—and for the next hour they wound their way up into the crowded park.

By now, it was mid-afternoon. Jacob told them everything he had read about Yellowstone, especially the facts about a huge mass of magma that lay under the swarming visitors. He told them that nearly the whole park was the caldera of a supervolcano, which nobody had known until they looked at it from space in the 1970s. He said that every 600,000 years or so, it would erupt and change the world's atmosphere for years. And the eruption was overdue. He told them that all the park's thermal springs, all the geysers and hydrothermal effects, came from the immense heat under the surface. He said there were tremors all the time, over three thousand in 2010, and there had been an earthquake earlier that year measuring 4.8 on the Richter scale. If it blew, it would cover half the United States in six feet of ashes.

"Thanks a lot, Jacob," Magdalena said.

They made it to the Grant Village campground by four that afternoon. All the spots nearest the lake were already taken, but they found a decent one, and in under fifteen minutes they had everything connected. Jacob insisted that they see Old Faithful—*not tomorrow, today, right now*—so when the car was free of the Airstream, they climbed back in. The boy had a strange, demanding urgency.

Soon there would be time to think, time to walk along the trails with this new Anna of his heart, this lovely lady carrying his child. He imagined the lake misted at dawn, alive and numinous before anyone else woke, taking her down through verdurous glooms and winding mossy ways into some grove no one could know, and loving her the way they used to when the world was young, when it was all shining, when it was Adam and maiden and the birth of the simple light.

EPILOGUE

Jacob

Along the Firehole River and over Craig Pass, he remembered a dream of a melting road and wheels full of eyes. He had dreamed it in the time when he forgot who he was, the time of the Name. Whenever he thought of the Name, inner peace and outer disconnection came over him, as though everything he saw with his eyes were a great illusion. He watched the cars ahead of them, not knowing what to expect.

They turned off the Grand Loop Road toward the Old Faithful Visitors' Center. Traffic was heavy, and the parking lot at Old Faithful, big enough for a football stadium, set his father on edge—huge tour buses, swarms of people from the ends of the earth. They went slowly up and down the lot, row by row, and they were starting their second run through it, his father growing critical of the human race, when finally a car full of Japanese tourists pulled out in the row nearest the geyser. Everyone in their car was holding up a cell phone, and a girl leaned far out of the front passenger window, equipped with a selfie stick.

"The real world now exists as material for smartphones," said his father. "Look at it—the reduction of reality itself to a set of images you can put in your pocket. Seized and possessed. The final conquest of the modern project."

"Dad! Geez. Give it up!" cried Magdalena. "We're in Yellowstone."

"Really, Walter. It's a just way of seeing things," his mother said.

"It destroys memory," said his father.

"So you remember everything without it?"

Jacob listened to the usual words of their argument, but already the old grudges and pains that used to be behind them were disappearing. A new playfulness made they seem younger—younger than he was. They touched each other, teasing and smiling.

The bleachers for watching the geyser were empty. They had missed the last eruption by fifteen minutes, and the next one wasn't for another ninety. His father wanted to go for a jog, a new habit he had acquired in exile, and he quickly disappeared up the asphalt walkway.

"We'll be in the visitor's center," his mother said. "Are you okay poking around by yourself, Jacob?"

"Sure." It was the first time she had remembered to call him that. As Magdalena walked with her, he could follow the ripple of male attention that surged after her like the Wave at a football game.

There were signs everywhere warning visitors not to stray from the trail. The appearance of solid ground could be deceiving; the lava crust could randomly give way, easily, at any time, and you could be plunged into boiling water or mud. He loved reading about it, even though it was sometimes gruesome. Some young employees at the Park had gone out one night to drink beer and had ended up falling through. He imagined the sudden scalding drop. He didn't even want to picture them. They came from somewhere; they had names.

He wandered up the shorter way, thinking about his new name. *Jacob*, who wrestled with God. Who changed his name, too, not *to* Jacob but *from* Jacob to Israel.

Crossing the bridge over the Firehole River, he stopped and looked at the water weirdly flowing over white encrustations. He imagined the magma hunched far down under them, hundreds of cubic miles of rock liquefied by heat. This whole place was an inevitable disaster—and the crowds swarmed over it happily, sure it wouldn't be today. Not today, not today with its ice cream and pretty girls and new baseball caps.

He moved on from the bridge up the trail. Everything looked like it was going to stay, but everything was really going away, even what you thought was still. Even these mountains were *going* in God's time. Maybe *faith that moved mountains* was a way of saying God's time. The time of the Name. In God's time, mountains rose stretching upward and turned over and shook themselves out and got old and lay down like dogs too tired to stir, then other ones sprang up, and the seas silted down, and rocks rose and the daylight was full of what the old seas had let drift down for millions of years. Everything was going. Life rose and ages passed and you were born and like the flicker of an eyelash you were gone and the going kept going right past you.

A big family came by, talking and pointing, and he stepped off the path to let them pass. A double stroller, two fat little babies whose parents spoke French.

Babies came into the going. He remembered when his father had told him that he couldn't be alive now if he had ever been dead. But the going you came into wasn't *you* when you were born, not the *you* you were conscious of. It was the going that would eventually be you. Meanwhile it ate and made a mess in its diapers and cried and slept until finally *you* started to show up at three years old or maybe four. You grew and then you were convinced *you* were the going, because you had a name, you were Buford or Jacob, but you were never the going itself. You couldn't even explain your own body's going. You rode in it and thought *I think therefore I am* but that was crazy because the going was more the *am* than you were. You fell into the going without any say-so, and when it stopped, the going didn't stop, it was just *you* that stopped and maybe that was not even you. You died, and another kind of going took over what had been you, and you became another kind of going.

What were you? He thought about Alison Graves' body rotted into the bed, about the Confederate soldiers in the cemetery. How could you make yourself into the going that didn't stop? The stillness deep in the going? His mother said that if people concentrated on their own breathing when they meditated, the breathing disappeared into God, into the word of prayer: because "God"—that word was not the Name—was the place breath came from and went to, He was behind the going, He was the Name, He was a stillness that was the seed of time, a kind of quiet, a kind of heat. But also the whole being of everything.

It all came clear to him for a moment and he stopped. You could say *I* but God was the I AM in the going of everything, including you. And everything was going, not just things that were alive. Rocks, trees, mountains, clouds. Everything was going.

And suppose it all ended now
    the earth like sodden paper splitting
    the river disappearing upward in steam
    magma erupting upward
    and dead in the center of it

he, Jacob, flame
    burnt away
    into a shape of burning bones
    jeweled and incandescent
    and borne into the Name

He felt the call of his future.

"Hey!" somebody was yelling, a strange, high, scared sound. "Hey!"

He looked around. People were lined up on the walkway far to his right, their hands over their mouths, staring at him. A man was gesturing to him gently, the way you would motion to man on a skyscraper, teetering there on the skyscraper's ledge, about to jump. Up the walkway, toward the bleachers, he saw his mother and Raïssa—Magdalena—break into a run; two men in uniform suddenly sprinted past them. All over the park, people were stopping to point at him.

He looked down.

He could not remember later just what he saw. It seemed to him that it was full of eyes that rose and broke at the surface. He could not summon back exactly what he felt, whether it was terror or exaltation.

A woman's voice called him, and he looked over his shoulder. A ranger came carefully across the lava crust behind him and reached out her hand. He took her fingers and stepped carefully toward her and she guided him back to the path.

"Are you okay?" she said, her voice trembling. "Did you not see the signs?"

I saw the signs. I saw signs within signs.

"What's your name?" she asked when he did not answer.

"I don't know," he said.

He had started to say Buford Peach, and then Jacob Guizac. But neither was right. Any name was just the word for his going, not the name of his call.

His mother and sister stood close by, reaching for him, but the ranger held them away until they crossed back under the rope. He struggled for recollection, looking at the people pressing around him in a circle, all of them alive, all of them part of the going that he was part of too.

A great roar came, and instantly everyone ran away from him, not looking back, as though he were the center and source of the disaster they had to flee.

His mother came to him and squeezed so hard it hurt. His sister held his hand when his mother let him go. His father came running up, his face hot. Behind them, the geyser was erupting early. They turned now to watch it. Up it leapt, leapt—again—again—and the mist drifted to leeward—and again—as it traced on the air its seed, its flower, its momentary leaf. And was gone.